To mi

Welcome to my World

K. Pierce

2-9-99

AN ANGRY WORLD
by
Kendall F. Person

Published
by
PEACE Books

Person, Kendall F., 1966-

AN ANGRY WORLD

Cover Design by Daniel Greely

ISBN 1-889214-01-9

...Thank you, Tanya Lynn Morning, for your encouragement and support.

Thank you, Mattie Brown for being my mother. I could not be more fortunate.

Thank you, Gail Clark, for your energy. Not possible without your cutting edge editing.

Thank you Crystal and Michael for spending kids' day with me.

Thank you Roshell, Derrick, Deon, Claudine, Claud (May he be resting in peace.) and Kevin. I love my siblings.

Thank you Person and Walker clan for being family.

Thank you Andrea, G. Anthony, Patrick, Simeon, Marguerite, Brian, Alan and Pierre for being my friends.

Thank you David, Stephen, Kenneth and Victor for the sands.

Thank you loyal readers for believing in the power of the written word.

Thank God Almighty, for the knowledge....

ABOUT THE AUTHOR

Kendall F. Person is a Commissioner on the
Sacramento Metropolitan Arts Commission where he
Chairs the Outreach & Education Committee. He was born
in Denver, Colorado in 1966 but was raised in
Sacramento, California where he presently resides.
He is a graduate of the University of California at Davis.
An Angry World is his third novel.

AN ANGRY WORLD

Written by
Kendall F. Person

Other Novels:

Capturing Spring
The Remembrance

PROLOGUE

THE END:
A SHORT STORY

T he choir members swayed in unison as the minister brought his powerful sermon to a close. Their beautiful voices chimed in perfect harmony as the congregation cried out for their spirits to be freed and their souls to be saved.

"Jesus! He saved my soul! Jesus!" sang the choir, of men, women, boys and girls. They recited the chorus over and over until there was barely a soul left standing.

The minister, knowing he performed his job well, wiped his brow and sat like a king on his throne, presiding over the masses that squeezed into the large hall every Sunday to hear the Word. His word. Deacon Edwards quickly pulled the handkerchief from the front pocket of his gray polyester suit jacket and began the demeaning but worthy chore of patting the Reverend—the Chosen One—until he was completely dry. Mother Edwards ran to her husband's side, after pulling the soft towel from her large handbag, and began the belittling but honest task of wiping her superior husband down until the heat of the church had evaporated and left him feeling cooled and relaxed.

The choir's rhythms began to subside and the congregation had begun to regain its composure as they looked at the large clock, which covered an entire wall, and realized it was almost time to go. Brother

Edwards placed his hanky back in his coat pocket. Mother Edwards sat in the front aisle which faced the stage and the members of the Young Adult Choir took their seats, one by one. Only then did the minister jump to his feet and dominate in the spotlight.

"Oh, brothers and sisters! The Lord is with us today. Isn't the Lord with us today?" he asked his followers even though he knew their responses.

"Yes, He is!"

"Preach, Reverend!"

"The Lord is good! Yes, He's so good!"

Every individual who had a tongue and knew how to use it, responded with his or her own enthused homage to God or to the Reverend, who was God-like to some. Hands flew in the air, swaying back and forth as the congregation thanked the Lord for giving them this day. They prayed as loud as their voices would carry, hoping the Lord would hear them and answer their prayers. They confessed their sins of the week and made empty promises of giving up alcohol, mistresses, lying and cheating. They shed tears of joy and sorrow. The parishioners became weak as they felt their sins wash away. A chosen few actually felt the spirit take control of their bodies and empty their diseased, infested souls of all their wicked sins...for another week.

The Reverend looked above the heads of his flock and smiled at the fact that they were his. It was his word they came to hear. He spoke of the sins of alcoholism and by the end of the testimony, every member who had even looked at a bottle of booze would swear off the wicked hemlock. But by week's end, they would swagger down Main Street reeking of the witches' brew, from head to toe. The Reverend knew that, but he did not care. He had their minds for the day and that was all that mattered.

The Reverend indeed loved the Lord, but there were bills to pay. They had moved into an elaborate temple with banquet rooms, wedding chapels, and offices large enough to hold private parties for the entire board and their wives. The Lord saw fit to bestow upon him a new house on the riverfront with five city acres surrounding his humble domicile. His yacht and his Jaguar needed repairs and his summer home in the Keys hadn't been renovated in more than a year. The

Lord had provided and it was up to him to take great care of the gifts he had received straight from the heavens and via the pocket books of his parishioners.

The flock regained its composure, the Reverend returned to his chair, and the altar boys began their long, slow walk down the aisles carrying empty baskets. Before the clock could strike the next minute, the baskets would overflow with green bills of great worth. White envelopes filled with checks of high value and green bills of even greater amounts. The children would drop in coins retrieved from their penny banks and the elders would drop in small donations, sacrificed from their pension checks.

The choir rose and began humming the Lord's prayer as the deacons and the mothers echoed the Reverend's message.

"Give, my brothers and sisters. For it is far better to give than to receive," shouted the Minister.

The Reverend looked down into the pit of naivete and became giddy at the sight of the baskets being filled. He once again leapt from his throne and echoed God's Word from on top of his mountain. The congregation became overwhelmed with the fact that they were giving to their Lord, their God up above. They danced and shouted and screamed: "Hallelujah! Hallelujah! Hallelujah!"

They screamed so loudly that the walls began to shudder and shake. The children's cries where drowned out by the emotional outbursts of their parents. The choir swayed back and forth with such vigor it appeared that the stage moved with them. The Reverend, alas, the Reverend held his arms up and out toward his flock proving he was their shepherd who would lead them home.

The celebration reached an earth-shattering pitch but somehow one of the parishioners heard the cries of the enraptured children. She opened her eyes just in time to see the last small child being lifted up by an invisible power, floating through the air and out the door. She rubbed her eyes as she knew that the Spirit they felt every Sunday was nothing more than a collective, emotional, spiritual outburst of mortal beings expressing their aggressive behavior and belief in the Lord that had been neglected on Monday, Tuesday, Wednesday, Thursday, Friday and Saturday. She screamed to the rest of the congregation, who were still lost in their own redemption, but to no avail.

The distraught woman, who knew that the truth, the Real End, was near, squeezed through the narrow rows of believers and dashed toward the stage. The deacon, who avoided becoming caught up in the service since he was on guard duty that week, caught sight of the woman. He immediately identified her as a traitor, a non-believer, a demon. He gave a nudge to his appointed side-kick and they quickly slid their hands in their pockets and felt for the small revolvers which were to be used only in a real emergency. Now was the time to act.

"Glory! Glory! Glory!" sang the choir.

"Sing, my choir! Praise Him, my people! The Lord is good. God is here!" shouted the Reverend, Mr. Holier-Than-Thou. The crying woman made it to the edge of the stage and reached up toward the minister, who was so deeply involved in his own thoughts that he merely shrugged her off as unimportant. The deacons, fearing life in the promised land might get ugly, raced to her side, tackling her in one swift motion.

The congregation looked on in awe, believing they were saving the helpless woman from evil spirits. Spirits that tried to take over the church's humble abode.

The Reverend, oblivious to the captive parishioner and feeling the world at his feet, summoned the altar boys to end their rounds and deliver the money to the vault room where it would be counted, then stowed away for safe-keeping. He tired of the ritual and was ready to enjoy the rest of the day counting his take. He picked up the microphone, attempting to command the attention of his followers. He looked around the church and thought it odd that they had not calmed down at the mere sight of seeing him near the speaker system. After clearing his throat, he spoke deeply into the microphone.

"Yes, my brothers and sisters. Let us take our seats."

The screams and cries intensified which made him a bit uncomfortable. What was happening? He glanced at the deacons, but they stared back at him, more uncomfortable than he.

"Alright, people. I need you to take your seats!" he shouted, but it did no good. The choir continued to sing, the parishioners continued to wail, and the deacons continued to stare.

The Reverend looked down to the front row, and, for the first time that day, realized his only child was missing. He quickly looked back up, frantically circling the room with his eyes, as the horror engulfed him. For the first time, he noticed the children had been called away by a force greater than he had imagined. He tried to jump from the stage to search for his son but his legs were unwilling to carry his body from the place in which they now stood. He glared at the large clock in time to see it strike twelve. But how could that be? It was one o'clock some two hours ago. As the long hand clicked into place, a large sound echoed throughout the land. The Reverend placed his hands to his ears and tried unsuccessfully to block out the sound of the first horn. But it was real, and it was here.

The double doors to the outside world opened and revealed a dark and desolate world. The sound of the second horn blared through the speaker system and men on white horses filled the corridor. The Reverend, who should have felt safe, gawked in horror as the heads of the horses turned into lions whose growls filled the temple with fury and power. The parishioners continued their celebration, either ignoring or becoming a part of the end. The minister did not know. The deacons did not know either. But the fire breathing lion-horses were coming toward them and they were unable to do a thing about it.

The sound of the third horn sent locusts buzzing through the air. Thousands upon thousands of the creatures swarmed the church hall and filled the air until it was black and thick.

With the fourth horn, the church roof cracked wide open, revealing a black sky and a moon that dripped red. All at once the minister and his deacons knew that the blood of the Lord had been spilled. It all became so clear. So perfectly clear to the Reverend now. Satan had hidden down in the depths below all these years and had finally established enough courage to challenge the Higher Power.

With the sound of the fifth horn, the congregation dropped to the ground and lay flat on their stomachs. The ground opened and ghosts of the past rose from the dead and lay next to the still-living parishioners. The blood plunged from the moon, landing on them all in large drops. The locusts swarmed their host and began feasting on the fresh kill.

The Reverend became sick but his eyes could not close and his legs would not move.

"Kill me! Kill me now! Have my sins been so great that I must be tortured? Have I not tried to serve you? Have I not tried to live by your Word?"

The minister no longer looked like the distinguished gentleman who only seconds earlier had ruled this tiny slice of the world. He now bowed down at the feet of the being whom he was supposed to be serving. He thought of his house in the Keys and boat in the marina and realized these possessions had no meaning. He received artificial fulfillment from his property and now he had to pay. "But why must the price be so high?" He asked the question, yet knew the answer. He knew that as the Chosen One, he had let his Lord down. He had led his flock astray and now the Wrath of God had to be unleashed. The vengeance had to be delivered.

The Reverend decided to give in to God's Wrath and let the Lord use him as he saw fit. He listened closely for the last two horns and prepared for the heat. The fire and brimstone would be hot. He would suffer eternally but it was meant to be so there was no need to repent.

The sixth horn sounded and the fire streamed from the mouths of the lion-horses, scorching the pillars, burning the balconies, and igniting the clothes the parishioners wore, into tiny fireballs that streaked across the halls. The room's heat rose to an unbearable degree, yet neither the minister nor his deacons burned. Rather, they were forced to watch their followers feel the brunt of the wrath of God, which was one hundred times worse.

The sound of the seventh horn could not come quick enough. The Reverend lifted his arms up to his Lord and begged for his forgiveness. Even though he knew it was too late. A strong wind ripped the roof off the top of the church and the Hand of God descended from the clouds. This was the most incredible sight any man had ever seen. Suddenly, the Reverend knew how Moses felt when the powerful Red Sea parted at his command.

The lion-horses and the locusts disappeared. The fires extinguished and the parishioners, unscathed, along with the ghosts, stood and walked out of the open doors. Dead-alive. Dead-alive.

Soon the only humans left in the entire hall were that of his holiness ("Don't call me that," uttered the Reverend to himself) and his deacons. They were still caught up in a vision which was very difficult to understand. Was it all a dream? Yes, that's it. That is it. The Reverend was dreaming and now he was about to awaken in his warm bed with down pillows and silk sheets. He would walk across the bedroom to his bathroom with the sunken tub and shower with the built-in massager and admire his view of the river. He would be happy again. But he would change.

"Oh, yes Lord! I'll change. Just let me wake up and I'll change for you Lord," shouted the Good Reverend.

The trance was broken. The Reverend and his deacons felt freed from their restraints and made a mad dash for the door. All three had different hopes for the future as the large double doors opened. However, they did have one common goal: to pray for a familiar world.

When they reached the front door, the Reverend opened it as wide as he could, revealing the most beautiful day he had ever seen. The sun was high in the sky, which was a most unbelievable blue. And the grass, oh the grass. It was breathtakingly green. *Green as what? Green as money,* he thought.

The trio stepped outside to welcome their guest when the Hand of God suddenly came crashing down and crushed them as quickly as He had made them.

The doors to the church silently swung closed and the rest of the congregation continued their day as if there had never been a Reverend or his deacons.

VERSE ONE

Bomb blast kills four. Irish Republican Army accepts responsibility. – London, England

Brooklyn stood over the inoperable washing machine shaking his head. He hated this laundromat, but it was cheap and near his marina. Every other washing machine was defective. Coming here was like a game of musical chairs trying to figure out which machine would wash, rinse and spin his clothes on the same quarter. He continued to stare at the tub of water, then came to the realization that the rickety machine wasn't going to suddenly spring back to life. He rolled up his sleeves, reached into the machine, and began the old-fashioned chore of hand-wringing the water out of his clothes.

He was somewhat upset, but soon realized he had nothing else planned on this depressing spring night. The rain clouds had hung around all day, completely drenching the water-soaked city. Sacramento had become accustomed to dry winters. After six years of drought, many transplants began to think that it really didn't rain in Southern California. Or Northern California for that matter. This year would be different. Either Mother Nature was worn out by her children's complaints or she felt the sinful people of the Golden State had suffered long enough. The long hot summer ended a bit early and by the end of March the residents had had their fair share of cold, windy, and especially, rainy days.

By the end of October, the blue skies were covered with low-hanging clouds. A chill set in the air causing the balmy temperatures throughout the state to dip well below normal. To the dismay of many, outside activities were being canceled across the state. San Diego's Bay Harbor, just a week earlier congested with boats and yachts, now played host to only the massive destroyers and cruisers that were permanently docked during times of world peace.

The shops at Marina del Rey in Los Angeles closed their doors and rolled up the boardwalk much to the chagrin of the many visiting foreigners. The story was much the same in San Francisco, Sacramento and Lake Shasta.

The weather forecasters called it "El Nino", the warming of the world's oceans which causes a drastic change in weather patterns throughout the globe. The temperatures in Sacramento dipped into the fifties and by mid-November the residents had already begun brushing dust off their winter coats. The frigid temperatures provided much conversation over water coolers and in the men's room but that was only the beginning. By late December the rain had started to fall. A little heavier than usual but most natives of the Golden State were jumping for joy for the six long years of drought had taken a toll on the reservoirs and many rivers and lakes that were now dangerously low. However, in early January the rain fell from the sky like never before.

An inch an hour, according to the weather forecasters. Incredibly the rains did not stop there. At months end, California was under water, reeling from the most severe flood to hit the region in sixty-seven years. The Sacramento valley was virtually at a standstill as several flooded communities tried to salvage the few remaining pieces of their lives. 'Twas the middle of February before the flooded out freeways could finally be repaired and the farmers able to tour their water-soaked crops and tally their losses.

Brooklyn was one of the lucky. Other than a stalled car and a ruined pair of Stacey Adams shoes, his home and those of his closest relatives were spared from destruction. As he wrung out his clothes, he continued to stare out the glass plated building. The rain had not let up and this was beginning to annoy him. He was tired of running for cover every time he stepped outside. He knew, though, as well as others, that the rain was a gift from God. For the first time in what seemed like an eternity, the grass was green and the trees stood proud and strong. But best of all, the many lakes, rivers, and reservoirs were full. For the first time in six years, he could cruise up the American River without fear of running ashore or having the jagged edge of a boulder destroy the bottom of his houseboat.

He finished wringing out his clothes, tossed them in the laundry cart that was provided by the laundromat and headed over to the dryers. It was a full house so maneuvering through the crowded, child-infested building was much like driving down the Capitol City Freeway at rush hour. Two small children played with toy cars in the middle of the narrow aisle. Their mother stood directly over her offspring, seemingly engrossed in her National Enquirer while pushing her laundry cart back and forth with her leg.

Brooklyn halted in his tracks. He opened his mouth to ask the family, who had set up camp, to excuse him but figured it was less of a hassle to simply walk around the row of machines. Brooklyn hated hassles. He walked around the middle aisle, excusing himself whenever necessary, silently hoping there would be a single dryer which was not in use. To his surprise, one was empty.

He quickly loaded his laundry, slipped two quarters into the appropriate slot and stood for a minute, watching his clothes spin around and around, much like his life. He pushed the laundry cart away, looked at his watch, and walked out to his car. He couldn't stand to sit in the laundromat. It made him feel like he had nothing to do except clean his clothes. While this was true, he still wasn't ready to admit his existence had come to this.

He slid into his convertible BMW, turned the key in the ignition backward and tilted his seat back as the soothing sounds of Barry White poured through the speakers. *Come here, come here, come here baby. Come here girl.*

He took another look at his watch and figured he had another nineteen minutes before his clothes dried. If he returned to the laundromat in twenty minutes, his clothes would either be dumped haphazardly into an unused laundry cart or sprawled across one of the folding tables. That always bothered him, but really, he didn't blame his fellow laundromat users. Nothing was worse than needing a dryer only to see one that contained finished its cycle but still had a shit load of clothes.

It was cold and wet but the sound of the rain hitting his vehicle while he listened to Barry lure a beautiful African queen into his den was a hundred times more comforting than watching the young brats fight over who got to put the quarter into the washing machine.

Brooklyn was a peaceful man. Anyone with vision could see that. But something about him caused tension, if not outright fear, to overtake many at first encounters. It may have been the way his eyes always appeared to be red. They were not red from lack of sleep or too much marijuana; but red with fire or with sorrow. Maybe it was the contrast of Brooklyn's fiery eyes with his maroon-black skin. Skin so smooth that more than one total stranger had asked to touch it, just to make sure it was real. Or maybe it was the way he would look at his host. Much like a holy man staring at a pariah or a hungry lion glaring down from a mountain top at the unsuspecting wildebeest. But more than likely, it was the combination of all three. He was the type of person who always had something on his mind. Something different. Something maybe beyond this world. He was well loved and well established. He excelled at the company he worked for and was elected President each year of the many organizations of which he was a member. But no one ever really got close to him.

Brooklyn had a gaze which could cut right through you. One minute he would be laughing, joking with the rest of the crowd and seconds later, the fire would return to those eyes as if there was a madman inside trying his best to get out or a lonely soul longing to be set free.

Brooklyn had started to fall asleep when the sound of the rain startled him out of his self induced trance. He glanced at his watch, hit his fist against the dash board, and jumped out of the car. He rushed back inside the building, partly from not wanting to get wet, but mostly to avoid having his clothes handled by strangers, only to discover the woman with the National Enquirer and pesky kids pulling his clothes out of the dryer. *Damn! One minute late,* he thought. He took long fast steps toward her, wanting to remain calm, trying to hold back his anger but unable to do either.

"What are you? A clothes dryer vulture?" he barked at the woman, who was still trying to read her magazine while dumping his clothes into the nearby laundry cart.

"Well, I didn't know when you were coming back," she replied, not backing down nor seeming a bit disturbed by the fire in his eyes. "I can't be at this laundromat all night waiting for folks to clear out."

"I'll get them." He walked between her extended arm and the dryer, sending a scorching look at the kids in the process. The woman stood back, finally finding something more interesting than her magazine, folded her arms, and waited patiently while Brooklyn unloaded his clothes, making room for hers.

Her name was Arizona. Never having been out of California, her mother got the fool notion to give her children names of places she most wanted to visit. The notion always made Arizona a bit sad to think that her mother had lived her life vicariously through the names of her children. That was about all that saddened her. She was a strong woman, in more ways than one. The father of her two kids had left long ago, at her request. Johnny had started out with so much promise but let the world convince him that he wasn't worth the rags on his back. Arizona couldn't have that. Not around her children. She enjoyed having a man around the house. She enjoyed his scent after he stepped out the shower and his huge hands wrapped around her body. She liked to see him put away a second helping of the food she ritualistically placed on the table and loved his manliness pressed against her, inside her, shooting through her. But having no man was better than settling for a weak one.

Johnny came home one Monday evening and collapsed in her arms. Tears rolled down his face and the loud sobs made his words barely audible. He had beat the pavement for over two months yet found not so much as a job flipping burgers. He complained of his inability to provide for his kids and his desire to buy his woman a dozen roses but being unable to do either. Johnny had expected sympathy. He also expected warmth and a soft shoulder to lay his head. However, on that fretful Monday, he received his walking papers. Arizona pushed him off her lap, waltzed to the door, opening it as wide as it would go, and ordered him to get out.

Dumbfounded, he became enraged and for the first time—and the last—raised his hand to the face that had unselfishly supported him. His unsuspecting blow sent her staggering backward. She turned toward her kids and telepathically told them to leave the room. Johnny dropped to his knees, with fresh tears covering his face and begged her for forgiveness. *Oh God, where's the bottom?* she thought.

She quickly scanned the room, spotting her oldest child's wooden bat. Johnny, now completely succumbing to the pressure of life, buried his face in his hands and wailed while shouting that nothing was going right. Nonchalantly, Arizona walked over to the bat, grabbed it with both hands and upon finding her way to her children's father, swung it with enough force to smash in the side of his face, knock out an entire row of teeth, and to forever take what little manhood poor Johnny may have had left.

Blocking out the past, Arizona found her way back to the present. She stared at Brooklyn, who seemed to be taking his time pulling out his clothes. The thought that he was being spiteful crossed her mind, but she knew better. He was not a spiteful man. His meticulous manner blended with his stoic aura. Tall and slender, but not too thin. Black as night without stars and eyes so red they matched the shirt that clung tightly to his thin, muscular frame. While not handsome, his looks commanded attention and respect, both of which he now had. She leaned back against the fully loaded washing machine behind her and let her beloved tabloid magazine drop to the floor.

Arizona could live without a man. She had done so for most of her life, but she preferred the comfort of a man. Blood began to flow through her veins, sending a wave of excitement to her loins. Imagination running wild, she had to calm herself and remember where she was.

"All finished," Brooklyn announced after dropping his last shirt into the laundry cart.

"Thank you," replied Arizona. "I'm sorry about rushing you. I just didn t know."

"It's all yours." The fire blazed from his eyes, chin went up in the air and he strolled away, leaving her speechless and breathless. His lingering scent engulfed her. She closed her eyes, refusing to allow his blatantly rude behavior to ruin the moment, and inhaled deeply.

"Mom. It's your turn." Her child spoke, disrupting Arizona's trance. She gave little Johnny a quiet smile and began stuffing clothes into the dryer. She quickly grabbed her children and sat with them in the waiting area. Luck was with her as her view of Brooklyn was uninterrupted. She pretended to read her magazine that little Johnny was so kind to retrieve, but really, she refused to let the fascinating man out of her sight.

Time passed and her luck expired. Someone, another man, cut off Arizona s vision by deciding to use one of the washers right where the red eyed man stood. The other man dragged over a large white basket and started the task of loading the washer. She almost stood up and walk around him, but her pride would not let her. Besides, she had never chased any man and as much as she wanted to, she figured it best to read her magazine and raise her children. The man who had just stumbled into her a full view, turned with his back to Arizona giving her a view of the back of his sweatshirt. "Ricky," she read, from the stranger's shirt, *I wish Ricky would get out of my way*, she thought.

Looking down at her children who had resumed playing, the foreign emotion of sadness entered her heart. She had taken their daddy away from them, believing with all her heart that no father was better than a worthless one. She refused to let that feeling find a home in her heart. Arizona buried her head in her magazine after stealing one last look in Ricky s direction.

Ricky poured two cups of detergent into the washing machine, concentrated, and then dumped an oversized load of colored, white and dark clothes into the single-load washing machine. As the water filled the washer, he pushed his clothes down below the water line, determined that all of his garments were going to get wet even if they did not wash clean. Ricky hated the laundromat. He hated waiting for the machine to finish its cycle and even more waiting for a dryer. Three weeks had passed since he had washed clothes and the stench of his smelly underwear was becoming too much for even him to bear.

After assuring himself that all of his clothes were swimming safely in the soapy water, he closed the lid and walked outside to smoke a cigarette. He remembered how things were back in the old days. There was no going outside when it was forty degrees and pouring rain just to take a toke. You could sit in the warmth of a restaurant or airport and just fire up. But the conservatives and liberal pretenders were getting their way. Big Brother now told him where and when he could smoke. Next he would be told that he couldn't smoke at all.

Ricky lived on the south side of town in a small rural area known as Hood. He wanted desperately to move back into the city but would have been a fool to do so. His father had passed away a year ago and left him a large house surrounded by a full acre of land. The house had been paid for and the taxes were cheap. He had thought of selling his home but that was before he became a part of the Movement. Now, it was the perfect place to meet, to plan and, if necessary, to hide. There was only one problem, the lack of wash houses.

Ricky worked in the city, delivering fuel for a local oil company. On days when he was forced to clean his clothes, he would toss them in the trunk of his car and drive to a laundromat to do so before jumping on Highway 160, southbound, toward home. Today was one of those days. The rain had not let up but this was furthest from his mind. A meeting was planned for tomorrow, at his place. One that could change the entire focus of his organization. One, in fact, that could change the entire course of this God-forsaken country.

An old alley cat rubbed his matty, furry body against Ricky's legs, catching him off guard, Ricky jumped back. Demonstrating a sigh of relief in discovering the creature was just an aging cat, he brought his foot back, then forward, landing a solid blow against the cat's back side. The steel toe of his boot collided with the tail bone of the cat, making an intense cracking sound which sent shivers down Ricky's spine. The battered cat dropped dead on the spot, another of life's casualties. He quickly kicked the animal underneath the nearest car and strutted back inside the laundromat to beat up on the washer if it wasn't finished washing his clothes. As he approached, a tall slender brother with red eyes, carrying a basket of neatly folded clothes, walked around him. A sister with two small boys pulled clothes out of a dryer; and a washer containing Ricky s garments spun out of control. The sound of thunder boomed through the air. A swath of lightning lit up the sky. And the lights in the cheap, dirty, crowded wash house flickered out. An adult's scream, the sound of kids crying, a mother's reassuring voice, then the eruption of gun shots.

Someone had told the story of the day of redemption, an old fool, a wise man, and a court jester. Each told the story differently, but in the end, all had read the same book. On a lonely, rain-filled night at an insignificant laundromat, someone had told the tale and, worse yet, someone else had believed it.

VERSE TWO

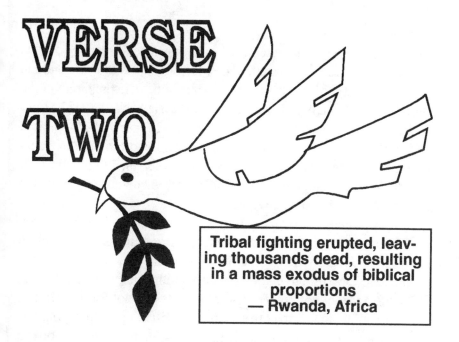

**Tribal fighting erupted, leaving thousands dead, resulting in a mass exodus of biblical proportions
— Rwanda, Africa**

He's got a gun!" screamed a stocky Mexican woman with an incredibly heavy accent. In unison, the patrons of the Sudsy Suzie Laundromat dropped to the floor. The power outage was brief and in no time the bright lights illuminated the building, making it brighter and hotter than ever before. Ricky held the gun out in front of him, moving his body back and forth, from waist level, like a cop expecting a villain to spring out of his hiding place at any moment. Sweat rolled down his face, lips pushed out and eyes gleaming only like a madman's could. Mothers shielded their babies and sons tried desperately to protect their mothers.

Another sound of thunder, another gunshot straight in the air. More screams, then calm. A soothing voice glided through the air, over the heads of the patrons, the defunct washers and directly into the ears of Ricky.

"It's alright, man. Just a little thunder. Everything's going to be okay," soothed Brooklyn, in the most calming tone he could muster. He had not dropped to the floor, but rather stood upright, deciding to meet his maker face to face, not hovering on the ground like a trapped mouse.

"That ain't no thunder, man. That's them. They're ready for us.

But don't you worry none cause I gots your back," replied Ricky, beginning his free-fall into madness. He had heard thunder but had mistaken it for gunfire. He, and others like him, were prepared for the shot that would be heard around the world. He packed a .357 Smith & Wesson in the waist of his pants. There was a sawed-off shotgun under the removable back seat of his car and two Uzis in the trunk, buried under the spare tire and jack. The leaders had told them that, like the Wrath of God, the shot would come when you least expected it, so it was crucial to be always ready.

Ricky stared at the man with the red eyes. To his right stood a well-built, honey-colored sister. She too stood upright, but, unlike the man, had fear in her eyes. Directly beneath her, lying flat on the ground, were two small boys. Her's no doubt. Ricky sensed that the fear drifting from her body was for her kids and not for herself, but she had nothing to fear. Not from him. The rest of the patrons, including the dime-store security guard, and useless manager, lay flat on the ground, covering their ears and doing their best to block out any horror that lay ahead.

This time the sound of thunder was so loud that even Brooklyn took a step back and grabbed his heart to verify he had not caught a bullet from the crazy man's gun. Ricky turned his head, being careful to keep the gun out in front of him, and looked outside. The steady rain had turned into a downpour. Small pellets of ice smashed to the earth followed by what appeared to be buckets of water. Lightning streaked across the sky and one, two, three seconds later another boomer roared through the night.

Ricky was wrong. They were not here. The red-eyed man was right. It was simply thunder. His arm dropped to his side, gun still in hand but now safety on, no immediate threat of danger. Arizona let out a sigh of relief and Brooklyn wiped his brow. The washer with Ricky's clothes in it stopped spinning. In a single motion, Ricky threw the lid open, pulled the bundle of wet clothes from the washer and shoved them in his basket. Without looking back, he turned toward the door and stormed out.

Brooklyn followed. Not knowing why, but feeling it was something he had to do. The man was sick and the sky, still sending down torrents of rain, was angry.

"Hey, man," Brooklyn called out just as he stepped out into the hellish night. "Are you alright?"

"What do you care?" replied Ricky, shoving the key into the driver's door lock. Water pounded him from all directions and in seconds he looked as if he had jumped into a swimming pool, completely clothed.

"You scared a few people."

"I didn't mean to. But I didn't hurt no one. I just shot in the air. I knew what I was doing."

"I'm just glad no one set off any firecrackers. You probably would have broken out an Uzi or something." Brooklyn laughed, trying to ease the tension that hung defiantly in the air. Ricky stole a quick glance at the trunk. The red-eyed man didn't know what was in there? No. He couldn't, Ricky thought. He turned back toward the stranger who now was standing ankle-deep in water. The thundercloud passed by taking the heavy downpour with it, leaving only a steady drizzle in its path. The key fit into the lock, he turned it right and the lock popped open. He started to jump in and drive away but realized that a warrior stood in his mist. He reached in his back pocket, pulled out a soggy card and handed it to the brother.

"Look, I can't talk now. I imagine that rent-a-cop is on the radio to the police department. The last thing I need is Johnny Law hassling me. I don't know if I would stand for it. But take my number and call me. I'm part of an organization that I know you will find worthwhile," Ricky said.

"What kind of organization is it?"

"It's one filled with brotherly love. That's all you need to know. Give me a call and I'll fill you in. I gotta go." In the car, like a flash of light, he sped off, sending a wave of water in his wake. Brooklyn looked at the card, slid it in his pocket and walked back inside.

"Did you get his name, sir?" questioned the security guard.

"Did you get his license plate number?" asked the manager. The patrons had decided to stand, now that the basket case had gone. They were pulling their clothes out of the washers and dryers as quickly as they could. Though their garments were soaking wet, half dry, and completely wrinkled, the patrons of Sudsy Suzy were getting the hell out before the suspected psycho could return.

"No. I didn't get his name. He just jumped in the car and sped off. It was dark and the rain was coming down so hard I couldn't see," stated Brooklyn with hands in pockets and card squishing between his thumb and pointer finger.

"Damn nutcase. Acted like he never heard thunder before. Thought we all was dead," barked the short, fat and completely flushed manager. His belly hung sloppily over his belt, and what little hair he had left was brushed carelessly across his head. His dingy white t-shirt and grimy jeans spelled out his story loud and clear. A nutcase shooting a gun on his shift was the most exciting thing in his life since being in the crowd when someone shot at the pope.

"Yeah. He was kind of crazy. Please excuse me." Brooklyn brushed past the guard and manager and returned to his basket that he had set aside temporarily. The crowd had thinned out, causing Brooklyn to momentarily wish someone would shoot up the place more often. Picking up his basket, he started for the door but then felt eyes on his back. He knew who they belonged to and for some unexplainable reason felt compelled to turn around and stare her in the face.

Their eyes met briefly, then Arizona's gaze fell. She felt awkward and embarrassed. She was a strong woman, a provider, a care giver and a survivor. But deep inside, so deep in fact it rarely saw the light of day, was a little girl yearning for love and affection. She picked up her basket, summoned her young and proudly walked toward the door. Within earshot of the mesmerizing man, she heard the soothing sound of his voice as she passed.

"Let me help you with that. It's coming down pretty hard outside and I would hate for you to have to dry your clothes all over again," stated Brooklyn, watching the lady walk by.

"So he speaks," Arizona replied but regretting what she had said.

"Hey, I apologize for my attitude earlier. Doing laundry just puts me in a bad mood. The name is Brooklyn." Hand extended, she placed hers in his. A man's touch: strong, dominant. The feel of a woman: delicate, warm.

"Arizona," she responded.

"Nice name. What do you say? Can I help you out?"

"No. I've carried clothes through worse. But I appreciate the offer. Maybe I'll see you here again. I'll let you carry them then. That is if the offer is still good."

"It will be. You be careful out there. It ain't nothing nice. Hey, fellas, you take care of your Mom."

"We will," replied the bashful boys simultaneously. Arizona continued her walk toward the door, hands full, boys in tow, smile on face. Brooklyn gave her a little space then proceeded afterward. Sudsy Suzy was almost empty now, except for the Batman and Robin wannabes still gabbing about the event like housewives over their favorite soap.

All was quiet. Washers and dryers completed their empty cycles. Playing children were now on their way to a safe haven known as Home, and Ricky was shooting holes in someone else's ceiling. Brooklyn strolled out the door, jumped into his car after popping the lock and shoving in his clothes, and raced home.

VERSE THREE

> **Locals cheered as neo-Nazis threatened Romanian Gypsies with Molotov cocktails.**
> **— Rostock, Germany**

The bombing at the Federal Building in Oklahoma City wasn't the only thing to rock Brooklyn's nerves that dreadful Monday morning. He had arrived at work, running a little later than usual, to discover that someone had rummaged through his desk. The bottom desk drawer, where he kept miscellaneous documents, was pulled halfway out and a large notepad protruded from the open space. He probably would not have thought anything of it had it not been the place he also kept his paycheck stubs.

His first inclination was to blame it on the cleaning people, but with all of the seemingly valuable items sitting atop his desk, they would have little need to rummage through desk drawers filled with papers they would scarcely understand. And besides, Brooklyn worked with the nosiest bunch of people the insurance industry had to offer.

Steaming at the collar, he walked toward the door, planning to go on a rampage accusing any who looked as if they could be accused of trying to see if the boss threw him a few more pennies than the rest of them. The radio was on, however, and hearing the horror of what his fellow countrymen in Oklahoma City were going through made the problem of the nosy co-worker seem so unimportant. The rage that had boiled in his blood, now subsided and gave way to grief that he could have never imagined.

A fanatical group or perhaps an individual had decided to plant powerful explosives outside of the Federal Building in downtown Oklahoma City. The blast completely obliterated the entire front section of the massive nine-story structure. People could be heard screaming and others yelling instructions as the horror of the day truly began to unfold.

After pulling his chair away from his desk, Brooklyn set his cup of espresso on the table and sat down hard in the cushioned chair. He turned up the radio and listened with disbelief as the radio announcer delivered the devastating news: "At nine o'clock this morning, as residents of this mid-western city began filing into work, a car bomb strategically planted outside of the Federal Building in downtown Oklahoma City exploded, completely obliterating the entire front section of the building. The powerful blast could be felt some thirty miles away and the debris from the building has completely littered ten downtown city blocks.

"There have been reports of injuries from apartment buildings surrounding this area where flying glass literally shattered all over town, sending thousands running for cover. But the real story is right here where you can see the remains of the Federal Building that once housed the Alcohol-Tobacco & Firearms unit which was responsible for the downfall of the Camp Davidian cult, in Waco, Texas, two years ago to the day.

"There have already been eight confirmed deaths, six of those children who were housed in a daycare center on the second floor of this once sound structure. City officials bleakly announced that they expect the death toll to rise as they continue to pull survivors and remains from the rubble.

"I know the question many of us are asking is, why here? Why Oklahoma City? A place that is far removed from the international politics that place so many of our other American cities in jeopardy. Oklahoma City: the heartland of America and the very buckle of the God-fearing bible belt. The alleged terrorists or madmen, if there is a difference, knew that by striking in a place like this, they would be blasting a hole through the very foundation on which America is built.

"We have come to expect tragedies in New York City and Washington, D.C. We may have been more prepared had this act been attempted in Chicago or Los Angeles, but Oklahoma City as the cowards knew, would be unprepared. They knew that our farmers and our farmers' children would wake up with the sun and begin harvesting the food that would feed the rest of their brothers and sisters that lived between the Atlantic and the Pacific. The vicious murderers knew that the religious residents of this quiet urban city would send their children off to school and head to work thinking of only how they were going to solve the problems that were left on their desk the day before. The people here were not ready for this nor are they ready for the scars that will mar their lives as they wake up each morning reliving the explosion that woke them up that quiet Wednesday morning putting an end to their sanity and serenity. This is Marv Starks reporting."

Brooklyn lifted his head and stared out the large picture window that decorated his tiny office. The nightfall had begun to give way to the new day. He watched with fascination as the day became brighter and the sky more blue. Thoughts of the open desk drawer flickered in his mind but he crushed this trivial matter and focused his attention on the beautiful sunrise.

The last storm had its fill with the valley and finally decided to move on, at least for the time being. Brooklyn closed his eyes and inhaled the flavor of the new season. He imagined the scent of the roses and the aroma of the fresh pine, but his vision dissipated. A single tear rolled down his face as he thought of the innocent children in Oklahoma City who would never smell roses again.

The sound of the telephone ringing reminded him that he was at work. He figured that he should probably act like it. Quickly grabbing a tissue, he blew his nose, took a sip of espresso, cleared his throat, and started another work day much the way he had started the ones before.

"This is Brooklyn," he stated into the receiver.

"Brooklyn, this is Dave Roberts of Roberts Oil Company. I was given your name by my agent as the person handling my claim," replied Mr. Roberts, sounding a bit disturbed.

"Yes, Mr. Roberts. How may I help you?"

"How may you help me? You can start by explaining this letter I received from the Department of Environmental Health. They say I'm out of compliance, and they are going to shut me down if I don't begin cleaning up the contamination out on Highway 160. What the hell is that all about? I reported this claim to you people four months ago. Why hasn't something been done?"

"Mr. Roberts, please fax me a copy of the letter and I assure you I will attend to it right away."

Brooklyn was the Environmental Claims Director in charge of remediating contaminated service stations, bulk plants and other areas at over one hundred twenty sites in three states. While it was not difficult getting files confused, this particular case came immediately to mind. Fortunately, notices from state agencies threatening everything from fines to a complete shutdown of operations were as common as dirty old men at a large bosom convention.

He worked for a midwestern-based insurance company that had enthusiastically insured oil jobbers until the owners realized they had interest in a financially unstable industry. Immediately upon graduating from college, he began his career at Wexington Mutual Insurance Company. They had representatives at a local career festival he attended in the final months of his senior year. The representative, John Kayfield, and Brooklyn had hit it off early on, and before he knew it, he was pushing paper and staring out the window, five days a week, eight hours a day.

Wexington was a good company. They were employee-oriented and treated every worker as a member of their own family, as long as you were in. If you were not, you knew it and it wouldn't take long before you would be ushered out the door, box in hand, foot print on derriere. Brooklyn, somehow, was in. Even with his maroon-black skin contrasting with the majority of the employees like a rich onyx swirling about in a winter storm, he had moved up the ranks quickly. His most recent promotion had its advantages but it was times like these that sent him longing for those carefree college days where attending classes was by choice and not a necessity.

He listened as Mr. Roberts ranted and raved about how he had paid his premiums every month and deserved to be treated with respect. At the end of their conversation, Brooklyn had managed to calm him down by assuring him that, "We here at Wexington do everything possible to protect the interest of our clients," and all that other bullshit that he had become accustomed to spitting out at the drop of a dime.

After hanging up, he sat back in his semi-comfortable armchair and debated on what he should do next. Files were piled high on his desk and the computer was beeping, signifying several memos needing to be addressed. He knew that he needed to work but today he just couldn't get focused. For the first time of the season the sun was shining, making him unable to concentrate on the piles of paper or Mr. Roberts' problems. He leaned back in his seat and thought about the night at the laundromat and visualized, once again, the woman named Arizona.

He pressed his eyes firmly shut so he could imagine her touch, taste her scent and see the pain in her eyes as he had done the night before. Her short hair, cut stylishly into a seventy-ish Afro mixed perfectly with her strong African cheekbones and heart stopping nineties figure. She wore large hoop earrings which dangled freely over her shoulders. Her golden brown lipstick added the final touch to a face so beautiful that only the hurt and pain in her eyes could mar her radiant glow. *Arizona*, he thought. "Damn, look at all this work," he mumbled as he shook the vision from his mind and resumed his ritual of pushing paper and watching the clock.

VERSE FOUR

More Bosnian Muslims found massacred, slain by Bosnian Serbs.
-- Sanki Most, Bosnia, the Balkans

As Arizona walked toward the bus top, she noticed that the clouds had returned, bringing with them a sense of gloom. Arizona had been in the house most of the day, trying to catch up on the housework she had been unable to do over the weekend. Now, she regretted not sharing in the few hours of sunshine they had been blessed with. She had walked her boys to the bus stop early that morning, and for the first time in what seemed like an eternity, noticed the sun making its way across the beautiful blue sky. It had been several months since the sun and sky had made a joint appearance making that morning seem like a dream, or a postcard from the edge. With the sweet taste of spring blowing through the open windows, clothes folded and put away and tonight's dinner thawing on the stove, she accepted the sacrifice and moved on.

A light wind blew across her uncovered arms, causing goose bumps to appear on her otherwise unblemished skin. A large thunder cloud moved through the sky, blocking out the warm sunlight in the process. Arizona, looking skyward, frowned and rushed toward the bus stop, silently hoping the bus would not be late. She reached her destination, slid into the narrow space between two other mothers after graciously exchanging greetings, and awaited the arrival of her boys.

Being in a domestic mood, she had taken two chickens out for the night's meal. Johnny could practically put away a whole fryer by himself. What they did not eat that night, she would pack in their lunch bags, the following day, and send her three men on their way. But as she planned the menu she realized that Johnny would not be coming back. The thought of being alone in her bed sickened her, but she held her head high and stood by her decision to make him leave.

Shoving one bird back into the freezer, she thought of the man she had met the night before. The memory was so vivid that she could almost smell his masculine scent and still feel his large, strong hands overtake hers. Envelop them. Protect them. Brooklyn had not backed down to the crazed man with the gun which proved he was either emotionally strong or as freaked out as Ricky. She hoped for the former but could not help thinking it was probably the latter.

Time passing, clouds forming, other mothers soon arrived and in no time, the bus stop resembled JC Penney's, the day after Thanksgiving. Arizona glanced at her watch and noticed the bus was running a little late. The sky darkened and a chill raced through the air. She looked toward the sky, which now was as black as night, and shook her head in disbelief. The rain was on its way.

"I might as well move back to Seattle," stated a young woman standing to her right.

"Hey, what's going on, Sonya? How long have you been standing there?" replied Arizona.

"I've been standing here for a minute or so. I would have said something earlier, but you looked like you were enjoying wherever your mind had taken you," replied Sonya.

"Does it really rain all the time in Washington?" Arizona asked.

"Just like this. One minute the sun is shining, and the next you are pulling out the umbrella."

"I just hope the bus comes before it gets started. Last thing I need is to get caught up in a downpour."

"I know we need the rain, but I for one am sick of it. I can't even get my hair done without it frizzin' up the second I walk out the door. You know what I'm saying, girlfriend?"

"I hear you. But this is Sacramento. It can't last much longer," Arizona replied.

"Guess who I saw yesterday?" Sonya asked, trying to add color to the somber conversation.

Arizona turned and faced Sonya, offering her her undivided attention. Sonya was a dear friend who would give you the shirt off her back and all that jazz, but had no real direction or goals. She spent most of her time downing others or making wishes that would never come true. Sonya grew up the product of the welfare system and was unable or unwilling to break the cycle. By the age of twenty, she had four kids and knew all of the social workers by name at the county building. Having nothing to do with her day, it was spent either with Oprah or the daytime soap known as Sacramento.

Normally, Arizona would not have entertained the conversation but she knew that Sonya was going to say Johnny, and for some reason, she wanted to know how he was doing.

"Don't tell me. You saw Johnny, right?" asked Arizona.

"Well, yeah. But that's not news. I see his trifling ass everyday with a bottle of booze in hand and beggin' for money to buy another," Sonya replied, letting out a quiet chuckle.

An arrow pierced Arizona's heart. Had she done this to him?

"What I was going to say is, I was down in Tracy at the prison. They call it a correctional institution, but it's a prison. I was there with my cousin visiting her husband. Girl, it's a trip down there. I mean all those fine men. Ooh, they can lock me up anytime."

"Who did you see?" asked Arizona, now tiring of the conversation and wishing more than ever the bus would come. Light sprinkles had begun to descend from the clouds and the chill had turned cold. A gust of wind flew by, catching everyone offguard, sending moans and groans through the tightly-packed crowd.

"Well. There we were in the visiting room talking to Lewis. That's my cousin's husband ... when out walks Donovan."

"Donovan?"

"Yeah, girl. You heard me right. Donovan James. I couldn't believe my eyes. I about died."

"What is he doing in there?"

"Well, from what I hear, he shot somebody. I couldn't get all the details because some damn fools starting fighting and they made us clear the room. But girl, I'll tell you this. Prison must not be all bad 'cause that man sure did look good. If you see him, you'd feel like a fool for letting him go."

"Oh yeah. He'll make a great husband. We could have our wedding reception at the warden's house."

"Whatever. Hey, we have to stand by our men in prison. They're still humans, they're still black and their dicks still get hard."

With Sonya's last word, the thundercloud gave way and all hell broke loose. The rain fell from the sky so hard and fast that the crowd was drenched before they could make it to cover. The wind picked up speed, sending large balls of water smashing into the backs of the mothers as they headed for nearby homes to find temporary shelter under awnings which were in eyeshot of the bus stop. Arizona and Sonya bolted across West El Camino Avenue toward a city bus stop which had a small covering. A crowd of people had already sought shelter inside the limited space, but they still managed to squeeze under the overhang. Arizona looked out at the streets which were now flooding, incapable of handling the vast amounts of water which pounded the surface. She stretched her neck, searching the street trying to locate the bus carrying her boys. She hoped they were safe, but the thought of not knowing gnawed at her heart.

"This is the craziest shit I've ever seen in my life!" bellowed Sonya, barely audible over the sound of the storm.

"I hope my babies are alright," shouted Arizona.

"They're doing better than us. The bus driver probably pulled over to the side to wait out the storm. They'll be here any minute."

Sonya attempted to comfort Arizona but really she was only trying to console herself. Unlike Arizona, Sonya did not work. She walked to the bus stop everyday at the same time to meet the arrival of her children. The bus was already fifteen minutes late and she couldn't help but think that a maniac was out there driving in this weather the same way he would drive on a sunny day. The torrential rains continued to fall, the streets continued to flood and the group of mothers, crammed under a bus stop on the corner of West El Camino and

Truxel, stared hypnotically down the street, awaiting the arrival of the Nat Turner elementary school afternoon bus.

VERSE FIVE

> Homeless children
> slaughtered by
> city police
> —Rio de Janeiro Brazil

The severe thunderstorm blinded Ricky's vision, but this didn't stop him from rolling eighty miles per hour down Interstate 5. Anyone acquainted with Ricky knew that when he was on a mission, there was nothing which could stop him. He had driven up to Redding, a small city located at the mouth of Shasta Lake, to deliver ten thousand gallons of unleaded gasoline. There wasn't much in the world that Ricky loved or even impressed him, but he was often overcome with excitement when he learned he would be heading up north. Although the majority of his trips did not call for crossing the lake, he would do so, just to see, to make sure it was still there.

Beautiful Lake Shasta's three hundred miles of shoreline made it one of the largest lakes in the Golden State. Nestled inside of the breathtaking Sierra Nevadas and accented by Mount Shasta, it was the perfect place to think of his perfect world. He would often arrive before dawn to catch the sun's rays softly pouring through the mountain pockets and bouncing off the clear water, creating mesmerizing sunrises, unequaled on either coast.

Delivering flammable substance was a hazardous job, but Ricky was generally a safe driver and conditions in California were usually good. On the way up, the sun had shone so brightly, he soon had forgotten about the wild rains that had plagued the city the past several months. This year, he had to be on his guard. One false move and he could find himself losing control and ending up a fireball on the following day's news.

Today, however, he drove like the maniac he was becoming. The meeting was scheduled to take place, at his house, in less than two hours. The trip had turned out to be a bust. The idiotic dispatcher had gotten his signals crossed and sent him north when he should have gone south. When he arrived at the service station to dump his load, the manager of the store promptly informed him that he had not ordered the gas but "would gladly take it off his hands if it was on the house." The stocky shop keeper let out a huge laugh before turning and walking away. Ricky stood there, wanting to pounce on the fool for wasting his time, but realized he had bigger fish to fry. The day had been a beautiful one, but now those damn clouds were beginning to block out the sun.

Ricky was a good driver and a hard worker. He showed up for work on time, put in extra hours when required and never complained about a thing. He despised working for the man, but for now, it was the only way. He refused to eat lunch with any of his co-workers, attend their parties or join their clubs. But he worked hard, therefore giving management nothing to complain about.

After relieving himself, he jumped back in the rig and headed southbound toward Sacramento and the meeting that awaited.

The speedometer hit eighty miles per hour. Ricky glanced at his watch, becoming confident when he saw the time. At his present speed, he could be home, showered and prepared, prior to the arrival of his first visitor. Light sprinkles started to appear on the windshield, but he hardly noticed. His mind was gone. Drifting through space, floating on the wind, trying to find the life that was meant just for him.

Ricky stood on the street corner, with the rest of the hoodlums, drinking, shooting craps, and complaining about the bum rap that life had given them. It was the second day of the month, so the corner of Rio Linda and South Avenue resembled a swap meet rather than a neighborhood intersection. Dimestore drug dealers stood on the corner, unloading their bags of dope by the gram. Young fools, thinking they were big time, not realizing the true drug lords dealt in nothing short of a kilo, leaving the petty matters to the corner hustlers and high school drop outs.

Dope fiends crisscrossed the street, attempting to get the biggest bang for their buck. All had a pocket full of money that the government was so good to provide at the beginning of each month. The kids were home, crying from either starvation or lack of attention, while their parents chased their pipe dreams with the money that was meant for them. The younger hustlers stood on corners, selling double ups, two for one rocks of crack, so to speak. They accepted cash, food stamps, and even an occasional blow job if the, bitch had big enough lips, as the saying goes.

When the sun set, the hookers would take to the streets. Some tricked because it was the only way to get their cherry popped. Others sold their bodies to support drug habits, but most prostituted to stay alive. The seedy, the needy, and the greedy busied themselves in their own private Idaho. Life's misfits; fighting for survival, striving to be at the top of the bottom of the pile.

Ricky was hunched over in front of an abandoned liquor store, shooting craps. He had lost forty dollars of his mother's money and was doing his damndest to get it back.

"Fuck that nigga!" shouted Ricky. "Ya'll niggas gonna give me a chance to make ma money back."

"Ricky, man. We don't have to do shit. Now, if you smile pretty, maybe I'll let you kiss my ass," replied Torion, as he counted the money he had accumulated, then shoved it in his pocket.

The other four men laughed loudly at Torion s remarks then gathered the few cents that remained on the ground.

"Come on, Brothers. That's ma mom's money. Let's shoot one more time. Double or nothing."

"Nigga, I 'm sick of you whining," shouted Kip. "Put your money down. Your ass throw a seven and the pots yours. Anything else comes up, you ain't got nothin comin." Kip threw a ten dollar bill on the ground. The single bill drifted in the air before landing next to the two large dice.

"That's a fool's bet. Keep the rest of your momma's money in your pocket," stated Torion.

"Fuck that. Let me get some of this," quipped Lance, tossing a ten spot on the ground.

In minutes, the pot had grown and the crowd had reassembled. Ricky felt in his pocket to make sure what remained of his mother's money was still there. His mother had given him a hundred dollar bill to do some shopping. He figured he would run down to the corner, make a couple of bucks for himself and be on his way. Lady Luck had not been with him today, and he wound up losing half of the old lady's funds. There was forty dollars on the ground, meaning he would have to match it. If he won, he would recoup his loss and be on his way. But if he lost...

Tension had grown inside of the private circle and something tugged at his heart. A faint breeze blew by his ear and he could have sworn he heard a voice tell him to, "Walk away," but he did not. He kneeled down, picked up the dice and rolled them inside his hand. His sweaty palms caused them to briefly stick to each other. He closed his eyes, said a silent prayer and rolled the dice forward. Eyes followed the small polka dot cubes as they tumbled down the makeshift craps table. Sounds of the ghetto persisted in the background. Young black men yelling, "Double ups!" Old hookers screaming, "Pussy for sale." Tires screeching, gun shots echoing, mothers crying, dice tumbling.

Ricky, however, only heard the sounds of the dice. He closed his eyes tightly and listened for the sound of his friends celebrating. He imagined his mother's angry voice and thought of other ways to get the money back. He could follow Torion and hit him over the head just as he walked into his house. He could borrow a gun from one of his friends and hold up an old lady as she tried to catch the bus, or, he could find a job and make money the old-fashioned way.

Seconds passed, then silence. The dice stopped rolling.

"Well, I'll be damn," uttered Torion. "I knew I should have took my butt home while I had the chance."

Ricky opened his eyes and stared at the beautiful polka dots that, combined, added up to seven.

"Yeah, niggas. How you like me now. Take your broke asses home." Ricky extended his arm to scoop up his money when an unrecognizable shoe stepped down on the pile of green.

"What the hell? You better get up off my money!" Ricky shouted, *looking up for the first time.*

"I'm sorry about that, Brother. Here let me help you," replied the stranger.

"Put your hands on my ends and you'll be pushing up daisies before the horn can sound," responded Ricky. He quickly scooped up his winnings, shoved the cash in his pocket and took a step back to absorb the apparently crazed man.

The stranger was not from the area. That, he could tell instantly. He was impeccably dressed and even donned a bow tie around his muscular neck. His hair and mustache were cut so evenly that Ricky instantly wanted to know who his barber was. He carried a book of some kind in one hand and a stack of papers in the other. He stood confident and proud, neither fearing his new environment nor being a part of it. Ricky watched him. Eyed him. Envied him without even knowing him.

"Hey, young brothers. The name is Malik. I saw you brothers over here shooting craps and became a little disoriented." His voice was calm, cool, yet self-assured and assertive.

"What the fuck is that suppose to mean?" asked Kip.

"It just means that you brothers don't even realize you have fallen into the master's plan. It means you young Brothers have been lost for so long you can't even understand that a better life awaits you. You're standing on a street corner, in the middle of the night, trying to beat each other out of the few pennies that you're fortunate enough to have in your pockets. You've been lost for so long that you can't even possibly see that you, my brothers, each of you are better than that. Hey, look. I have to get out of here. I'm on my way to a place where my people know who they are and are proud of it. You all are welcome. Come and we'll help you understand who you are my African brothers.

Malik handed a flyer to each person in the crowd before gliding back to the bronze Cadillac that sat on the corner awaiting him. Ricky, Torion, Kip, Lance and Johnson stood in silence, staring at the mystery brother until he was completely out of sight. When the car was finally gone, they bowed their heads and read the with great interest the piece of paper that was put into their hands. Finishing first, Ricky looked up and turned his head in the direction of the now invisible car. He looked back down at the flyer, folded it up, and slipped it into his pocket with his mother's money.

The sound of the pounding rain forced Ricky back into the present. He clicked on the windshield wipers but the water landed on the windshield with such force that they did little to nothing to improve his vision. Glancing out of the side window, he realized he was almost home. He looked down at his watch and became a bit alarmed when he noticed he only had thirty minutes to make it to his house. Ricky hated to be late. With outright disrespect for the force of nature, he pressed the gas pedal with his right foot and sent the six-axle Mack truck into warp speed. The speedometer pushed past the ninety-mile-per hour mark and continued to accelerate toward a velocity it had never known.

The wipers flipped back and forth, causing water to splash harder against the window, making it impossible to see. The freeway turned into a river as the truck began to glide on the water like a sailboat floating across the open sea. He crossed the bridge and now could finally make out the skyline of the city. His heart pulsated with joy as he thought of the meeting, his life, the man, the mission, his destiny. Sweat poured down his face as he squinted to peer through the sheet of water which ran continuously down the front window.

Heading northbound on the same interstate, a school bus, filled with quiet children, inched its way toward the usual exit. All of the school children were strapped safely in their seat belts. All except one. Little Johnny Tyler knew his mother would be waiting for him and the excitement of seeing her was too much to keep him in his seat. As they reached the familiar exit, he unbuckled his seat belt and found his way to the front of the bus.

The trained bus driver drove at a snail's pace, imagining the future doctors of the world were in his care. He put on his right blinker as he spotted his off ramp and began to make his way over so that he could carefully take the exit. The kids were depending on him. The mothers and the school had put their trust in him, and he was not going to let them down. The freeways had become shallow swimming pools, and, the sky, a large black mass, but he was almost there.

Arizona and Sonya peered out of the covered sheltered as they spotted the familiar school bus which carried their offspring. Their burden eased, each exhaling, in relief.

"That yellow bus never looked so good!" shouted Sonya.

"I know that's right," echoed Arizona.

The big rig with the Roberts Oil logo posted in large letters on both sides, maintained its speed for a second longer. But the water had risen too high and the truck's weight was unable to penetrate enough to keep its wheels on the ground. The trailer section began to hydroplane. It wagged back and forth across the lanes, like a hyperactive dog excited to see its master. The driver of the vehicle finally felt the weight of his cargo and mistakenly forgot all the driver's sense he had ever been taught. On a flooded out freeway, pulling two trailer cars with a full load, he grabbed the steering wheel with both hands, leaned back, and slammed on the brakes with all his might.

The tail car disconnected from the vehicle, flipped over the meridian and crashed into the Nat Turner Elementary school bus before its driver could exit the freeway. The force of the vehicle sent the school bus into the air, flipping over once, and crashing down on its hood. Tires rolling, rain splashing, mothers screaming.

The main chaise, with Ricky inside, went into a tail spin, hitting the guardrail once, and causing only a minor dent to the double-banded iron bars. As it continued to spin around, the rail broke loose, sending one hundred sixty pounds of man, ten tons of steel truck, and five thousand gallons of unleaded fuel tumbling into the American River below.

VERSE SIX

> Government squashes
> peaceful protest.
> Violence erupts.
> —Tieneman Square, China

Brooklyn let his pencil drop to the desk then rubbed his hands hard through his short, handsomely groomed hair. When he was younger, he wore his crop in a very neat box cut. After turning thirty, he felt the style too juvenile and decided to wear his hair cut close to his head. He thought it made him look more mature. He glanced at the clock, looked down at his now-clear desk and for a brief moment, a wave of relief engulfed him. When he arrived at work earlier that morning, a mound of paper had greeted him at the door. He had managed to plunge through all of the mail and memos even with the battery of phone calls he had received.

Leaning back in his chair, he stared out the window just as the rain finally let up. Instantly, a small hummingbird appeared and fluttered outside his window. The large pine tree dripped with water but the deep green color was priceless. California, being the real wild west, was usually as dry and brown as the Sahara desert. However, with the abundance of water that had graced the land the past several months, it now resembled the Emerald City from the Wizard of Oz.

The hummingbird knocked against the window in an apparent attempt to get inside. The hard substance startled it a bit, but curiosity overcame her as she again tried to break down the glass barrier. With her second unsuccessful try, she fluttered its wings and appeared to meditate in space. Brooklyn stared at the beautiful bird and she stared back. They were mutually fascinated but did not know what to think of one another.

Brooklyn, for a brief second, wished he could be the purplish blue bird with the red face and pointed beak. The freedom it must have felt to be able to soar anywhere in the land made all other beings small in comparison. The hummingbird, for only a moment, wanted so desperately to break down that invisible wall and sit where he sat. Eat what he ate. Feel what he felt. A being so intelligent that it could protect itself from the rain by invisible barriers made her existence seem so unimportant. Brooklyn reached toward the window, wanting to be there, trying to be free. The hummingbird, giving it all she had, slammed her body at full speed against the window pane. The barrier did not budge. Although, for an all-too important moment in time, Brooklyn flew and the bird crossed his legs in the swivel chair in the office.

"Hey, there, Brooklyn."

"Uh? What?" Brooklyn stuttered.

"I'm sorry. I didn't mean to startle you," said Remmy, laughing a little under her breath.

"No problem," responded Brooklyn, somewhat embarrassed but recovering quickly. "Just staring out the window."

"Wishing you were there, huh?"

"Well, now I do. A few minutes ago it was raining like all hell. This weather doesn't know what it wants to do."

"Tell me about it. I'm sick of it. I feel like I've been living in an aquarium. Hey, look at your desk. Someone's been working hard."

"Had to. You know I'm going on vacation in a couple of weeks and the last thing I need is to come back to a war zone. I figure if I stay on top of things, and you nice people sort of maintain my desk while I'm gone..."

"Oh no. Every man for himself. Don't think I'm going to be doing double duty while you're sunning down there in Jamaica. You really like that place, don't you?"

"Love it. Something about Jamaica. It's just hard to explain. You gotta do it one day."

Remmy walked into the office and had a seat in the guest chair that sat directly across from Brooklyn. She wore her shoulder-length sandy blonde hair loosely and it swayed back and forth while she walked. Remmy was one who cared about her appearance and spared no expense to make sure everyone else knew it. A peach-colored Ann Klein suit adorned her perfect Size 6 frame. The skirt was cut two inches above her knees giving any man who cared to look a sensual view of her flawless cream-colored thighs. Even with only four steps to the chair, her runway walk caught Brooklyn's eye even as he fought off the temptation to stare. Remmy knew he would do so. She wanted it that way.

After carefully sitting down, she positioned her self in a manner that would give her audience the best seat in the house. She slowly crossed her legs, causing her tailored-made suit to inch up a little further. Perfect.

"I'm bored," Remmy announced, sounding very sexy without really even trying. The faint aroma of Obsession drifted from her body and across the desk to waft around Brooklyn, capturing him in her spell.

"How are you bored?" he replied, fighting off the erection starting in his pants. "If you don't have enough work to do, I m sure I can help you out."

"Oh, I have plenty to do. There's a car accident every hour, it seems. I'm just sick of it. Why don't we call it quits and go open the doors at The Peppermill for Happy Hour. I could use a Long Island right about now."

"A Long Island? Sounds like you want to get things started right. I'll have to pass. I have some things I need to do."

"You have to check in with your honey, I suppose."

"Yeah. Something like that. But I'll take a rain check."

The rain had completely subsided and afterwards the sun's rays gently streamed through the uncovered window. Brooklyn's jet-black skin glistened under the spring sun. His long arms and large hands extended behind his back while he tilted back in his arm chair. The redness had returned to his eyes even though there was no hate in his heart. He tried to imagine what was going on in Remmy's mind, but was unable to do so any more than he could read the little humming-bird.

Remmy repositioned her legs, revealing the other thigh, just as smooth, just as white. She had moved to Sacramento seven years ago after accepting a position with the fastest-growing insurance company in the industry. For her, this job was a dream come true. The small town in Wisconsin in which she grew up held no future unless one's aspirations were to become a farmer or a farmer's wife. She desired neither. Her parents refused to allow her to leave the state to attend college, citing money as the main issue. But upon her gradua-tion day, she walked across the university stage, accepted her tassel, and headed immediately for the airport to board the 747 that would take her to the Golden State.

Yes, her friends and family thought she was crazy for wanting to go to such a place that seemed plagued by natural and man-made disasters, but she didn't care. California was two thousand miles away from Shaboygen, Wisconsin. There was only one thing on her mind: freedom. Freedom from waking up at the crack of dawn to milk the cows. Freedom from her mother trying to hitch her up with every town boy who could carry two barrels of hay and chew snuff at the same time, and freedom to find her dreams. To ride the wave of life or get caught up in the fantasy of her dreams. The thought of earth-quakes, fires, riots, and floods never entered her mind as she boarded the jet—on the first boarding call—and walked straight ahead.

Her mother waved from the concourse with one hand and wiped the tears from her eyes with the other. Her father stood tall and proud with his overalls nearly up to his chin and a straw hat covering his balding head. Cousin Mary Lou and Aunt May bowed their heads in prayer and asked the Lord to watch out for their foolish kin as she entered the world of the wicked and the sinful. Remmy Johnson missed all of this for she never looked back.

Now she sat across the table from a black man, a taboo where she was from. This was California, however, and she could sit across from any one she damn well pleased. Her fondness for Brooklyn was inexplainable. Maybe it was the fact that she had never said more than two words to any black person prior to moving out West. Maybe it was the way she imagined her snow white body molding with his maroon-black manhood. Or maybe it had nothing to do with color. Just maybe, Brooklyn was a tall, dark prince who simply lit a match under her burner. Imagining his long, strong hands caressing her, and picturing his sweaty shoulders rubbing against her was enough to make her scream out when she was at home, all alone. And more than enough to have her father slap her face.

"The bell has tolled. I guess that means we can get out of here, said Brooklyn," purposefully breaking the silence.

"It's four-thirty already? Time flies when you're not working. Brooklyn?"

"Yep."

"Aren't you even going to say thank you?"

"Sure, Remmy. Thanks for keeping me company. I couldn't of pushed another piece of paper."

"Not for that. For the Kisses I left you."

"Kisses? What kisses?"

"Right there in your bottom desk drawer."

Brooklyn rolled back in his chair and pulled open the bottom desk drawer. It was full of the usual loose papers. He looked up, now somewhat confused, and said, "I don't see a thing?"

"Keep looking."

He pulled the drawer out as far as it would go and discovered a small glass jar filled with Hershey's chocolate Kisses. Extending his right arm, he removed the jar and quietly closed the drawer.

"So, it was you who was rummaging through my desk. You better be careful. You almost got an ear full. But, thanks."

"Just a little something. I know you don't eat chocolate, but that doesn't matter."

"No, but I'm sure you do." Brooklyn tried to retract his last statement but his attempts were useless. The words carelessly flew from his mouth and he was helpless to do anything but watch them land on Remmy's ears. *What was he doing?* he thought. "I better get going," he said aloud.

As they both rose—she, to walk out, he, as a sign of respect—a graying older man appeared in the doorway. The awkward scene dissipated and both felt a little relief that Brooklyn's comment could be set aside.

"Perfect. Just the two people I need to speak to."

"What'cha got, Larry?" questioned Brooklyn as he turned off his computer and reached for his suit coat which hung over his chair.

"Looks like we got another roll-over on our hands."

"Ah, shit," Brooklyn gasped. "I'm not even through cleaning up the one I've got."

"Well, you know what they say," Remmy offered. "Better you than me. I'll see you tomorrow."

"Not so fast, Remmy. You're not getting out of this one. Apparently, the truck was a double tanker. It was speeding down Interstate 5 during a downpour when it jackknifed. The second tank disengaged, flipped over the meridian and smashed into a bus full of school kids."

"Oh-my-God. Are they alright?" questioned Remmy, with deep concern in her voice.

"We don't know. That's all the information I got. Melanie heard it over the radio."

"Then how do you know it's one of our policyholders, Larry?" asked Brooklyn.

"I know. You're not going to like this, Brooklyn."

"Why is it that I never like anything?"

"The radio announcer stated that the truck belongs to Roberts Oil."

"Roberts Oil? Damn! Anyone but Dave Roberts! Wait a minute. Didn't you say it was a double tanker?"

"Yes."

"Did they say what happened to the other tanker?"

"Yes. It went into the river."

Brooklyn clasped his hands together, closed his eyes and looked toward the ceiling. "Please say it was empty. Come on. Have just a little mercy. Let it have been empty."

Laurence had been with Wexington for over thirty years. In eight short months, he would retire with full honors. He had handled all lines of insurance and dealt with all types of disasters. At one time, he would have shown emotion as well, but the years had hardened him. He now examined every claim for what it was...a claim. An empty envelope that would soon fill with paper containing information about the unfortunate sap who happened to be in the wrong place at the wrong time. Whether they were sound asleep inside of a burning house, sitting on a collapsing bridge at the onset of an earthquake or riding down the freeway during a rain storm. Whether it was a small child or a toothless old man, it didn't matter. They were merely claimants to him, and money was all he could offer.

Brooklyn and Remmy were still young, and, thus, sympathetic to those involved in serious accidents. Hearing that children might be hurt brought tears to Remmy's eyes and an unfriendly insured brought fury to Brooklyn's. But old man Larry would deliver the news, let out a self-indulged chuckle, and head down the hall, preparing to go home. No more claims for him.

"They think it was full. The news report says as much as ten thousand gallons of fuel could be floating downstream into the Sacramento River. You'd better notify Home Office. This could be a big one. Tell them to set the reserves at three million dollars for the environmental cleanup. Remmy, I'm not sure how many students were on that bus, but Melanie says it's a mess down there. The bus, it seems, flipped over on contact. Chances are slim that many of those children survived. You better set auto reserves at one million dollars and someone had better notify Dave Roberts that he may not have enough insurance to cover this one."

Laurence said his peace, chuckled quietly to himself, and strolled down the hall thanking the Lord that he had only eight months left.

VERSE SEVEN

Religious leaders
plot to kill
Jesus Christ
—Jerusalem

M y babies are in there! You have to do something!" Sonya wailed.

"Ma'am. You have to stand back!" yelled the rescue worker. "We're working as fast as we can. Paul, you have to keep these people back! Get on the radio and tell them we need help down here, right fuckin' now!"

The thunderstorm had passed and the wet streets were the only hint that four inches of rain had recently deluged the city. Blue skies acted as the backdrop, while the sun lit up the remains of the day accompanied by a dazzling rainbow. A flock of birds sailed through the air, finally being able to enjoy the season of spring. The beautiful setting, however, had been completely overshadowed by the horrendous chain of events which continued to unravel.

The school bus rested on its hood, trapping the children inside. Rescue workers arrived on the scene in record time and at once initiated efforts to free the children. The tanker that had broken off from the Roberts Oil truck had come to rest ten feet from the bus, leaving minimal room to work on freeing the trapped children. With limited space, not knowing the extent of the injuries the small children had received, and with mothers frantically running about, the rescue squad took deep breaths and attempted to work the miracles expected of them.

Paul had managed to pull Sonya back, who had fought her way to the bus despite the string of policemen acting as a barricade between the bus and the assembled crowd. Interstate 5 had been completely shut down, creating five-mile back-ups in both directions. The group of other grief-stricken mothers managed to maintain control as they held vigil some fifteen feet away from the familiar yellow school bus.

"Come here, Sonya," coaxed Arizona, reaching out for her friend. "They're alright, girl. You'll see. Just stand here with me, and let the people do their job."

"But my babies are in there! I can't just stand here! I got to help them!" screamed Sonya, still trying to get around Paul who was now almost willing to let her past.

"You can't help them like this. Let them do their jobs. The kids need us to be calm. They need us to be here for them when they get out."

Arizona's calm, reassuring voice finally penetrated the fear which enveloped Sonya as well as several other panicked mothers. Sonya backed away, allowing Paul to concentrate on other pressing tasks. Sonya staggered toward Arizona, who managed to catch her frightened friend in her arms before she could collapse. The other mothers, now bound by a cruel twist of fate, gathered around Arizona and Sonya, obliterating the panic, replacing it with a strength. With hope. With love.

Paul rushed toward the rescue truck and radioed in to the hospital, the fire department, and the entire fucking National Guard for help. Returning to the scene, he stopped in his tracks just to catch his breath, one more time. He had only been driving ambulances for four months, and up until now, had never really been tested in an emergency. Sure, there was the occasional heart attack by the seventy-year-old diabetic or the young mother experiencing false labor for the second day in a row. But no amount of training could have ever prepared him for a situation like this. One that would test his emotional stability as well as his physical fitness. His kid rode a bus similar to this one. It could have been his son hanging upside down in the middle of Interstate 5.

Exhaling, he looked toward the sky and silently thanked the Lord for stopping the rain and made one small request, "Please Lord, let the kids be okay."

"The door won't open. The spring must have broken under the weight of the bus," stated the man in charge.

"Do you think we should break the window?" asked the second-in-command.

"I don't see any other way."

"But the glass may hit the children," stated Paul. "Has any one tried the back door?"

"No, we haven't. Let's give it a try. I want all the gurneys moved to the back. All hospital personnel, be on standby. We don't know what we're going to find," replied the man in charge.

The sound of sirens blocked out all the normal noises of the city. Rescue trucks, fire trucks and police cars arrived by the dozens, creating a spectacular array of lights, sounds, and colors. Women in white prepared bandage wraps. Men in white assembled gurneys and men in blue continued to hold the public at bay. Television crews arrived on the scene and quickly set up their cameras, allowing the entire valley the chance to watch the drama unfold.

Paul steadied his nerves as he reached for the handle of the bus' back door. His trembling fingers slid around the flattened knob and turned. The door clicked, then popped open. The man in charge slid a gurney inside, in the remote chance a small body was wedged against it.

"It's all clear," said Paul as he stuck his head inside the bus. "Are you guys okay?" he asked, praying that he would get a response. A dozen tiny voices responded in unison, "We re okay," forcing him to bow his head in prayer one more time. "Thank you, Lord."

"Just stay where you are. I'm going to come in and help each of you get out."

"Okay," the children responded.

The previous school year, Georgia Gibson, the president of the PTA, had decided that the school buses were not safe enough for her children. She went on a mission, collecting enough support and signatures to force the school board to agree to put money into modern buses. The new buses arrived on the first day of the following year, and, after a careful inspection by Georgia and the local safety inspector, they were put on the streets, allowing Georgia to rest easier.

The impact of the collision would have been enough to knock most of the children out of their seats and through the windows, if not for the fact they were wearing their safety belts. The bus was eerily quiet as the majority of the children remained in a state of shock which prevented them from screaming out for their mommies and daddies. A few sniffed and whined, but even they would have made more noise if one of their classmates had stepped on their toes during recess. Paul looked through the open space and saw a dozen tiny heads, still in place but turned upside down as if they were stalled on the top loop of a giant rollercoaster. The sturdy bus had cushioned their landing and, for that, Georgia Gibson would instantly become a heroine.

Paul crawled through the open door and beamed as tiny heads began appearing.

"You come to get us?" asked a little brown-faced boy, resembling his mother, Sonya.

"Yes. We've come to get you. Are you hurt?"

"I don't think so. Is my mommy here? I'm not suppose to leave the bus with anyone but her."

"She's here. She's right outside. I want you to get on my back and I'll take you out, okay?"

"Okay."

Paul situated himself on all fours in the small space between the roof and the seats that where almost pushed into each other. He unfastened little Tommy's seat belt and the frightened child smiled, then slowly crawled on top of the nice man who now looked like a horsey. After making sure the little tike was safe on board, Paul crawled toward the door, allowing the man in charge to lift the little guy from his back.

A loud roar went through the crowd as they cheered the safe arrival of the first student. Bright lights beamed from the newscasters and those watching at home clapped their hands and rejoiced as they made out the tiny head that appeared from the bus. Nurses quickly took hold of little Tommy so that he could be examined to assure he was not injured. The mothers, no longer willing to remain behind the barrier, stampeded through the officers who reluctantly let them pass.

Tears filled Sonya's eyes as she spotted her child. "My baby! My baby!" she screamed. "Thank you, God!" she prayed, silently.

Paul, who was fast becoming the man-of-the-hour, saw none of this for he had already crawled back through the twisted remains of the bus to gather more children. The rescue was going wonderfully as the majority of the eighteen children appeared to be in good spirits. He called out more hellos and was answered each time by bubbly-eyed students waiting patiently to be freed.

Child after child was passed through the door, and mother after mother rejoiced at the sight of her offspring. One child, a little girl named Shondra, emerged with a broken leg, so was unable to climb atop of the horsey. Paul carefully placed the tot in his arms and carried her out, calling out for a stretcher as he appeared outside of the door. He handed the child over and slid back into the tunnel which was now becoming as dark as a secluded cave hidden in the wilds of the African jungles.

Outside the bus, Arizona stood over the stretcher where Nigel, her youngest son, sat patiently, while the nurse practitioner gave him a complete examination. Arizona kept one eye on Nigel and the other on the bus, awaiting the sight of her other child. She noticed darkness had overtaken her city and looked toward the sky. She shook her head as she spotted yet another band of black clouds accumulating. "Come on rain. Hold off for just a second longer," she pleaded. "Just wait until they get my little Johnny out."

Across the freeway, about thirty feet down, were two large cranes fishing for the tanker which had plunged into the river. Ricky had freed himself from the truck, well before it sunk, and managed to swim the short distance to shore. In a state of shock, the rescue squad found him sitting on the river bank staring hypnotically at the trail of fuel that littered the river. With police cars following, he was whisked away in an ambulance when upon asking him questions about the accident, he began spitting up mouthfuls of blood.

Several teams from the Department of Environmental Health's

emergency response unit walked up and down the riverbanks tossing in large oil diapers trying to soak up as much product as possible. Only hours after the largest petroleum spill in Sacramento's history, dozens of dead fish had begun floating upside down on the river's surface.

Inside the bus, Paul scanned the area one last time as he was sure he had retrieved everyone. Turning to leave the bus, for the last time, the strangest thought crossed his mind. He had recovered seventeen kids from the bus but no adults. Using his common sense, he realized that there had to be at least one unaccounted for adult. He crawled forward, finding it more difficult to move toward the front. The seats and ceiling were practically sandwiched together, making it nearly impossible to pass through.

"Mark, toss me a flashlight!" Paul screamed toward the exit.

Seconds later, a cylindrical black object rolled toward him. Reaching forward, he grabbed the flashlight and clicked the on button in the same stroke. He turned toward the front of the bus and moved the light up, down, then side from side. He moved closer, but was blocked from working his way to the front of the bus by the wreckage. He managed, however, to stick his head above a large chunk of metal and immediately became thankful that he had not eaten earlier. Directing the flashlight's beam toward the front door that was nothing more than mangled metal and glass he spotted a man jammed against the door with a steel bar protruding from his body. Blood was splattered throughout the area, and if Paul had not even been sure of his own name, he was absolutely certain of one thing: this man was dead. He turned to crawl out and alert his co-workers to what he found, when his light flashed on a small frail body wedged between the dash board and a seat. Paul stared at the figure for a second. He knew he should move, but he sat, frozen in his tracks. He could hear trickles of rain against the bottom of the bus that was now actually the top. He could sense the dread that had come over the mother who had not yet been able to hug her child. And, with the use of his light, he could see the small fingers of the child flex and retract...flex and retract.

Turning quickly, he scurried toward the exit, allowing the light to drop and roll toward the front of the bus. Frantically, he stuck his head out of the door and shouted, "There's a kid pinned at the front of the bus! I can't get to him, but he's still alive! I saw him move his fingers! You have to hurry! It looks like the dashboard is pushing in on his chest!"

The crowd reacted at once. The rescue workers raced to the front, yelling out orders as they went.

"We need a crow bar!"

"Get a doctor!"

"Get the hell out of the way!"

The reporters repositioned themselves, to be certain they and the people at home would not miss a thing.

The mothers turned toward Arizona who was now lost, floating in another world. Had they said a little boy was pinned? No. It couldn't be her Johnny. It could not be her Johnny. Sonya raced to Arizona's side, grabbed her, held her, stared her in the eyes, and told her that everything was going to be alright. Arizona shook free from her grasp, ran toward the bus with arms extended, and screamed with the pain of a thousand mothers. "Not my babyyy!!!! Not my baby!!!" With the roar of the lioness, the storm clouds broke loose and unleashed another wrath upon the city. The plague of a million years had come. The vengeance which had been promised was here, and the angry world did not quite know how to react.

VERSE EIGHT

A boat, carrying seven hundred Haitians, sunk after being turned away from American soil.
—Caribbean Sea

Okay, okay. I got it. You don't have to rub my fuckin' face in it. Damn! How could this happen. Stephen, call a meeting tomorrow with the board. Damn right, at 8:00 a.m. We're not planning for the Texas shuffle. We've got a crisis here. Get ahold of everyone and tell them I want them in my office by 8:00. And that means you too, Stephen. We've got to stay on top of this."

Dave Roberts replaced the phone on the hook ever so gently and walked toward the large picture window. He wanted to slam the receiver down, but could ill afford another heart attack, so he did all he could to keep his pressure down.

Night had fallen over the city and the millions of lights twinkled like tiny stars in the vast galaxy. Mr. Roberts, the way he preferred to be addressed, had worked hard in building the lucrative oil company that his father had passed down to him. Unlike his predecessor, however, Mr. Roberts did not care to be holed away in the foothills, so he moved downtown and leased the penthouse in the tallest building in the city. He could never understand why men worked so diligently to accumulate life's treasures then moved to secluded areas where no one could see all that they had achieved. The hermit life was not for

Mr. Roberts.

His house, an authentic Victorian, sat five blocks from the state capitol building on one of the few hills in the valley. The gardener arrived twice a week to assure that not a blade of grass was even a millimeter taller than any other. His chauffeur kept his Jaguar, Mercedes Benz, and Range Rover gleaming, while his wife maintained the interior of their home. Yes, Dave Roberts had made it, and he wanted everyone to see.

Staring down at the city he had conquered, heart pounding at an erratic pace, he inhaled small pockets of air and thought of all that he had to be proud of in his life. A ball of sweat rolled down his forehead which he carefully wiped away. He had to stay calm. His whole life was floating down the Sacramento River, but he had to stay fucking calm.

Slowly turning away from his prized view, he stumbled toward the bar which adorned the south wall of the luxurious penthouse, which sat smugly atop the Renaissance Tower. A flamboyant Persian rug covered a large section of the floor with fur so white and soft that nearly all visitors felt compelled to slip their shoes off and let their toes glide through the comforting texture. An original oil painting of George Washington graced the north wall with art from around the world filling the spaces ever so delicately between.

Reaching the bar, Mr. Roberts poured himself a double bourbon— no ice—and downed it in one gulp. The fire burned his throat, but he hardly noticed. He quickly refilled his glass and returned to his marble desk: dark green, with a shine so bright the reflection of his treasures could be seen. He sat hard in his seat and thought about his life. He had been through hell and high water, managing always to come out on top. But now, eighteen children had been hit by one of his trailers, and dead or not, it could mean trouble. And to top things off, half his load of valuable crude oil was now floating down the river of one of the most nature-loving cities in the whole fucking state.

Who had they said was driving the truck? Was he speeding? Had he been doing drugs? Contemplating the questions that shot through his mind, he rolled the now-empty glass of bourbon in his left hand, while clutching a Mont Blanc fountain pen in the right. He pounded

the pen repeatedly against his desk until the point broke, leaving drop-
lets of ink in its wake. He looked down in time to prevent the ink from
ruining his starched white Perry Ellis shirt and tossed the useless instrument into the waste basket. Hearing a knock at his door, he wiped
his brow, placed the empty glass on the table, and ordered the intruder to, "Come in."

"How are you doing, Mr. Roberts? I hope I'm not disturbing
you."

"Come on in. I can't be any more disturbed than I already am. Fix
yourself a drink on the way in, and while you're over there, make
mine a double."

Craig Peters, the operations manager for Roberts Oil, walked over
to the bar, quickly preparing two drinks before making his way to the
high-back English chair facing Mr. Roberts. Craig rarely drank. In
fact, he only did so in the face of his boss. He hated the taste of
alcohol but would do anything to please Mr. Roberts even if it meant
putting poison in his system, or stabbing his closest friend in the back
with the jagged edge of a Kenyan spear. Mr. Roberts longed for the
constant reminder that he was somebody, that his fifteen minutes had
now lasted a full hour, and Craig was just the one to give it to him.

"Here's your drink, Mr. Roberts." He passed the glass with the
two shots of bourbon, no ice, to his superior who now had managed
to hide all of the anxieties he was feeling.

"How was it down there?" asked Mr. Roberts.

"Well, sir. It's not pretty, but I'm glad to report it's not as bad as
it could have been."

"How many kids are hurt?"

"All of them were a bit shaken up, but..."

"I don't want to hear about the fucking little brats that were shaken
up! You know what I mean Craig! How many of'em are dead?" Mr.
Roberts roared, now standing halfway out of his chair. He slammed
his drink on the table, spilling half the contents. He quickly put his
hand to his heart, took five tiny breaths and returned to his seat. Steaming, like a fire-eating dragon discovering an intruder within his midst,
he suddenly imagined himself a female praying mantis in the presence
of her mate. *She stood up on her hind legs and rubbed her front two*

legs together. Her mate, worn out by the deadly mating ritual, laid helplessly before her, wanting to run, to vanish, but unable to do either. She grasped her front legs together, closed her beady eyes and sucked in the stringy saliva that hung from her mouth. Finishing her prayer, she lunged forward, devouring her mate as viciously as he had loved her. Emitting a quiet chuckle, Dave Roberts shook free from his fantasy and stared toward the messenger who, now red-faced and bug-eyed, stared back. Craig Peters felt exposed, vulnerable as if he could be attacked at any moment, but knew there was no turning back.

"The bus driver died, but most of the kids are okay. There is one little girl with a broken leg, but they think she won't have to spend even one night in the hospital."

"Damn. How much is the auto policy worth?"

"You have an underlying policy with a million dollar limit but, fortunately, we purchased the umbrella which adds another four million dollars."

"Then we should be okay. I mean how much do you think a dead bus driver's worth?"

Mr. Roberts' last question scorched Craig's ears. He knew that a lot of money, perhaps the entire company, was at stake, but to hear him put a human life into those terms, sickened him...for a moment. "What are the limits on the environmental policy?"

"We combined the two last year. With our clean record, the marketing representative didn't believe the separate policies to be necessary," answered Craig.

"So we have only one fucking policy to pay for this mess?"

"I'm afraid so. But, Mr. Roberts..."

"What about the oil? How much were they able to recover?"

"No one knows for sure. But they have a hundred people down there. You know how this city is about their rivers. From what I was able to find out, they think they can recover a large portion of it as long as it doesn't rain again. They're working real hard down there. They shipped in an oil water separator that was used in the big Dunsmuir spill. The damn thing's enormous. Looks like it can suck up the entire river."

"Good, good. I just don't want those environmentalists to make a big fuss over this. We don't need any bad press. I want everyone to do whatever is asked. I want *us* to come off looking like the victims."

"I hear you, sir. But I have to tell you..."

"Tell me what? What else do you have to tell me?"

"A little boy was pinned inside the bus. The rescue workers managed to get him out, but he's in a coma. He's only seven years old and they had to pry the dashboard off his chest. Kid's on a life support system, and chances are not good that he'll pull through. I have a seven year old, Mr. Roberts."

Craig finished delivering his message in time to watch the king accept the fact that his kingdom had begun to tumble down. The tension that Dave Roberts had tried to keep from reverberating throughout his body manifested in his hand and exploded. The glass, containing about one shot of Bourbon, was crushed in his hand. Blood seeped from open wounds caused by the broken glass. The bourbon trickled into the cuts, ironically preventing infection from occurring.

Craig stood up, trying to find his way to the door before the ax could fall on him. When he reached the exit, a faint voice drifted through the air. "I want the locker cleaned out of whoever was driving the truck. In fact, clean out the garbage and send it to his house. I don't want to see him."

"Yes sir."

"Craig? Who was it?"

"Who was what, sir?"

"Who was driving the fucking truck?"

"Richard Swift."

"Richard Swift? Which driver is that? The name doesn't ring a bell."

"They call him Ricky, sir," stated Craig as he walked out the door.

Mr. Roberts sat hard in his seat, ignoring the nagging pain of his hand and loud thud of his heart. He turned, facing the city lights, and thought back to a conversation he and his grandfather had had on his grandfather's farm in Jackson, Mississippi.

"Dave..."

"Yes, Grandpa?"

"You see them niggas over there working in the field?"

"Yes, Grandpa."

"That's all they good fur. You hear me? Don't ever truss'em as far as you can see'em. They some mean sons of a bitches an will try to get over on you any way they can. Boy, you's got to remember that you's a white man an therefore a better man. Make sure they knows that an you'll be alright. Ever let them get close to your woman, an they try to stick their black dick in her, then she ain't no good. Let'em play with yur kids an they'll grow up to think they's ya equal. Give'em a decent job an theys will destroy yur business. Ya hear me boy?"

"Yes, Grandpa." Little Dave stared out into the open field and watched the Negroes picking their cotton like they did everyday. He had never paid them much attention, but now that his grandpa had spoken, he would always keep one eye open. *"Thanks, Grandpa."*

Mr. Roberts stood up, walked to the window and leaned against it upon arrival. For twenty years, he had poured his heart and soul into his oil company. Twenty years before that, his pappy had done the same. Escaping the backward state of the South, they went West, not finding but working for their pot of gold. Forty years of Roberts blood was now contaminated by a nigger.

If the kid died, if the rain came, his life would be over. And, for that, he would be sure to take the nigger's life too.

VERSE NINE

> An eleven-year-old murderer was murdered himself today.
> —Chicago, Illinois

The glow of the morning sun was as breathtaking as any human could ever wish. It stalled in the sky, midway from the top, to give all who were awake the chance to bask in its beauty. On the outskirts of the historically proud African-American community called Oak Park stood a fifteen-story structure which blocked out the wondrous vision for those poor souls who had the misfortune of stubbing their toes or breaking their necks. The Medical Center had been established by the city of Sacramento and later taken over by the University of California. Hundreds of aspiring young doctors passed through its hallowed halls each year in search of the power of healing. The Medical Center stood as proud as the sun with the wisdom of one hundred years buried deep within its foundation. The trauma center had seen it all; the birth of crack-addicted children, shoot-outs, and even earthquakes. No single incident was too large for the hospital to handle, no surgeon mighty enough to save the lives of those whose time had come.

In Room 213 of the hospital, Arizona sat by the bedside of her oldest child, little Johnny. It had been three days since the accident, yet neither of them was able to move from their spot. Little Johnny lay in a coma, shut off from his world, while Arizona was unable to find strength to do anything more but lean over the bedside and stroke her son's hand. The heart monitor sat to the right of the bed. Every few minutes she would look at the indicator ball and breath a sigh of relief as it continued to slowly bounce across the screen. If it ever stopped...*well, it just wouldn't. Not to her Johnny.*

A nurse walked around to the other side of the bed, not wanting to be the one to disturb the grieving mother. She picked up the child's hand, checked his pulse, then replaced it ever so gently by his side. After assuring the intravenous drugs were still hooked up properly, she walked over to the window, opened the shade, and let God's beautiful sunlight brighten the dimly-lit room.

Nurse Janice, on her way out, glanced over toward the little boy's mother, then quickly looked away. She was going through her own private hell. She had decided some time ago that she no longer enjoyed the emotional elevator ride that was so much a part of her chosen career. She had watched more children die then she ever cared to think about, and yet it still was not easy. Nurse Janice had no kids of her own, deciding the pain of possibly losing one was too much for her to consider. So, instead, she learned to love temporarily. She learned to love all the children that were placed in her care as if they were her own; but, she also learned to let go. She looked around the small, white room and marveled at its ability to hide all of the pain so conveniently under its sterile white walls and fitted sheets.

Turning to walk out, she bumped into a man who had appeared in the doorway.

"Can I help you?" asked Nurse Janice, leery of the strangely dressed individual who emitted a putrid odor from his body.

"No. I'm where I wanna be," replied the man. He was missing the top row of his teeth, which made his speech sound slurred, almost inaudible.

"I'm sorry, but only family is allowed back here at this time. Visiting hours don't begin for another hour."

"I am family, woman. That's my son in there!" he replied, fighting back a mix of anger and tears.

"Oh, I'm sorry. I didn't know. Go on in," she replied, stepping around him and continuing on to the next room, oblivious to whether she had hurt the father's feelings.

The quiet exchange had not broken Arizona's trance. Unmoved, she continued the vigil which had cost her five pounds, ten gray hairs, and a host of bags under her once-beautiful and mysterious eyes. Johnny had not seen her since the day she had thrown him out. Flashes of their happy and tragic past danced in his head while he contemplated his move. He looked down and scowled at the condition of his clothing but refused to let his misfortune keep him from checking in on a child that he had been robbed of.

"Arizona," he croaked.

Her head lifted but did not turn toward the sound of the voice. Simply moving her head in the affirmative, she acknowledged his presence. Johnny walked toward the other side of the bed, trying desperately to maintain the pace of his heart. The sun had now fully lit up the room allowing him a clear view of his son and the woman he used to love.

Little Johnny lay still. Tubes sticking out of every part of his body made him appear like an oversized puppet ready to come to life at the dollmaster's command. His tiny eyes were shut tight and his small beautiful face was expressionless. Johnny's eyes began to burn as the first wave of tears formed, readying for departure. He kneeled on the other side of the bed, faced Arizona, and reached out his hand, allowing hers to finally find the comfort she so richly deserved.

"Hi, baby," he said.

"Hello, Johnny," she replied. "How are you doing these days?"

"Can I take the fifth? Believe me, I could be doing better. But hey, I'm alive. What have the doctors said?"

"Nothing."

"Nothing? But they gotta say somethin'."

"They do. But what they say doesn't mean nothing. He's in a coma. He's alive, but that's all they know."

"A coma? How long is he suppose to be in that?"

"They don't know. He could wake up today, he could never wake up. How's that for narrowing it down?"

"Where's Nigel?"

"Over Mama's."

"How's he doing?"

"Oh, you know Nigel. He's running around as if he wasn't even on the bus."

"No. No, I don't know Nigel. I don't know either of my kids and now one of 'em I might not never know. You wasn't right, Arizona. I was tryin'. God in heaven knows I was tryin'. You put me out like I was some no good bum, leaching off you and not trying to do right by my kids."

"Not now, Johnny. I don't want to discuss that now. We can't change the past so let's just let it be."

"Let it be? Woman, that's all I've got is the past. Look at me. I ain't got shit, but the memory of my two kids to keep me from blowin' my brains out, and you want me to forget that?"

With a steady flow of fresh tears rolling down her face, Arizona slid her hand away from Johnny's and clutched her son's instead. She knew Johnny would come, but she had not had the energy to decide how she would react. Her pride would not let her even consider the fact that she may have chosen the wrong path, but her heart ached so much she only wanted the pain to go away. She wanted Johnny to go away.

"What do you want from me, Johnny? Do you want me to say that I destroyed your life? Do you want me to say that if I had let you stay one more day you would have been the better man because of it? You're the same man that you always were. I didn't make you start drinking. I didn't take away your self-respect. You did all that by yourself. So don't come here and accuse me of taking away your manhood over my son's hospital bed. 'Cause he don't need that. He don't need no negative energy, and, at this point, neither do I."

Silence filled the room as Arizona wiped the tears from her eyes and focused her attention on the little one. Deciding to let Arizona's statement pass, Johnny stood up, walked toward the window, then stopped halfway.

"How long have you been here, baby?"

"Three days."

"Have you eaten anything?"

"No. I'm not hungry."

"You have to eat. He may not need a deadbeat dad, but he don't need no anorexic mom either. Why don't you go on home and get some food and some sleep. I bet Nigel would love to see his mama."

"I can't leave my baby here all by his self."

"I'll stay with him. No matter what happened, he's still my son. Go on home. I won't leave here until you get back. I promise."

"Will you call if anything happens?"

"Of course. Go on home, girl. You look as bad as me."

"I hope I don't smell as bad."

"Same old quick tongue. Let me go to the house and take a shower..."

"Don't even say it, Johnny Rex Tyler. I'll be back this evening. Are you sure?"

"Woman, go on home."

Arizona stood and the sound of her popping bones could be heard across the room. Johnny smiled as good memories pushed out the old. The sight of her brought them all back: her feisty spirit, mouth-watering cooking, and sexy long legs that could wrap around his back, forcing an almost instant ejaculation. He watched as she bent down and kissed their child's forehead, rubbed little Johnny's hand then turned, heading for the door.

"Johnny," she said, stopping before making her exit.

"Yeah?" he replied, hoping she had reconsidered her position on his going to her house.

"Thanks for coming."

"You don't have to thank me, woman. That's my boy right there. This is the only thing old Johnny has ever done right in his life. That's my son too, Arizona. You hear me?" Voice trailing off, he refused to let her see him cry ever again. She sensed his need to release and left the room, giving him time to spend alone with his son.

After stopping by her mother's place and giving Nigel a great big hug, Arizona walked into her own house and headed straight for the bathroom. She looked under the bathroom sink, grabbing the first bottle of bath oil she found. Turning quickly, she moved forward, reached for the nozzle to the hot water and turned it all the way to the right.

Minutes later, she found comfort surrounded by bubbles, drenched in warm water. Other than the burning candles, all was dark, though not quiet. She had taken the time to search the house for her favorite cassette disc, depositing it into her bathroom disc player before slipping into the tub. *So much trouble in the world...,* wailed Bob Marley as his melancholy Caribbean rhythms wafted through the room. *He's right, she thought.*

Half an hour later, she was pulling the drapes closed in her bedroom, preparing to climb into her inviting bed and catch up on overdue sleep. She had taken several small bites out of her turkey and mild cheddar sandwich, but her appetite had not returned. Just as her head hit the pillow, the phone rang. Mouth gaping, heart pounding, tension building, she stared at the telephone. She was afraid to touch it for fear that she would hear a message of doom.

...third ring...fourth ring. "Answer it," she said aloud.

"Hello."

"Hello, may I speak with Arizona Tyler."

"This is she."

"Ms. Tyler, my name is Remmy Steel of Wexington Insurance Company. How are you doing?"

"I'm sorry. I don't need any insurance."

"Oh, no. I'm not a salesman. I'm the auto claims supervisor. We insure the vehicle that was involved in the accident with your son's school bus. I wanted to set up a time to meet with you to discuss the accident."

"What did you want to discuss? I gave a statement to the police at the hospital. I really don't feel like reliving it all over again."

"I'm sorry. I know how you must feel, but we must have a statement directly from the claimant for our records. We need to know how the accident occurred, and the condition of your son. If you want to be compensated for your damages, you will have to..."

"If I what? If I want to be compensated for my damages! My son ain't no car! My house didn't burn down, you inconsiderate bitch! My baby is in a coma, fighting for his life! And *you* have the audacity to call me talking some crazy mess about compensation! I'll show you compensation! You hear me, I'll show you compensation!"

Slamming the phone down, she stood up trying to douse the fire boiling in her veins. She had never thought about being compensated for her pain. Her mind had focused only on the recovery of her son. Had the world come to the point that every tragedy had to be rectified by unearned money? Would compensation, as the witch on the phone had put it, replace the laughter that would no longer fill the house if little Johnny never recovered from his coma?

New worries filled her consciousness, making sleep an impossibility. A glance at the clock showed the time at 11:00 a.m. She snarled at the phone, returned to the closet, dressed, and darted to the hospital to be with her son.

VERSE

TEN

Brooklyn? Do you have a second?"

"Just," he responded, without looking up. "This recent spill is driving me crazy. Not to mention, I've received five other new claims in the past four hours."

"I'll come back," Remmy responded in a soft, almost somber tone. Accustomed to her bubbly spirit and seductive voice, he turned, abandoning his work, and gave her his full, undivided attention.

"Hey, lady. What's going on?"

"I don't want to bother you. I'll come back."

"Bother me. Please. Come on in and have a seat. Tell me what's on your mind?"

She stepped inside the office, finding little comfort in his guest chair. There was a knot in her stomach that wouldn't shake loose. Butterflies had declared an all-out war and no matter how many breaths she took, they refused to call a truce.

"I've just spoken to the claimant from hell," she finally said.

"Welcome to the club. But don't worry, there's more. And probably worse," replied Brooklyn.

"Don't say that. I'm not sure I can deal with it."

"Trust me. Not only will you learn to deal with it, but find humor in it as well. What was this one's problem? He wants ten thousand dollars for his 1976 Pinto?"

"Not exactly. I called the mother of the kid who's still in the hospital from the big accident on Interstate 5."

"Ooh. Touchy."

"Tell me about it. I mean, you'd think I was the one driving the truck the way I was treated. I'm trying to help her."

"What did you say, Remmy?"

"I just told her that if she wanted to be compensated for her loss she would have to answer a few questions. You know, the usual mumbo gumbo."

"I'll be honest. I'm no expert when it comes to bodily injury, but I may have tried a different approach."

"Like what? I generally don't have problems settling claims, especially when were not disputing liability."

"Remmy. How many claims have you had where you had to contact the mother of a seven-year-old kid who had to be rushed to the hospital only three days previous?"

"Well, I can't think of any off the bat."

"Put yourself in her shoes. She is probably worried to death, and the last thing she wants to talk about is the value of her child's injury. That is, if she has any amount of decency. Just call her back, apologize, and move on. Tell her that when she is ready to talk, let us know. Until then, explain to her our benefits package and let her know if there is anything we can do, to give you a call."

"You make it sound so easy. I think I really blew it. Brooklyn, why don't you handle this one for me?"

"Oh, no! I'm up to my ears in cleanup. The last thing I want to deal with is a hysterical mother..."

"Are you being a hypocrite?"

"It came out that way, didn't it?"

"Yep. What do you say? I'm sure Larry won't mind. In fact, he might prefer it. You know he thinks you're some kind of insurance God or something. You do this for me and I'll prepare for you the best dinner you've ever had."

"You can cook?"

"Of course. What do you think we midwestern girls do on the farm during the winter months? Do we have a deal?"

Remmy leaned forward in her chair to offer Brooklyn a good look of her exceptionally blue eyes. With her right hand, she pushed her long, sandy blonde hair behind her face and fluttered her eyelashes toward the African knight of her dreams.

Trying to remain stern, attempting not to let his emotions run rampant, he adjusted himself, returning her gaze with one of his own. Brooklyn had never touched a white woman. He was neither intrigued nor repulsed by the pale race, but the opportunity had simply never arisen. He often wondered why so many successful African-American men found it necessary to desert their race, but beyond that had no hidden desire to be with one. However, to him, women were women. Soft, precious, and on any given night, moist and tight.

He looked across the table and thought that Remmy was someone he could make love to. But what did that mean? He was actually afraid to find out. Brooklyn acknowledged the darkness of his skin, but never felt it was anything of which he should be ashamed. What if he started to feel for her? To love her. Wouldn't his fellow Americans think of him the same way he thought of the Clarence Thomases and Ward Connerlys of the world? Brooklyn did not want such an experience. While he was not completely color-conscious, neither was he colorblind.

"You don't have to fix me dinner, Remmy. I'll handle it for you. Bring me your file so I can review it prior to calling the claimant."

"Thank you, Brooklyn. I owe you one. If I may make a suggestion?"

"Of course."

"You might just want to sneak up on her. If my intuition serves me right, she'll hang up on you the second you tell her where you're from."

"I don't think it s a good idea to just drop by her house. She may have people staying with her."

"Her son is at the medical center. The staffing personnel wouldn't give out specific information on him, but I know he's still there. I bet if you go up there, you'll find her. I called fifty times before finally reaching her at home. Something tells me she is one of those mothers who is rarely going to leave her little boy's side."

"That may be a good idea. Do you remember her name?"

"Oh yes. I couldn't forget it. It's Arizona Tyler. Very fitting. She's a real monsoon."

"Arizona? Couldn't be," he whispered to himself.

"What was that?" she responded.

"Oh, nothing. Get me the file. I'll try and get up there tomorrow."

"Thank you, Brooklyn. Larry wants us to stay on top of this one."

"Believe me, I know. Have you spoken with our friend, Dave Roberts, yet?"

"No. I was kind of hoping you would speak to him first. He kind of scares me."

"Oh, he's alright. I'll take care of it. I better get back to work."

"Yeah. Me, too. Hey, just let me know when you would like to have dinner. You don't have to be afraid. I don't bite."

"How do you know that I don't?"

"I don't. But I'm not afraid."

Bat of the eye, show of the thigh, twitch of the lips, and a shake of her hips, Remmy Darla Foxforth waltzed out the door.

Brooklyn returned to his own work, picking back up the new Roberts Oil file, Remmy had left with him, and scanned the most recent report. He attempted to call the driver, Richard Swift, for a statement. He needed to contact Roberts as well (he refused to call him Mister) but was putting it off. For what reason, he did not know. Something told him that now was not the time to contact him. Richard Swift had not answered the phone or returned any of his calls previously. Brooklyn had assumed that the driver had been released from the hospital, but maybe he was wrong. He picked up the telephone and dialed 4-1-1.

"This is Brenda. What city, please?"

"Sacramento."

"Go ahead, caller."

"The Davis Medical Center."

"Which department?"

"Do you have a patient information?"

"Hold please for the number."

An electronic voice came and delivered seven digits that Brooklyn quickly jotted down: *734-2011, please make a note of it.*

He returned the receiver to the phone, held it down for a few seconds, then dialed the number just obtained.

"UC Davis Medical Center, how may I direct your call?"

"I'm trying to find out if you have a patient in your care."

"What is the name and when would they have been brought in?"

"Richard Swift. S-w-i-f-t. Around three days ago."

"Yes, he's here."

"Great. What room is he in?"

"We can't give out patient information over the phone, sir."

"Can you tell me his condition?"

"I'm sorry, sir. You will need to speak with his doctor or a family member. We're not allowed to give out patient info..."

"I know, I know, over the telephone. Thanks for your help."

Brooklyn leaned back in his seat, scratching his head with his ink pen. It had been a long, exhausting day, and he still had the afternoon to go. He felt himself losing his grip on this claim and suddenly wondered if he ever had any control. Every phone call led him on a wild goose chase. The Environmental Department of Health had completely taken over the clean up, which meant he could expect an enormous bill at the conclusion of the case. None of the employees at the oil company had any substantial information. Of the two men who could offer any true insight, one he couldn't locate and the other he was hesitant to call. Now, to top it off, he had to make contact with a grieving, hot-tempered mother named Arizona Tyler. For a brief moment, he had hoped it might be the same woman he had met at the laundromat several nights ago, but, even if it were, she would either not remember him, or not be in any condition to get to know him.

Time inched forward. Despair and discontent filled the air as Brooklyn gazed up at the calendar hanging on his wall, next to his picture window. In two weeks, he would be on vacation. Going back to the Caribbean, Jamaica to be exact. The taste of acki and salt fish. The gentility of the West Indianian people and the flavor of ganga entered his conscious and took him floating far, far away:

The hot and humid air greeted him as he stepped off the 747 that had flown him across the Caribbean Sea and onto the landing strip in Montego Bay. The green brush of the mountains that formed the incredible background was the first thing to catch his attention. He had not expected mountains. The tourists rushed off the plane, cameras around necks, straw hats on heads, and money in hands as they began immediately searching for their luggage and locating their tour buses which would take them to the portable America on the islands. Resorts that reminded them of home. Brooklyn, however, did not wish to be locked away at a resort, manned by entrepreneurs whose only desire was to make the American tourist as comfortable as possible so that they would spend all the money they brought with them and, perhaps, phone home for more. He packed lightly, pulling his large backpack across his shoulders. He stepped outside the airport and became mesmerized by the lush vegetation and enchanting palm trees.

The natural beauty of the island was quickly eclipsed by the proud and stoic faces of its people. Jamaicans, the people of African descent who had gained their freedom from their oppressor in much the same fashion as their brethren across the sea by demanding their independence from the British government in the 1960's. They showed a certain pride in their country that he had never seen in all his travels across the United States. Feeling the inviting sea air and marveling at the clear island waters, Brooklyn realized at once that he found Eureka, and it wasn't in northern California.

Ringggg! Ringggg! Ringggg!

"This is Brooklyn," he responded into the receiver, after damning it for disrupting his daydream.

"This is Mr. Roberts. I know you've already heard about the spill, and the accident. I'm assuming you people are on top of this."

"We've set up two claims. One to handle the spill and the other to deal with injuries and property damage."

"Have you heard anything about the kid in the coma?"

"You mean the one who had to go to the hospital? He's in a coma?"

"You haven't found that out yet? What am I paying you people for? To sit on your asses while I do all the work! Damn right he's in a coma. I have enough insurance to take care of him, don't I?"

"I believe so, Roberts. We will do everything in our power to settle the claims against you within your policy limits. However, I have to place you on notice that any claim in excess of your stated limits will be your responsibility. You'll be receiving a letter giving you the exact details in a couple of days. I have a few questions for you while I have you on the line. How much fuel was your driver carrying at the time of the accident?"

"Our records show about eighty-nine hundred gallons."

"Do you know how much was recovered?"

"Only about half spilled. Of that, I hear the department of Health has been able to recover about two thousand gallons."

"Hmmm. So about two thousand gallons is still floating downstream?"

"It looks that way. I'm going to have enough insurance to cover this, right? I mean, I pay $60,000 a year in premium. You're going to take care of me?"

"We're going to do everything we can. I have one more question?"

"Yeah?"

"Have you spoken to your driver, Mr. Swift, about what actually happened? I can't seem to get ahold of him. I think he may still be in the hospital."

"No, I haven't, and I don't think we ever will. We fired him that same day."

"Do you know if he had been drinking or doing any drugs?"

"I wouldn't doubt it. You know how those black people are. Always doing something. Hey, look, I have to get off this line. Keep me posted. I want to know what's going on every step of the way."

And with that, Mr. Dave Roberts of Roberts Oil Company hung up the phone leaving Brooklyn in a state of shock. He slowly hung up the telephone, and stared once again out of the window. The hummingbird returned, but whatever he saw on the other side of that invisible barrier was more than enough to send him packing. The redness intensified in Brooklyn's eyes and the anger in his heart. He couldn't imagine a person so ignorant or so incredibly backward that he did not take the time to think that the person on the other end of the phone just might be the object of his hatred. Or maybe old Dave Roberts did know but didn't give a damn. Either way, Brooklyn's blood turned ice-cold.

A small man with an appearance identical to Brooklyn, dressed entirely in red, appeared on his left shoulder. Brooklyn stared at him in disbelief and listened to what he had to say.

"Ha, ha, ha." the small man snickered. *"Don t worry about it, Brooklyn oh boy. You've got that cracker's life in the palm of your hands and he don't even know it. Calm yourself down, sit tight, and justice will prevail. You'll see."*

Brooklyn turned toward his right shoulder and stared at the small man's exact twin with the exception that this man was dressed entirely in white.

"Now, Brooklyn. You can't fight ignorance with ignorance. You are paid to do a job and to do it well, regardless of who you are doing it for. Just shake it off. You've heard worse. And besides, he knoweth not what he sayeth."

Sitting straight up, Brooklyn now gazed straight ahead. Two weeks to go, and he would be on vacation. Maybe, this time, he would not come back.

VERSE ELEVEN

Famine has stricken the land. The children are starving to death.
—Somalia, Africa

Well, if it isn't Superman. What's up, Ricky? I see you recovered from your dive off the American River bridge."

"I m cool, Martin, man. A little sore, but I'll live."

"I didn't think you was coming back to work here. I mean after the accident and all."

"Why not? I've still got to pay my bills."

"Well, you know how Mr. Roberts is about his trucks. I just kinda figured..."

"Well, you kind of figured wrong. Fuck Mr. Roberts. It was an accident. Any fool can see that. Rain was comin' down so fast I didn't know if I was comin or goin'."

"Damn. I bet you thought your ass was dead when you started heading for the river."

"Man, you'll never know. It's like they say. I mean, there it was. My whole life, right before my eyes. And it wasn't pretty. It just made me realize that I need to take care of business. No more lollygagging around. Hey, where's my lock?"

"Wouldn't it be on your locker?"

"If it were on my locker I wouldn't have asked! What the fuck! Where's my shit?"

Martin peered into Ricky's locker and acknowledged the empty space. He had been on a long haul, down to San Diego, and had heard over the radio of the accident but not of any of the events that had followed. Ricky stood in amazement as he tried to figure out if he had cleaned out his locker and simply forgotten he had done so. The small, dingy locker room filled with steam as another co-worker ran hot water, preparing for a shower, and a long night with his honey.

Martin had no idea what he should say. He knew, deep in his heart, that Ricky had been fired but did not care to be the first one to enlighten the man with the dreadful news. Dave Roberts took great pride in his fleet. He would often inspect the trucks and was known for docking the pay of a driver if so much as a ding appeared on the shiny chrome. He had been in the rain himself, but had chosen to drive with due care. Having nothing to rush home to and valuing his life more than any pressing meeting, he had made it home in one piece. And, better yet, the truck was in one piece also.

Looking up at Ricky, who appeared to be figuring out the first piece of a complex puzzle, Martin felt sorry for him more than he would have if it were anyone else. Ricky worked hard. He was seldom late and appeared to be so very lonely. He figured the job must be his life, and now that it was over, he would have to start again, but was confident Ricky could do it.

Ricky, on the other hand, began to scratch his head and pick through the array of thoughts that gathered inside. *Why would his locker be cleaned out? Had he been fired? Who would have the audacity to put their hands on his things?* He turned and sat on the bench directly in front of the locker and retraced his steps the hours before leaving for Redding.

He had arrived early, determined to make it up and back before the meeting. He had rushed in, collected the day's assignment from the incompetent dispatcher and walked toward his truck. Maybe he had not stopped at his locker, but the lock... he never removed the lock. Then, like a bolt from the heavens, he remembered. He remembered it all. He had stopped by the print shop on the way to work and had copies of the nights agenda printed to pass out to all of his guests. The meeting had been an important one and, therefore, the agenda full, but, fortunately, as it turned out, not specific.

It suddenly became so clear to him. He had been fired and they had violated his space by cleaning out his locker. The bastards couldn't even wait for him to gather his own belongings. They had to rid the land of his vile existence before he could return and wreak havoc on the weak and the humble. *Those bastards,* he thought. "How could they have cut my lock?" he wondered aloud.

"Maybe they thought you was going to be in the hospital a lot longer and thought there was something in there you might need," offered Martin, rather sheepishly.

"Cut the shit, Martin." Ricky fired back. "You know I've been fired. Those bastards couldn't wait to get rid of me, could they? I've worked hard for this company, but I guess that didn't make no difference. Did it, Martin?"

"Maybe if you go talk to Mr. Roberts he'll reconsider."

"What? Bow down to my oppressor. Request permission to continue serving the master. Fuck that, and fuck you!"

"Mr. Swift," called a strained voice from the direction of the manager's office. Ricky turned and looked toward the door in time to see the entrance of Craig Peters. He was accompanied by a fat security guard who hadn't even taken the time to stop eating his jelly doughnut. "May we see you in the office?"

"See me for what? Where's the stuff that was in my locker, Craig?"

"You mean that racist propaganda that was in Locker seven? It should be sitting on the steps of your house. We had the Federal Express man pick it up yesterday. I'm sorry, Mr. Swift, but your services are no longer needed here. If you would step into my office, we'll need to collect all of your keys prior to turning over your final check."

"Fire me! For what?"

"For what? There are witnesses who say you were driving like a stone cold maniac. You sent one of the company's best trucks off the freeway and hit a bus-load of kids in the process, and you stand before me asking why you're being fired. You should just be glad we don't decide to prosecute you for reckless endangerment. Now hand over your keys, and I will be sure to drop your final check in the mail."

Before Ricky could respond, the back door to the small and now crowded locker room was kicked in. The water to the shower turned off, and Barry, the only other African-American employee of Roberts Oil Company, innocently stepped out of the shower and appeared in the room with nothing but a towel wrapped around his waist. Dave Roberts stood at the back door like Clint Eastwood making his first appearance of any given movie. Silence surrounded the room as all eyes shifted to Mr. Roberts.

"Hey, fellas," stated Barry, walking over to his locker to dress himself for the night ahead. "Good to see you, Ricky. We thought you was a goner. Man, I think you're in the wrong profession. You could have taught Houdini a few tricks. What's going on there Craig? Martin? Hey, what's up, Mr. Roberts? Damn, whose birthday?"

Barry bopped over to his locker, which sat between where Ricky and Craig stood. Martin had backed up and now leaned against the wall which led to the main building. The door which Mr. Roberts entered was at the far end of the cube-shaped room and offered the only true exit, unless you wanted to walk through the entire store. The security guard finished his doughnut, pulled up his pants, then leaned against the lockers behind Craig. No one returned Barry's greetings, a first sign of trouble. Mr. Roberts walked toward the crowded circle in his usual nonchalant manner. He had popped a pill earlier to control the erratic pace of his heart and was in no mood to get it stirred up again. He had fired men before. Some went out like a sick hound, head down, with their tails between legs. Others pounded their chests like a gorilla trying to ward off an intruder. He handled them all the same, but with this one, he sensed real trouble.

"Ricky," he said quietly. "I'm sorry it had to come to this, but we simply cannot have drivers who don't use safety precautions. That's a pretty big spill you caused, and I'm sorry but we can't take the chance on it happening again. Now, give us your keys, and we'll cut you a check right now. We'll throw in a week's severance pay. I know it'll be a little tough going, but you'll make it. A strong buck like you should have no problem finding another job."

"It was an accident, Dave. I'm sure I'm not the first one to have one," Ricky responded, just as calm, just as relaxed.

"It's Mr. Roberts to you. Like I said, I'm sorry. Now, I'm going to have to ask you to leave the premises, or you'll have to be escorted off."

Barry pulled up his pants so fast, he stumbled backward, bumping into Ricky, who caught him before he could fall. Ricky tried to make eye contact, looking for support, but Barry, with two kids and a pregnant wife at home, turned away, continuing his dressing ritual. He pulled a sweat-shirt over his head and grabbed his shoes and socks. Desperately, he thought of just walking out of the door with his shoes in his hands but decided against it.

"Don't worry, Barry, man. You're okay. Massa here needs at least one of us to meet his quota. Two was just too many, and now one of us has gots to go." Ricky's statement was made to Barry but directed toward Dave Roberts. A sneer spread across both of their faces as the showdown began.

Two men, both of the same nation, hated one another for no other reason than being of a different color. Dave Roberts hatred was historical and deep. He had been taught that blacks were his inferior and therefore could be treated in any manner in which he saw fit. Being a businessman, he was forced to deal with them on a day-to-day basis, but not once did he ever learn to trust, love or respect them. And now, the other side had played the race card. He had opened the door so wide that all of his backward ideology could fit inside. Ignoring the degenerative condition of his heart, he ran his thin fingers through his graying hair while imagining a perfectly sized rope hanging over a perfectly sized tree.

Richard Swift's hate for white people was newer but no less sinful. Such hatred had festered in the souls of his father and grandfather. They were incapable of acting upon it. Of extinguishing the fires that burned within them by making their aggressors pay for their aggressions. Ricky had almost followed in their pitiful footsteps but was fortunate, for on an ordinary night, while shooting craps with the other young fools, he had found an organization, or better yet, the group had found him. The knowledge, pride, and self-respect he was taught was invaluable. Discovering that his history began far before slavery enlightened him, but at the same time angered him. The realization that his culture had been stolen from him had been enough to push him over the edge. Oh, yes, he had to work for them, but only long enough to gain the power to extract his revenge.

"Now look here, nigger. If you don't get to steppin', I'm going to be forced to call the law and they'll have to lock you up. But, hey, on the other hand, you'll be able to see your dad. Probably the first time in years," Mr. Roberts chuckled.

"You son-of-a-bitch!" Ricky screamed. "I'll kill you! You hear me!"

Ricky lunged toward Mr. Roberts, who anticipated the attack. Without hesitation, he reached for the long steel pipe which leaned against the side wall. Ricky was too quick for him and landed a blow to his right jaw. The two of them fell to the floor and tussled about while the security guard stood motionless, not knowing what to do.

"Get this black-son-of a bitch off me!" shouted Mr. Roberts.

The rent-a-cop jetted toward the melee, finally realizing stopping the fight was part of his job. Barry, wanting to stay as uninvolved as possible, but was unable to stop himself, stuck his leg out as the porky guard rolled by, causing him to trip and stumble. The guard hit the ground with a thud, only inches away from the man he was assigned to aid.

Craig Peters and Martin looked at one another, then simultaneously ran toward the brawl, grabbing Ricky around the waist and shoulders as soon as they reached him, but not before he scored a final blow to his opponent's now-swollen nose.

"Calm down, Ricky. Come on man, just calm down!" shouted Martin.

"Get his ass out of here! Do you hear me? Get his ass out of here!" demanded Mr. Roberts, attempting to rise but finding this somewhat difficult.

"I'm a man, you red-necked, blue-eyed devil! And I'll be treated as such! I don't need your job, Massa Roberts ! You know why I don't, 'cause it ain't gonna matter! You hear me, Massa Roberts! It ain't gonna matter, 'cause there ain't going to be nothin' left for you to deliver to. Now, let go of me fools, so I can get the fuck out of here!"

Martin and Craig unhanded the screaming man, who pulled a set of keys out of his pocket and dropped them on the floor before storming out the door. He ran to his car, stuck the key in the lock, planning to jump inside and speed away. With adrenaline at peak level, he had completely forgotten that he had checked himself out of the hospital just hours earlier, at the objection of the doctor. Suddenly feeling light-headed, he rested his back against his car, then leaned forward, realizing he was about to vomit. Grabbing his stomach, he lurched forward and regurgitated a large wad of blood which splattered on the asphalt before him. Taking a deep breath, he held in the next round, fearing his guts would come up, then crawled inside his car.

His mind was working so fast that, for a moment, he drew a blank. Nothing made sense, not where he was, not where he was going, or even who he was. He stared out of the car window at his own blood and wondered what was wrong with him. Closing his eyes, he recalled that night in the laundromat. He remembered the thunderous noise and listened to it resound in his mind over and over again. He had not been mistaken. He had heard the sound his leader had told his group about. The shot had traveled around the world and had landed in his ears. He looked up toward his former place of employment, and with all the vitality of a hunter on the first day of the season, his mission became clear. The war had begun, and he had to prepare.

Inside the locker room, Mr. Roberts ran cold water over his face and sloppily washed the blood away. Craig, at his side, had offered his assistance, but it was blatantly rejected. A fat lip, blackened eye, and bruised nose were small casualties that he could handle any given day. The nigger had stormed out thinking he had really done something, but it was he, the owner of Roberts Oil, who had really won the battle. Without a job, what would Ricky do? Probably nothing; just like the rest of them.

Preparing to return to the office, he locked gazes with Barry who had decided not to leave until the entire ordeal was over. A gleam appeared in Barry's eyes, then he slowly and quietly turned away.

Mr. Roberts walked passed him and thought to himself, *he's next.* "Come on, Craig. We have more pressing matters to attend to," he said.

VERSE TWELVE

Dormant volcano erupts,
burying entire village.
—Colombia, South America

ightfall settled over the city, and for the first time in what seemed like an eternity, a million dazzling stars lit up the night. They were all there: the Little Dipper, the Big Dipper, the Milky Way and every creation ever imagined by the innocent minds of small children. The North Star gleamed so brightly one might have imagined that it was waiting on the three wise men, trying to show them the way to salvation, sanctity, the promised land.

The valley residents wandered aimlessly below, unmoved by the display of lights that may have acted as their guide, if only they had taken the time to look. Instead of noticing the stars, they bickered and plotted, schemed and imagined ways to hurt, belittle, disgrace, maim, and kill one another. Had not there been one person who pondered the meaning of life on that starry night? Would not a soul look into the darkness and believe that the answers to all of life's ills were buried in the stars or the moon?

There had been a break in the series of powerful storms which plagued the city over the past several months, but no one really seemed to notice. To them, the storms were but a nuisance which would soon pass. For this was California, the Golden State, and it would not rain for long. How many of the residents had actually gone to bed at night, after saying their prayers thanking the Creator for the life-giving rain which had forsaken them for so long? How many people had cursed the sky when the black clouds began to form because they were prevented from washing their cars and taking long overdue dips in their backyard swimming pools?

The foolish people of Sacramento—the holy land—had never taken the time to even understand the name of the place in which they lived. Every Sunday the church pillars over-flowed, filling to capacity. The annual Baptist convention was held, booked solid months ago, and confessions at the glorious cathedrals had lines of parishioners waiting at the doors. But the priests, ministers, and reverends should have simply told their flocks to look up at the sky on this star-filled evening and thank the heavens that they were alive to see such a glorious night. Perhaps, they should have tapped into the mind of little Johnny Tyler who lay peacefully in his coma, cherishing every bit of his untimely solitude while the world continued to chase their tails, spinning further and further away from what they were actually trying to catch.

Arizona sat in one chair in the far corner of her son's room nearest the window. She had pulled up the empty garbage can, turned it upside down and rested her feet on its bottom. Nurse Janice had brought her a blanket which she pulled all the way up to her chin, to block out the slight breeze that drifted in through the cracks of the window seal. Johnny sat in a fold-up chair, which one of the orderlies was so kind to fetch, at the foot of his child's bed. His legs extended out, barely resting on the hospital bed, but enough to keep them elevated, allowing him at least a decent night's sleep. The life indicator ball continued to bounce across the small, green screen of the heart monitor machine. Even with no one watching to make sure it did not stop, it continued its rhythmic cycle...beep...beep...beep. Little Johnny, while enjoying a level unknown to many, was still of this world giving his grieving parents something to hold on to.

Nurse Janice returned to her station, exhausted and depressed. She acknowledged the presence of her replacement and breathed a sigh of relief upon realizing her shift was over. In record time, she made her way out of the hospital and over to her vehicle, which was parked in the safe confines of the parking garage. She waved to the friendly security guard, but, too tired to speak, jumped in her red Celica, spotting it easily in the deserted lot, and headed home.

Boarding the on-ramp at Stockton Boulevard, she allowed two vehicles to pass before easily merging into the middle of the freeway. Half asleep, she hadn't noticed the vehicle speeding behind her. The crazed driver blinked his lights then swerved out of her way, refusing to reduce his speed. Janice, fully jarred awake, somehow knew that the erratic driver really had no place to go. She turned on her music, cracked her window, and allowed the night air and night sounds to soothe her, guiding her home.

Ricky sped by, cursing the woman in the red Celica who had pulled onto the freeway and right into his path. The slight interruption had caused a break in his thoughts, but it was short-lived. He soon returned to his inner musings which were at the very foundation of his madness.

After leaving Roberts Oil Company, he stopped at the first bar that he saw. Slamming down a shot of Jack Daniels, he thought of his promise to the organization. Unsure of himself, for the first time in years, he needed something to calm his nerves, to take away the pain and ease his mind. The whiskey sent fire shooting through his body but the taste made him long for more and more until the courageous bartender refused to serve him another drink. Ricky knew better. The organization had taught him that liquor was wicked. *It was the white man's way of maintaining control of one's mind, of keeping him subservient and shameful,* he remembered the leader saying. At the time, however, none of that mattered. He had not been in touch with any of the members since days before the accident and had no way of knowing if they had kept the energy going or let it die. He had just lost his job and now had no way of contributing his share to their dwindling funds. He had broken his vows, gotten drunk off hemlock and also discovered—all in the same day—that the little boy he had hit was in a coma. A young African soldier, taken out before his prime, and simply because he had been careless.

Tomorrow would be another day. He would wake up refreshed and rid his body of the vile liquor he had guzzled. Making contact with the key members would be the first task on his agenda. Finding a job, any job, would be the second.

Having changed freeways miles back, he took the Meadowview Road exit off of Interstate 5, turned right on Highway 160, and headed for home. His house would be there for him. His father had made sure of that. Passing the marinas, he glanced over and took notice of how high the river had risen. There had not been a flood in ten years, and even then, his house had escaped serious damage. If the rains hung around much longer, and the levees were unable to handle the swollen river, this time he might not be so lucky.

Refocusing his attention on the road, Ricky briefly laid eyes on a tall figure appearing to remove something from the trunk of his BMW at Scott's Marina. With the aid of his headlights and the dim lights of the marina, he managed to catch a quick glimpse of the man's face. For a moment, Ricky thought he knew the man, or at least thought he may have seen him before. On any other night, he would have approached the black man, hoping to pull the future warrior within their ranks, but with nothing on his mind except getting to his humble abode, Ricky hit the accelerator and raced home.

Brooklyn pulled his briefcase out of the trunk of his BMW, closed it shut, and headed down the pedestrian ramp of Scott's Marina. He had purchased a houseboat five years before despite the objections of his parents and friends. Now the watercraft was the envy of all who boarded.

The still night was the first to catch his attention. After so many months of fighting his way down the ramp and damn near losing his balance as he attempted to board his vessel, it was a pleasant change to be able to once again stroll down the ramp and enjoy the calmness of the water and the peacefulness of his neighborhood on the river.

Scott's Marina was located in the tiny town of Freeport only fifteen miles south of Sacramento, making the commute almost nonexistent. Tiring of the daily ritual, Brooklyn decided he needed to make some type of change in his life. Knowing that he would never move away from Sacramento, he chose to at least move to the water giving him the permanent feeling of being on an eternal vacation, far, far away. On long, hot weekends he would boat downstream and patronize the many friendly river towns in his path. Being on the river was like living in a different world. The people were always friendly and the water always welcoming and refreshing on any lonely day.

He paused during his descent and looked toward the sky, noticing for the first time the many stars that had set up camp. Suddenly a feeling of euphoria overwhelmed him, and for a moment he was moved by something completely inexplainable. However, as quickly as it came, it dissipated, leaving Brooklyn helpless to understand what it meant and incapable of bringing it back.

Reaching his boat, the third one from the end, he looked back at the row of similar vessels docked against the side of the pier. None rocked and few demonstrated any signs of life as the majority of the water dwellers deserted their boats during the trying winter months. Brooklyn, finally unlocking his door, stepped inside. With a click of the switch, the boat was illuminated, filling the space with man-made light which enabled him to find his way around. He dropped down onto the small sofa that just fit in the cramped quarters of his fifty-foot cruiser. He reached for the remote but decided the night was too peaceful to be disturbed with the unmonitored sounds of television. Instead, he chose to turn on his compact disc player, letting the sounds of Beres Hammond lure him away to his favorite island in the Caribbean.

After turning up the volume to his stereo, he stood up, walked over to the door, turned the lights off, and walked up to the deck. The stars still lit up the night, relieving his mind. The unobstructed sky is what he had come to see. He found a seat on one of the two lawn chairs that remained fixed on the upper deck, leaned back, and tried to figure out what it all meant. Not just the night or the stars, but also his life, his mission and why the world had decided to take out its revenge on that little boy in the coma and his poor mother.

Pushing down from the gulf of Alaska, another storm had taken shape and was headed for the Golden State. Still a day away, it had time to mix with the warm air of the pacific and grow into a sizeable creation. While the inhabitants of the city turned in for the night, Mother Nature's onslaught began picking up speed.

The man-made levees had been built to withstand any gale-force wind that She could throw at them, but the small minds of men could never imagine what was really in store. For the true power of destruction lay not with the force of nature but within the anger and hate and pain to which the world had become so accustomed. Fearing rainstorms, hurricanes and earthquakes, the residents had built buildings and roads to withstand them all... all but the self-destructive power of themselves.

VERSE THIRTEEN

Massive earthquake
flattens port city.
—Kobe, Japan

It was the third knock at the door which woke Ricky from his sleep. He had pounded the pavement every day for one solid week before finally landing a position as night watchman at the Folsom Dam. He hated the job. It was a long drive up to Folsom, and the pay wasn't worth the gas money it took to get there, but it was something. And for now, that's all that mattered.

The digital alarm clock read 11:30 p.m. Extremely tired but intrigued, he dragged himself out of his comfortable bed, reached for the sweats that hung around his headboard, and headed for the front door. The house had a slight chill, forcing him to grab a sweatshirt out of his walk-in-closet on the way toward the front. The knocking continued, a little louder than usual, sending a jolt of pain through Ricky's already tension-filled, hung-over head.

"I m coming! Cut out all that fuckin' knocking!" he shouted.

"Well, open up the door. It's stormin out here," replied the voice from the other side. With that, Ricky swung open the front door and greeted his old friend, Torion. Torion barged right by, trying to escape the rain that had literally drenched him from head to toe. Torion's fiery red hair and walnut-colored skin appeared to shine as the dim light reflected off the sprinkles of water which dripped off his body.

"It's still raining out there?" asked Ricky, rhetorically.

"Naw. There's an elephant spraying people as we walk by your house. Of course it's still raining! Look at me. Were you sleep?" quipped Torion.

"Yeah, man. But I'm up now."

"Where have you been? First you leave us hanging, not even bothering to show up for your own meeting. Then you disappear. Ricky, man. What's your problem? Are you still down? Are you getting afraid?"

While Torion's words slipped out, Ricky grabbed him about the throat and backed him up against the wall next to the door that still hung wide open. The gale force wind blew in large drops of water that landed in large thuds right next to where the two ended up. Ricky pressed hard and Torion, regretting what he had just said, gasped for air while wondering what he could do to get Ricky off of him.

"Don't you ever question my state of mind. Do you hear me, Torion? I brought your ass into the organization and I'll take your ass out. Alright, my Brother?" His voice remained calm and his glare fixed on his target.

"Come on, man. Get off me. What's up with you, Ricky?"

"Nothing's wrong with me. Do you hear what I'm sayin ? I'm the same man I always was. Okay?"

"Alright, man. Alright. Just be cool."

Ricky loosened his death grip then finally let go of Torion altogether. He reached over, casually shutting the door before finding a seat in his living room, pointing to an empty chair, apparently offering his guest a seat.

"Have a seat, Torion. Hey, I'm sorry about that. Things aren't going the way they should be right now, but I'm okay. Everything is gonna be okay."

"Man, you better not pull that crap no more. I ain't your enemy. I think you have forgotten that. You almost made me forget my promise and fuck your ass up!" stated Torion, accepting the invitation to have a sit down. He found a chair directly across from his host, sat back and prepared to hear whatever it was that Ricky was going to say.

Of the old gang, Torion had been the last to join up with the organization but now he was one of its most inspiring members. His promptness, loyalty, and dependability made him a favorite among the top brass but his timidness kept him from rising in the ranks. He was tired of making excuses for how the world had spit on his race and was prepared to do something about it, as long as it did not involve immediate danger. He knew that just being a part of such a freedom-fighting organization might cost him his life—which he was prepared to offer—but he didn't necessarily want to see it coming. If he were in a building and a bomb exploded, or he was the victim of an ambush, then so be it. But outright combat, he wanted no part of. So rather than become a front line soldier, he worked as the messenger, the henchman, a behind the scenes figure rather than a front man. He was accepted with open arms by all the members, for they knew that, if the time ever came, Torion would protect their backs.

"Did you hear about that accident on I-5?" asked Ricky.

"You mean that nut who was speeding and hit those kids?" Torion responded. "How could I not. It was all over the news. I heard the screwball was driving like a bat out of hell in the middle of a thunderstorm. Why? What about it?"

"That screwball was trying to go to a meeting that was planned at his house."

"How did you know that? Wait a minute. Wait a freakin minute. Don't tell me that was you. Ahh, man! What in the world was you thinking? I mean we would have waited. We could have rescheduled. There's still time."

"That's just it. There is no more time. While we are still trying to firm up our game plan, they're pressing forward. Setting their goals, preparing for the battle."

"What are you talking about? Everything's still cool. That's what I came over to tell you. Malik says not to worry about rushing things. We'll take our time and plan things right."

"What? Malik's a fool! The time is now. Didn't you hear it?"

"Hear what?"

"The shot. They fired the warning shot. Now they all know, and instead of us responding, Malik wants to start backpedaling. Well, we're not going to do that. We're moving forward."

"Ricky, man. I can't follow you. I don't know where you're coming from. Malik says it's all good. We have time."

"They fired me."

"From the oil company? Why?"

"'Cause I'm black, that's why! What are you thinking, Torion! What in the world is Malik thinking that he feels there's more time? There is no more time! Do you understand me! The war has begun and we're right smack in the middle of it. You go back and tell Malik that I have a plan. A plan that will make them all know we are here and are for real. Let him know that we need to meet. Soon. Tomorrow night. My place."

"Hey, I thought the newspaper reports said the man driving the truck went over the embankment into the river."

"Yeah, yeah, that's right."

"Are you okay? I mean you look alright, but man you must have fallen twenty feet. How in the world did you get out?"

"I just did, okay. They took me to the hospital but I told them I was alright. They tried to keep me, but I couldn't let them. I had to make sure everything was going okay and I'm glad that I did, 'cause from what you're telling me, everything ain't okay."

"You checked yourself out of the hospital? You don't look well. You should have stayed in for awhile. At least until you knew that everything was okay."

For the first time since he walked through the door, Torion finally looked straight at Ricky. Not just a sideways glance or indirectly, but a meaningful observation. He looked at Ricky's eyes, which were swollen and watery. He observed his skin, which appeared pasty and clammy. He watched the sweat pour down his friend's face, continuing to stain his already-drenched sweatshirt. Torion's knees knocked together, and his feet took turns nervously tapping, then pounding the floor. Ricky was falling apart right before his eyes, and he had no idea what he should do about it. He wanted to get up, leave, run away from this place, but he was too afraid to do anything but sit and watch his friend slide into a dark world which he could not comprehend.

The house, which was never spotless but usually presentable, was completely strewn with clothes and newspapers. Unwashed dishes sat on the dining room table, which was adjacent to the living room in which the two men were seated. A quick glance at his watch gave Torion all the excuses he needed. 11:30 at night. It was time for him to go.

"Look, man. You better go back to sleep," Torion advised. "I'm going to get on out of here. I'll tell Malik what you said, but he'll probably want to speak with you tomorrow anyway. I'll tell him about the meeting, but I don't think he can make it."

"Oh, he'll make it. Tell him I got a plan. Tell him we'll be ready, okay? Tell him that for me, Torion." He felt the vomit coming up but didn't want Torion to know. He walked to the door, opened it wide enough to allow his guest easy passage. Ricky, stood behind the door to see his friend out and shield himself from the rain. Torion jumped to his feet and marched out the door. With the wind battering his face and the unyielding rain tormenting his body, he stopped on the last of the three stairs and turned to face his comrade. They had grown up together. Made some good choices, some bad, but through it all they had remained by each other's side. Since then, Torion's life had taken on more meaning but Ricky's less, regressing. Ricky was heading the wrong way on a one-way street, plummeting into the abyss and unwilling or incapable of doing anything about it. Torion had noticed it before: the quick temper, the sporadic ideas and the intense hatred of European descendants. Hatred so strong that Torion could see the demons working inside Ricky's eyes whenever he talked about the war. Oh yes. Torion was as much a part of the African-American race as his brothers, but he was more human than black.

He looked at his friend, who was now closing the door, and yelled words of encouragement. "You take care of yourself, Ricky! I'll be back to check up on ya!"

Inside, Ricky stumbled toward the bathroom, kneeling by the toilet when he finally made it inside. The sandwich he managed to get down, the small can of soup, the glass of orange juice, and what seemed to be all of his guts ended up in the soiled white bowl. Managing to find his way back to his bed, he collapsed on top of the blankets. He was unable to find enough strength to wrap the covers around his frail body, so he fell asleep exposed to the cold.

Torion reached the ranch style-home located off of the Garden Highway directly on top of the Sacramento River on the north side of town. Several cars were parked in the driveway, but the dark house appeared deserted. He hopped out of his vehicle and sauntered up to the door, admiring the array of luxurious automobiles on his way. Reaching the entryway, he grabbed the round steel handle and tapped it against the solid oak door three times, then stopped. Seconds later, he heard three knocks which he answered with two more knocks, a pause, then another two taps. The door opened, allowing Torion access to Malik's humble abode.

He was met by the scent of drakarian aroma incense and the flickering lights of the many candles burning throughout the house. No furniture cluttered the front room, which boasted a full length Liberian carpet accented in rich dark colors and spectacular designs. Four large oil canvasses adorned the four walls. Each reflected a slice of African-American culture including the haunting painting of a Negro ghost hanging from a tree surrounded by white men in white capes. Blood trickled from around its neck, running down the rope and onto the hands of the Imperial Wizard of the Ku Klux Klan while his flock laughed, in the background.

Torion walked inside and was greeted by Malina, Malik's queen and woman behind his throne.

"What's going on, Malina?" asked Torion.

"You, Torion. Where have you been? Malik expected you over an hour ago," she replied. Her voice was light and sexy, almost erotic, and very manipulative. She had deep brown skin, glistening with the light of the candles. Hair cut stylishly short was wrapped around her shapely head which attracted men to her seductive body. Legs, long. Breast, round. Walk, enticing. "Come on in. We're all in the back room." Torion did not wish to covet his leader's queen, but his heart was not free from lust, so he did, (but he did not touch).

Descending the two steps, he entered a large room filled with people, *his* people. The soothing sounds of Impromptu escaped from the speakers, circling the room, allowing the perfect ambiance to go with the perfect setting. The entire back wall was made of glass, giving anyone who cared to look a phenomenal view of the river which was now level with the banks of Malik's and Malina's backyard. The rain continued to fall from the sky but the residents of the ranch house on Sacramento's elite riverfront stayed warm and dry.

"Torion, what's up with you, my brother?" asked Malik. His voice was as deep and strong as the first day they had met. "Not like you to be late. Is everything cool?"

"That knucklehead is on time even when he's running late," responded Rapone.

"You need to be more like him," echoed his girl, Raven. "How are you doing, Torion? Don't pay them no mind."

"I'm not. You guys think it's ever going to stop raining?"

"Who knows? I just hope it stops before the river gets much higher. Last thing I need is water to be coming up in here," replied Malik. "Have a seat, little man. We're just exchanging positive energy."

Torion found a seat by the oversized picture window, faced the group, and closed his eyes to maintain calm before he started to talk. He felt all eyes were on him, but refused to let that speed up his pace. He would speak when he was good and ready. Rapone broke the silence.

"You alright, man?"

"Yeah. I'm cool. I just came from Ricky's."

"Ricky? Where is he? What's he up to?" asked Malik.

"He s not doing too good. It was him."

"What was him?"

"The guy who crashed into the school bus then went off the bridge. That was Ricky. He was speeding down the freeway trying to make it to the meeting. He must have lost control."

"Oh my God." Malina put her hands over her mouth, shocked into silence.

"He's alright, isn't he?" asked Raven.

"I don't know. I mean, he looks okay. No broken bones, but he kind of looks sick. He checked his self out of the hospital. He kind of looks like he's sick on the inside. You know what I mean?"

"I'll go by there tomorrow," Malik announced in his authoritarian way.

"That's what he wants, Malik. He wants all of us to go over there tomorrow. He wants to have a meeting with the entire organization."

"That brother always wants to work," interjected Rapone. Even when he doesn't feel well, he wants to keep things moving forward. I'll go with you, Malik. We'll make sure he gets some rest."

"He doesn't want rest, Rapone. He said he heard it."

"Heard what?" questioned Malik, moving forward to guarantee he didn't miss what Torion was about to say.

"The shot. He was fired. He said he was fired because he's black, and then he said he heard the warning shot. I don't think so though, Malik. I think he's just tired. He's sick. I didn't hear it. Did any of you?"

"We might not have been listening," stated Rapone. "I thought I was paying such close attention, but maybe I didn't hear it."

"Malina, get on the phone and call Darius. Tell him we need to meet over Ricky's house tomorrow night. What time did he say?"

"7:00," Torion replied.

"Tell them to spread the word. I want everyone there. And don't be late."

"I think we just need to slow down," cried Torion, but it was too late. The women had walked into the back room, and Malik had headed toward the shelter with Rapone following. They walked out the sliding glass door, braving the elements, and walked into a steel shed sitting next to the house. Once inside, Malik pushed the wheel barrel to the side, bent over and pulled back a large piece of sod. Underneath was a trap door with a steel-bolted padlock. Malik quickly pulled keys from his pocket, popped the lock, and began descending a ladder, entering the dark and damp hole in the earth. Torion and Rapone followed suit, carefully stepping down into the mist of darkness, with golf-ball size raindrops pelting the steel roof.

When all three men were inside, the hatch was pulled closed. The censored-light switched on, giving the snake's den an eerie glow. The cramped quarters contained several shelves, each housing several dozen boxes of ammunition. Rifles, AK 47's, pistols, and hand guns hung from the ceiling. Each were tied by fishing wire, resembling a mobile designed for a baby Hitler. Several tin pails lined the south wall of the bomb shelter; they overflowed with grenades. Machetes, Swiss army knives, and daggers lined the north wall. An extraordinary map of the Mother Land was painted throughout the shelter, completely surrounding them. Engulfing them. Enraging them.

Malik began the chant, with the others soon following. A loud boom echoed through the air, setting the tone for this night, the night that Malik had been waiting for. He had been the one to deliver them but now realized that Ricky was the chosen one, for Malik had not heard the shot. What he did know was that it was real and it was here.

Boom, tap tap tap boom. Aheeee! Boom tap tap tap boom Aheeeee! The chant grew louder but the thunder drowned out their cries, caring nothing about their celebration. The revolution they had heard about was here, and they cared not that the revelation came from a false prophet.

On the other side of town, buried within the brush, sat a small wooden structure owned by Dave Roberts. On most nights, the cabin remained empty less the raccoons that set up camp in the absence of human residents. But tonight, the midnight oil was burning bright. Several men, hunched over a map of the city, absorbed the words of their leader. Dave Roberts stood at the head of the table, pointing to key locations around their homeland that had suddenly become a war zone.

The walls were decorated with swastikas, Dixie flags and other paraphernalia that reminded them of the good old days. Days when white men ruled the world without challenge and without resistance. An open closet door revealed white cloaks, dangling from hangers and a cracked spare room door revealed enough arsenal to set the entire city ablaze. It was not the entire city, however, that they wished to burn to the ground, but simply the area where the enemy had set up camp.

Lightning brightened the sky. Thunder chilled the night. And hate filled the room as the showdown had begun.

VERSE FOURTEEN

Avalanche traps school bus inside of tunnel. Rescue workers work tirelessly as nightfall approaches.
—Albertville, France

he Federal Bureau of Investigation lived up to the promise made by the attorney general, Janet Reno, as the second suspect was apprehended in the bombing of the Alfred P. Murrah Federal Building in Oklahoma City. Terry Nichols was arrested in his home in rural Michigan after a search of his premises and other areas frequented by him turned up materials which may have been used in the making of a bomb. He will join Timothy McVeigh, who is already being detained after he was stopped for speeding about an hour after the explosion. However, still at bay is John Doe Number three whom investigators believe was at the scene just minutes prior to the explosion which has killed one hundred sixty-eight people and shattered the lives of thousands more. Janet Reno has issued a statement that terrorist charges as well as destruction of federal property will be brought against all of the suspects involved in this cowardly and sinister act.

In local news, a small child is still fighting for his life at the University of California Medical Center. Young Johnny Tyler remains in a coma ten days after a fully-loaded oil tanker collided with a school bus. A spokesman for the hospital has issued a statement saying that his condition is unchanged, but his parents are praying for his recovery. No criminal charges have been filed against the driver of the vehicle, however, KCRA news has learned that the driver, Richard Swift, has been relieved of his duties as a delivery driver of diesel fuel for Roberts Oil Company. We will keep you informed about this tragedy as additional events unfold.

Well, spring is here, but you wouldn't know it by the weather. We'll have a full forecast, coming up in just minutes...

Click. With the press of a button, the thirty-inch television, sitting inside the black Italian stone cabinet, next to the oversized picture window with the incredible view of the city, was turned off. Franklin Jackson (a.k.a. Frankie) always placed the television next to a window or sliding glass door to remind him that no matter how gripping any particular show was, it was simply make-believe. He would often glance out the window to make sure that the world did not sneak anything past him. Grown men who glued themselves to their televisions disgusted him. They were called couch potatoes but Frankie thought that name was too good for them. With the world as their playground, they instead chose to find entertainment and self-worth in a small electronic box controlled by other men.

Frankie used his television as a device to keep up with what the rest of his countrymen were doing rather than as an outlet or an avenue of escape. His state-of-the-art, surround-sound system was programmed to pick up news networks from around the country, which he watched with great interest. His obsession with the news was due to his desire to be prepared to tackle any conversation which arose during his hectic days. Mostly he watched TV so that he would be the first attorney at the scene. Ambulance chasers, he and his associates were often called. Regardless of the name he was given, he had made a million bucks in the business. Representing innocent victims of a devastating accident had bought him a thirty-foot yacht which he kept docked at the Alameda County Marina in Oakland. It also enabled him to purchase a sprawling art deco home along the banks of the river in the posh neighborhood of Garcia Bend. And it helped him make the monthly payments on his Lamborgini which was parked in the third stall of his four-car garage.

Frankie hadn't always been so fortunate. His father had worked hard, assuring that his wife and three kids had food on the table and a roof over their heads. As he looked beyond the television and out the window, he recalled how his father would come home from working at the steel mill. Dirt covered Frankie's father from head to toe, his back just a little less straight than the day before. The old man wanted nothing more than a hot bath, a warm meal, and to rest, until the alarm clock went off the next day. He thought back to that dreadful Christmas Eve when his mother had sent him upstairs to wake his father so that he could watch the children open their gifts. Instead, Frankie found his father face down on the bathroom floor. The doctors declared it a heart attack, but Frankie had believed with all his heart that his father was just too tired to get up. Three days later, the family paid their last respects, lowered his father into the ground, and filled the hole with the same earth removed earlier from it to make space for the deceased.

Frankie vowed that if he were going to have a heart attack it wouldn't be from working in a steel mill but from spending too much time partying on the sandy beaches of Kenya or the calypso night spots of Trinidad and Tobago. Using the money his father left him, he put himself through college and then through law school, graduating at the top of his class. Turning down many offers from prestigious law firms, he instead created his own organization, specializing in personal injury.

In the beginning, things were rough. More times than he cared to remember, he thought of throwing in the towel and accepting a job with an established firm just to have a steady income. Hard work, perseverance, and an incredibly generous jury soon catapulted him into the big time. He had represented an employee against the same steel mill that had robbed his father of his youth in a case that involved a client's severed foot. The employee had been loading a paper bailing machine by kicking paper into the chopping blocks rather than utilizing the broom and shovel provided by his employer. During his last kicking motion, he slipped on a piece of loose paper, lost his balance, and slid forward into the machine just as its jaws clamped together, completely crushing his right foot from the ankle down. The foot could not be saved and was later amputated. Frankie was able not only to convince the sympathetic jury of the gross negligence of the steel mill by arguing that the work environment was hazardous. He also persuaded the jurors that his poor client's entire life was virtually destroyed because of it. The jury took less than five hours to find in his client's favor, awarding seven million dollars in lost wages and general damages. From that day forward, slick Franklin Jackson never even considered working for another man, ever again. As the verdict was read, he bowed his head, closed his eyes, and said softly, "This is for you, Dad."

Frankie strolled over to the window, wanting to soak in the entire valley all at once. At last, the rain had subsided. A million trees swayed in the persistent wind but the sun now shined, allowing the soggy residents time to temporarily dry out. From the top floor of the Renascence Tower and on a clear day, he could see the silhouettes of the snow-capped Sierra Nevadas. For today, he only needed to see as far as the medical center. A little put off that he had not reacted sooner, he thought about the little boy who had taken up residence in one of its rooms. He then thought of his own seven-year-old son and suddenly felt the pain of the innocent child's mother and father. The sorrow they must be feeling was enough to block out the sun.

When he initially received word of an accident, and after making the determination that the possibility existed for a big pay off, he would rush to the hospital, hoping to be the first of his kind on the scene. Frankie's confident demeanor and convincing speech were too much for the withdrawn families, coaxing them to instantly sign on the dotted line, accepting his services in representing their interests in a court of law. He had been engrossed in a trial when the tanker hit the bus and had not investigated the loss. But now, after posting his twenty-third straight courtroom victory, he had time to fully donate to defending the poor little boy whose only wish was to make it home safely from school.

The reckless driver had probably been drinking and surely had a record a mile long for other drunk driving offenses, or so he could make a jury believe. And the company, Roberts Oil, they were certain to have a list of citations for lack of a driver's safety class or other active precautionary measures to ensure the safety of their employees and others. Best of all, there was an insurance policy out there ready to be tapped into.

Franklin Jackson took one last look out the window before walking across his dazzling Oriental rug to his hand-carved portable closet. Opening the french-style doors, his eyes caught the attention of the circular mirror which hung against the north wall, adjacent to the picture window. He stood in its path, admiring himself and the seven-hundred dollar Armani suit which had been tailored to his figure. At six feet four inches, his height alone commanded attention, but his strikingly good looks and thin but muscular frame dominated the show. Honey brown skin glistened silky-smooth like polished mahogany, hypnotizing hazel colored eyes and white teeth were so straight they were even envied by his dentist. He was balding on top but the wavy hair that remained on the sides and on the back of his head was more than enough for his loving wife to run her fingers through. Make no qualms about it; life was good for Frankie and he made damn certain that it showed.

Tiring of basking in his own glow, he reached into the closet, grabbing hold of his ankle-length rain coat and umbrella. He walked over to his desk, closed the law book he had been reading, dropped a legal pad and some notes into his leather briefcase, then clasped it shut. Lasting four weeks, the last trial had worn him out, but he couldn't resist this one. An innocent little boy was lying in a coma as his parents grieved by his side. Doing all they can to stay strong for their child, they probably were not aware that they had been wronged by the negligence of Roberts Oil. Someone had maliciously ripped the foundation of their lives out from under them. Somebody had stolen precious days from little Johnny Tyler's life. His parents needed to know that although monetary compensation would not aid him in his recovery, it would send a message to the greedy businessman that their son's life was worth something — worth a lot of somethings.

Franklin took another look out the window and noticed the rainbow. He laughed aloud after catching a glimpse of the direction it had taken. The rainbow stretched east, toward the foothills, better yet, in the direction of the hospital. A hospital housing a seven-year-old boy in a coma. He grabbed his hat, turned off the lights and rushed

out the door determined to follow the rainbow to the pot of gold that
awaited.

VERSE
FIFTEEN

Typhoon makes a direct hit on seaside city, resulting in monumental flooding.
—Indonesia, Southeast Asia

"Knock, knock," said Sonya while peering into the partially open hospital room door.

"Hey, Sonya. Come on in," replied Arizona. She was unable to see her friend but easily recognized her voice.

Sonya walked into Room 213 as she would have walked into any other room. Seeing little Johnny lying in the hospital bed—eyes closed, skin darkened, laughter faded—her pace slowed. Her spirits dampened, she continued on, trying to hold in her pain as best she could. Arizona did not get up to greet her, as she had sat in the uncomfortable chair next to the window for so long that it seemed she had become a part of it. Sonya did not mind. She crossed the small room and embraced her friend the second they were in arms length. Arizona accepted the hug, although she was drained of all emotion.

"Oh, girl. How are you doing?" asked Sonya.

"Well, I'm fine. My baby hasn't woke up, but other than that, I'm just fine," replied Arizona. She pulled back, not wanting to replenish her supply of tears. She was tired of crying. She had cried so hard for so long that it almost pained her when she felt another sobbing attack coming on. So instead of allowing a release of her pain, she withheld it. She motioned Sonya to take the chair which had been recently occupied by her ex-husband.

Sonya fought hard to hold the pain at bay but it was useless. As soon as she caught a glimpse of the child, the dam burst and the river of tears poured from her eyes. She plopped down in her seat, burying her face in her hands and wept openly. She cried not only for little Johnny but for her children as well. It could have been one them. God help her. It could have been one of them.

Arizona stared out the window, giving Sonya the opportunity to let it all out. She always thought it absurd when people told her not to cry when she hurt. What were tears for? Crying relieved the mind and heart of the excess burden it carried. Tears eased the pressure on one's shoulders and somehow helped to take away the pain. *Go ahead and cry Sonya,* she thought humbly. *Go ahead and let it all out. Cry for Johnny. Cry for Tommy and cry for every kid who was on that God-forsaken bus.*

"I m sorry, Arizona. I know you don't need this."

"You have nothing to be sorry for. I'm glad you came. Even if all you can do is sit there and cry, I'm still glad you came. I know my baby is too. And when he wakes up, he'll tell you. They say that when you're in a coma, you're still alert to what's going on. So go ahead and cry for my baby so he'll know that you care. So he'll know that there is a reason for him to wake up. 'Cause you know what, Sonya? I'm all cried out. So while you're at it, cry for me too."

A new wave of sorrow overcame Sonya who shook frantically like a heroin addict who desperately needed one last hit. Arizona picked up the box of Kleenex on the table next to her chair and carried it over to her grieving friend. Sonya removed two tissues from the box and blew her nose hard, trying her best to regain control.

Minutes passed. Arizona returned to her seat. Sonya managed to catch her breath, after a trip to the restroom, dousing her face with water. The sun's rays drifted inside the room, feeding life into the two plants which Arizona's mother had brought by when she visited with Nigel, allowing him to see both his mother and his brother. The bouncing indicator ball continued its flight across the screen, leaving faint green lines in its path. Beep...beep...beep...

Arizona was the first to speak, breaking the overbearing silence which had swept over the entire room. "You'll never believe this. This lady called me from the insurance company of the guy who hit the bus. She was talkin' crazy. Told me she would compensate me for my damages. Can you get over that? Like my baby is a pair of shoes or a broken ladder."

"Was her name Remmy something or other?"

"Yes. I think that is what she said her name was. Remmy Steel. How did you know that?"

"She called me, too."

"I don't believe it. My son is lying in the hospital fighting for his life and she has the nerve to try and offer me money for my damages. I hope you gave her a piece of your mind."

"Well, not exactly. I mean, she was just doing her job. And besides, I deserved to be compensated for what I went through."

"I guess. It just seems like everything is measured in terms of money. Where's the compassion, the humanity?"

"Girl, you're living in la-la land. Nowadays it's about how much and how many. I will admit that my situation is a little different considering Tommy, praise God, walked away without a scratch, but hell, when that woman called me, I acted like the world was comin' to an end. I mean, the money is just sittin' there and more than anyone else it's rightfully yours. Hell, you add a new dimension to pain and suffering."

"What did she say? I mean, after you put on your performance?"

"She apologized for my tragedy and said she would like to compensate me for my pain and suffering. She offered me five thousand dollars. Five thousand dollars. Just like that."

"What did you say?"

"What did I say? I told her I thought that was fair, and how soon could I get it? That lady sent that check and a piece a paper for me to sign out that day."

"But what if Tommy has additional problems? I mean, what did the doctors say?"

"They said he was okay. A bit shaken up. But kids are resilient. They bounce back. How's Nigel doing?"

"He's fine. Driving Mama crazy."

"See what I mean? Girl, you can get money for him, too. You better call that lady back. You're going to have hospital bills. Look how much time you've missed from work! They owe you that money, Arizona. Call Remmy Mill or Steel or whatever her name is back, and get what you are due."

"You're probably right."

"Probably! I know I'm right. I don't have the number with me but when I get home, I'll call and leave it on your answering machine. Hell, for how much drama you're going through they'll probably offer you fifty thousand dollars for Nigel alone."

"I'll think about it. What else is going on outside this hospital?"

"Same old shit. I went back down to the prison with my cousin and I'm not going to tell you I saw that fine ass Donovan again. I told him what happened, and I hope you don't mind but...but..."

"But what, Sonya? You better not have given him my phone number! The last thing I need is some convict calling me collect asking me to send him a letter."

"He just wanted to say hi and lend his support."

"Sonya!"

"I'm sorry. Hey, accept the first call and I'll pay for it. But I'll tell you one thing, if you see him you'll be making that drive down to Tracy every week."

"Not in my lifetime."

"Suit yourself. But prison don't take away nothin' but their freedom. Has that trifling ass Johnny been up here?"

"The entire time."

"You're kidding. Don't tell me he managed to smuggle that cheap wine onto the hospital grounds?"

"He hasn't drunk anything. He just left a couple hours ago. I let him go to my house to take a shower and get some decent food."

"No you didn't. You let that bum into your house? I hope it's still there when you return."

"He's okay, Sonya. He may be a lot of things, but Johnny loves his kids, and he has always respected me. It was me who threw him out, remember? He didn't walk out on us."

"Yeah, but look what he's done with his life since. A big, fat nothing.

"I think all that is going to change. There's something about your oldest son being in a coma that suddenly makes you wake up and smell the coffee."

"I guess. Hey, I'm going to run. I need to go pick up Tommy from school."

"Not letting him catch the bus I take it."

"Not yet. I can't. Do you need anything?"

"Just your support."

"You know you got that. I'll be by later on in the week. If you need me to sit here while you take care of business, just give me a call. I'll be happy to."

"Thank you."

"Be strong, sister."

"Is there any other way to be?"

"Same old Arizona. Bye, girl."

Sonya and Arizona met in the middle of the room, and leaned on each other for love and encouragement. They were two mothers, fighting back the pain which tried to creep into their lives with nothing but total destruction on its mind. Using the strength passed down from their mothers, they pushed on and continued to survive in a world in which only the fittest thrived.

Sonya walked over to little Johnny's bedside, lightly kissing his cheek and petting the top of his head. She refused to cry, for she did not want him to see her upset. Instead, she turned her head away, catching a glimpse of the machine of life. At first glance, it looked evil, like a demon trying to steal a soul from a helpless victim, but as she focused her eyes on it, she found it soothing and peaceful. "You keep bouncing, ball. You hear me. Don't stop bouncing."

Arizona had returned to her seat and was again gazing out of the window. The world continued to function, just as it did for a lady named Yolanda Jackson who had stood in the same hospital room only one year before, who had prayed for the life of her child. Sonya, not believing in long good-byes, quietly walked out the door as nonchalantly as she could.

An hour later, Arizona heard a light tap on the hospital room door. Somewhat lonely, she eagerly invited her guest in. "Come on in. The door is never locked." Turning away from the window, she laid eyes upon the finest man she had ever seen. The black suit he wore, the polished boots covering his feet, and the Rolex watch around his wrist took a backseat to the man that held it all together. *"Who is this tall brother with the baby smooth skin coming to call on me?"* she thought. "Can I help you?" she croaked.

"How are you doing ma'am? Are you Arizona Tyler?"

"Yes I am. Who wants to know?"

"I'm sorry to bother you at a time like this, but unfortunately, there may be no better time. My name is Jackson, Franklin Jackson. I'm an attorney practicing right here in Sacramento. If I may have just a minute of your precious time. Oh, my God. This must be him. The little angel I've heard about. Such a fine young man. How old is he? About seven?"

"Exactly seven."

"I have one at home the same age. Believe me when I say my heart bleeds with yours as you live through this nightmare."

"Thank you. What did you say your name was?"

"Franklin Jackson. But my friends call me Frankie."

"Well, Mr. Jackson, what may I do for you?"

"You may do nothing for me. It's what I may do for you. May I sit down?"

Mesmerized by his looks, charmed by his style, and bored out of her mind she figured what would it hurt to hear what this man had to say. If she didn't like it, she would make him leave. In the meantime, he was a sight for her tired eyes.

"Please do," she replied, trying to appear indifferent but doing a terrible job at it.

"When I was ten, I watched one of my uncles hop around on one leg because the other had gotten blown off when the motorcycle he rode exploded. The mechanic had carelessly put his engine back together. Well, my uncle just shrugged it off as a freak accident. He went through life on one leg while that mechanic lived a comfortable life continuing to perform careless repairs on other customers' vehicles. My uncle didn't know that this mechanic should have bought him a wooden leg. That dime store mechanic, caring not about the safety of his customers but simply about the size of his invoices, owed him for his pain and suffering. He owed him for his lost wages and loss of enjoyment of life. Hell, he even owed my aunt because from what I hear old Uncle Jack just wasn't quite the same after losing that leg, if you know what I mean.

"What I'm trying to say is that the owner of the truck who hit your son's school bus owes you. Blinding rain fell from the sky, and yet Mr. Swift felt he had to make it to his delivery on time or else face the consequences. Roberts Oil Company didn't care about the safety of your son, Mrs. Tyler. They only cared about making a buck, just like that mechanic who caused the accident which took away my uncle's leg. Do you see what I'm saying Mrs. Tyler? Roberts Oil Company owes you. They owe you for every day that you sit here looking at your son who can't look back. They owe you for every day that you miss hearing his voice, helping him with his homework, or just holding him in your arms. Do you hear me?"

The pain was suddenly replaced with anger as Arizona thought about the rich oil distributor sitting somewhere in his mansion eating lobster with his wife and playing golf with his children. She thought about the driver, how he probably didn't even know or care about the chaos he had caused in her life. *How could they do this to her? How could they take away her happiness and act as if nothing had happened?* She would not let them. She would show them and Ms. Remmy Steel what she was made of. It seemed Franklin Jackson was just the man to do it.

"I got a call from an insurance company," she said, giving Frankie her undivided attention.

"Whose was it?" asked Frankie.

"The oil companies. A lady by the name of Remmy Steel. She said she wanted to compensate me for my damages. She gave my friend, Sonya, five thousand dollars. Sonya said I could probably get fifty."

"As Frankie laughed, his deep, baritone voice resounded throughout the hospital. He grabbed his stomach which was starting to ache and continued laughing as Arizona stared back at him in confusion.

"Why are you laughing? Do you think that's too much?"

"Too much? Mrs. Tyler, if you allow me to represent you, I'll get you one hundred times that amount. You have a little boy in a coma, brought down by the careless act of a large oil company. When we're done with them, they'll be asking you where you want the oil to go."

Walking into the hospital, side by side, were two men who had yet to be formally introduced, although they had spoken over the telephone several times before. They arrived in separate cars and from different directions, but for a common cause. Brooklyn walked indoors with Dave Roberts next to him, to his left side. Neither bothered to thank the other for opening the main front door to the hospital, for each had only one thing on his mind. The white man carried a teddy bear in one hand and a box of candy in the other. The black man carried a briefcase in one hand and nothing in the other.

Reaching the elevator at the same time, they finally acknowledged each other with a brief nod of the head, then stepped into the open elevator. The ride up was quiet and uneventful. Dave stared at the lights while Brooklyn read through some notes he had taken from Remmy's claim file. The elevator stopped on the second floor, opened, and allowed the men easy access to the spacious but crowded hallway. They both turned right, following the direction of the arrow toward Room 213.

"Are you following me?" asked Brooklyn, jokingly.

"It seems that way," responded Dave, reluctantly.

Neither one really believed the other was headed to the same destination but as they approached Room 213, still side by side, their suspicions rose. Out of the corner of their eyes, they looked one another up and down, but couldn't figure out the connection.

When they reached Johnny Tyler's room, they both stopped. Then they stared in surprise at one another.

"Are you coming to see the little boy?" asked Brooklyn.

"Actually, I want to see his mother," Dave Replied. "I own the company involved in the accident, and I just want to let her know how sorry we are."

"You own Roberts Oil Company?"

"You've heard of it. Yes. Yes, I do. My name is Dave Roberts. And you are?" Dave asked politely. Hand extended, he waited for the black man to return the greeting, but he did not. Brooklyn's eyes turned a deeper shade of red. His lips tightened and dark skin seemed to emit a cold which stung Dave, forcing him to take a step back. "Are you their attorney?"

Brooklyn took a deep breath, not knowing how to respond yet certain he had to do something. Roberts Oil Company was one of their biggest accounts, so he had to be cordial. However, the man had insulted him. He had insulted his race, and for that, Brooklyn held him in contempt.

"I'm the Environmental Claims Supervisor from Wexington Insurance Company. How are you doing Dave? I'm Brooklyn Hunter."

Dave's mouth dropped open as he lowered his hand to his side. His complexion changed from peach to deep red, matching the color of Brooklyn's eyes. The Americans looked at each other. They gazed deeply into each other's soul to try and guess what the other must be thinking — a useless exercise. Two men, each of the same nation, neither of the same race, bound together by a common cause not knowing what to do.

On the other side of the door, Arizona had accepted the ink pen from Frankie's hand. She quickly glanced through the three pages of legal mumbo jumbo, and without further consideration, signed on the dotted line. She now understood that she deserved to be compensated for her damages and that is what she intended to do.

VERSE SIXTEEN

Poaching of the African Elephants has been outlawed. May be too late to prevent extinction.
—Zimbabwe, Africa

Brooklyn Hunter. How are you doing?" Mr. Roberts asked, extending his hand.

"I'm doing okay, Dave Roberts. It's a pleasure meeting you," responded Brooklyn, smiling through gritted teeth, offering his hand to Mr. Roberts. The shake was mechanical. Up and down, hands barely touching, a meaningless exchange.

"It's good to see you here. I was just dropping in to check on the kid. Hey, why don't you deliver these things for me, and I'll leave so you can do your job." Retracting the right hand, he now extended the left, offering the gifts he brought for the little boy who unknowingly held the fate of Roberts Oil Company in his hands. Brooklyn looked down at the bear and box of candy and became sick inside. He knew that there were those who would feel personally responsible for the accident and not feel at peace until they knew that the child would be okay. But something about this man made Brooklyn realize that was not the case. Dave Roberts had only one thing on his mind: money.

If the mother refused to accept a settlement for her pain and suffering or the life of her child, the man who stood before him would walk away laughing, unmoved by the civility she displayed. If he knew his company were free from harm, would he still come bearing gifts?

Brooklyn thought not, and for that he could not accept the deceitful items, client or no client.

Mr. Roberts continued to hold out his arm and Brooklyn, now dazed and confused, stared hypnotically at the bear who appeared to be laughing at him. Taunting him. Disrespecting him. Mr. Roberts, now noticing Brooklyn's confusion decided to speak and break the God-awful silence which burned between them.

"Hey there, Mr. Hunter. May I call you Brooklyn?"

"You always have."

"Now, Brooklyn, sometimes people say things without thinking but that doesn't mean they meant any harm. You know how foolish we Americans can be. But that doesn't make us any less respectful and understanding of our fellow citizen. Am I making myself clear?"

Brooklyn nodded, lips held tightly together, unable to speak for fear of what might come out.

"Now, let's go in together and show a united front. Even if I may have offended you earlier, of which I have just offered my apologies, you still have work to do. I pay sixty thousand dollars a year in premiums, and I don't expect personal feelings to interfere with what is best for my company."

The burning sensation entered Brooklyn, erupting into an inferno. Mr. Roberts must have noticed the fire in his eyes, for he immediately took a step back. Brooklyn bit hard on his tongue. He forced his thoughts to travel elsewhere in the world. He thought of his vacation, the river, his home, and of anything else which would help him maintain control. Roberts Oil Company was one of their biggest insureds, so he had to control his actions, but he was a man. He could not let this blatant display of disrespect go unnoticed.

"Mr. Roberts. May I call you Dave?"

"I prefer Mr. Roberts, but for the sake of argument, yes, you may call me Dave."

"Now, Dave. I have been working for Wexington Insurance Company for five years and have prided myself in the fact that I have always done what was best, not only for the client but for Wexington as well. I don't always agree with what anyone says and I sure in the hell don't try and pretend that we live in a perfect world. I refuse to allow another American, as you put it, to control my emotions and therefore my judgment and job. But Dave. You have to realize that I am a grown man. Being a grown man entitles me to the same amount of respect that you are entitled to. Have I made myself clear?"

Now the rage engulfed Dave. But unlike Brooklyn's, his heart was weak. He slowly turned his head, took in five ragged breaths, and turned back to face the black man who, like the comatose boy, had two hands on Dave's destiny. As his heart began to relax, his mind picked up momentum, sending thoughts and emotions swirling about. He thought of the man he had to fire, then pondered the words of his grandfather as he acknowledged the aggressiveness of the new nigger who had entered his life hell bent on destroying it. Why was this happening to him? He had been a good man, a good Christian, but the demons were starting to rise, intent on devouring everything he had worked for. He would not let them succeed. Two generations of Roberts' blood was worth fighting for.

While staring at the white man in front of him, Brooklyn thought back to his fourth grade teacher at his all-white prep school. He remembered staying after class at the request of his professor and being a bit nervous about what his mentor was going to say. He liked Mr. Allen, but there was something about him that had always made Brooklyn feel insecure.

"Brooklyn?" asked Mr. Allen as he leaned over his fourth grade student's desk. "What do you want to be when you grow up?"

"I told you at show-and-tell. I want to be a doctor, Mr. Allen," replied Brooklyn, smiling proudly as he spoke.

"I was hoping that you were just trying to impress the other kids. Brooklyn, unfortunately, you'll never be a doctor. Negroes just aren't mentally fit for such a challenging position. Now, you're good with your hands. Set your aspirations on being a toll-taker or a sign holder. Maybe even a bathroom attendant. There's a future in that. Well, hell. You can save enough money to maybe buy you and your family a house one day. Now won't that be something?"

Brooklyn looked hard at the foolish white man who stood before him. Even at nine-years-old he felt more sorry for the teacher than he did for himself. He knew that he had been treated differently, but when you're a kid you don't want to believe this to be the case. Now the boogeyman his grandmother had warned him about had appeared, but the pride instilled in him at a very early age was too much to be overcome by such a worthless man.

Every morning when Mr. Allen awoke, he stared into the mirror and thought how lucky he was that the good Lord had graced him with pale skin. It was at these moments in which nothing else mattered, not the fact that his wife was sleeping with the mailman. Nor was it an issue that his oldest son had not been to school in the past seven months. And it definitely was not the fact that he was fifty-one years old and still trying to prove himself to the principal at the local elementary school. He had but one thing of which he was proud: that he was white. This filled him with enough emotion to fill the City of Angels three times over.

Brooklyn stared at his teacher who stared back. Neither of them flinched nor turned away in shame. They say a picture is worth a thousand words, and by God, when that young child finished staring him down, Mr. Allen believed it. Brooklyn thought back to the great kings and queens who had walked the earth before them. His young mind drifted to the prominent philosophers, explorers, inventors and orators. The beautiful and the gentle; the great Africans who were a part of the world in ways others could only envy.

Mr. Allen's face suddenly reddened with shame, as he realized that even if his pupil had elected to be a carpenter, he could build a greater house than he. Mr. Allen now understood that if life had taken Brooklyn to the heartland, the young boy would be a better farmer than he. And at only nine years old, Brooklyn Joseph Hunter had to let his teacher know how he felt.

"My Grandmother said I could be whatever I wanna be. She said that the boogeyman would try to tell me differently, but I wasn't to believe him. I'm going to be a doctor, Mr. Allen. And if you get sick, I'll still try to make you better. Mr. Allen?"

"Yes, Brooklyn."

"Are you the boogeyman?"

"No, Brooklyn. I don't think so."

Mr. Allen, broken and defeated, yielded to his young pupil, al-

lowing him safe passage out of the door.

Twenty years later, the same battle continued, only with a different player. It was the same old game. The same old game, in fact, the immigrants had played since the day the Mayflower had landed on Plymouth Rock.

"Let's go in," said Brooklyn, finally gaining control. "I'm sure his parents will be happy to see you. After all, you didn't have to come."

"I've never done this before," admitted Mr. Roberts, letting down his guard. He paused uncertainly, then asked, "What do I say?"

"Just let them know that you wish them all the best. People think they always have to come up with a profound statement, but that's just not true. Let's go in. We have a job to do."

Brooklyn knocked on the door of the semi-closed hospital room. A light voice from the other side of the door told them to, "Come in," and they did so without hesitation. In single file, they trailed through, mentally preparing for any possible situation which might arise.

Upon entering the room, their eyes met and Arizona remembered first. How could she forget a man so intriguing, so black, so mysterious. She stared at Brooklyn who in turn stared back at the woman of his dreams. It was her. The same Arizona, only the worry of the past days had drained a part of life from her beautiful face. A tall, muscular man stood next to her. He was impeccably dressed and well-groomed. His eyes also locked in on the strangers who walked through the door.

For a moment, Mr. Roberts' heart stopped. He followed after Brooklyn and now stared into the faces of two black adults: a man and a woman. Glancing to his right, he saw the little boy whom his driver had injured. A little black boy. He panicked. *"Oh God!"* he thought. *"Grandfather, you were right. You were right. They're coming to get me. They're going to try and kill me!"* The conversation was only in his head but to him, it was as real as if his grandfather were standing in the room.

Managing to pound his chest with a fist without anyone noticing, he jump-started his heart which now bordered on total destruction. Believing he was dreaming and attempting to end the nightmare, he closed his eyes, shook his head from side to side, then refocused on the intimate circle. The niggers appeared to be laughing at him. Their lips grew into large pancake-shaped saucers. Eyes bulged, and stupid smiles displayed huge razor-sharp teeth. He wanted to scream, yet nothing would come out.

Tension crept into the room like poisoned gas in a Japanese subway. Brooklyn, however, managed to speak, allowing Mr. Roberts to feel at ease.

"Arizona?"

"Brooklyn, right?" she asked.

"You remember my name," Brooklyn replied, sounding surprised.

"How could I forget a name like Brooklyn? It's not a common name."

"I'm honored. I wish our informal reunion could have been under more pleasant terms."

"Life's funny, ain't it?"

"Yeah. It is."

"How did you know I was here? I mean, did you know it was my son?" Arizona asked.

"To be honest, I didn't. Arizona, I work for Wexington Insurance Company. You spoke with one of my co-workers about a week ago. Her name was Remmy Steel. I've taken over the handling of this case. This is Dave Roberts, the owner and CEO of Roberts Oil Company, the company involved in the accident with your son's bus. We wanted to come by to let you know that if there is anything we can do to make things more comfortable while you are going through this trying time, to please let us know."

"That's very kind of you. I was kind of rough on your co-worker. It's just that she caught me off guard."

"You don't have to explain. We get so caught up in our jobs that sometimes we forget the emotional side. How's he doing?" Brooklyn asked, glancing for the first time at the bed.

Unable to allow his client any more rope in which to hang herself, Frankie jumped into and took over the conversation. "I'll answer that, Ms. Tyler. His condition is unchanged. He's in a coma."

"Are you his father?" questioned Brooklyn.

"No. I'm his attorney. Franklin Jackson." Frankie took three steps forward, then offered his hand to Brooklyn, who shook it readily. He did the same with Dave Roberts, who reluctantly returned the greeting, introducing himself simply as, "Dave Roberts."

"I'm sorry, gentlemen. It was nice of you to come by, but I'm going to have to show you to the door. We're having an attorney-client conference and before long visiting hours will be over. Let's exchange cards, and I'll give you a call in a few weeks. Hopefully by then, the doctors can tell us something substantial."

"I understand," replied Brooklyn. He exchanged cards with the attorney, then turned to follow Mr. Roberts who was already exiting through the door. Before leaving, he turned back toward Arizona and spoke slowly, so she would hear his words and understand that they were coming from the Brooklyn she had met in the laundromat rather than Brooklyn, the insurance representative. "Arizona. I'll say a prayer for you."

"Thank you, Brooklyn," she replied. "Thanks for coming by." He turned back toward the door, missing the tears that began to appear even though she fought to hold them back.

Frankie put his arms around her, and she collapsed in his arms. "It's alright. You'll see. Everything will be just fine. You're in Frankie's hands now. I'll take care of you."

They stood in front of the window holding onto one another hoping to find the answers to life's cruel game. Arizona's silent tears turned into loud sobs, forcing Frankie to hold her tighter, then tighter more. Business was business, but he had a seven-year-old at home and could not help but respect the intensity of pain this innocent mother was forced to endure. *You'll pay, Dave Roberts. Oh yes. Frankie'll make sure of that,* he thought, savagely to himself.

Outside the hospital, Mr. Roberts scurried to his car, which was parked in a nearby lot. His face completely flushed, heart beating erratically, he knew he had to get home and double up on his medicine which he had forgotten to take that morning. His vision becoming blurry he noticed that everyone passing by had black skin: the old lady on the corner; the young man walking his dog; even the fucking police officer directing traffic. What was happening? What in the fucking world was happening? Suddenly, a blast went off in his head. The sound of a space shuttle rocketing toward orbit; a mine bomb exploding on contact; a cannon at the onset of the war. Dave Roberts covered his ears but the sound was so loud it nearly drove him to tears. He uncovered his ears and looked toward the sky, understanding the time was now do or die.

Still inside the hospital, Brooklyn sat in the lobby reading a magazine; only, he wasn't reading it, just pretending to do so. He peered over the pages waiting for Franklin Jackson to walk by. When he did, Brooklyn would return to the little boy's room. He had to see Arizona...again.

VERSE

SEVENTEEN

Bison shot as they roam off of wildlife reservation.
—Yellowstone National Park, North America

i. May I come in?" asked Brooklyn, peering through the well-traveled hospital room doorway.

"You would know the answer to that question better than me," replied Arizona.

"This isn't business. I promise you. I wanted to come see how you were doing, that's all."

"Well, then I guess it's okay. You'll excuse me if I don't get up. It's been a rough day."

"There's always tomorrow."

"Yeah, I know. I just don't think I want to deal with that either. Come on in and have a seat, Mr. Hunter."

"Please call me Brooklyn. Mr. Hunter's for work and I don't necessarily like it then either, Ms. Tyler."

"Arizona."

Brooklyn strolled through the archway and across the small hospital room. He took the first seat he saw, which happened to be the one usually occupied by Arizona's ex-husband. However, Johnny wasn't there, so it was his for the taking. Finding it impossible to do otherwise, he stared at little Johnny, who remained in a coma, still hooked up to the machine of life.

Little Johnny looked so peaceful that for a moment, Brooklyn wished he could have traded places. He had a good life. Still, the chance to go into an obscure world and glide through the vast unknown was more tempting than he could resist. Breaking his trance, he quickly glanced at the heart monitor machine temporarily hypnotized by its motion. Looking at the long tube protruding from the child's arm to the intravenous drugs that hung in a clear plastic bag from a long pole, Brooklyn noticed the faint smell he associated with death. He realized something he had only briefly thought about in all of his years in insurance. The claimants they dealt with were not simply pieces of paper. They were human beings, breathing, eating, running, laughing, playing beings. They had lives to live which were directly connected to the lives of others. He thought Remmy had learned the hard way, but being abused over the telephone was nothing like sitting in the room of one of the innocent victims of a fluke accident. A victim in which you were supposed to make it all better by offering a pile of money, but not too much because the policy holder would not like that.

His mind finally returned from its short trip. Brooklyn decided to focus his attention on the woman he came to see. He took in a deep breath, held it for a few seconds, then blew it out in a soft, steady flow. Arizona, for a moment able to escape her continuous bout with depression, stared at Brooklyn with great interest and curiosity. Normally not an avid believer in fate, she nevertheless wondered if the Tarot cards had something in store for the two of them. After all, it had to be more than a coincidence that their lives had again touched.

"I haven't seen you at the laundromat lately," stated Brooklyn.

"I haven't had much to wash," she replied.

"I hope you don't mind me coming back up here. I just felt like there was a reason for my presence."

"Sure there was. You have to save that man's company. You have a job to do."

It has nothing to do with my job. If that were the case, I would have went home when your attorney asked me to leave. I just hope that, whatever it is, it's all good. I mean, first that guy shooting at the thunder and now this.

"They say life's a funny game," Arizona stated.

"Funny, not angry," replied Brooklyn.

Brooklyn knew that he had to think quickly to change the direction of the conversation. He had not come up to discuss how cruel the world was. That was a given. When he had exchanged words with her on that stormy night, he had felt something powerful come over him. Not quite certain what it was, and given a second chance to find out, he knew he could ill afford to use such knowledge unwisely.

"Have you been here since the accident?" he asked.

"Yes. Every day. I tried going home once, but it was too unbearable."

"You're a strong woman. I admire your courage."

"I don't get it when people say that. What do you admire about my courage? That's my son over there. What else am I supposed to do?"

"I guess it's the only thing people can think of saying."

"But you don't have to say anything. Words aren't always necessary to convey feelings and emotions. Actions speak louder than words, or are those meaningless words too?"

"That's what I remember about you. Not afraid to say what's on your mind or to remove a stranger's clothes from the dryer."

"Don't tell me you're still holding that over my head? I mean, I said I was sorry. But I won't say that it's people like you who turn washing clothes into a main event."

"I'm not sure how I should take that statement," said Brooklyn, lowering his voice and narrowing his eyes.

Arizona raised, at last repositioning herself so that she faced him, smiling so faintly that only those who wished to see would notice. Brooklyn had made that wish. "Take it any way you like. But I won't tell you how I meant it."

"You know what you need?"

"Okay. Now you're going to tell me what I need. Is this where you're supposed to say you'll see me again? Save it, Brooklyn."

"No, really. I was just going to say that you need to relax. Does anyone ever come up here for you?"

"His father."

"Your husband?"

"No. His father."

"Good...I mean, oh, I see. How would you like a nice, quiet dinner on the river? Give your mind a chance to release some of that tension. I won't keep you away long."

"On the river? Thanks, but the last thing I need is sitting in some crowded restaurant trying to act like I'm enjoying myself."

"Not at a restaurant. At my house."

"You have a house on the river?"

"Literally. I live on a houseboat."

"That sounds crazy. I never heard of any African-Americans living on a boat. Alright, Friday. You're going to mess around and end up lost at sea."

"People say that. But once you experience the peacefulness of being on the water, you'll never want to come back on shore, let alone live there. Here." He reached in his pocket, fished for his wallet and pulled out a business card. Sliding the ink pen out of his shirt pocket, he wrote down the address to his marina on the back. Returning the pen to his pocket, he stood up, walked over to Arizona and handed her his card.

"I better go," he stated. "I would love for you to come by whenever you feel like you need to be set free."

"Believe me when I say that's a tempting offer, but I'm in no mood to climb into anyone's bed."

"I was hoping you wouldn't take my invitation like that. The water. Remember, I was talking about the water. It s so soothing. Come for dinner. You'll feel like a whole new person. You need to get outside a little. If not with me, than with your mother, your best friend. I'm sure your little boy knows that even if you're not here, you're with him."

She took the card from his hand and laid it on the corner table. Arizona knew that she could not continue to sit in the hospital every day. Her bills were stacking up, sick leave from work was running out, and atrophy setting in, but the thought of leaving her child frightened her. She felt, like so many other mothers would, that she needed to be here in case he woke up or the life indicator ball stopped bouncing. Brooklyn stood before her resembling the Prince Charming she had always dreamed of. This fantasy prince had been a part of her life when she most needed him and she did not want to let him go. Falling into a trance, her mind tumbled backward in time awakening memories from her past.

"Arizona!"

"Yeah, Mom."

"Get in here! I need to say a few things to you."

Arizona ran inside the house, leaving her brothers and sisters in the backyard playing a game of freeze tag. Her pigtails flopped around her shoulders as she bolted through the door to find out what her mother had to say. She stopped near the entrance, hoping that whatever was on her mother's mind would not take too long. After all, she was winning.

"Yeah, Mom?"

"Your teacher called. She said you're having problems at school. Said you're having trouble making decisions. At first, I thought that was the silliest thing I ever heard and questioned why she would call with such nonsense. But then I thought maybe this teacher knew more than I did, and I ought to talk with you about it. Now, you have to remember, Angel, decisions are what life is all about. What school do I go to? What job should I take? Which man do I choose? You're going to be making decisions for as long as you live. Maybe longer. So just remember there really is no right or wrong, cause you can always correct your mistake. And if you can't, that don't matter neither. No one gets them all right. Okay, baby?"

"Yes, Mom. Can I go play now?"

"That's your decision."

"Arizona? What's going on?" she heard a voice say, bringing her back to the present. Brooklyn stepped back, turned around, and joined Arizona in receiving the person at the door. Johnny walked in, cleaned up, rested, and smelling of Boise d Ebene cologne. The rags he had worn the last time he saw Arizona had been replaced by a stiff pair of black jeans and a plain but clean white t-shirt. His hair was not cut but was at least groomed and presentable.

"Johnny. You made it back," exclaimed Arizona, sounding relieved.

"Of course I made it back. But I can see you weren't expecting me," barked Johnny in an accusing manner.

"Please, Johnny. This is Brooklyn Tyler. He's from the insurance company that represents the guy who hit little Johnny's bus. Brooklyn, this is my son's father, Johnny."

"Nice to meet you, Mr. Tyler." Brooklyn walked toward Johnny, extending his arm as he approached. Johnny extended his, and the two gripped hands once they were close enough. "Hey, Arizona. I better go. I have a few things I need to take care of. It was nice talking with you. Whenever you think of the water, it'll be there. My best to you, Mr. Tyler."

"Thanks," Johnny replied, letting go Brooklyn's hand and walking into the room. Brooklyn stole one more look at Arizona before disappearing, deciding it best to leave the family alone.

Not caring if the insurance man was out of earshot, Johnny immediately started to speak. "What did he have to say?" he demanded.

"That if we needed something to give them a call," Arizona calmly replied.

"What did you say?"

"Well, I couldn't say much. I was advised by my attorney to not say anything."

"You have an attorney? What's going on? Why didn't you talk to me about that?"

"What? Johnny calm down before I..."

"Before you what? I let you throw me out once but it won't happen again. I told you. This is my boy, too, and you better start acting like it!"

"I can't do this today. I know he's your son, but I've raised him. I'm the one who has taken care of him."

"And look where he is!" Johnny fired back.

Like a bomb, the words exploded inside Arizona's ears. She knew that there was nothing she could have done to prevent the accident, but it was only normal to blame herself. Johnny's accusations destroyed the protective shell she had built up allowing her pent-up emotions, her heart, and her soul to all come tumbling down.

"It s not my fault!" she screamed, leaping out of her seat. "There was nothing I could do! What could've been done?"

"I'm sorry, Arizona. I didn't mean that."

His words were like bandages over a severed limb. Her screams turned into sobs which ended in silent tears as she dropped into the chair nearest to her son's bed. Grabbing the blanket, she clutched it with such force that large veins appeared, making her hands appear old and feeble. "I couldn't do anything, baby. You know that, don't you, little Johnny. Mama loves you. She would never hurt you," she murmured repeatedly, tears rolling down her cheeks.

"I'm sorry, Arizona. Please don't cry." Johnny placed both hands on her shoulders, rubbing them gently, softly. He had not meant to hurt her, but she had hurt him, and the pain still clung around him like a disease, festering until it was out of control. "We're both under a lot of stress. Hey, that shower and change of clothes has done a lot for me. I couldn't believe you still had some of my old clothes at the house. Why don't you go home and do the same. Maybe even get a good night's sleep. Then tomorrow we can talk the way we need to. Come on, baby. Come on and get up."

"There was nothing I could do, Johnny. He always took the bus."

"I know, Arizona. I know."

Accepting his offer, she stood, trying desperately to pull herself together. She knew she had to get out or go crazy. The small amount of sunlight that shone threw the window wasn't enough to lift the cloud of doom that lived over her. Where could she go? Going home would only continue to depress her. Her mother's house offered little comfort and Sonya's much less since she didn't feel like rehashing their earlier conversation and, in fact, didn't want to discuss the accident at all. She closed her eyes, vying to make a private wish. For tonight, she only wanted to think of a happy world, one where everyone and everything was at peace. She wanted to smell the faint aroma of honeysuckle hanging in the air and watch the warm sun cast a glow over the city, calming the turbulent waters.

She walked over to the corner table and picked up the card which lay on its top. She folded the card in her hand, turned toward Johnny, and said, "That's a good idea. I do need some air. I'll be back in the morning." She grabbed her green leather purse, walked over to her son, kissed him lightly on the lips, and strolled toward the door. Before leaving, she felt compelled to say something to Johnny. The decision I made about you and me wasn't easy, but I had to make it. If I had to make the choice all over again, maybe it would be different. But I don't and I refuse to feel guilty over something I can't change. I do want you to know that I'm sorry you missed a part of their lives. They are your sons too, Johnny Cornelius Tyler, but I'm not your wife. With that, she turned her head and walked out the door.

*****

"Were the directions okay?" asked Brooklyn, welcoming Arizona into his houseboat.

"They were fine. I have never been to a marina. I didn't even know they were here. Except the one in Miller Park," replied Arizona, as she climbed on board.

"I have to tell you that I wasn't surprised when you called and said you were coming."

"Uh-oh. Don't get too full of yourself. I just didn't want to stay home. I didn't even enjoy my bath."

"I told you. I think there's a reason for us knowing each other."

"Haven't you figured it out yet? You seem to have all the answers," teased Arizona.

"If I had all of them, I'd be living in that boat right there." He pointed out of the window, giving Arizona a full view of the river. A forty-foot yacht floated southward, drifting past the window, but going slow enough to allow Arizona time to notice every detail. The fantastic vessel seemed surreal to her. Tall elm trees lined the river's banks, and a flock of ducks raced around its edge. She could not see the ship's inhabitants. Somehow this was for the best, for she could imagine herself inside, sipping champagne and boating into the happy world she had only dreamt about. "Why don't you have a seat on the lower deck. I'll get us going before I serve dinner." Brooklyn's voice was as soothing as the waters. Arizona felt as if she were floating on a cloud and loving every minute of it.

"We're leaving the dock?" she asked.

"Of course. You don't think I would have you in my home and not show you a tour of my backyard, do you?"

"I just didn't know. I love your home. You're right. I could live here."

"Becoming a believer already? You haven't seen nothing yet. Walk up the stairs. I'll be up as soon as I get us going." Directing her to the lower deck, she walked up the three steps and stepped into a room similar to her own patio. The two chairs which faced outward enticed her. The deck itself was small, but looking out of the plastic window which covered the port of the boat, she realized how big Brooklyn's home really was. She made her choice of a seat and sat back, absorbing the beauty surrounding her.

She had become so lost in the scenery that she had not noticed they were moving. She stood upward and, after turning around, saw Brooklyn standing on the top balcony appearing as if he was spinning a wheel, she then realized he was obviously driving the vessel. She looked at the river, sat back down, and for the first time in two weeks discovered that she could still smile.

Arizona admired the other boats as they passed the marina. She found it hilarious how all of them had names on the back which seemed to symbolize what their boat meant to each owner. There was an enormous sailboat which read *Peace*. Its sails were so high up she wondered how it was able to pass under the bridges that it had to go under. Another medium-sized vessel with green trim and a dark green canopy covering its deck was named *Fantasy Island*. Two men on this boat held fishing poles and drank beer while they awaited a bite from the unsuspecting Trout. The watercraft that really caught her attention was a smaller boat. Its clean, fiberglass shell and navy blue canopy made it stand out above the rest. Arizona read the letters that spelled out its name and laughed out loud. *Capturing Spring*. "How fitting," she said aloud.

"Huh? What was that?" Brooklyn yelled.

"Oh, nothing," she replied.

Reaching the end of the marina she took in a deep breath, wanting to taste the air, to drown in the world she had now entered, never to return. Thick pine trees acted as a wall, shielding the river from the unhappy world she so desperately wanted to escape from.

Now on a set course, Brooklyn placed the clutch in neutral, allowing the current to take his home into its grasp and do with it as it saw fit. He loaded his compact disc player, pressed play and joined his guest on the deck below. Bob Marley eased through the speakers, delivering his precious island music to the here and the now.

"Are you ready to go back?" asked Brooklyn.

"Are you kidding? I could stay out here forever. Thanks for having me," she replied.

"It's beautiful, isn t it?"

"Beautiful doesn't give it justice."

"No. But you do. Have you ever danced on the river?"

"I've never been on the river."

"Stand up."

"What? Are you crazy? I'm not going to dance out here."

"There's no one here but you and me. Come on."

He offered her his hand, which she hesitantly accepted. She stood up, and he hastily removed the chairs to allow them use of the entire dance floor.

Good friends we have. Good friends we lost. Along the way. In dis great future, you can't forget your past. So dry your tears, I say, Mr. Marley wailed through the aquatic speakers.

"This is my favorite song," she said.

"Somehow I knew that," he replied.

They faced one another, each with their guard down and vulnerability up. The orange glow emitting from the sun gave way to the red glare which hovered above the blue water. A light breeze blew from the north giving the water enough momentum for the boat to continue gliding downstream. The hypnotic tunes of Bob Marley caught the world in its grasp. The mysterious palm trees swayed to its rhythm. A flock of birds hovered overhead. And two people who were determined to seize the day, laughed and cried and unforgettably danced the night away.

VERSE EIGHTEEN

Nation in a panic as Mad-Cow disease discovered. Government contemplates slaughtering entire stock.
—United Kingdom, British Isles

A s expected, the sunset was spectacular. Apparently the real spring had finally arrived, and the residents of the Sacramento valley wasted no time in enjoying it. For the first time of the season, the temperature had topped the seventy degree mark, and the day's warmth had remained, allowing joggers to run without returning home soaking wet. Traffic was especially heavy since many people felt inclined to simply drive around the city, enjoying the glorious evening which was in store.

A grayish-blue Range Rover, carrying five members of the All-African Children Militia, rolled down Highway 160 on its way to the southern portion of the city to a meeting which was long overdue. Torion sat in the back seat, staring out of the window at the glorious Sacramento River. He had lived in Sacramento his entire life and had never ridden on the water. Consequently, he was previously unable to relate to its tranquility. Today, however, he took in all the sights which had eluded him for so long. His mind raced with the speed of the vehicle as he thought of the events the militia had in store. Butterflies mixed in his stomach, but he took in large breaths of air, trying his best not to let them take over.

As they passed Scott's Marina, he noticed two people, a man and a woman, who appeared to be dancing on the lower deck of a decent-sized ship. A bit taken back that the couple was black, he managed a smile and thought that the world could not be all bad. *Two African-Americans, dancing on a luxurious boat, cruising down the river without a care in the world. What the hell am I doing wrong?* he thought.

He wanted desperately to join them, but instead, he had become a part of an organization of hate and envy. The militia had accepted him as family. When he was hungry, they made sure he ate. If he was without residence, they provided shelter. And when the world seemed to bring him down, they were always there to pick him back up. In return, he dedicated his life to their cause, even though, at times, he didn't believe the cause was worth fighting for. Definitely, not worth dying for.

He pressed his ear to the window, trying to hear the music that the boat people found so intriguing, but all he could hear was the voice of their leader sending messages of hate through the speakers of the deluxe automobile.

"Oh, yes, my children," the leader intoned through the speakers. "We are trapped in a society that only wants us here so that none of them will have to lurk in the muck at the bottom of the dirty barrel. We were stripped from our homeland, carted across dangerous seas. Strapped to one another like animals and forced into acts not fit even for trolls. Four hundred years, children. For four hundred years we picked their cotton, tended to their children, and were raped by their men as if our very existence was simply to please and work for the master. But as all empires in the evil past of Mother Earth, this one will fall as well."

Torion's hand twitched as something inside of him told him to reach past Malik and ram his fist into the stereo to prevent the leader from spewing his hate-filled message any further. Lacking the bravery of his hard-working father, he did absolutely nothing except continue to covet the boat people. He did not covet their boat, however, but rather the inner peace which emitted from their pores and surrounded them like Thule fog on a cold winter morning.

Veering left off the highway and before reaching the Hood town bridge, the troupe followed the lead car down main street. A host of other vehicles—twenty-two—to be exact, wound their way through the tiny neighborhood on their way to the home of Richard Swift. Unaccustomed to a steady flow of traffic, the residents of Hood stopped their daily activities to give their full attention to the string of vehicles infiltrating their haven. There were no cemeteries in the area, so they knew it was not a funeral procession. Not having any theaters, dance halls, or other sources of entertainment, the residents were puzzled as to what exactly could be happening in their neck of the woods. With the passing of the last car, they returned to the world which was familiar to them. One which was safe and secure. One where the last thing on their minds was an imaginary shot which could turn friends into foes.

One by one, the cars located places to park in the vicinity of the house. Ricky waited on the porch for the arrival of his visitors. He left work early, complaining of chest pains, to assure he would be home. He had missed the first meeting, and it would take an act of God to make him miss another. Staring up at the sky, he growled, cursing to himself. Disgusted by the strange weather, and longing for the consistent days of summer, he wished he controlled the sky and everything that fell from it.

When the first person stepped out of their vehicle, he turned and walked back inside the house. There would be no small talk today, just business and only business. Like the sound of a row of pop bottle rockets igniting at the California State Fair, car doors were open, then quickly shut, signifying the group was ready for a gathering. Set to meet and plan out their attack before their attackers could beat them to the punch.

Malik was the first to enter Ricky's house. Dressed in fatigues which were designed in the majestic colors of the African national flag, he looked like the warrior he wanted to be. Unblinking, he nodded to his host and immediately sat in one of the three chairs located at the head of the room. Ricky had spent the entire night pushing all of the furniture out of the way so that there would be enough room for his visitors. He expected over a hundred people, traveling from as far away as Oakland. Standing room only, he could accommodate them all. Malik, his beautiful wife, Malina, and the secretary, Rapone, would need seats. Malik would deliver the message that the leader had prepared, and as custom dictated, Malina would remain at his side.

The smell of Jade incense filled the air as the members of the Northern California chapter of the All-African Children Militia filed inside. Mood: somber. Tension: heavy. Fist: clinched. Malina took her seat adjacent to her husband, and Rapone completed the half-circle just as the last member walked inside. All eyes focused on the deliverer as he prepared to give the greatest speech of his life.

"Greetings, my children," Malik echoed loud enough for all to hear.

"Greetings Sir Malik," the adult children replied in unison. Their voices were as crisp and clear as a Sunday choir at morning service.

"Would you step forward, Brother Richard."

Ricky pushed through the dense crowd until he was inches away from the speaker. The crowd stretched back to the kitchen, but everyone managed to fit. Torion found a spot up front. He would have preferred to hide amongst the people, finding comfort in being a face in the crowd, but he needed to know what was being required of him. He did not want to hear the voice drifting from a distance over a dozen heads. He wanted to see who was speaking as the message was delivered, wicked though it would be.

"Turn and face your family, and tell them what you heard."

"I heard it! Ricky yelled. I heard the shot! The one our leader told us would come!" Gasps rang through the pack, and questions were hurled through the air.

"When?"

"What did it sound like?"

"I didn't hear it!"

"How do you know it was the one?"

"Please, my children. Let him speak," responded Sir Malik.

"I didn't know for sure when I first heard it. A man at the laundromat convinced me it was thunder. But I know it wasn't. It couldn't have been."

"Tell them what happened to you," coaxed Malik.

Ricky appeared to choke back tears but continued speaking. "I was fired from my job. I was fired from a job where I had slaved for the man for five long years, but he bought another buck and didn't need two of us. The other buck bowed down to the master. When I refused, my boss called me a nigger and threw me out like vile trash. Then you know what happened? I heard it again. This time I was sure. I know he heard it too."

"But we're not ready!" shouted a voice from the back.

"Who said that?" demanded Malik, rising from his chair. The crowd parted, leaving a skinny, younger man exposed.

"I didn't mean that," the young man stammered nervously. "What I meant was..."

"Nathan. Come forward!" Malik commanded.

Nathan grudgingly walked forward. He felt his skin burn as eyes peered at him. His heart skipped a beat, but his feet continued to move forward, closer to his leader. When he was within arms length, Ricky moved out of the way, allowing a face-to-face encounter between Malik and Nathan.

"Do I detect regret?" Malik questioned.

"No, Sir Malik. I just didn't think it would happen so fast."

"What do you mean fast? It's been four hundred years! How much longer do you wish to walk in the shadows of your oppressor? How much longer do you need to scrape the bottom before the fire in your veins ignites and demands to be on top?"

"I didn't mean it like that. I just thought that it would be different."

"Different how?" interjected Rapone. "Did you think they were going to send us a telegram informing us that they were ready? I don't think he's down, Malik. Are you down, Nathan? Can I count on you to protect my back, or are you going to be hiding in the dugout waiting for a sign that only you can see?"

"Is it any different than a shot that only one man heard?"

The eyes shifted toward Torion as he stood waste deep in regret. The words had escaped his mouth by accident, but at least they had come from the heart.

"Torion? Was that you?" asked Malik, completely stunned at what he heard.

"It was him," Ricky interrupted. "Torion's weak. You've placed all your trust in the weakling, and now he's showing his true colors. He has never been down."

"You know that's not true, Ricky. I've put everything I've had into this organization, and I care more about it than most of you in here. That's why I'm not going to ask my brothers and sisters to give their life because you've mistaken thunder for the shot!" Torion fired back.

"Yeah! How come the rest of us didn't hear nothing?" stated another voice near the door.

"How do you know it was real?" replied still another.

Malik could tell they were on the verge of pandemonium, which he could not allow. Shot or no shot, he was ready for the war to begin. He could not allow traitors to betray the organization and take others along with them. He had already spoken to the leader who had commanded his army across the nation to take up arms and prepare to fight. Malik refused to lose ground on his turf to a handful of men who had turned out to be mice.

Quickly, he jumped atop his chair and screamed to his congregation at the top of his lungs. "Mmmyyy Cchildrennn! Listen to me! What do we want? Do we want to be caught off guard like our forefathers were? Shall we sleep through the night and let them come for us and put us back in chains while we bicker amongst ourselves? Ricky heard the shot. I know he did because I heard it too. I heard it and so did the rest of you, but you're just too afraid to admit it. The time is now, my children, and we won't let it pass!"

Pandemonium erupted, but the kind that Malik had hoped for. Cheers filled the house as clenched fists punched the air. The army had assembled, and now it was ready to attack. Drowning in a sea of enmity, Torion, Nathan, and a small handful of other dissidents stood solemnly. The wall they had accepted as love vanished, leaving only shards of broken promises and chunks of rotted trust. Torion felt himself becoming sick, so sick that he had to get out before the malignant seed could grow inside of him. Nathan must have felt it too, for he turned and tried to find his way toward the door. Ricky glowed as the thought of Dave Robert's death entered his mind, but he noticed, out of the corner of his eye, the traitors attempting to sneak away. Opening his mouth as wide as it would go, he pointed his finger in the direction of the betrayers and yelled with all the strength of a lion king perched on a mountain-top. "Judas!! Get them! It's Judas!"

Falling victim to mass hysteria, the crowd transformed from a peaceful demonstration into a vicious mob, out for blood. Enjoying the power his words had created and reveling in the mob mentality, Malik joined the fracas, sending orders from high on his throne.

"Get them! Don't let them get away. We mustn't let them get away! Judas must die. You hear me, my children? JUDAS MUST DIE!!!"

*****

On the other side of the river, imbedded in dense pines four scores of men in white robes danced mockingly around a burning cross. Nightfall had overtaken the valley, causing the blaze to appear larger than the night itself. Bottles of beer lay strewn about the circle. Each man had one bottle in his hand, turning it bottom up to assure that all of its contents were entering his body.

Dave Roberts wore a purple robe, indicating that he was the King, the Imperial Ruler, the granddaddy of hate. Tiny slits were cut into his hood, allowing him to watch the festival unfold. Hidden, but no less present, a sinful smile was pasted on his face as the thought of stringing up the ignorant nigger who had attacked him danced lovingly in his mind. His great grandfather had told him of the old days. He had waited a lifetime for them to return. Now, in his fiftieth year, these days had come back.

Earlier, stumbling away from the hospital, he had heard the shot. It was so loud that he wanted to place his hands over his ears and deafen the noise but refused. He wanted to hear it. He wanted to be sure it was the one but really, it didn't matter. The niggers had raised up, and he was determined to put them back down. The world belonged to his kind, and the time had come to let everyone know it.

The Klan also had detected treason among the ranks. Hog-tied to stakes driven into the ground, two men lay spread-eagled, stripped of their worldly possessions and exposed naked to the world. They had tried to convince the drunken mass that they had made a mistake, but the angry mass refused to listen. Instead, like a hungry gator, they turned on their own, determined to rid their circle of useless white trash.

The cloaked rebels joined hands, creating a large circle around the cross which still flickered in the warm night air. Bond tightened, immoral fabric sewn, the group of well-established hoodlums raised their arms in unison and began singing their song of hate:

America. America. God shed his grace on thee. And crowned thy good, with brotherhood, from sea to shining sea...

VERSE

NINETEEN

Drunken preacher builds
ark. Takes pair of every
living creation on board.
–Mountains of Ararat, Turkey

I t had been two weeks since devil's night erupted into a
full-fledged massacre. The hate mongers continued their
cowardly plans of destruction while the rest of the citi-
zenry moved through their daily routines, oblivious to
the evil smoke that simmered beneath them.

In a mid-sized office building, tucked away in a large suburb,
Brooklyn pushed paper from one side of his desk to the other. He
always performed quality work, but on the eve of his over-due vacation, he could not have cared less about the problems of his insureds.
For an unprecedented fourteen straight days, the sun shone giving
way to the long hot days of summer. The mercury on the company
thermometer hovered around the eighty-degree mark, giving the employees the false impression that the worst of the winter weather had
come and gone.

The friendly hummingbird fluttered outside his window but Brooklyn did not have the time to look. Instead, he pushed the work from
one side of his desk to the other, intent on finding the neatest position
for the files to be in when he returned. His plane left at the crack of
dawn, and he hadn't even packed. He contemplated sneaking out of
the back door but, with his luck, the old man would see him leaving

early and question his motives.

A quick glance at the clock offered some relief. In two hours he would walk out of the front door of Wexington Insurance Company and not think of it again for an entire fourteen days — heaven. The sound of the ringing telephone caused goose bumps to welt up on his arms. Lacking the desire to deal with anyone's problems, he thought of just letting it ring, but with two hours to go, that would be a hell of lot of noise.

"This is Brooklyn," he uttered into the receiver in the most professional voice he could muster.

"Mr. Hunter? This is Franklin Jackson. I represent Johnny Tyler and his mother, Arizona."

"How're you doing, Mr. Jackson. I believe we met at the hospital," responded Brooklyn, attempting to recapture his professional aura.

"Please, call me Frankie. And yes, we did. I apologize if my behavior was a bit abrupt, but Ms. Tyler and I had so much to talk about."

"I understand. How is the little guy doing?"

"His condition is unchanged. I'm not sure how familiar you are with his situation, but it doesn't look good. To put it bluntly, very few people snap out of a coma. They usually pass quietly, only noticed by the flat line on the heart monitor machine. Poor little guy. He's only seven, you know."

"Yes, I know. Well, Mr. Jackson, er, I mean Frankie. How may I help you today?"

"Well, two things. I don't know about you, but I don't think there is much to discuss in regard to this case. Little Johnny was minding his own business, on his way home from school of all places, when a tank from a delivery truck owned by Roberts Oil Company, your insured, smashed into his bus, putting him into a coma. I imagine you wouldn't dare try arguing comparative fault or any nonsense like that. Juries wouldn't be very sympathetic to that. They like little boys."

"Something tells me you didn't call to just rehash what we already know."

"Smart man. I guess we can cut the chase. I received your letter outlining your client's policy limits. I must admit I was a bit disappointed to see a company Roberts Oil size carrying only a five million dollar policy, but who am I to tell another man how to run his business."

"Five million dollars is a large policy."

"Is it? I guess in your line of work you have to put price tags on everything. So, what kind of price tag would you put on Johnny's head?"

"I wouldn't put it quite like that, Mr. Jackson. As a reputable insurance carrier we strive to ensure all settlements reached are fair and reasonable. We do not simply..."

"Cut the crap, Mr. Hunter. I've been a lawyer for too long to sit through that crock of shit every time I speak with one of you claims people... but you do sound convincing."

"Are you telling me your client is ready to settle?"

"She will be. When I tell her that you've offered to pay your policy limits in exchange for a release, she'll settle."

Brooklyn dropped the receiver on his desk and turned his head toward the clock on the wall, which now resembled a robotic prison guard, blocking his road to freedom. A palsy fifteen minutes had passed. He thought of pouncing on the guard and ripping its mechanical guts from its plastic body. Eyes reddening, he glared at the guard, holding him prisoner in his four by four cell with only a pile of paper and a telephone which allowed only calls from money hungry parasites. Smoke began emitting from the numbers and a fire ball erupted underneath it. The entire room filled with a poisonous gas, making it difficult for him to breath. For almost two whole hours, he would be forced to breathe the poison while the dreaded guard hanging on the wall mockingly moved forward at the pace of a snail trying to climb out of a pot of glue.

Brooklyn and Arizona had spoken to each other every day after that beautiful evening on the river. He learned to know her better than most of the people he had known his entire life. They laughed about their pasts, cried about the present, and prayed together about the future. He had become the only bright spot in her dreadful days and she offered him a ray of sunshine to an otherwise dark and empty world.

Though a million words formed between them, they never mentioned the reason he had come by to see her that day. Not wanting to rain on their parade, they refused to discuss the fact that he was the man who would give her money for the worth of her child's life, a thought that sickened them both, but one that could not be avoided.

He picked the telephone up again, after catching his breath and spoke into the phone. "Mr. Jackson. I'm sorry, but it is not possible for us to pay you five million dollars for this claim. However, we empathize with the Tylers and are willing to discuss a fair and reasonable settlement based on Johnny's medical bills. We will also be willing to make an additional payment for the pain and suffering that has been caused by this tragic accident. Please send over copies of all the hospital bills and the doctor's report so that I can accurately evaluate this claim and extend an offer that I'm sure you and your clients will find fair."

"Listen. I've gotten twice as much as we're asking for a much smaller injury. Before you go deciding to ignore my fair and reasonable offer, you need to think hard about taking a case like this to trial. Before I'm done, they'll be calling it Tyler's Oil . I'll get the information you requested, but I don't want to hear you come back with anything less than five million dollars."

"Well, you may not be happy with the offer I extend, but your clients may be. You will relay our offer to your clients, won't you?"

"Without a doubt. Which brings me to the next item on my agenda. I can't control who my client spends her time with, but I'll say this. If I find out you discussed this case with Ms. Tyler, we'll own Wexington as well. I'll get that information to you via the mail. You have a good day."

Brooklyn put down the receiver on the phone then pulled his airline ticket out of his open briefcase. Kingston, Jamaica. Kingston, Jamaica. He read the itinerary over and over just to make sure it was real. His life had somehow ended up like his home: set adrift on memory bliss, as the saying goes. With no woman in his life to call his own, he at least had met a person with whom he felt at ease. Now, because of his job, that relationship was also in jeopardy. Where had he taken the wrong turn, and why couldn't he locate the path of serenity?

Refusing to work a second more, he tossed the ticket back in his briefcase, snapped it shut and started the process of preparing for the end of the day. With a full hour to go, he decided to sneak out and risk the chance that Larry would see him. Right now, he didn't give a damn. He was losing a piece of his mind and refused to let another piece float away with it. With the computer, radio, and adding machine turned off, he stood up with briefcase in hand, and walked toward the door. He stuck his head out, checking to be sure the coast was clear, then strolled quietly down the long, empty hallway.

Stopping at the first aisle he came to, he peeked around the corner, then continued his journey. Exit now in sight, he already felt a burden lift from his frame. He ducked behind the large partitioned area which housed the secretaries, sneaked passed the copy room, and tiptoed around the small cafeteria. He turned the door's knob to the right, took one last look over his shoulder, and flew out the door.

He was halfway to his car when he heard someone call his name. "Brooklyn!"

The voice was light and friendly, but still he was hesitant to turn around. Imagining it was someone running after him at the request of Larry, he was willing to follow through on his plan and face the consequences when he returned.

"Brooklyn! Wait for me."

Turning around, he was mildly surprised at noticing Remmy running in his direction, blond locks blowing in the wind. Her long tan legs moved with ease in her two-inch heels. He decided he would wait and see what she wanted.

"You weren't going to leave without saying goodbye, were you, Brooklyn?" she said, after finally catching up to him.

"Well, being that I'm sneaking out a little early, I figured it best not to announce my departure on the intercom."

"Got short-timers itch, huh?"

"Like you wouldn't believe. I'm leaving very early in the morning and believe it or not, I haven't packed."

"I believe it. You men are all alike when it comes to things like that. You got somebody to help you?"

"Just myself."

"I'd be happy to come over and send you off. You might as well have a home-cooked meal from a midwestern gal before you head over to the islands."

"Thanks for the offer, but I don't want you to go through the trouble. I'll be all right."

"Well, I'll just stop by to see you off. Besides, I've never been to your boat. I think that's so romantic living on the water. I'll bring some rum. You might as well start your vacation now. What do you say? Remember, I don't bite."

"What the hell. Packing's a bitch. If you're willing to do the dirty work, who am I to stop you. I'm at Slip 37 at Scott's Marina off of Highway 160, near Hood."

"I've been there before. Isn't Cheshire Queen docked there?"

"Slip number one."

"Great. I'll see you at six. How's that sound?"

"Sounds like a winner. I appreciate your help."

"My pleasure. I better get going before someone finds both of us gone. Don't want unwarranted rumors to start flying."

Like a cat, Remmy turned around on her toes and strutted back into the building; derriere moving side to side, hair dangling over her shoulders. Brooklyn stared at the woman. Thoughts of having her entered his mind as blood rushed to his groin, causing a pulsating sensation in his pants. You need a woman, he thought as he reluctantly turned and uncomfortably walked to his car.

*****

"You found it okay?" said Brooklyn, opening the door wide enough for his guest to walk through.

"Piece of cake. Wow, Brooklyn. I love your place. Reggae, huh? Getting ready?" she replied in an incredibly sexy tone and finding it impossible to not look past her host as she spoke. "What an incredible view. I can't imagine waking up to that every day."

"Yeah. It's pretty nice. I can't imagine it any other way. Make yourself at home. I'll fix us a drink."

"I'll do it. Just show me the way to the kitchen. I make the best rum punch in the state."

"What do you know about rum punch? You've been to Jamaica?"

"No, but I get around."

He showed her to the kitchen, allowing her unlimited access to his home. The area was small, so he stepped out of the way so she could work her magic. She settled her bag on top of the counter, then reached inside the freezer and grabbed a tray of ice.

"Where do you keep your glasses?"

"Right up there."

He pointed to a small cupboard above the stove. She reached inside and pulled out two short glasses. The rum smelled good as she poured it out of its vial and mixed in the sweet red juice. A speed boat raced by, ignoring the no wake zone, causing Brooklyn's boat to rock side to side. Remmy kept her balance, but the ice slid off the counter and crashed on the floor. They both bent down to pick it up. Their bodies touched, sending a swath of fire through each of them. Brooklyn backed away. Remmy smiled, then slid her tongue across her thin lips. She tossed the ice into the sink and continued to mix the drinks: two parts rum, two parts punch. When she was through, she handed a glass to Brooklyn who led her up the stairs of the lower deck .

When he arrived, he was shocked to see Arizona dancing to the music of Peter Tosh, moving her savory body to the grooves pounding the deck. With the sun high over-head, she looked like a native islander, beautiful, sexy and black. He shook his head hard, not believing what he saw. When his eyes refocused, she was gone.

"Oh, I just love it, Brooklyn. Why have you never invited me before?"

"Never knew you were interested."

"You have got to be kidding! Who wouldn't be interested in making love..." Remmy caught herself, now somewhat embarrassed she lamely finished her thought. "I mean, relaxing on a boat. I want one."

"You wouldn't regret it. Have a seat. Take a load off."

She accepted his invitation. Crossing her legs, the split in her summer dress revealed soft, creamy thighs. Leaning forward to glance at the flock of ducks floating by, her unblemished breasts were exposed.

Falling back into the seat and sipping on his drink, Brooklyn realized for the first time how beautiful Remmy really was. He had only thought of her as a co-worker, but now that they were out of the paper-pushing element, he began to see her in a whole new light.

"How's the Roberts Oil claim going?" she asked.

"Shitty. But then what did you expect? I don't know how I'm going to keep the payoff within his limits. I spoke with a guy down in the Department of Environmental Health. He says he thinks the clean-up bill will top a million bucks. We've already exhausted over a hundred thousand on the kids and we still have the little girl with the broken leg, and the little boy in the coma to deal with."

"Better you than me. I don't think I could handle all that stress."

"You would've done fine. You just have to put yourself above it. Hey, let's change the subject. I'm officially on vacation. Speaking of vacation, I better pack."

"I'll help."

"Don't rush. Finish your drink."

"Nonsense. We'll get you packed then finish the bottle together."

Simultaneously, they downed the drinks and went back inside the cabin. The bedroom was a small but comfortable room on the stern side of the cruiser. Remmy ducked under the low-hanging entryway and stared at the strange art lining Brooklyn's walls. Three wooden masks hung over the headboard. The middle one had long dreads covering its face and extending down its sides, and the two smaller ones to either side of the larger mask had large hollow eyes and thick, protruding lips. Each of them gave her the creeps. She quickly looked away from the walls and down to Brooklyn.

He bent over, pulling a suitcase from inside a compartment built into the wall. The muscles in his arms flexed and his smooth dark skin glistened as the diminishing sunlight poured in through the portholes. Remmy rushed back to the kitchen to refill her drink; three parts rum, one part sweet juice. She returned to the bedroom, already feeling the buzz from the first one and watched the warrior glide around his tiny room, pulling clothes from each hidden compartment. She looked back at the mask, then back to Brooklyn. All the while she sipped on her rum, enjoying the tingling sensation the combination was giving her. The music that oozed from the speakers was starting to feel good, which she contributed to the liquor she consumed.

Deciding to cut her trips short, she returned to the kitchen one last time and brought the bottle of rum and carton of sweet punch with her. While Brooklyn disappeared into the bathroom, she filled his glass, changing the combination in it to four parts rum, one dash sweet juice. Another selfish boater raced by, sending the boat rocking frantically about. Unable to keep her balance this time, she fell onto the bed, spilling her drink on the descent. Brooklyn, reappearing from the bathroom, rushed to her side, concerned that she might be hurt and oblivious to the drunken state she was in.

"Remmy! Are you alright?"

"I m fine, handsome," she replied, slurring her words as she spoke.

"It takes a little getting used to, doesn't it?"

"I love it. Every part of it. Oh, this is so romantic. Don't you think so? Don't you think it's romantic?"

"What? Falling on your face?"

"No, silly. The water. The sun. A man and a woman. Come here, Brooklyn."

She turned over, spreading her legs so the dress revealed more than just her thighs. Arms extending upward, she beckoned for him to touch her, to feel her — taste her.

Not at all trying to fight the temptation, Brooklyn went to her. Their lips were the first to touch. Hers: soft, sweet, wet. His: strong, thick, comforting. Tongues intertwined, they wrapped themselves in each other's arms and rolled about on his bed, moving closer to the ecstasy which hovered overhead.

The boat rocked as others passed by. Brooklyn moved with the rippling waters, refusing to let it disturb his groove. He raised up briefly, pulling his shirt off, revealing rippling muscles and chocolate-sweet skin. His black hands rubbed hard against her white legs as she licked and bit at his ear lobe. For a moment, all was there and nothing was missing. She was simply a lonely woman longing for a man's touch and he was merely a sad soul wanting no more than his share of happiness. There was no black, no white; no hate and no pain...until they spoke.

"Brooklyn. I knew this day would come. You couldn't resist me. Ha, ha, ha, Remmy laughed. There isn't a black man alive who can turn away when a white woman offers him a chance to taste."

A power boat drifted by, two ducks quacked, fighting over food and a dog barked from a distance. Brooklyn noticed none of this. He leaped off the Jezebel and backed against the wall. Ashamed, he reached for his shirt and quickly pulled it over his head. The redness returned to his eyes, and hate filled his heart. He wanted so badly to see the stars. He wanted to look at them and try to figure out what they meant. Where were the answers to peace? To salvation? He didn't know, and at that moment did not give a fuck.

She recoiled, wondering why she had let those words slip from her mouth so easily. She was not a little girl any more. She would be held accountable for the words which dripped from her lips like venom from a cobra's jaws. Growing up in her secluded town, they had always been taught that black men worshiped white women. Who told those stories? She now wondered. Fearing the intensity of the power in his eyes and mourning the possibility of losing a friend, she searched her mind to come up with the right thing to say.

"Brooklyn. I'm sorry. I don't know what made me say that."

"I've been told that alcohol makes one say exactly what is on one's mind. From the looks of that bottle over there, I guess you just might have a lot more to say."

"I didn't mean it like it came out. What I meant was..."

"Remmy. You don't owe me an explanation. You said exactly what it has been thought since the Mayflower landed. But I'm going to give you an opportunity to be one step ahead of your fellow Americans. Contrary to popular belief, to most black men, black women are the most beautiful, amazing, and awesome creatures to walk the earth. Being a man, I saw some pussy in front me, so I was going to take it. But being a black man, I think I'll wait for the real thing. Hey, look, if you hurry you can catch some more rays before the sun goes down."

Remmy burst into tears. She dressed quickly and scrambled to get out of the bed she had made for herself. She cried for the hate that was imbedded in the country's fabric. She cried because she hadn't really meant any harm, and in some ways, realized that this was worse. Mainly, she cried because she really liked him; not just because he was black, but because he was a man, one of the sweetest and kindest she had ever met.

Brooklyn knew all this but was unwilling to admit it. He had not made the rules, but he would be damn if he was always going to be a victim of them. Dave Roberts, Remmy, Larry, they were all just alike. No matter how much he had hoped things would change, he knew with all the impact of a bullet train hitting a brick wall that he would not see that change in his lifetime.

He watched her as she ran out of the bedroom; sobbing, regretting, retracting. He stepped up on his lower deck and watched her scurry across the plank and up the ramp into the parking lot. He watched but did not say a thing. He just watched Remmy scurry away and thought about his life and how shitty it had become.

When she was out of sight, he returned to his bedroom to finish packing. He shoved clothes into the open suitcase, not caring if they were wrinkled or if anything matched. He knew that he had to get away or risk losing his mind.

Noticing the half-full bottle of rum, he picked it up, sat down on the bed, stuck the open end inside his mouth and leaned his head way back. The rum burned down his throat, but the fire put out the more deadly one which had begun to fester in his thoughts.

Remmy had been right. Brooklyn was a kind man, but he was also a smart one. He had come to the realization that living in an angry world, unfortunately, meant that he was angry too.

VERSE

TWENTY

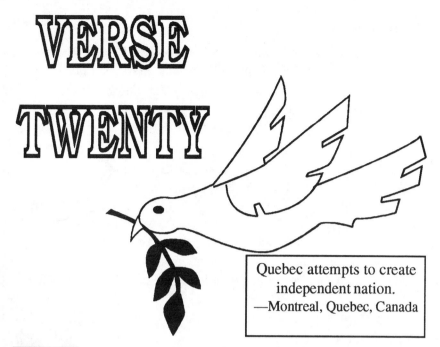

Quebec attempts to create
independent nation.
—Montreal, Quebec, Canada

After a long and tiring day at work, Arizona walked through the door, dropped her purse on the coffee table and her body on the couch. With Nigel at her mother's and little Johnny still in the hospital, all was quiet. So quiet in fact, she panicked for a moment, wondering where her little ones could be. She quickly stood, deciding to go looking for them, then slowly sat back down. Like a thirty-ton weight, the whereabouts of her two sons came to her altering her emotions from panic to dread.

Initially, she was reluctant to go back to work, but once she walked through the doors of the State Lottery office, she was glad she had returned. Her co-workers met her at the door, surprising her with a cake and well wishes. Diving into the pile of work left for her, she was able to temporarily forget what had kept her away for so long. After work, she was pleasantly surprised that the traffic was especially light and the weather, delightfully beautiful. She easily cruised along the Capitol City Freeway, taking the WX freeway to Interstate five and exiting at West El Camino, the location of the accident. With thoughts of her precious day, however, she passed by the accident scene without remembering the devastation which had been wrought.

Now at home, she stood, walked into the kitchen and poured

herself a large glass of apple juice. The ice-cold taste felt good and relieved the dryness in her mouth. She had started to head for the bathroom and prepare for herself a nice warm bath when she heard a knock at the door, forcing her to delay her evening plans. Finishing her drink, she walked back to the front door and prepared for her visitor.

"So, how was the first day back at work?" asked Sonya, smiling as she walked through the front door.

"Hey, what's going on Sonya?" returned Arizona, smiling in return as she closed the door after her guest stepped inside. "Have a seat. I want to check my messages. I just walked in myself."

"Oh, I'm not staying. I just wanted to find out how your day went. I need to go meet Tommy at the bus stop, and I don't want to be late."

"He's catching the bus now? Good for you, Sonya."

"Yeah. I figured it was about time. Some things I have to place in God's hands."

"Ain't that the truth. Well, work was fine. I'm glad I decided to go, because it helped to get my mind on other things. I still go up to the hospital every day, but like you just said, it's all in God's hands now. And how was your day?"

"Same ole shit. As soon as my youngest gets to the first grade, I'm going to get me a full-time job. Of course I said that when Tommy turned five, but look what happened."

"It's hard, I know. But you just have to set your mind to it and follow through. It's up to you. Believe me. If we sat around waiting for a fairy godmother to make our dreams come true, we would all be standing in the soup line."

"I know that's right. Hey, did you call that insurance lady back?"

"Not exactly."

"Girl, you better call her and get what's due. Just think what you can do with all that money."

"Well, I didn't call, but it's being handled. I hired an attorney. And girl, he's black and beautiful."

"What! You go, girl. Hey, don't let this one go, and if you don't want him, send him to me. Damn, why didn't I wait? He's probably going to get you a hundred thousand dollars."

"You think so?"

"Of course. You saw what Johnny Cochran did. What's his name?"

"Franklin Jackson."

"You go, girl," Sonya replied and looked down at her watch, all in one motion. "Look at the time. Let me get out here. Keep me posted."

"I will. Thanks for coming by."

Sonya walked out of the door with Arizona closing it behind her. Her beautiful day continued. Walking into the bathroom, she turned on a combination of hot and cold water and mixed in a generous portion of bath oil. She thought of checking her messages, but decided she would put it off until after her bath.

Later, after turning on the compact disc player, she ripped off her clothes and climbed inside the newly run bath water. Her senses were ignited simultaneously, with the sound of Mary J. Blige and the feel of the water hitting her at the same time. *My life, my life, my life...in the sunshine.*

"Sing it, girl," Arizona shouted into the candle-lit bathroom. She ducked her head underwater, allowing the water to run through her hair and down her face. It was times like this when she loved her short hair most. Just when the bath oil had sufficiently relaxed her, the telephone ringing caused her heart to skip a beat. She tried to calm herself down, battling the overwhelming tendency to become alarmed as she heard the phone. But for the time being, it was a losing battle.

The telephone rang twice, three times, and then a fourth before she pulled herself out of the tub and raced down the hall in her splendid birthday suit, completely covered in soapy water.

"Hello," panted Arizona into the phone.

"Arizona?"

"Yes, this is Arizona. Who's speaking?"

"This is Johnny. You sound kind of different. I didn't recognize your voice. How're you feeling?"

"I'm good. I'm dripping wet, but other than that, I'm good."

"Why did you have to go and say that for, woman? You know I get lonely."

"Alright, Johnny. We'll change the subject. What's going on? Is everything alright? How's little Johnny?"

"Well, that's what I've called to talk about."

"What? Is he okay? Is my baby okay?"

"Relax, baby. Everything's fine. The doctor just said he needs you to come down here as soon as you can."

"Why Johnny? Tell me! I can't take no games right now. Is everything alright with my baby?" Indescribable terror raced through her veins as the worst possible scenario skipped across her mind. The indicator ball had stopped. She knew that was what her ex-husband had called to say. Why would the doctor want to see her? Continuing to hold the phone next to her ear, she stood quietly, refusing to breathe too loudly. She braced herself, wanting to comprehend what she was going to hear next, the first time around. The sound of the words— dead and Johnny—were two that she never wanted to hear in the same sentence, again.

"Come on, Arizona just relax. I said everything's fine. His fingers moved today," Johnny calmly replied.

"He woke up? Oh, my God! He woke up?"

"No. But his fingers moved."

"What does that mean? Is he slowly coming out of his coma?"

"They don't know. It could just be reflexes 'cause he's still completely out of it. But that one nurse, the one who always comes in with the blankets."

"Yeah, Janice. What about her?"

"You know she's been here several years. She thinks he was dreaming. Maybe a nightmare, maybe not. But she thinks that he was either dreaming about the accident or about one of us. Maybe he was hugging one of us in his dream. Or maybe my little buddy is in there fighting for his life. His fingers moved, baby. He can do this. My little boy can do this." Voice cracking, arms weakening, Johnny dropped the phone on top of his son's bed and let the tears fall after it.

Johnny had taken the misfortune of his child and learned from it. The torn clothing, foul odor, and bottle of Mad Dog 20/20, were completely gone. He had a full-time job as a custodian at Burbank High School. With the work came benefits which he utilized right away. Making his first trip to the dentist office in twenty years, he finally purchased dentures and did away with his Leon Spinks imitation.

Wanting to be ready, he did all this for his son. He wanted so badly to set a positive example for his boys that he had sworn off liquor—cold turkey—and replaced it with Seven-up. He swore his old lady would never see him cry again, but he could not refute what was meant to be. He had cleaned himself up, and now it appeared that the little boy with his namesake might get a chance to see his father again.

Arizona had already dropped the phone, pulled a summer dress over her head, and headed out of the door. Emotions running in all directions, they canceled each other out, leaving her numb and cold. "His fingers moved. His fingers moved," she continually uttered to herself. "Are you coming back to me, baby? Come on back to mama. I miss you so much." She said aloud. Faster than the speed of light, she jumped in her car and headed in the direction of the now-faded rainbow.

*****

"The bodies of two African-American men were found floating in the Sacramento River near the town of Rio Vista. Their bodies were pulled from the water by the Coast Guard after they were spotted by a group of fishermen entering the Delta. The deceased have been identified as Torion Michaels and Nathan Tucker, both of Sacramento. Investigators have announced that the men appear to be victims of a hate crime and are conducting their investigation accordingly. Both men had swastikas painted across their foreheads and chests. The police reported that the men had been beaten so badly that forensic experts had to piece their skin back together in order to identify the racist markings.

The African-American community is outraged as is the town of Rio Vista. The mayor has been quoted saying, "We do not condone those cowardly acts in our town. Members of all cultures are accepted and respected here. The Coast Guard is scanning the waters for more possible victims. We will keep you advised.

"In other news..."

"Johnny." The sound of his name tore him away from the evening news, which was fine with him. Not wanting to hear any more about crazy skinheads killing brothers, he pressed the power button on the remote control, eliminating the nightly news anchor team and their depressing presentation.

"Hey, baby. Damn! What did you do? Blink your way here," he replied.

"What time is the doctor coming back?" she asked, running toward little Johnny's bed.

"He'll be back in a minute. Hi, Arizona."

"I'm sorry. How are you, Johnny?"

"I'm good. Kind of makes you feel a little funny."

"Funny how?"

"To think that he's in there moving around."

Johnny's words pushed Arizona onto the bed as she found a seat next to her son. Trying to hold her tears back was useless. The first tear landed on her son's smooth, bare arm. The next one landed on the white blanket covering little Johnny's body. The third and fourth were too close together to be counted separately but both fell on her dress which hung loosely on Arizona's thinning body.

Johnny remained in his chair. He wanted to comfort her but knew she needed this time to be with their son. Minutes passed. The doctor finally appeared. His gray hair, slicked back, attempted to cover the large balding area on top of his head. His stethoscope hung around his neck, and he held a slim, black chart in his hand. He looked tired and worn but not out. Still with ten years to practice, he refused to allow fatigue to set in. Knowing there was no way to retire early, he did not wish to wake up the next thousand mornings, painfully anticipating the day ahead.

"Mr. and Mrs. Tyler," he said formally.

"That's us. Arizona, the doctor's here." Johnny replied. She turned toward the doctor who walked toward the family circle and stood just off from the center. With the parents' full attention, he wasted no time in getting right to the point. He had compassion, and it would show, but he was a professional first and would not sugarcoat any of the news he had to relay.

"Nurse Janice told me your son's fingers moved. We immediately ran tests to try and get other responses, but nothing came up. We even had an orderly monitor him for several hours. Unfortunately, he didn't move again. The only explanation we can offer is that it was just a nervous response."

"Does it happen to all coma patients?" questioned Arizona.

"Well, that's the strange thing. It doesn't. Almost never. That's why we were so intrigued. His vital signs haven't changed. No other movement before or since. I'm hesitant when I say this but the medical profession is not omniscient. Some things we just can't explain, this being one of them. But I can say that it can be looked at in a positive manner."

"Is there anything else that can be done? Have all the tests been run?" Johnny asked, with hope beaming from his eyes.

"Yes they have and no, there's nothing further we can do. All you can do is what you've been doing, showing your son your love and support. You know my number. Call me if you have any further questions."

"Thank you doctor. We appreciate all you've done," replied Arizona. Turning back toward little Johnny, she kissed his forehead and whispered words of encouragement. She then stood, walked toward the window, and found her usual seat. Johnny watched her, waiting for her to speak before he did. He had been here awhile. The situation had already settled in his heart, but she would need time for it to settle in hers.

"I was a nervous wreck all the way here. I didn't know what to think," she said.

"I know. He's going to pull through, woman. He's making his start," he replied.

Before she could respond, the phone rang. Their eyes met, hearts skipped beats and both felt reluctant to answer the phone, hesitant of discovering any drudgery that may await on the other side.

"I'll get it," said Johnny. Standing up, he walked toward the phone which sat not more than arm's length from Arizona, picked up the receiver and spoke into it. "Hello."

"Hello. This is Frankie Jackson. May I speak with Arizona Tyler, please?"

Before responding, he put one hand over the receiver and turned toward Arizona. "It's that attorney brother. You want to speak with him?"

"Not now. Tell him I'll call later. Tell him what happened. He'll be glad to hear the news."

"I'm sorry Franklin, but she can't come to the phone right now. This is Johnny's father. What can I do for you?"

"Oh, how are you doing, Mr. Tyler? I was just calling to see how the little one was doing?"

"Well, his condition hasn't changed, but he did move his fingers last night."

"You're kidding? What did they say that meant?"

"Nothing definite, but the doctor said it was a good sign. We're hoping that it will happen again. I think he's gonna be alright. I think my boy is gonna make it."

"Good! That's good news. My prayers are with you. I'm going to need to meet with the both of you in the next few days. We've made a demand on the insurance company, and I need to supply them with a few things. Doctors' reports, medical bills, and the like."

"Arizona. The attorney brother wants to meet with us. How's tomorrow evening?"

She nodded her head in the affirmative.

"Tomorrow's fine. About six o'clock here at the hospital. Let's meet in the main cafeteria. I don't want to be talkin' no crazy talk in my boy's room."

"I understand, Mr. Tyler. I'll see you both tomorrow."

Frankie hung up on his end and walked toward his decadent picture window. The sun had started to set, but his office faced the east, thereby missing yet another amazing sunset. He gazed out the window for a second, but tore himself away and sat hard in his seat. He had work to do.

He had never known anyone to survive a coma and damn sure had not heard of anyone's hand moving and didn't quite know what that meant. He did know, however, that if the boy lived, he could kiss the five million dollars goodbye. Suddenly, time was of the essence. He would have to gather all the information that the claims person had requested and negotiate a settlement based on the fact that the boy would most likely die.

It was times like these that he hated his profession, but it was also these rare occasions which required that all emotion be set aside. He wanted the kid to live; he had a son himself, but he could walk away with close to two million dollars if the boy died or at least if Wexington thought he was going to die.

Picking up the pen, he turned all of his attention to the case involving the seven-year-old boy in the coma. He would have to settle this one soon. The possibility was too great that if they went to trial, the boy could be out of his coma. *What would that be worth?* he thought. "Not five million dollars," he said.

Back at the hospital, The Tylers stared at the their son, hoping he would move again. They did not care about the diminishing value of their claim; but were concerned only about the life of their child.

Beep....beep...beep...

VERSE

TWENTY-ONE

Agrentina Challenges Great
Britain in territory dispute.
—Falkland Islands, Agrentina

Man, I wish I could of got today off. First real warm night of the year, and I'm stuck inside this tomb."

"Quit your complaining. Summer's just startin. You'll have time to fuck off."

"That's a lot of water out there."

"Shit. Most damn rain I've ever seen. At times, it seemed like the sky was just going to cave in."

"One thing's for sure."

"What's that?"

"The fuckin' drought is over."

The two men high-fived each other just as Ricky walked in carrying a radio in one hand and a flashlight in the other. His gray uniform, which imitated the clothing worn by police officers, looked peculiar hanging on his thin body. His raw hate of authority formed a hazy aura around him. Stan and Jeff, the night staff, glanced at Ricky then resumed back to their conversation. It seemed every other month the agency was hiring a new security guard to canvass the area, which seemed unnecessary. The Folsom Dam was nestled in the posh hills of northern California's gold country and the only real disturbance was an occasional wildcat howling in the distance. The prior guards, Stan and Jeff figured, must have become bored and ditched the steady work with something that took a little more brain power, like a kiosk attendant or a valet parker. Like clockwork, a new guard would appear, work for around thirty days, then walk out the door, never to be heard from again. Used to this revolving door of so-called security guards, Stan and Jeff never bothered to get to know any of them. Acknowledging the watchman's presence with a nod of the head was the most they usually extended.

Ricky looked at the white men and felt relief when they did not speak. The last thing he was inclined to do was carry on a meaningless conversation with the enemy. The war had begun, and he trusted no one. He looked back in their direction, but not directly at them. The entire front section of the room was made of glass. The view it offered was a magnificent contrast to the drab concrete structure to which it was attached. The dam faced west, giving the staff a picture perfect view of the sunset. Stan and Jeff noticed the security guard staring through the window and turned their heads in time to see the Lord's amazing grace. The sun's golden rays beamed off the navy-blue water, reflecting the darkening night sky. The array of trees, now strong and healthy, stood proud with their rich green vegetation. The abundance of rain was now accented by the powerful sun making for an absolute ideal combination. For an undisturbed moment in time, the world had become perfect; perfect for the haves as well as the have-nots, perfect for the boys and the girls, perfect even for the blacks and the whites.

Time passed as did the moment along with it. And so went the chance for the world to achieve its humanity. Like so many other acts of God, few noticed its beauty, or its total serenity. Once the sun had finally set, the perfect moment would be over. Ricky would continue his stroll around the building, Stan and Jeff would return to their conversation and the world would continue to follow the path of destruction.

"Man, was that a sunset or was that a sunset?" asked Jeff, wiping the sweat from his brow. "I've never seen anything like that in my whole life."

"California, man. Only in California. Did you see that dude?"

Stan asked Ricky.

"Unreal," replied Ricky. The question had caught him off guard resulting in a casual response. He turned to walk out, preferring to scope other parts of the building when he heard another question hurled at him. Hearing the speaker a little closer, he stopped and turned around. One of the white men was walking toward him. Barely managing to refrain from panicking, he tightened the grip around his flashlight. Would they attack in a place like this? He didn't know but would not wait to find out. If he saw hate in the man's eyes, he would strike, as he was not afraid to draw first blood.

Stan walked toward the nervous security guard with a broad smile across his face. As he neared, his right hand extended outward, relieving Ricky's mind for the time being.

"How're you doing, man? The name's Stan."

"Richard," he replied, extending his left arm, his right hand so tight around the flashlight he felt veins pop.

"Did you see that shit? I mean did you see that shit! Prettiest damn sunset I've seen in my life! Looked like it was straight out of a fantasy."

"Damn, Stan. Alright! The sunset was cool. Leave the man alone!" yelled Jeff, somewhat embarrassed at his co-worker's enthusiasm.

"No problem," replied Ricky, loosening his grip. "It was somethin to see. Stopped me in my tracks."

"Damn, I wish I had a camera. Oh, well. Maybe we'll get another just like it," said Stan.

"There will never be another one just like it. But at least you saw this one," Ricky replied. "If we all realized some things you just don't get twice, maybe we would take better care of our lives."

"I heard that!" shouted Jeffrey. "What are you? Some kind of poet in disguise? You work here as a watchman at night and by day you're super poet?" Stan and Jeff laughed. Ricky chuckled, while thinking of a reason to get out of this conversation, but he was drawn to the window. The natural picturesque display that was spread out on the other side of it was too much for him to resist. Stan saw his interest and decided to invite him for a closer look.

"Take a closer look. Kind of makes you respect Mother Nature a little more. Never want to litter again. Hey, Jeffrey, this is Richard."

How're you doing, Richard. Ricky and Jeff walked toward one another. They met in the middle, performed the unusual ritual then both turned and walked toward the front of the window. As they approach the work station, Ricky was taken aback by the complicated network of cables, switches and levers. He had lived in Sacramento his entire life, always knowing the Folsom Dam was there but never making the short trek to see it. He imagined the dam to be just an oversized lake with a wall keeping the water separate from the earth. Now he stood at its very mouth and realized it was so much more.

The Folsom Dam was built in the early 1940's, initially a mammoth sized hole dug at the valley's edge near the foothills at the base of the Sierra Nevada. After an average winter, the snow would melt, sending water running down the mountainside, through the rivers, and up into the dam, giving the residents enough water to last through the area's dry summers. The dam was so enormous that all of Northern California depended upon it as a source of natural, safe water. Sitting at the top of Folsom Lake, on a hill high enough for a person to see the skyline of the city, the dam resembled a fortress.

"What is all that stuff?" asked Ricky, curiously looking down at the complex panels.

Returning to their seats, Stan and Jeff grinned as they prepared to explain their jobs, which neither of them did very often.

Stan spoke first. "A little bit of everything. Most of the switches are for lights around the dam and the building. You'd be amazed how much electricity it takes to keep this place going. Kind of ironic, ain't it?"

"Why would you need lights around the dam? People can't be in this area, can they?"

""They're not supposed to be. We sometimes get knuckle-headed boaters who think they're cool by boating inside of the barrier. They have no idea what would happen if one of the gates broke while they were there messing around," kicked in Jeff.

Surprisingly, Ricky's interest perked up. Never having seen the dam before he started working there, he was fascinated with its ultimate strength. Enough time had passed that he deemed the white men safe, so he relaxed, removing his hand from his flashlight. Afterall, not everyone knew about the upcoming war.

"Remember last August when one of the gates broke?" asked Jeff.

"I remember that. I live near the river, so I pay attention to its height. On one of the hottest days of the year, the river was damn near to the top of its banks," said Ricky.

"Yeah. That was the result of only one gate breaking. Forty thousand cubic feet of water per second poured through the broken gate. Gate was open for over six hours. Are you getting a feel of what I'm saying? Lot of water in here. Some crazy boaters making past the guard and markers would of been pretty sorry."

"Damn. How could that happen? It would seem like this place would have safety locks all over the place."

"We do. But even the safety for the safety lock can go out. Gump happens. The state poured in ten million dollars to reinforce the walls. Smartest thing they ever spent our tax dollars on. If an earthquake ever hit here and cracked the walls, boy, you could just kiss Sacramento good-bye. Probably Vacaville and Stockton too," added Stan.

"Good thing earthquakes don't happen in Sacramento," said Jeff.

"No, but they happen in the mountains. How do you think they got to be mountains? But that's what they got us here for. To monitor this monster twenty-four hours a day."

"To the night owls," boasted Jeff. The troupe raised their hands in a mock toast. They toasted for the beauty of the sunset. They raised invisible glasses for the water. But more importantly, they toasted to the strength of the dam.

"I better get going on my rounds. Thanks for the info," said Ricky, turning to walk away.

"Any time, Richard. I hope you stay with us awhile. Most night watchmen don't last a month. I think they have a hard time with living the vampire life," joked Stan.

"I'll be here. For as long as it takes."

"Huh?"

"Nothing. I'll be here. You fellas take care. And good luck."

Stan and Jeff watched curiously as Richard Swift left the room. They looked at one another, shrugged, and continued their previous conversation.

As he walked down the ramp of the circluar room, he thought of why it had to be. Determined to be the fittest, he knew he had to fight, but wondered why it had become necessary. During times of crisis, the races pulled together, caring more for survival then superiority. When the rubble had been swept away and the last house rebuilt, though, each group returned to its own neighborhood and its own world.

The grounds were especially quiet. Walking outside, he was met with a cool breeze that blew in from the east. The mountain chill slid down the hill and rested on the same peak which housed the building where he now stood. Reaching in his pocket, he pulled out a pack of Marlborough Lights, shook one loose and lit it after placing it between his lips. He inhaled, then let out a short cough. He needed to quit smoking, but cigarettes were the only pleasure he had left, so he decided against it.

He had fought off a round of vomiting earlier in the day and felt another one coming on. He hated that he had eaten a large lunch, but the hunger pangs had become unbearable. Food just never seemed to taste good any more. Rather than eating for enjoyment, he did so now because nourishment was necessary for survival. Leaning back against the building, he thought back to the meeting with the All-African Children Militia. He thought back to Torion, his life-long friend, and continued to hope he was right. *Had that really been Judas?* he thought.

"Judas must die!" screamed Malik from his throne. "Don't let them get away!"

"What are you talkin' about, man? I'm not Judas!" screamed Torion as the angry mob stormed toward them. "I told you, he's crazy! Ricky's fuckin lost his mind!"

"He is the chosen one!" retaliated Malik. "The traitors are here to persecute him. Brothers and Sisters, don't you see! The devil will come in many disguises! The devil has arrived!"

Torion's and Nathan's flight toward the door was useless. At least thirty people remained in their path, leaving but one option open, to scream like hell.

"Get the fuck away from me!! Help! Helpppp!!!"

A strong, tall man slapped his hand across Torion's mouth and another man, equally as intimidating, landed a blow to Nathan's right jaw, knocking the latter unconscious. The other members of the militia followed suit, throwing jabs, kicking, scratching, and punching the men as if Torion and Nathan were inflatable dummies used for the purpose of taking out one's aggression.

One especially solid blow connected with Torion's stomach forcing up a thick wad of blood and yellow gunk. A bottle smashed on top of his head, bringing him to his knees, but leaving him conscious. Being less fortunate than Nathan, who remained unconscious, Torion felt a foot hit his back and another connect with his chest. He felt excruciating pain and could hear his bones breaking, veins burst, and his spinal chord snapping. Falling flat on his face, eyes open wide, he resembled a frog in mating season. He had one final chance to look at his brother, Nathan, who had actually died ten minutes earlier, but the wild mob continued to attack.

Torion's world became dark, then in seconds, nothing. The party was over. Returning to what few senses they had left, the melee ended. Not wanting his people to dwell on what they had done, Malik summoned his henchmen to grab the carcasses and go. Ricky shoved his way to the back room, grabbed a couple of old blankets, and threw them over Judas and his dead helper.

With a quarter of a mile to the nearest house, all was quiet around Ricky's. The men threw the bodies in the car and drove off quietly through town. Ricky sat in the car with Torion's body. The still night added to the silence as they drove down the highway not saying a word. What had they done? They had killed their own and mistakenly called them Judases, but as a harrowing a deed as it was, it was over, and now they had to move on.

Reaching a desolate area south of Rio Vista, two men accompanied Ricky and three more emerged from the second car. They all jumped out of the cars and carried the bodies of their friends. Before burying them in the river, one of the henchmen pulled a quart of oil from the trunk of the car. Popping it open, he poured it on the dead men's bodies. Drawing a swastika on Nathan's and Torion's chest the best way he knew how, he made the rest of the troop hold off for a minute as to let the hate signs dry.

Enough time elapsing, they hurled the bodies into the river and drove off.

It had been Judas, Ricky thought. *There was no Torion. There was no Torion. There was no Torion,* he repeated to himself, over and over again. Flicking out the cigarette, he walked away to continue his rounds.

As basic a job as it was, the job was just the diversion he needed. The total seclusion allowed him to come up with a plan to assure his people's victory. The shot had been fired. The war was on, and the militia still had not come up with a viable plan of attack. Walking past the room where the two men were, he looked through one of the small windows which lined its walls. The men were sitting in their chairs, continuing their conversation about the sunset, and the spectacular summer that was sure to come.

Ricky looked at them for a minute then lifted his eyes and stared past them through the windows in the background. He started to turn away when something caught his eye. His gaze locked, his attention focused, he zoned in on the water while recalling the conversation he had earlier with Stan and Jeff. Forty-thousand cubic feet per second... That's just one gate... Those boaters would be sorry...

Heart thumping, stomach closing, Ricky ran into the men's room and threw up his last meal. Skin clammy, sweat drenching his starched shirt, he realized the vision had come. He shook his head from side to side, mouth open, allowing the remains of his dinner to fly out. Staggering over to the sink, he doused his face with cold water, then stood and looked at himself in the mirror. He became frightened, afraid to accept it, but it was too late. His destiny had been revealed to him. The time to deliver was now. Hate built up within him, despair filled his soul and the sound of the bomb exploded between his ears. Ricky at last knew what he must do, and he intended to see his destiny through.

VERSE

TWENTY-TWO

Anti-abortionists declare war on Planned Parenthood. —Boston MA

Brooklyn stepped off the plane and it all came back to him: the beautiful Jamaican women, the breathtaking mountain backdrop, and the tantalizing scent of ganja. Deciding on a different flavor, he changed planes in Montego Bay and hopped on the next flight to Kingston, the nation's capitol. The greeting he received in the city was much different than the one he had received in the countryside. The taxi cab drivers in Kingston already knew their fares. In Montego Bay, he was immediately surrounded by dozens of men trying to out bid each other for Brooklyn's precious American dollars.

He slung his backpack over his shoulder, picked up his mid-sized suitcase and walked to the street curb. Raising his right hand in the air was all it took for the cabbies to come running.

"Where you need to go?" asked one driver in his heavy Island accent. The sun was shining, but a dampness hung in the air. He could still hear the sea crashing against the jagged rocks. He could see the skyline sitting on the edge of the island overlooking the clear waters of the Caribbean Sea. He could see Blue Mountain Peak, sitting proudly in all its natural splendor. More importantly, he could see his people.

"New Kingston. How much?" Brooklyn responded, managing

to sound less like a tourist than the first time he had visited.

"New Kingston, mon. You have U.S. money?"

"Yeah."

"Twenty-five dollars, mon."

"Never mind. I'll catch the next one."

"Alright mon. Alright. Fifteen. New Kingston's far."

"Fifteen's cool."

Brooklyn opened the door and was met with his favorite aroma: marijuana. The naughty dreads dangled around the driver's head as he jumped out of the car, rushing to Brooklyn's side to help him with his luggage. Popping the trunk open, the cab driver picked up the bag off the curb and dropped it inside, then slammed the trunk shut. Brooklyn removed his backpack and set it on the backseat.

When Brooklyn finally sat down, he was pleasantly entertained by the island music. He didn't recognize the performer, but it didn't matter. Reggae was reggae.

They drove down the narrow road which wrapped around the bay. Water lapping on both sides of the curved thoroughfare, Brooklyn sank down in his seat and breathed a sigh of relief.

"You're from New York?" asked the cabby, deciding to make conversation.

"California," replied Brooklyn.

"California. It's pretty nice out there, huh?"

"Yeah. It's pretty nice. Have you ever been?"

"No, mon. I've never been to the states. I wanna go. I'm saving. I got a sister who lives in Washington. I'm going to stay with her when I get enough money."

"It doesn't cost that much."

"You talk like an American, mon."

Passing through the city, Brooklyn was amazed at how many people were on the streets. Hundreds of cars raced along the broken roads. Thousands of pedestrians paced up and down the sidewalks, determined to get to where they needed to go. He watched three children running along the gutters, still in their matching brown school uniforms, having fun as they playfully chased each other through the streets of the city.

The avenues of Kingston were a far cry from those to which he was accustomed. Though used to stray dogs and wandering alley cats, he could not help but stare at the mass of goats who seemed as comfortable in the urban mecca as in any spacious pasture.

"This is a big city. It's much bigger than I thought," said Brooklyn.

"Yeah, mon. A million people live here, mon."

"A million? Your're kidding!"

"No, mon. Three million on the whole island. What did you think?"

"I don't know. I just didn't think it was that big. We don't get much positive information about black nations in the states. The only time you see any black nation on T.V. is when there's a drought or a war. The only big cities we see are London and Paris. Places like that."

"You ever been to London, mon?"

"Never. I've got too many other places I have to go first."

"Beautiful women in London, mon."

"Beautiful women in Jamaica."

"Yeah, mon. What hotel in New Kingston are you staying at?"

"At the Devon House. I heard that's the best place to stay. Do you think so?"

"Yeah, mon. You'll like it there. Lots of beautiful women."

After turning right, the taxi began its gradual ascent up the hill to New Kingston. The traffic thickened, and the old part of the city was replaced by the new district. Tall, colorful buildings towered over the streets. Brooklyn scanned his new surroundings, determined to catch it all.

"This is Freedom Park," the cabby announced, pointing to a statue which guarded the grounds of Kingston's most famous park.

"Who are those statues of?" asked Brooklyn.

"Bob Marley. Marcus Garvey. Martin Luther King. All of'em, mon."

"Wow! Man, I love this place."

"Everyone loves Jamaica. Irie, mon. No problem here. Did you read the big sign in the airport?"

"I'm not sure. What did it say?"

"It said, mon, that we have our problems, but our grass is still green, and our sun still shines."

"It's pretty wild. Most people who come to Jamaica never see this. Most of them don't make it any further than the beaches. Not me. I want to see it all."

"The whole island? I'll take you, mon. You renting a car?"

"No."

"I'll show you around. I'll give you my number. Give me a call. I'll show you the whole island."

Crossing through a busy intersection, they turned into the parking lot of the Devon House. The Victorian styled inn was accented by towering palm trees and exotic vegetation. A number of people sat on the patio, under tall ancient trees, enjoying their acki and salt fish and other local delights they had chosen. The precisely manicured grounds expanded in a full circle around the house, which was located adjacent to a restaurant where some people dined.

A number of pavilions were set up near the entrance. Authentic Caribbean art decorated the area, causing Brooklyn to force himself to refrain from leaping out of the car and making sporadic purchases of items he did not really need. The taxi came to a stop, but before the cab driver lost his fare's attention, he reached for a pen and began jotting a phone number on a piece of paper.

"This is the Devon House," the cabby told Brooklyn. "Call me, mon. I'll show you around."

Looking at the card, Brooklyn smiled, opened his door, and climbed out.

"Thank you, Conrad. I'll do that. I'm Brooklyn, by the way."

"What's up, Brooklyn. Welcome to Kingston."

He handed the cabby the agreed-upon fare, latched his backpack to his back, and picked up his suitcase which the cabby had so politely retrieved. He turned toward the entrance and walked straight ahead, enjoying every step of the way. After checking into the inn, he would take a quick shower and rush down to the restaurant. He didn't want to waste even one valuable second locked away in a hotel room. He could do that at home.

Nightfall had arrived, but it hardly made a difference. The lobby mercury read eighty degrees, but the swamp-like humidity made it feel even hotter. Brooklyn strolled across the grounds and through the restaurant. The crowd had multiplied, but the waiter had no problem locating a seat for his new guest.

"Are you here by yourself, mon?"

"Yeah, mon," Brooklyn responded energetically.

"Oh, a New Yorker."

"No. California."

"Los Angeles?"

"Sacramento."

"Sacramento. You left your lady friend back there? How come she didn't come with you?"

"Don't have one."

"You'll find one here. Lot of good Jamaican women. What would you like to drink?"

"Do you have Red Stripe?"

"Yeah, mon. That is a Jamaican beer. Brewed right here in Kingston."

"I'll take one. And keep them coming."

"Yeah, mon."

Brooklyn pulled the pamphlet out of his pocket as soon as the waiter walked away. He had two weeks to see the island, and he planned to do just that. Kingston alone had so much to offer: the African Caribbean Museum of Modern Art, the Bob Marley Museum, Blue Mountain Peak. The list went on and on.

When the drink arrived, he raised his glass in the air, making a silent toast: Here's to you, Jamaica. He then downed his drink while already thinking about his next one. He was on vacation and was damn sure going to act like it.

VERSE

TWENTY-THREE

Man opens fire on hotel guests. No reason cited.
—Sydney, Australia
– Down Under

ould you look at that line," exclaimed Arizona.

"Oh, well. We're here now," responded Johnny. "Nigel would probably kill us if we didn't go in. Isn't that right, son?"

"Yep. The line's not that long, Mommy. You can sit down. I'll wait," promised Nigel.

"That's okay, baby. I'll stay here with you."

"The line's moving real fast anyway, Arizona. This is your day to relax. Just kind of go with it. We don't have anything else to do," Johnny replied.

"I guess you're right. Things a Mother won't do."

Arizona, Johnny, and Nigel stood in line in front of the Marine World Africa USA Theme Park. The sun hovered high overhead, accented by a cloudless sky. Thousands of people arrived early, planning on beating the crowds, but their plans backfired as the line went through the main entrance, down a packed sidewalk and around a curve a quarter of a mile away.

Nigel, feeling neglected, had awakened the night before at his grandmother's house, screaming for his mother. Having no success in calming him down, Grandma phoned his mother who rushed over, giving him the much-deserved attention he needed.

"I'm sorry, baby. I know this has to be hard on you too," she said as she rocked her youngest child in her arms that night. "You keep hanging in there for Mommy. For your brother too."

"I wanna go home. I don't wanna stay over Grandma's no more!" Nigel exclaimed.

"I know, baby. But I need you to do this for me just a little while longer. I know it's hard for you to understand. But right now, I need you to be a big boy to help me out."

"I'm not helping you being over here."

"Yes, you are, Nigel. More than you'll ever know. Hey, I'll tell you what. You go back to sleep, and this weekend, I'll take you to Marine World. Is that a deal?"

"Can Johnny come?"

"Johnny's still sleeping, baby. But when he wakes up, you can tell him all about it."

"Mommy? Can I ask you somethin'?"

"Of course. You can ask me whatever you want."

"Is Johnny going to die? My friend, Joshua, said that his mother told him people die when they get a coma. Does Johnny have a coma?"

She continued to rock her youngest child hoping that the answer would come. How do you tell your five-year-old that his big brother may not make it? This was a question she never thought she would have to ponder, yet now here was her youngest child demanding a response to this very question. Like so many mothers, she was determined not to cry in front of her child. His world was his mother and if he even sensed it was unstable, all the boyhood strength that God had instilled in him would simply disappear.

"Mommy doesn't know the answer. It's in God's hands now. If God decides He needs your brother in heaven, then he'll take him. But I'm praying to him every day. I'm praying, and I'm begging that he lets my boy stay with me a little while longer."

His mother's soothing words comforted his soul and caused his eyelids to droop. No longer afraid that he had been abandoned, he drifted back to sleep enabling Arizona to finally release her emotions. She let her tears roll down her face but wiped them away before they could land on her son. Carefully, she put him back into his bed and laid down next to him. Pulling the blanket over their bodies, she kissed him on the forehead and rocked him to sleep.

Nigel had been thrilled when the day of their big trip had finally arrived. To Arizona's amazement, they were passing through the park's front gates and in no time they had entered another world. Children's music played over the intercom as hundreds of kids wandered happily from one side of the park to the other. A one-hump camel walked by in the distance. A young man carried a baby orangutan in his arms, and swarms of ducks intermingled with the crowd.

Nigel's eyes grew so wide, his parents thought they were going to pop out of their sockets.

"Alright, Nigel. Today is your day. What do you want to see first?" asked his father.

"I wanna see the sharks! Let's go to the sharks!" screamed Nigel.

"This place is huge," said Johnny.

"It should be for twenty-six dollars a person," replied Arizona, a bit sarcastically.

"Hey, don't you worry your head none about how much it cost. Today is on me."

"I'm going to give you the money back for my ticket, Johnny. You don't have to do this."

"Can I, woman? Would you sit back and let someone spoil you for a change?"

"Look, Mommy! Look at the playground!" yelled Nigel.

A monstrosity of a jungle gym sat to the east of the shark exhibit. Hundreds of children dangled from its uneven bars and crawled through the colorful tunnels. Vendors surrounded the area as some youngsters dragged their parents from the balloon vendor to the cotton candy seller and back again, from the hot dog man to the stuffed animal woman, and back again.

Reaching the shark exhibit, they were pleasantly surprised at how short the line was. Wasting no time, they found their place at the end of the line and inched forward as the line continued to push ahead.

"Wow!" exclaimed Nigel. "Look at the sharks!"

"It's amazing how they do this," said Johnny. "Whoaa! Look at that one, little man!"

He pointed upward as the family unit glided along on the automated sidewalk. The exhibit was truly an architectural masterpiece. The entire tunnel was one large aquarium. Sharks swam by on both sides, while Johnny pointed to a bigger one which shot by overhead. The patrons were right in the middle of the sea without even getting wet.

Passing through the tunnel, they ended up in a large room which resembled a cave. Huge, stuffed sharks and other exhibits lined the walls and remained preserved in glass cases. The family walked back and forth to each one, attempting to be a part of the entire experience.

"What time is it, honey, I mean, Johnny? Remember the killer whale and dolphin show begins at noon," said Arizona.

A slow smile spread across Johnny's face as he inhaled her words. "It's only ten o'clock. We're okay. Where to next, little man?"

"Joshua said he liked the walruses. I wanna see the walruses!" Nigel demanded.

"It's your world. On to the walruses," declared Johnny.

"Isn't it a beautiful day?" asked Arizona.

"Very," Johnny replied, looking directly into her eyes.

For a moment, she gazed back. He went first but she soon followed as they took a trip down memory lane; the day they met, the first time they made love and the birth of little Johnny. It all felt so good, so right. Not wanting to start something she couldn't finish, Arizona turned away, refusing to give her ex-husband false expectations. *He's different now,* she admitted to herself. *Somehow, I think the old Johnny's back.* Turning her gaze back toward him, she noticed for the first time that he had regained his dignity. His hair was now cut short and even, beard, trimmed and well-groomed. A fresh fragrance surrounded him, and that smile she had been so crazy about lit up his boyish face. She had loved him once. She had chosen to have his children, to be his wife. She looked down at his second son and pictured his first in her mind. So much of Johnny was in them that she wandered how could she ever think she could ever stop loving him.

"Ha, ha, ha! Look at the big one blowing water through his mouth! They're silly!" laughed Nigel as he peered at the walrus family through the thick wall of glass. The sea mammals were contained in a huge swimming pool which resembled their own natural habitat. A trainer stood inside the barrier on one of the tallest rocks tossing fish to the walruses after they completed their assigned tricks. Children screamed and laughed as the creatures entertained the masses in order to receive their day's rations.

"This is really nice. When Johnny comes home, we've got to bring him here. I'm sure he would love it," said Johnny.

"You think he's going to come home?" asked Arizona, backsliding a bit.

"Woman. He's coming home, and that's that. I've got too many things I want to do with my family. I can't be no two-time loser, Arizona. I can't lose my boy twice."

Without giving it any thought, he bent down and gave her a light kiss on her lips. His touch felt good, just like it used to. Arizona did not kiss him back, nor did she resist. Her knees went weak and her heart skipped a beat. Pink clouds formed in her mind and fireworks went off around them. She needed this day. She was so tired of being alone, and so sick and tired of being sick and tired. She, Nigel and Johnny all deserved this day. Arizona Tyler intended to hold on to it.

"We better get going to the dolphin show if we want to get seats up front," said Johnny.

"Not too close," replied Arizona.

"Please, Mommy," begged Nigel. "I want to sit right by them so I can tell Johnny I touched'em."

"Please, Arizona. Can we sit in the front row," whined Johnny mockingly.

"Well, alright little boys. I think you're enjoying this as much as Nigel," she responded looking at Johnny.

"I still got a little kid in me that's not afraid to come out every now and then."

Following the arrows, they headed in the direction of the Killer Whale Pavilion. A crowd of people roamed in the same general direction, causing Johnny to pick up Nigel so they could pick up the pace.

Walking to the top of the hill, they soon stood inside the enormous arena with an open tank surrounding its center stage. They arrived just in time to secure seats up front. The crowd came in directly afterward. In no time, the arena had filled to capacity and the female trainer took center stage. "Ladies and Gentlemen. Welcome to Marine World Africa USA! Home of the world's greatest killer whale and dolphin show!" The trainer spoke with the aid of the microphone, making her voice crystal clear. "We are sure you will enjoy the show. Without further ado, give a great big welcome to Shosho, Rabin and Tango, the dolphins!!"

The crowd went wild, cheering so loudly they shook the tarp which covered the part of the arena where the audience sat. Nigel leaped up, clapping his hands together as he cheered. Johnny slipped his arm around Arizona as she cooed with excitement at the sight of the dancing dolphins.

Shosho, Rabin, and Tango were either true entertainers or very hungry. They jumped through flaming hoops, danced the hula, and in perfect synchronization, jumped over an elevated bar. The trainers tossed them their reward of sardines, while the crowd gave them one of applause and praise.

Just as the spectators reached their emotional peak, two steel gates opened on both sides of the stage, allowing God's creatures access into the arena. Their names were Willie and Shamoo. The largest killer whales in cohabitation took center stage, electrifying the already high-voltage audience. Ten tons of mammal circled the pool, shot out of the water, then splashed down in front of the crowd, completely drenching the first three rows.

"Oh, my God! We're drenched!" exclaimed Arizona, loving every minute of it.

"Do it again! Do it again!" shouted Nigel, exploding with glee.

"I can't think of any better way to cool down!" said Johnny while wringing the excess water out of his shirt.

"Do it again! Do it again!"

Arizona and Johnny laughed, amused at the delight in their son's face. The sun remained high in the sky and the sky remained forever blue. Laughter filled the air as the playful beasts earned their keep.

There were no tears and no sorrow here, only smiles, smiles that added a final dimension to a perfect day. In a world so used to hurt and pain, it was nice to discover the silver lining hiding beneath the rainbow.

VERSE

TWENTY-FOUR

> Korean airliner shot down
> by Soviet missile.
> —Mediterranean Sea

"How much?"

"That depends on what you wanna do."

"I want the whole thing. How much is that?"

"Twenty dollars will give you the night. Give me fifty, and I'll take you to the moon."

Ricky reached over the passenger seat and unlocked the door to let the whore in. She was dressed scantily in a tight leather skirt cut barely below her hips. Her red halter top resembled a bra more than any t-shirt. A blonde wig adorned her head contrasting drastically with her black skin.

She opened the car door and stepped inside. Ricky watched as she sat carefully, positioning herself to produce her most seductive pose. She closed the door, and Ricky drove off into the night.

"What's your name, brother?" asked the prostitute.

"Richard," he replied, his voice hoarse and thick as if he were speaking through a jar of honey.

"Where we goin'?"

"Does it make a difference? I got you for the night."

"You the man. Just as long as you bring me back to where you got me."

"I wouldn't leave you stranded, sister. Now cut out all this talking. I ain't payin for no conversation."

"Oh, you one of them johns who likes to get off in the car. Why didn't you say so? Where's the money?"

"Here," Ricky replied, reaching into his pocket to produce two twenties and a ten. "Been there. Done that. You ready for me, baby?" Ricky asked sardonically.

"To the moon, right?" she replied in her rehearsed sensual tone.

"To the moon, baby."

Roxy, her stage name, reached over and unzipped the john's pants. Putting her hand inside, she rubbed her fingers through the hair on his groin. He reached over her hand and turned up the volume of the cassette radio. Kaycee's remake sifted through the speakers as the sound of the soulful tune filled the car: *If you think you're lonely now. Wait until tonight, girl...*

Driving no more then twenty-five miles per hour, he turned off Broadway onto Second Avenue, attempting to allude the police or other cars which might get too close. He kept his eyes on the road, but nevertheless found it impossible not to daydream. He imagined he was a nomadic warrior, defending the lives of his family as they clung together, engulfed in fear.

Roxy pulled out his penis as the warrior held up his spear, attempting to save his terrified family.

"Mikeyla!" screamed at his wife. "Be careful Mikeyla! That lion will kill you!"

"Stay back Adora! Hold the kids back. I'll show this beast who's king."

The lion leapt toward him, but Mikeyla was quick and he jabbed the spear at the angry lion who had gone mad with fever. The long knife managed to nick its target, which only irritated the beast more.

Roxy managed to get his entire manhood in her mouth, slowly working her head, bobbing up and down. At first, he lightly rubbed his free hand gently through her hair, but as she continued to take him to the point of ecstasy, he became more forceful, pushing her head down with each thrust. Willing to please her john at any cost, she allowed herself to be handled like a rag doll, an animal, a whore.

The lion circled Mikeyla, waiting for the perfect moment to strike. Choosing to die with honor rather than run away in fear, he steadied his spear, staring right back at the wild beast. He turned on his tiptoes, not wanting to make any sudden moves. As expected, the lion attacked first, leaping at its target with paws extended forward, mouth as wide as it would go. Mikeyla pulled back on his weapon, then thrust it forward and upward, trying to make sure his one lunge counted.

Ricky pushed Roxy's head down with his hand and up with his torso. It was all in there. He could feel a tingling sensation, signifying the time had come. Roxy felt Ricky's manhood expand, then grow hot. She sensed the pulse then thrust harder, wanting to be the one in control.

Meeting the lion halfway, the spear went into the lion's body forcing a desperate growl from its open mouth. The lion crashed to the ground, still kicking and bucking with the long end of the spear protruding from its chest. Mikeyla knew he had to finish the job or be devoured himself. Leaping on top of the beast, he wrapped his hands around the spear and shoved deeper into the lion's flesh. The sounds of its plaintive cries could be heard a mile away. Antelope and zebras raised up their heads and leapt forward, initiating a stampede. Shoving the spear repeatedly into the dying lion, Mikeyla felt a certain exuberance he had never known. The pride in knowing he was the king, ignited his senses and filled his soul with fire.

Pulling to the side of the road, Ricky threw the car in park and turned up the cassette player. *Every freakin' day and every freakin night...* Sensing a climax building in his loins, he grabbed the back of the car seat with both hands and thrust his hips forward. Being a pro, Roxy sensed the coming explosion and geared up for the blast. *Every freakin' day and every freakin night...* Not wanting to cancel one another out, they worked together guaranteeing the absence of a dud. Positive to positive, negative to negative. She squeezed her lips around his manhood and welcomed D-day.

"Ooohhh, shittt! Oooh, shitttt!" His howls drowned out the sound of the band, as the end of the song approached. He put both hands on her head and pushed down one last time, just to make sure she knew he was king.

"Did you see it?" she asked, opening the car door to spit.

"See what?" he panted, still recovering.

"The moon."

"Yeah. Yeah, I saw it. It was nice."

"Damn straight. That's why I get the big bucks. Are we staying here?"

"No. Let's ride. Do you wanna ride?"

"It's your night, brother. Just as long as you bring Roxy back to where you got her."

They boarded the Capitol City Freeway from Alhambra Boulevard, heading northbound, for no particular reason, just because this route offered easy access. The lights of the galleria blazed in the background and two strobe lights crisscrossed through the dark night sky. A wailing ambulance with flashing lights exited the southbound lanes heading to Sutter Hospital in an attempt to save someone's life.

"Why do you do this?" asked Ricky.

"Oh, no. Don't start giving Roxy no morality talk. Not after the way you just got off," she replied.

"Believe me, I would no more tell someone how to live her life than I would allow someone to tell me how to live mine. It was just a question. I just wanna know how a fine sister like you ended up driving down the freeway with a man you never seen before in your life."

"I wanted to make easy money. What's easier than fuckin'? Nothing too deep about it. Let me ask you something, or don't I get to talk?"

"Go ahead. You're off-duty for the moment."

"Why you gotta pay for it? Your woman don't know what she's doin'?"

"I don't have a woman. I don't have nobody, really. But I guess that's the way it's meant to be."

"Well, I don't think this is where I'm meant to be. I'm gonna get out of this business. Try and get myself a respectable job. So my daughter don't have to be ashamed."

"Do you believe in destiny?" asked Ricky.

"I don't believe in nothing that I can't buy. Last time I checked, you couldn't buy no destiny. Why? Do you?"

"I have to. That's the only logical explanation for why I have to do it."

"Do what? Ah, shit! You ain't one of them weirdo john killers?"

"Sister, if you only knew. Don't worry, I would never hurt you. But there's a war going on and nobody seems to know. Nobody but me. That's why I think it's my destiny. Cause I heard it."

Passing Arden Fair, Roxy looked to the right and marveled at the huge shopping structure. She had lived in Sacramento all her life and remembered when it had been nothing more than a glorified strip mall. Now with Nordstrom's at one end and Sax Fifth at the other, the little mall that could had hit the big time.

On the west side of the freeway stood the Hilton Hotel. Bringing class to the area, the Hilton had demonstrated that this City of Trees had arrived. Ricky continued driving on the freeway, not understanding what they were doing but enjoying it nevertheless. On any given night, Roxy was paid for her services, though none of the other johns ever said anything more to her than a few terse words. The man driving the car seemed crazy, but at least he was willing to engage in polite conversation.

Ricky hated the fact that he was unable to resist the sinful act of fornication but could not resist sexual gratification. Disgusted with what he done, he tried to add something extra to the night, to somehow take away his shameful physical pleasures. Besides, he needed someone to talk to. Someone whom he could care less if she understood, only that she listened.

"What did you want to be when you grew up?" asked Roxy.

"Nothing," Ricky responded.

"Come on. I entertained your conversation, now you have to entertain mine."

"I wanted to be an astronaut. Wasn't that a ridiculous notion?"

"I thought I was going to be an actress. I always pictured myself lounging on the deck of my beachfront home, sipping a martini with close friends. Maybe I aimed too high."

"Yeah, maybe."

Exiting the highway at Watt Avenue, Ricky followed the street

north, picking up Interstate Eighty just passed the light rail station.
Several people stood at the bus stop, waiting patiently for it to arrive.
He zoomed west, in the direction of the City by the Bay. McClellan
Air Force Base sprawled on the east. Hundreds of acres, designated
as a war zone. Military cars busily moved about, always on guard,
ready for any kind of attack.

"Are you from here?" she asked.

"Born and raised. What about you?"

"Same. Maybe that's my problem. Maybe if I had of gone away I
would be in another line of work."

"Do you really believe that? Or are you just telling yourself that
to make you feel better?"

"Does it matter? Either way, I'm still here, ain't I?"

"I believe it don't matter where we live. God has a mission for
each of us and no matter what side of the map we call home, our
destiny will prevail."

"So I guess you're saying that I was destined to be a hooker?"

"No. I m saying that there is a master plan for all of us. Now what
you do with your life while you work out that plan is a different story.
But in the end, none of that matters."

"Now tell me, Mr. Know-it-all, what's your destiny?"

The freeway had emptied, leaving only a few scattered cars with
flickering headlights beaming in the night. On the north side of the
highway, Arco Arena lit up the sky as the Sacramento Kings defended
their throne. Ricky imagined the point guard throwing up a three-
point shot in a final ditch effort to win the game.

An airplane flew overhead, departing from the international airport located just a few miles north. Switching to Interstate five, Ricky
headed south, concluding his circle around the city.

"My destiny?" he asked. "My destiny is to change the world."

"That s too vague. Give me something I can feel," she replied.

"I'm going to lead the revolution. For every brother that's ever
been beat. For every Native American that's ever been lied to. And
for every Mexican who has been escorted back across the border. I'm
going to lead all of us to salvation. To control. To power."

"In this revolution, will people die?"

"Has there ever been one where people haven't?"

"I don't know. But I don't want people to die. I don't wanna die."

"Ahh, sister. Don't you worry about a thing. With what I got planned, they're going to be in such awe, they will hand the throne over. You'll see."

Approaching the bridge which crosses the intersection of the Sacramento and American rivers, Ricky remembered the crash. Like a flash of light, the entire horrible incident played back in his mind, the rain, the bridge, the bus. Stomach now in turmoil, he was glad he had chosen to neglect dinner, not wanting to show his weakness to Roxy.

They passed over the bridge without incident and headed toward the skyline which resembled the land of Oz. Ricky continued down the freeway absorbing the feel of downtown. Old Sacramento sat to the west. With its mixture of historic western architecture and cobble stone roads, the story of the real wild west would be forever told. To the east, buildings of modern America stood forty stories above the ground, displaying on their walls man's ongoing attempt to reach the heavens on his own.

Ricky exited 15th street off of the Capitol City Freeway and took it to Broadway. Reaching First Avenue minutes later, he pulled up next to the same curb where he had picked Roxy up, allowing her the chance to go.

"Hey, one trip to the moon a night is enough for me," he said.

"It's your money. Thanks for the ride," she returned.

"You be careful out there. They'll be looking for you."

"Just as long as they got money, they can look all they want. You take care of yourself. You're the one leading the revolution. Ha, ha, ha," she laughed. "I hope we win."

"I hope we win, too. Hey, stay away from the river for awhile. Tell your friends. It's not going to be safe."

"Ha, ha, ha." Roxy let out another laugh then quietly walked away. Having more money in her pocket than she was used to earning in an entire night, she decided to throw in the towel. For the first time in a long while, someone had brought her back to where they found her. No long, cold walk. No being shoved out onto a busy street. The crazy revolutionary had showed her some respect. Now it was time to go home.

Reaching over to lock the door, Ricky made a U-turn, getting back onto Broadway. Turning left on Highway 160, he headed home. For the first time in years, he felt at peace. The night had somehow acted as confirmation, as the ultimate guide. It was time. Time for a change.

Off the coast of California, deep in the Pacific, the famous cooling Delta breeze changed directions. The rains which had tormented the citizens had gone, and unsuspecting to the valley residents, the heat was on.

VERSE

TWENTY-FIVE

After taking bite of forbidden fruit, man and woman cover themselves in shame.
—Garden of Eden, Middle East

Malik! What went down? Who knocked off the crackers?" screamed Ricky into the receiver.

"What crackers? What are you talking about, Ricky? It's too early for guessing games," responded Malik.

"Turn on the news. Channel 3. They pulled two white boys out the river. Same place where we threw Torion and Nathan."

"Shut up, Ricky. Don't say nothing about that over the telephone. Somebody could be listening. Just shut up and come right over. I'll call Rapone. I didn't order any hits! What's going on around here?" Malik demanded angrily.

"I'm there," Ricky responded, not really listening to Malik's last comment. He slammed down the receiver and rushed around the house in a mad search for clean clothes. The anchorwoman had talked about the two white men having the words white trash carved into their chests with a pocket knife or another sharp object. The coast guard had pulled the decomposed bodies from the waters surrounding the Carquinez bridge near Vallejo. No motive had been established, but investigators thought it might have been in retaliation for the vicious murders of the two African-American men who were pulled from the Delta two weeks before.

Worried, yet exhausted, Ricky fell asleep with the television on. He was jarred awake by the sound of the commentator's voice giving the joyous news of the deaths of the white men. While ecstatic that the militia had managed to strike first, he was disappointed that he was not in on the plan.

Ricky had already decided it best that, rather than taking pot shots at individual men, it would be better if he took them out all at once. Too late. First blood had been spilt. It would not be long before their blood was next.

Racing out of the door, he tripped over a pile of trash that had accumulated in the living room. Hitting the floor hard, yellow phlegm flew out of his mouth, followed by four hard gasps. He had decided to give up on eating, preferring the hunger pains over the bouts of nausea, but his body refused to cooperate. Now, instead of an undigested hamburger, bodily fluids littered the floor. When he finally managed to catch his breath, he leapt back to his feet and raced outside.

At only eight o'clock in the morning, it was surprisingly warm outdoors. Sun high in the sky, it burned down on the city, scolding it for complaining about the rain. Seventy-eight degrees already, according to the thermometer on Ricky's porch, at barely eight o clock. It was going to be a hot one. Summer had arrived.

Ricky pulled into Malik's driveway, parking behind Rapone's car which sat next to one of Malik's. Running up the stairs, he paused to regain his composure before knocking. The sickness in his stomach was becoming more sporadic and less controllable. He refused to allow anyone to see him when he was in such a condition. He would close the door to his bedroom, even though he lived alone, to be certain the world was closed out.

Feeling slightly better, somewhat in control, he knocked two times, waited for the response, then repeated the ritual. Door swinging open, Malik stood in the entryway wearing brown bermuda shorts to his knees and a sleeveless tank top revealing his bulging muscles. He wore a stern expression, indicating he was to be taken seriously.

"Good. You made it," said Malik, initiating the conversation. "Come on back."

"Of course, I made it," Ricky replied indignantly while following Malik to the back room which showcased the wall of glass. Rapone and Malina awaited Ricky's arrival, sitting in the back room, already alert and attentive. They turned toward Ricky as he descended the stairs. A layer of smoke floated in the air, as incense burned in all four corners. There was no music, only total silence.

"It's plastered all over the news," said Rapone. "It's all over the news! Who could of done it? We called all over town, and none of the brothers knew anything about it."

"Do you think they could have been lying?" interjected Malina, in her distress forgetting protocol in speaking before her husband.

"But why would they lie about it?" responded Malik, reclaiming the stage. Standing while the others remained seated, he demanded answers. This was his war. The leader had put him in charge of the revolution and he would be damned if someone would try to steal his thunder, successful hit or not.

"They weren't lying," Ricky quietly chimed in. I know what happened. It came to me on my way over.

"What happened, Ricky? Do you know something about this?" asked Malik.

"Someone else heard the shot too. We're not the only ones who know about it. Don't you see? Others are ready for the fight too. Other brothers and sisters have taken up arms in preparation for the war."

"Damn! Do you think so, Malik, man?" questioned Rapone.

"I don't know." he responded. "I don't know, anymore. Anything's possible. They think that it's in retaliation for Nathan and Torion. They think we've already struck back. Those red-necked thugs are at home scratching their heads."

"No they're not," responded Ricky. "They're home, strengthening their position. You know them white boys don't give up. They've been fighting for as long as we have. Longer. You see, our problem is that we've always thought small. We need to think big. Outsmart them with a new plan, not the same shit they've come to expect."

"Keep talking, brother. Are you getting this, Rapone?" asked Malik, so completely engrossed in Ricky's words he momentarily forgot he was the one in charge.

"Don't worry, brother. I'm with you." Rapone responded.

"You see what that white boy in Oklahoma did? Well, that ain't nothing. Fuck a building. I say we go for the whole fuckin' city." Ricky held center stage as his audience stared at him in awe.

"Blow up the city? Are you crazy? We can't do that. First of all, we don't have the capability. Secondly, you know how many of our lives would be lost?" responded Malik.

"Who's talking about bombing the city? I'm sayin' we flood this motherfucker. You know I work at the dam, now, in the same building as the boys who monitor it. They control the gates. If we can take control of those gates, we can put this whole city under forty feet of water. Ha, ha, ha! Hell, them white boys in Washington would be willing to negotiate then. We pull off some shit like that, we can have them bowing at our feet."

Ricky had returned to his days of old. No longer did he care about the militia's ethic codes which forbade swearing, drinking, and fornication. He was now a street bum, shooting craps on the corner of Rio Linda and Grand, trying to win his mother's money back. He was a child, crying out to his mother, begging her to give him food, love and affection. He was a fetus waiting to come out.

All sanity departed, leaving Ricky lost. Reality had bade him goodbye, leaving Ricky wandering in a galaxy where he alone controlled the world. Everything he said was magic. Every thing he did, golden. Make no mistake about it, Richard Swift had completely lost his mind.

"Ricky, man. Have you lost your mind?" asked Rapone. The question sounded rhetorical, but really he wanted to know the answer. "Look, brother. This ain't a movie. This shit is real. We can't be blowin' up no dam! Look, we stick to the plan the leader outlined. We have enough guns to last us a year. We're ready."

"Guns! Are you fuckin' crazy!" The madman screamed at Rapone, who jumped at the sound of Ricky s voice. Even Malik took a step back, not recognizing the man that Brother Ricky had become. "Them crackers got enough guns to last a decade! Who do you think we bought our ammunition from? Haven't you been listenin to me? We've got to think big! Am I the only one who understands what's going on around here? I heard it! I heard the fuckin' shot!!"

Unable to hold it back any longer, Ricky pushed his hand in his stomach, bent over and lurched up everything inside. Yellow phlegm, green glub, red blood shot out his mouth. Sensing fear within his organization, Ricky now accepted the fact that he was on his own. How could he expect them to understand? It was his destiny and he would go it alone. Ricky turned toward the living room and made a mad dash for the front door.

"Ricky, man, wait!" yelled Rapone.

"Brother! Brother! Are you alright?" yelled Malik.

"Oh, my God! What's wrong with Ricky? What's going on?" shrieked Malina.

Ricky ran out of the door, down the driveway and into his car. He turned the engine on, threw the car in reverse and peeled out, leaving tire tracks in his wake. Inside the house, Malina was now in complete hysterics, screaming toward her husband. "Torion was right! He's crazy! Ricky's crazy, and now Torion is dead! It's all falling apart, Malik!"

"Shut up, Malina. Just shut up! What do you think, Rapone?"

"I don't know, man. It's all gettin' so fucked up I don't know what to believe anymore. But I know one thing. We gotta count Ricky out."

"What do you mean count him out? He's the chosen one. How do you count the chosen one out?"

"Cut it out, Malik! Who are you trying to convince? Sounds like yourself to me," interrupted Malina, no longer afraid to say what was on her mind. "Torion was right, and you know it. We should have listened to him. Now look, there's people dead already and for what? The only shot was in Ricky's mind, and he's lost that."

"She's right, man," Rapone interjected. "You better call the leader and tell him it was a false alarm. A fuckin' mistake."

Speeding down the Garden Highway, Ricky turned up the volume of the car's tape player and absorbed himself in the sounds of the Messiah's voice. Listening to the hate-filled message, growing more angry by the minute, Ricky could not wait any longer. White against black, good versus evil, all of that no longer mattered. He was a man above men, a warrior among warriors, a god among gods. The task was his alone, and he was up to the challenge.

Departing on the usual exit, he turned left off of highway 160 and zig-zagged his way through the small town. Reaching his house, he noticed an unfamiliar car parked out front. Not expecting any visitors, he pulled into his driveway while keeping an eye out for the enemy. He could see the driver in the other car. It was one of them. A young white woman sat in the driver's seat pretending to read through some notes. *Who is she? Is she a lookout, a ploy?* he wondered to himself.

After turning off the car, he reached under the seat, checking for his automatic weapon. Good, it was still there.

Inside the car, Remmy Steel looked away from her notes in the direction of the man who had just arrived. Looking at the address on the house, she compared it to the one in the claim file. Deciding to relieve some of the pressure from Brooklyn's workload, and as a form of an apology, she had decided to locate the driver of the truck to obtain his statement about the accident. The police report listed his address, but the majority of the data related to the children and the oil spill itself. With a policy limits demand, they would need to obtain all the facts in order to accurately evaluate their insured's liability.

Assuming the black man was Ricky, she opened her car door and stepped out onto his front lawn.

"Hi. My name is Remmy Steel. I'm with Wexington Insurance Company. I'm looking for Richard Swift."

"Why are you looking for him?" questioned Ricky, his hand completely wrapped around his rifle.

"We represent Roberts Oil Company, and I understand Mr. Swift was the driver involved in a pretty big accident. I just need to get his statement about what actually happened."

"I'm Ricky." The madman looked around to make sure no one was in sight. With a better-than-average comfort level, he agreed to the interview, took his hand off the gun, stepped out of the car and invited her into his house. "Just a statement? That's all you need? You're not trying to pin anything on me, are you? It was raining like hell. I didn't mean to hit those kids."

"That's what we need to know, Mr. Swift. We need to find out, in your own words, how the accident happened. We're on your side. I promise, I won't take up too much of your time."

"Okay. Come in."

Remmy followed Ricky into the house. Just doing her job, trying to rescue a tarnished relationship, she unknowingly entered a snake pit. Her blonde hair glistened in the summer sun. Her pale skin absorbed the sun's rays, slowly tanning her light complexion. She wore a smart business suit, matching pumps, and carried a briefcase and cellular phone. She had everything she needed to conduct her business and be on her way.

In a rush, she had raced out of her office, telling no one where she was going. Brooklyn would be back in a couple of days, and she wanted his desk to appear as if he never left. Following Mr. Swift into his house, she noticed the tawdry manner in which it was kept. What did she care? How he lived was his business.

Closing the door behind his guest, Ricky turned and stared at the white woman. He watched in fascination as she pulled a dictaphone from her pocket. Since his drapes were never opened, the only light indoors came from the sun which crept in through the blinds.

"Alright, Mr. Swift. I can take your statement just like this. Let me check my dictaphone to make sure it's working properly."

"Who sent you?" he growled, ignoring what she had to say.

"I'm sorry. I'm from Wexington Insurance Company. I thought you heard me when we were outside. Let me give you one of my cards."

Lifting her briefcase, she balanced it in her hands, burying her head in the space. Ricky excused himself, attempting to outsmart the devil's helper, and sneaked into the other room. When he returned, she had closed the briefcase and set it on the floor. She extended her right hand outward, offering him her card.

"Here you are, Mr. Swift. Are you ready for the interview? I promise, I'll be quick."

"They sent you, didn't they? How did they find out where I was?"

"Your address was on the police report. It's standard practice to obtain the statements of all parties involved in an accident. We don't have to use the recorder. Let me just ask you a few questions, and I'll be on my way."

Using her feminine intuition, Remmy realized she was not dealing with a happy camper. Feeling a little nervous, she regretted walking into this man's house. She had figured she would get basic information and vacate the premises, just as quickly as she could. The day was a beautiful one. She did not have the time to get caught up with a distraught witness.

Ricky stared at the she-devil, certain he saw horns beginning to grow. Flames appeared behind her as he realized she was trying to take control. Free-falling through the abyss, floating in a black hole, Ricky swam in psychotic oblivion, entering a world where only few had gone.

There are those who would say Charles Manson is the Prince of Madness. Others might give the title to Jeffrey Dahmer or Timothy McVeigh. Years from now, when a new history book was written, the populace would agree that Richard Jason Swift had conquered this throne.

"Remmy. Is that what you call yourself? You come into my house, wearing a disguise, thinking I was too dumb. You can't fool me devil! Do you understand me? You can't—fool—me!!"

The sun reached its full peak as the valley baked underneath its rays. A half mile from the house, a neighbor mowed his lawn. Seven parcels down, a mother tended to her young. In the house that Ricky's father built, however, a revolution was going on. Most had thought the fight would be black against white. Many believed it was going to be man versus woman. Some thought it would be a battle between good and evil. Few would actually understand that the real war was between the sane and the demented.

Inside his house, Ricky pulled the gun from behind his back. The silencer on, cabins full, he pointed the gun at his guest. No longer resembling a woman, the devil had dropped its disguise. Giving no further consideration, Ricky pulled the trigger, emptying it at point-blank range. Remmy's lifeless body collapsed. It exploded into a hundred pieces as each pellet entered her delicate frame. In an instant, Remmy Victoria Steel's California dream was gone.

Wasting no time, Ricky grabbed Remmy's car keys and hurried outside. After entering her vehicle, he jammed the keys into the ignition and pulled her car into the second stall of his two-car garage. Racing inside, he began cleaning up the mess. Assuring that all of the blinds were closed and curtains shut, he wrapped her body in several large plastic bags. Taking a seat on the couch, he lit a cigarette and placed it between his lips then waited for night to fall. He could take out the garbage on the way to work.

VERSE

TWENTY-SIX

Guerrilla warfare at peak level.
Bombs strapped to children.
—Ho Chi Minh City, Vietnam

ou see, the problem with this country is we gave away too much of the control. Trying to give an inch, them damn niggers and spics took a mile. You know what?"

"What, Mr. Roberts?" answered the bartender as he reluctantly poured his patron another drink.

"My grandpappy should have been president. Hell, if he had sat in the White House, we would still be saluting the Confederate flag. No, ice! How many times do I have to tell you? No ice!"

"I think you've had enough, Mr. Roberts. Why don't you go on home and sleep it off. I'll call you a cab."

"You're not going to call me nothing but another drink. Don't you know who I am? I'm Dave Roberts, owner and CEO of Roberts Oil Company."

"I know, Mr. Roberts. But right now, you're drunk. So, to keep your wife from suing me in the morning, I'm going to call you a cab."

Before the bartender could turn and reach for the phone, Dave Roberts hurled his whiskey glass forward, sending it sailing directly over the bartender's head. The glass crashed into the mirror, sending shards of glass shattering in a thousand pieces. The other two drunken patrons jumped up, stumbling, and staggered out of the door.

The bartender looked at the shattered glass, then back at Mr. Roberts. He had tended bar for over twenty years and had had run-ins with the best of them. Having everything from knives waved in his face to guns pointed directly at his head, flying glass was the least of his concerns. When the sun rose, Mr. Roberts assistant would saunter inside, offering to pay for any damage caused by his employer. Jake of Jake's Bar & Grill would graciously accept the compensation and not give the incident any further mention. It was the same old ritual he had participated in many times before. If some old, rich fart wanted to get drunk and bust up a couple of glasses, who was Jake to stop him? Especially when he paid handsomely for the goods.

Tonight, as Jake attempted to close up shop, he noticed something a little different about Mr. Roberts. His eyes were bloodshot from too much booze or from lack of sleep. His skin was pale and clammy as if he had seen a ghost and lived to tell about it. Something was obviously wrong with this neurotic fool and, being the exceptional bartender that he was, he intended to find out.

"Hey, calm down, Mr. Roberts. I'll give you one more. How's that? Just tell ole Jake what the problem is."

"Damn right you'll serve me. I probably paid for most of this shit in here anyway. Fill her up and no fuckin' ice."

"No ice. Right, Mr. Roberts. Now what seems to be the problem?"

"The problem is too many niggers and not enough of us," Mr. Roberts replied in his usual hate-filled, alcohol-induced voice.

"Since when has that been a problem for you? You're a big man in this town. Why would you let get someone get you so riled up that you come in here and drink yourself crazy?"

"Because they're everywhere, that's why. I can't walk out of my fuckin' door without bumping into them. And now they're trying to take my business over. They're trying to ruin my life. Damned blacks even convinced some of us to help them, but we fixed that white trash, didn't we?" Recalling the recent night in his mind, a grin spread across Mr. Roberts' face as he remembered throwing the turncoats into the delta.

"Huh? How did you fix them? I don't think I'm following you,

Mr. Roberts."

Dave Roberts looked directly into Jake's eyes, trying to decide if the bartender was a fighter of the Cause. Mr. Roberts had patronized the bar for several years but only now realized he had always done all the talking. What did he know about Jake other than he could never remember to leave the ice out of his Bourbon. He looked at Jake's skin and saw that it was the same color as his. What difference did that make? Traitors were being discovered in the ranks and Jake could be just one more.

Jake waited patiently to hear a response to his question, then decided he was going to get nothing but the rambling words of a babbling drunk. Deciding he had better things to do with his night, he turned away from the conversation and began cleaning up the glass.

"Did you know there's a war going on, Jake?"

"You mean over there in Bosnia? Hell, I don't even consider that a war anymore. It's more like a way of life."

"I mean right here. It's going on all around you, and you can't fucking see it?"

"Probably cause I ain't all liquored up. Now, I'm going to call you a cab. You'll feel much better in the morning, Mr. Roberts. Those little men who are trying to get you won't be there when you wake up."

"Whose side are you on, Jake?"

"I'm on yours," said Jake, making another attempt to reach for the phone. Mr. Roberts grabbed his arm again, preventing him from dialing the numbers.

"I said I don't want a cab, Jake. I'll drive myself home. You just put what I drank on my tab, and Craig will be here in the morning to take care of it. He'll take care of that cheap glass as well."

Mistaking Mr. Roberts' command for drunken chatter, Jake snatched his arm from his grasp, picked up the phone and began dialing the number to the Yellow Cab Company. With only three digits dialed, Jake stopped dead in his tracks. Mr. Roberts had walked around the bar and was now pointing the long end of a pistol at the bartender's head.

Sweat appeared on Dave Roberts' fist. His frail fingers shook with intensity as the alcohol he had consumed mixed with the medicine already in his body, creating a deadly mix. While usually unmoved by such a cowardly display of power, Jake, horrified, began producing his own sweat. He now realized Mr. Roberts just was not quite himself. Worse yet, he feared, the liquor had nothing to do with it.

"What are you doing, Dave? Put that gun away and go on home before someone gets hurt," said Jake in the most calming voice he could muster.

"That's Mr. Roberts to you! Or haven't you learned to show a man respect when he's pointing a gun at your head?"

"Mr. Roberts. Put your gun away and we'll pretend nothing's happened. Look, I'm putting the phone down. I won't call a cab. You can drive yourself home, and I'll stay here and pray that you make it home safe. How's that? Now put the gun away. I told you, I'm on your side."

Dave Roberts slowly lowered the gun, then slid it back inside his pants. Bourbon seeping through his pours, hate radiating from his eyes, his face twisted and contorted, the drunken man barely managed to speak.

"I told you I don't want a fucking cab, Jake! Now what part of that don't you understand?"

"I understand that you're a grown man. I understand that you've had a lot to drink. I also understand that you have a gun. Where I'm from, if a grown, drunk man with a gun doesn't wanna take a cab, he don't gotta take a cab. You be safe out there, Mr. Roberts. I gotta tend to the bar."

Jake picked up a wet dish rag and began the mundane chore of washing down the drink that the drunk man had spilled. Carefully, he picked up the broken glass and deposited the fragmented pieces into the nearby garbage bin. He had purchased the bar ten years ago from an old friend who decided he wanted out of the business. Immediately changing the name to Jake's Bar & Grill, Jake ordered bar furniture and pictures which suited his personal style and taste. Literally, by walking the streets, passing out flyers and offering personal hellos, he established a loyal following of beer-guzzling white and blue-collar workers. With the glory of owning a building, though, came the agony of defeat. Drunk patrons starting fights, demanding more than they could handle and occasionally even pulling a gun, but Jake took it all in stride. He would clean up the broken glass, have his assistant order a replacement and continue to serve his loyal constituents who only wanted the liquor to take away their pain.

Dave Roberts staggered out of the door and stumbled his way toward the green Range Rover parked in the adjacent lot. The sun had set long ago, but its warmth could still be felt. Reaching his vehicle, he pulled the keys out of his right pants pocket and popped the lock. He climbed inside the automobile, put the key in the ignition, then sped off into the night.

*****

"Oh, Sonya. It was so nice! Expensive, but nice. You ought to have seen Nigel. I mean, when the killer whales appeared, I thought he was going to have a heart attack. Johnny wasn't much better. I felt like I was with two kids."

"Go look in the mirror, Arizona."

"Look in the mirror? Why?"

"So you can see your glow. I thought it was lost, but it was just hidden for a little while. Good for you, girl. But if you ask me, you should have been with that insurance man you were telling me about or that attorney. Haven't you heard a leopard never loses his stripes?"

"Sonya. Leopards don't have stripes."

"Tigers, cheetahs. You know what I meant. I'm just saying why go down the same road that didn't lead you anywhere the first time around?"

"Well, maybe the road has been repaired. Maybe that road isn't a dead end any more. A tiger may not lose his stripes, but that doesn't mean he can't find a new way home. Besides, I didn't say Johnny and I were getting back together. I just said we had a nice time. Is there anything wrong with that? And besides, I told you. Frankie's married. I don't do married men."

"Humph! Has Donovan called yet?"

"No. And he better not. How many times have I got to tell you, Sonya, that I ain't interested in no man behind bars! Do you want some more wine?"

"What the hell. I don't have any place to go. I don't have four men fighting over my honor. I'll check on the boys while you pour."

Sonya stood up, stretching her arms upward in the process. She wasn't much of a drinker so the Cabernet Sauvignon had immediately gone to her head, causing a light and relaxing buzz. Arizona refilled their glasses and watched in fascination as the red wine fell like a crimson waterfall from the bottle to a glass. Her mind had been so absorbed with little Johnny that even the simple task of pouring wine excited her. The smooth texture, faint aroma and tantalizing taste reminded her of the carefree days in which she only had to worry about herself. She thought about the days when she and Johnny would walk barefoot along the riverbank and devour bottles of wine before going to a private location where they would make love for the remainder of the night. Now, there were bills to pay, mouths to feed and children to take care of, but she didn't mind. In fact, she preferred it that way.

Minutes later, Sonya returned from Nigel's room and rejoined her friend on the living room couch, ending Arizona's unexpected trip down memory lane. Grasping her glass, Sonya raised it up, to make a toast.

"You'll never believe this," said Sonya. "Those boys are sound asleep, laid out on the floor. I picked them up and put 'em in bed. Couldn't believe it. I have the hardest time making Tommy go to sleep when he's at home."

"You know kids. They do whatever they wanna do," replied Arizona.

"You know what, Arizona?"

"No. What, girl?"

"You are alright by me. I don't care what those other people say."

"Tell those other people to go to hell," Arizona replied, laughing at Sonya's comment. Their glasses touched, creating a clinking sound, a happy sound.

"Well, there's something I have to tell you. Are you ready?" asked Sonya after taking a sip of her wine.

"I don't know. Am I going to like it? I'm too drunk to hear news that I won't like."

"You should. Anyway, I'm getting married."

"What? You're getting married? To who? When? Where? I didn't even know that you were seeing someone."

"I've been seeing him for awhile. Nicest brother you ever want to meet. Always tells me how beautiful I am. You ought to see how he reacts when he sees me comin'. He even writes poetry. For me."

"What's his name?"

"Jacob. Jacob Laurence."

"Jacob Laurence? From the old school? I thought he was in prison."

"He is. I told you I've been going down to the prison with my cousin to visit her husband. Well, I met Jacob while I was there. You've got to meet him, Arizona. I just know you'll think he's everything and more."

"But, Sonya, he's in prison. What can he do for you? What can he do for your kids?"

"He's not going to be there forever. He only has three more years, then he's eligible for parole. I love him, Arizona."

"I wasn't expecting this. I want to be happy for you, but I just can't. You deserve better. You deserve someone who can take you dancing and for walks along the beach. He can't do any of that. And girl, I know you heard how women marry these men in prison, and as soon as they get out they leave 'em for another woman. How can you be sure he isn't just marrying you for conjugal visits?"

"They're called family visits and, I know, Arizona. I just know. Look. I want you to be my Maid of Honor but if you're not with it..."

"I'm with whatever makes you happy. But I got to speak my piece. I just think you're better than being a prisoner's wife."

"But you don't even know him."

"It's not him that I'm concerned with. People make mistakes. I'm not casting doubt on the type of person he is because he got caught committing a crime. Unless it was murder. Please say it wasn't murder."

"Robbery."

"That's a relief. Anyway, what I was saying is that it doesn't matter to me that he made a mistake. People change. I've learned first hand of that. But what I'm talking about is the life that it involves. I mean running down to the prison four days a week. Being searched and questioned about your comings and goings. Conjugal, I mean family visits, with an armed guard posted outside the door. I just think you deserve more Sonya. You deserve better. We both do."

Silence filled the room as Arizona's last words floated through the air. Sonya had recently turned thirty and suddenly became painfully aware of her biological clock. Never married, she felt her time was running out. With no job or education, she had given up long ago on finding Prince Charming. All she wanted now was someone to hold her, to love her, and to make love to her until her body filled with warmth.

She was hesitant about telling anyone about her engagement. At this point, however, it no longer mattered. She was going to marry the man she loved and didn't give a damn what anyone thought of it...except Arizona.

The wine caused Sonya's emotions to erupt. Unable to even attempt to hold back the tears, she let them trickle down her face and slide into her untouched glass of wine. Arizona moved closer, putting her arms around her friend, finding comfort as much as providing it.

"I'm sorry, Sonya. I am happy for you. I just want you to make sure you're doing the right thing, that's all. I'm happy for you."

"He told me that I was beautiful, Arizona. I can't remember the last time anyone has told me that."

"Hey, allow me to make a toast," said Arizona, letting go of her friend and reaching for her wine glass. Sonya followed suit, after wiping the remaining tears from her eyes. "To Sonya and Jacob. May they have no problems in walking through the security gate."

"Funny," Sonya replied after taking a long sip. "Alright, my turn. To Johnny and Arizona. May there be room enough in the bed for the three of them. Arizona, Johnny and Mr. Jack Daniels."

The ladies let out loud whoops which echoed throughout the house.

As their laughter filled the air, their pessimism vanished as quickly as it had appeared. Arizona refilled both glasses as the two women continued to offer sardonic toasts, leading to yet more uncontrollable laughter.

Much later, when the wine bottle was empty, the semi-intoxicated ladies decided they had had enough.

"Girl, let me take my drunk butt home," Sonya slurred.

"Well, since you're walking, I can let you go. Otherwise, I would have had to take your keys," replied Arizona.

"Let me go wake up Tommy."

"Just let him sleep. I'll drop him off in the morning."

"Are you sure it's no problem?"

"Be quiet. You know it's no problem. Just call me when you get home so I'll know you made it."

"Thanks, girl. With my other kids over my mother's, I'm going to sleep in tomorrow. Oh. You never did answer the question."

"What question?"

"Will you be my Maid of Honor?"

"I would be honored to be your Maid of Honor. Just as long as the guard who searches me is a strong, tall, dark brother."

"Thank you, Arizona."

"No. Thank you."

Sonya walked outside and was pleasantly surprised by the warm night air. With only four blocks to go to get to her house, she decided to walk off her buzz by taking the long way home, even though it would only add four minutes to her journey.

As she walked along the quiet streets, she hummed *Here Comes The Bride* and pictured how she would look walking down the makeshift hall of the prison's visiting room. *I now pronounce you husband and wife,* she thought to herself. "That sounds nice," she said aloud.

Stopping at the red light, she noticed a car weaving across the road in the distance. Unmoved by the condition of the driver, she stepped off of the curb when the light turned green and began walking across the street.

On the adjacent corner, the driver of the vehicle, Dave Roberts, stopped for the red light just as Sonya stepped off the curb. Mr.

Roberts squinted and took another long swig of the bottle of bourbon that he had pulled from the storage compartment. He noticed the figure crossing the street looked somewhat unusual. Squinting his eyes further, he focused on what he thought to be a creature with a long protruding tail and elongated arms which dragged on the city street. *Now that's odd? What would a monkey be doing running free?* he thought. As he sat at the red light, he realized that there was no monkey, a black woman was crossing the street. Rage grew in his veins as he thought of the old days when niggers would get out of the way when they saw a white person approach. Irrational because of the deadly combination of medicine, alcohol and hate, Mr. Roberts was unable to contain the blind fury he felt. He pressed down on the accelerator, ran through the red light, and headed straight for the person crossing the street.

By the time Sonya noticed the speeding vehicle, it was too late. The maniac driver was heading directly toward her leaving only enough time to beg the Lord to take care of her children.

"You, nigger bitch! Get the fuck out of my way!!" Mr. Roberts yelled.

A final prayer. A scream. The sound of a collision. Then silence. When the smoke cleared, Sonya Lynn Vaughan lay dead in the middle of West El Camino and Truxel and Dave Roberts joyously sped off into the night.

VERSE

TWENTY-SEVEN

Jim Jones orders mass suicide,
believing redemption is at hand.
—Guyana, South America

At only seven o'clock in the morning, the sun was already out in force. Brooklyn walked up the stairs of Wexington Insurance Company, wiping the sweat from his brow as he did so. Looking up at the sky, he marveled at the strength of the sun and wondered why it had picked Sacramento on which to unleash its wrath so early in the season.

He had returned from Kingston in good spirits. Still high from his Caribbean experience, he had awakened that morning with a renewed outlook on life. Rising with the sound of the rooster, he chose a tall glass of water over a hot cup of coffee and read the morning edition on the lower deck of his houseboat. Bypassing all of the main news stories, he breezed through the comics and scanned the sports section before jumping into the shower.

Walking into the office, he was overcome by a sense of deja vu. He had been away fourteen days but it seemed like an eternity. On the last night of his vacation, he had studied the warm waters of the Caribbean Sea and the thousands of twinkling stars. Clearing his mind, his consciousness, and his soul, he had found serenity in inhaling the last of his half pound of ganga and final ounce of rum. He would return with nothing but good cheer and good thoughts.

"Good morning, Brooklyn," said Joan, the receptionist, pleasantly. "How was your vacation?"

"Fantastic," Brooklyn replied. "Just what the doctor ordered."

"Bet you wish you were still there."

"No. Actually, I'm glad to be back. You know what Dorothy said, 'There's no place like home.' Was I missed?"

"Oh, you know you're always missed. Just wait until you listen to your voice mail, then you'll know how much you were missed."

He continued down the hall, exchanging greetings with his co-workers and pausing frequently to relay the tales of his trip on the way to his office.

"Jamaica, man!" shouted Bruce over the walls of his small cubicle.

"Well, if it isn't the world traveler," teased Marsha from behind the water cooler.

"It was wonderful. Everything was just perfect. Paradise," Brooklyn declared after each comment.

Finally managing to duck inside his office, his optimism drooped a little as he discovered a mound of gray files on his desk. The office was very dark since he had closed the blinds before his departure. Immediately, before he could fall into a state of depression, he opened the blinds and allowed the sun's rays to pour in. He stared out of the window, wanting to see the hummingbird, but it was nowhere in sight. Feeling a bout of pessimism creeping through his body, he popped a compact disc, that he purchased from a cabbie back in Kingston, into his portable disc player. The sounds helped to calm his nerves, but could not completely shake the notion that he had returned to the real world.

He sat down, turned on the computer and began organizing the files on his desk. He thought about getting a cup of coffee, but the office felt only slightly cooler than outside. Instead, he buried his head in the stack of papers, attempting to lose himself in his work.

"If it isn't Brooklyn! So, you decided to come back after all. I almost shipped your belongings off to the Caribbean. I figured you found some West Indian woman and set up camp."

"What's going on, Laurence? I'm not going to tell you that very thought crossed my mind. So what's new around here?"

"Same book, different cover. But I'm two weeks closer to retirement."

"Counting the days, huh?"

"No. More like the minutes. Don't you wish your work went on vacation when you did? Make life a hell of a lot easier."

"Too easy. Then it wouldn't be life. I'll manage."

"I know you will. You got a call from a Mr. Jackson. Joan told him you would be gone for a while so he wanted to speak to me. Looks like he's ready to settle."

"He's always been ready, just for more than I'm willing to pay."

"I hear ya. It looks like he's seeing your way a little more. I read the file and I see he was initially requesting policy limits. He's dropped his demand to three million."

"Wow! That's a big drop. I wonder what happened?"

"Who knows. Maybe the kid is doing better."

"You think so?"

"It's a possibility. You probably should give him a call and see what the deal is. I hear Dave Roberts has got a hard-on over this one."

"Is the file still in your office?"

"Actually, Remmy has it."

"Remmy? I didn't think she wanted to touch this one with a ten-foot pole."

"Maybe she wanted to help you out. You know Remmy."

"I'll go down to her office and see if she still has it."

"She isn't in. She's been out of the office for a couple of days."
"On business?"

"I'm sure, but she didn't leave a note. Joan said she bolted out like a bat out of hell. I imagine she'll be in first thing in the morning. She never likes to leave her desk more than a couple of days at a time. Catching up stresses her out too much."

"Yeah. You know Remmy. I better push some of this paper."
"Welcome back."
"Yeah."

Laurence walked out of the door and headed back to his office.

He felt a little guilty for not checking on Brooklyn's desk, but the feeling would soon pass. He had already paid his dues. Now it was time to sit back and bide his time until retirement. In three months he would walk out of the door, down the steps and drive out of the parking lot of Wexington Insurance Company for the very last time.

Brooklyn pulled up the file number on his computer screen and proceeded to search for Franklin Jackson's telephone number. Pulling up the phone list, he scanned down to the J's and stopped when the computerized indicator covered Frankie's number. Picking up the phone, he dialed the seven digits. While the phone rang, he took several deep breaths, preparing for the confrontation that he had avoided for the past two weeks.

"Law offices, how may I direct your call?" said a soft, monotone female voice on the other end of the receiver.

"Brooklyn Hunter for Franklin Jackson."

"What file are you calling on?"

"Jonathan Tyler."

"One moment, please."

Silence, then a click as Brooklyn was transferred to the appropriate line.

"Mr. Hunter. Welcome back. How was your trip?" asked Franklin Jackson.

"Too short."

"I can imagine. Jamaica is my favorite island. Which part did you visit?"

"Kingston. I stayed in Montego Bay last year."

"My wife and I usually choose Negril. Seven miles of white sand beaches, please, don't get me started. Anyway, what may I do for you?"

"Well, actually I'm returning your call. I understand you spoke with my manager, Laurence. He tells me you've reconsidered your demand."

"Not really. I'm just trying to help you out a little."

"Ha, ha, ha! Thanks for the small favors. How's the little boy?"

"The same. Doesn't look good. Not many people are known to come out of comas."

"Yes, but it does happen."

"I've discussed the situation with my client, and we have decided to lower our demand to three million. He's an innocent, seven-year-old child. Brought down before his prime by a careless driver. Hell, three million's a gift. About the time I'm finished with Roberts Oil Company, I'll have the jury demanding his head, along with a substantial compensation package."

"Your client is still alive. He could recover fully and be able to live a long, productive life. I can't pay three million. At this time I'm prepared to make you an offer of $750,000.00 Why don't you take that to your client and see what they say?"

"Is that offer on top of the medical bills?"

"Yes. We'll pick up the hospital bills and will reimburse his parents for their loss of earnings and out-of-pocket expenses. Why don't you take the offer to them and see how they respond?"

"Do you actually consider this offer to be fair and reasonable?"

"Yes. Yes, I do."

"Well, I don't. In fact, I think it's an insult. I guess a little black kid isn't worth the same as a little white one."

"What? Have you forgotten what I look like, Mr. Jackson? Don't try and play the race card with me, 'cause it won't work. My job is to pay claims that we are legally obligated to pay. When making a payment, I take into consideration the nature of the accident, the injury, and the claimant. Not the color of the claimant's skin. So save your self-righteous lecture for the jury, Mr. Jackson. The offer stands at $750,000.00, plus expenses. Take it to your clients and let me know. Have a nice day."

Slamming the receiver down on the phone, steam blowing out of his ears, Brooklyn realized his vacation was over. He glanced out of the window just as the hummingbird flew by. Used to the bird pausing and staring inside, he leaned forward, pressing his face against the pane. The hummingbird, realizing it had passed by its destination, made a U-turn and headed back toward his soul mate. Just as the bird approached the window, a pine cone fell from a large tree, hitting the hummingbird on top if its head. The weight of the pine cone caused the bird to lose its balance, causing it to plunge toward the ground.

Through a cruel twist of fate, a hungry alley cat lay underneath the tree, waking from its slumber by the scent of falling bird. Looking up, the cat sprung to life, hardly believing that food was falling from the sky. Realizing its life was about to end, the hummingbird tried to recover and fly away, but before it could regain its senses, the feline quickly pounced on its meal, devouring the tiny morsel as if it was the only piece of food it had seen in days. In reality, it really was.

Sickened by the animal act of survival, Brooklyn turned away from the window and slunk back in his seat. The world was spinning faster and faster, refusing to allow him or anyone else to jump off. He thought about his vacation, which only sent him into a deeper state of depression. *Oh, God. Where's the bottom?* he thought. "This office," he said out loud.

Before he could pick up his pencil and once again attempt to earn his keep, he heard a loud scream from the front office. He jumped out of his seat and dashed in the direction of the cries. The entire office was on its feet, listening for another emotional outburst so that they could follow the direction of the wails.

"Oh, my God! Oh, my God!" screamed Joan from the reception-ist booth.

With Laurence leading the way, the staff rushed toward Joan, who sat behind the receptionist booth, crying with tissue in both hands. She shook frantically as a river of tears rushed from her eyes. Her sobs grew as she rocked back and forth, obviously disturbed by some-thing.

"What's wrong?" questioned Laurence. "What on earth is going on?"

Not saying a word, she reached down to the radio and turned up the volume. Instantly, the sounds of the announcer shot through the speakers and into the ears of the onlookers:

Recapping our top story, a fifth body was discovered, this one in the American River near the Lake Natoma bridge. Police say she had been shot several times before being dumped into the river. They believe she was already dead prior to being discarded but this can-not be determined until an autopsy is performed. Incredibly, she had been wrapped in several black plastic bags, along with several items which police refuse to identify at this stage. However, we have learned that the victim has been identified as Remmy Steel of Carmichael, California. No motive has been given for the heinous crime, but investigators believe it could be another race- related incident. The words White Devil were scrawled across her bare back with her own blood. The mayor has called a special meeting to discuss this growing surge of racial violence that has strangled the city in the past few weeks. Our own Troy Tatum will have a special report on this deadly epidemic tonight following the six o'clock news.

In other parts of the city, a woman was run down as she crossed the street in the Natomas area. One eyewitness says it looked as if the person driving the car deliberately hit her before speeding off...

Not waiting for group condolences, Brooklyn burst out of the door and leapt down the stairs leading to the parking lot. Pacing himself, he ran through the lot until he hit Fair Oaks Boulevard, then turned right and followed the longest street in Sacramento County to its end. Gradually picking up speed, he soon found himself running for his life at full throttle. He ran faster and faster, pushing himself to the very limit. Running. Thinking. Breathing; freeing his mind, trying to understand why the world had turned so ugly and attempted to pinpoint the time that this had happened. He only wanted to be free from a society who had learned to accept hate as a way of life. A community that embraced pain and scoffed at happiness as something a person received only two weeks out of every year.

Crossing Madison Avenue, his energy ran low and he collapsed outside of the Orangevale Community church. Completely out of breath, he looked up at the distinguished steeple and screamed at the top of his lungs.

"Why don't You help us?! Why don't You come back and help us!!"

Falling to the ground, he burst into tears, regretting what had been his final utterance to his friend. Remmy was dead. Now he could never take his angry words back.

VERSE

TWENTY-EIGHT

Six Million murdered
during the Holocaust.
—Eastern Europe

In a world filled with so much pain and suffering, we must search out the clouds of joy that the Good Lord assures us is there. So quick we are to blame others for our hardship that we no longer move toward the perfect world which God made for us. We hide in our homes with bars around our doors and windows and live our lives as if nothing is wrong. I'm saying, there is something wrong. Something deadly wrong with a society that has come to accept crime and hate as a part of our everyday existence.

"The Lord even gave us another chance at a clean world when he sent the rains coming for those forty days and nights. He washed away the filth which had decayed our souls and made them clean and pure. It didn't take us long to sour the taste of the apple. As soon as the land dried, we again dirtied the soil and polluted the waters.

"When will we learn that life is precious and divine? When will we see that God Almighty put us here for the purpose to love one another? To live in perfect harmony and make the world he gave us a more beautiful place to be?

"Now, another one of his seeds has been ripped from the earth before it had the chance to bloom. Sonya Lynn Vaughan was a good person, a loving mother, a caring friend. She was walking across the street on her way home from enjoying the evening with a friend. She was at peace with herself then, and she is at peace now. But we must not let her death be another one that goes unnoticed. There has to come a time when the human race has to say, 'Enough is enough!' Because if we don't, God help us, 'cause this time around it won't be with a rain. This time when He comes back, it'll be with fire. And Noah's Ark will be the first thing that goes up in flames!"

The minister concluded his powerful eulogy as the organist raised the volume of her solemn tune. The small but colorful choir dressed in their bright red robes, stood and added lyrics to the tune being played. St. John's Baptist Church was suddenly filled with an overwhelming sense to release all of its burdens. Finally, someone had realized that the world had gone mad, and it was up to the inhabitants to stop it.

The minister raised his arms, signaling that the congregation should rise and view the remains of Ms. Vaughan for the last time. Arizona gently took hold of Tommy's hand and led him up to the casket containing his mother's embalmed body. The line of people formed quickly, and the cries grew louder. To the left of Arizona, Sonya's mother collapsed, overcome by grief. Her two adult sons, fighting back their own pain, helped their mother stand so that she could pay her last respects to her only daughter.

When Arizona and Tommy reached the casket, she rubbed her dead friend's hand after dropping in a single rose and a picture of the two of them that they had taken several months ago.

"I love you, friend," stated Arizona, fighting back a wave of tears.

She held onto her dignity, knowing that someone had to be strong for Sonya's son. Little Tommy, not truly understanding what all the commotion was about, looked at his mother. He turned his head sideways, trying to understand how she could remain asleep through all the noise. He looked back at his grandmother who was now on her feet but shaking uncontrollably and screaming toward the ceiling, saying things that made no sense.

Frightened, he turned back toward the casket, finally realizing something was terribly wrong.

"Mommy," he cried. "Mommy, wake up!"

"Come on, Tommy. It's time for us to go," replied Arizona through low sobs, no longer able to hold back her grief.

"No! I want my mommy! Mommy, wake up. I'm afraid."

"Tommy, your mommy can't wake up. She's gone to heaven. But she's gonna watch out over you from there. Okay, little man? Your mommy is okay."

"Noo!! I want my mommy, Aunt Arizona. I want my mommy to wake up!!!"

To a child, death is not a concept that is easily understood. It is a word in the English language which a young child may have heard several times in his short life without ever having had to endure the misery it can cause. To children, dogs die, birds die, but not their mothers. And definitely not their dreams. At five years old, less than four feet tall, and only fifty-four pounds, young Tommy had turned into a volatile pile of dynamite. Light years ahead of his peers, the precious child was suddenly thrust into an adult world where the word death had taken on new meaning. Like a bungy jumper with a broken chord, his frail little mind crashed to the earth, shattering his world into a million pieces. His mommy was dead. Now what was he supposed to do?

"Don't die, mommy! Please, don't die! Don't leave me, oh Mommy, please don't leave. I'll be good. I promise, I'll be good!"

On a hot spring day, in one of California's hottest valleys, a storm cloud formed over the city of Sacramento. In a rare ecological event, the cloud burst, dumping an inch of rain on the city in only ten short minutes. The sound of the rain battering the windows jarred the congregation and sent the minister stumbling back to his seat. He bowed his head in prayer and begged the Lord for forgiveness. So intense was little Tommy's pain that the angels in heaven grieved openly as they had done for another little boy named Cedrick Jackson who had died a few years before. They grieved for Jason who had lost his life in an earthquake and for Torion who was bludgeoned to death by ignorant people whom he had loved and thought had loved him.

The angels in heaven were used to screams. They were used to tears and people pleading for understanding and for their prayers to be answered. They were used to dying men, who had spent their entire lives sinning, asking for forgiveness on their death beds. They were used to all that, and more. But the sound of a child's agony still seemed to carry a weight of its own. The sound of a child gasping for air, for hope, for relief, made even the oldest angels, who had seen and heard it all, plug their ears and break down into tears. For the holiest of them all knew that the promise of a better life held no serenity for a child who had just lost his mother. As Tommy's cries became overbearing, heaven wept openly, dousing the land in tears which the citizens mistakenly believed to be rain.

The minister prayed, crossed a T across his chest, then prayed harder. Realizing the world had done itself in, his only hope was to save as many lives as time would allow. Resuming his place as head of the church, the shepherd walked up to the microphone and attempted to lead his flock to salvation.

*****

Across town, under the attack of the same thundercloud which rained down on St. John's Baptist church, the East Lawn cemetery hosted a memorial for Remmy Steel. Her body was already on an east-bound plane, heading to Green Bay Wisconsin where the Shaboygen Funeral Home would pick her up and prepare her body for the funeral planned there.

An eight-by-ten glossy photograph, sat inside a beautiful bouquet of flowers. With no choir, the room was quiet except for the few hushed sniffles of Remmy's somber co-workers and friends. Brooklyn sat in the front row, between Laurence and Joan. He reached in his shirt pocket and pulled out a dry handkerchief. He passed it to Joan who had used up an entire box of Kleenex, even before the sermon began.

"Thank you, Brooklyn," she mumbled. "She was such a good girl. Why would anyone do this to her?"

"I don't know," he replied. "Larry, you've been around for awhile. Maybe you know the answer to that ageless question?"

"Which one would that be?" asked Larry.

"Why does the caged bird sing?"

"If I knew the answer to that, I'd be a rich, happy man. Only the caged bird knows and he can't speak. At least not in a way that we can understand."

"I guess, you're right. Hey, I'm going to get out of here. It's getting hard for me to breathe. I'll see you in the office tomorrow."

"You take care of yourself, Brooklyn. Remember, dying is a part of living."

"But murder isn't."

Quietly walking out of the door, he made it to his car just as the rain subsided but not before being drenched. Turning the key in the ignition, the vehicle sprung to life. He rolled out of the iron gate, making a left onto Greenback Lane and boarded Interstate 80, westbound. His windows were down, but the sudden downpour and hot weather created almost unbearable humid weather. Rolling up the window, he clicked on the cooler and leaned back in his seat, deciding to take a ride around the city.

Exiting on Dry Creek Road, he rolled past Sunset Lawn Cemetery and turned into the driveway, feeling the urge to pay a visit to his father's gravesite. Immediately following his arrival, a long caravan of vehicles, led by a black hearse and two police escorts on motorcycles turned in after him, livening up the otherwise deadening surroundings. Brooklyn took the path on the left, while the procession took the right. Stopping on opposite sides of the large grassy area which was covered with headstones, statues and flowers, both parties departed from their vehicles and slowly walked toward a canopy which sat over an empty grave.

Brooklyn stopped a few feet short of the canopy, bending down upon ascending on his father's final resting place. Dropping to his knees, he bent over the headstone and posed the same question to his father which he had asked his boss earlier.

"Hi, Dad. Hey, I was just passing by and decided I would stop in for a short visit. Now, I know I don't come by often, but I've been a little busy. But I promise, I'll make time. You know what, Dad? I wanna pose a question to you. When I was little you seemed to know everything there was to know, so I figure if anyone could answer my question, it would be you. So tell me, Pops. Why does the caged bird sing? Mom says it's because he's happy. But how could that be? I mean, I wouldn't be singing if I was locked up in a cell barely big enough to spread my wings."

"My fifth grade teacher says it's because he's sad. But after a certain amount of time, wouldn't you just get used to your environment? Would you wake up sad every day of your life knowing there was nothing you could do to change it?

"My friend, Remmy, well, she used to be my friend. Anyway she said the caged bird sings 'cause that's all he knows how to do. It's not a matter of him or her—political correctness you know—being happy or sad. It's just what it does. Well, what do you think, Dad?"

Brooklyn closed his eyes, trying to imagine the words his father would say. He stepped back in time, conjuring up an image of the old man as young Brooklyn sat in his lap, waiting for words of wisdom to fall from his father's lips.

"Well, Brooklyn. They're all right," his dad would say. "What do you do when you're having fun?"

"I laugh," answered Brooklyn.

"What does your mother do when she hears good news or goes to weddings?"

"She cries."

"And why do you wake up in the morning and go to bed at night?"

"'Cause you make me?"

"Besides that. Why do I wake up in the morning and go to bed at night, smarty pants?"

"I don t know?"

"'Cause that's what we do. When we get tired, we sleep. When we're rested, we wake up. When we get hungry, we eat. For no other reason, that's just what we do."

"You know everything," breathed a young Brooklyn in awe, mesmerized by his father's knowledge.

"Not everything. But what I don't know, your mother tells me."

Loud sobs broke his trance. He looked toward the group of mourners who had congregated under and around the canopy and wondered who they were mourning.

Arizona stood on the outer edge of the canopy. The tight-fitting black dress, dark sunglasses, and black scarf hid the emotions of the lady underneath. Deciding it best, one of Tommy's uncles had taken him home so he would not have to witness the burial of his mother. Arizona's head had started to pound from the moment she awoke, but now it felt like jagged boulders were swirling about. She blocked out the words of the minister, not wanting to hear anything more about death. Removing her sunglasses, she rubbed her eyes and began to scan the surrounding area.

Like a fairy tale, a dream perched on the highest plateau, their eyes met and, for the first time since the day dawned, hope entered their minds, enabling them to face another day. Not finding it difficult to believe, the two knew something magical had happened. *Is she my guardian angel?* Brooklyn thought. *Is he my Prince Charming?* Arizona wondered to herself.

He nodded in her direction and she understood. They were in different worlds right now but destined to meet in the same one. Tuning back in to her friend's service, she caught the tail end of the minister's speech.

"Ashes to ashes, dust to dust. May Sonya Lynn Vaughan rest in peace."

Reaching out again to his father's spirit, he imagined how his father would end the conversation. *"Now don't spend too much time thinking about that caged bird while you're free. You need to figure out what makes you sing and do it everyday."*

Exactly four hours later, Arizona stood on the lower deck of Brooklyn's houseboat while he turned up the music and prepared for departure. Minutes later, they were drifting down the river, dancing to the mystic grooves of the Caribbean. They had found what had made them sing and were determined to do it every time they got the chance.

As they drifted down the majestic Sacramento River, however, the sun's rays grew more intense. At seven o'clock in the evening, the ship's mercury still read 100 degrees. The vessel glided across the water and over an oil slick which had not been contained by the Department of Environmental Health. The profound heat caused the oil to boil, and a tiny spark ignited. The wake from the boat, fortunately, doused the spark before it could amount to anything worth mentioning.

VERSE

TWENTY-NINE

Forty Million killed
during slave trade.
—Western Hemisphere

ire season started early this year. In El Dorado County, a wild fire presently is burning out of control. It started late last night and has already consumed two thousand acres of land. The towns of Cool, Georgetown, and Pilot Hill have been evacuated as the course of the inferno has shifted directions and has panned out across the foothills.

Firefighters from ten counties have been called in to combat the blaze, but it seems to be a losing battle. Three deaths have already been blamed on the fire as residents in its paths pack what few belongings they can put in their vehicles and scramble to evacuate. The Sacramento County fire chief has declared that this is the angriest blaze he has ever seen. It has spread so fast that the firefighters are almost helpless to contain it before more homes are consumed. Their only hope is that they bring the fire under control before it descends on the heavily populated city of Folsom.

In Placer County, a three-alarm blaze was reported only minutes ago at the Hewlett-Packard shipping facilities. The Roseville Fire Department has requested aid from Sacramento County to help combat the blaze before it spreads to surrounding communities. The fire departments in the five-county Sacramento metropolitan area are

*already stretched razor thin due to the foothills fire. There were no
known reasons for either blaze at the time of this report. We'll keep
you informed as the news unfolds.*

"Nurse Janice, it sure is hot in here. Is the air conditioner on?"
asked Johnny, sitting beside his son's hospital bed.

"Yes, at full blast. It's so hot outside, the cooling system can't
work hard enough," replied the nurse. "Why don't you drink a cold
glass of water? It may help you cool off. How are you doing, anyway, Mr. Tyler?"

"I'm living. Thanks for asking. I guess we're in for a long, hot
summer."

"It looks that way, but I can't remember it being this hot so soon."

"It happens. I lived in the valley my whole life and I've seen some
pretty hot ones. But, I have to admit, I hope it doesn't stay consistent."

Nurse Janice turned, walked out of the door, and down the hall to
the next patient who was in need of her assistance. Johnny walked
over to the window, grabbed the pitcher sitting on the table, and poured
himself a tall glass of ice cold water. The chilling sensation felt good
as the precious liquid slid over his tongue, down his throat, and into
his belly. He finished his drink, set the glass back on the table and
resumed his position in the chair.

It was dark in the room because the blinds were drawn. Johnny
had wanted the natural light to radiate through the room, but the sun
was much too hot to allow it inside. Picking up the remote control, he
scanned through a myriad of TV stations, trying to find something
carefree and humorous. Tiring of the news from the wicked world, he
instead chose a cooking show, hoping it would not be a deliverer of
bad news. The chef's menu appeared on the screen as Johnny licked
his chops, realizing he had not eaten a thing all day.

*Good afternoon and welcome to Frederick's Kitchen. Today, we
are going to make a potpourri of delectable items for your taste buds.
On our menu, we have chicken chili—sure to be a hit for any occa-
sion, corn salad, a great substitute for that traditional green salad,
fish burritos, much lighter than beef or chicken, and mussels shipped
in directly from Puget Sound. Okay, folks. Let's start cooking,* said

Chef Frederick.

Deciding to win his way back into Arizona's heart through her stomach—hell, it worked for men—he quickly scribbled down the ingredients and watched through squinted eyes every move the chef made.

First, you brown the ground beef, seasoned lightly with salt and red pepper. Not too much salt. There's enough in the salsa and chili powder to keep that blood pressure up as it is.

"Light on the salt, green salsa..." said Johnny as he scribbled down the recipe.

Chop up one small red onion and place it directly into the simmering salsa. Be sure to keep the burner on low so that the salsa simmers and doesn't boil.

"Simmer, don't boil. Red onion, chopped..." Johnny repeated.

"Daddy."

Place a dozen chicken wings into the oven after seasoning with cayenne pepper and poultry seasoning. Preset the oven to about four hundred degrees. This will cook your chicken through and through while maintaining its natural juices.

"Daddy."

"Natural juices, keep on low. Set at four hundred. Huh? Did someone say something?"

"Daddy. Where's Mommy?"

Johnny broke out in a cold sweat all over his body. He froze in position, his head toward the television, pencil in right hand, and feet on a stool. Once, in a drunken stupor, he had passed out in an alley after downing two pints of cheap liquor. While unconscious, voices erupted in his head asking him what he was doing, telling him to get up out of the alley, clean himself off and go take care of his kids.

As he sat in the hospital room, listening to some fat chef explain how he got that way, the voices reappeared. This time, though, they sounded familiar. In fact, they sounded like his oldest son. Attempting to turn around, Johnny struggled in the arm chair, helpless to move from his present position. Like a small child waiting for someone to say, *Simon says* or be tapped so that he could move again.

"Daddy."

The voice spoke again. Completely engulfed in fear, Johnny Tyler urinated in his pants. The urine seeped down his leg and soiled the chair which had served as his support for so long. Finally, his total paralysis disappeared and he slowly turned his head toward his son's bed. He could still hear the beep of the heart monitor machine. He could hear the fat cook gabbing about salad and chili. He could hear the sound of his heart pounding inside his chest, but all the other sounds were minute in comparison to the one that was coming from the direction of the bed.

"When did you get here, Daddy? When did Mom let you come back?" said little Johnny, sitting up in bed.

Color drained from Johnny's face as the sensation that he was talking to a ghost would not leave him. Then he turned and saw his son, sitting up in the same bed that so many thought would become his tomb. His eyes were red and tired, skin clammy and hair unkempt, but he was smiling. Talking. Asking his father where was his mother and when had she let his father return home.

"Nurse! Nurse, get in here!" screamed Johnny, not believing what he was seeing. He had given up alcohol but the effects could be long lasting. His mind was playing a cruel trick on him, and he needed someone else in the room to help him calm his frayed nerves.

In a flash, Nurse Janice reappeared in the room. An orderly accompanied her, and before long, a doctor ran through the door to find out why a man was screaming in such a shrill voice.

"What's wrong, Mr. Tyler?" asked Nurse Janice.

"Look!" Johnny replied.

Johnny pointed to his son who was now a bit frightened himself. Stunned by his father's strange behavior, he had not noticed where he was. With the appearance of the staff in white and the outrageous behavior of his estranged father, little Johnny finally noticed that he was a patient in a hospital room.

"Nurse Janice, go call Dr. Severson, ASAP. Mr. Tyler, I need you to get hold of your son's mother and tell her to come here right away. I want a full staff in here immediately so that we can run some tests. Oh, my God! I think we saved one," said the doctor, who appeared to be in state of shock himself.

The nurse and orderly scrambled around the room, taking steps to implement the doctor's orders. Johnny, in disbelief, walked to the telephone and dialed Arizona's phone number. The room filled to capacity as blood pressure straps, temperature gages, and intravenous drugs were hauled in for the purpose of making sure the little kid in the coma was a-okay.

Three rings. Four rings. Five rings. On the sixth ring, the answering machine picked up.

Hello. No one is in to take your call right now, but if you leave a message at the beep, I promise to get back to you. May God bless you and have a nice day. ...beep

"Arizona. This is Johnny. How're you doing, baby? Listen, come on up to the hospital. I have to talk to you about something. See ya soon."

An hour later, the room emptied, leaving only Doctor Severson, Johnny and his son. All three exhausted but nonetheless had smiles on their faces.

"That's quite a scare you put everyone through, young man," said the doctor kindly, patting little Johnny on the head.

"What happened? Why am I in the hospital?" little Johnny asked.

"I'll let your father have the honors telling you all about it. Mr. Tyler?"

"Yes, doctor?"

"Your son is going to be fine. We're going to want him to stay in the hospital for a couple of days. When he gets home, try and put some weight back on him and monitor his progress. I believe he's out of the dark. He's definitely out of the coma."

"Thanks, doctor."

"Congratulations, Mr. Tyler. You're very fortunate."

"I'll count my blessings every day for the rest of my life."

Doctor Severson, with his chin up, chest out quietly strolled out of the door. It was times like these that he was glad he had chosen the medical profession. 'Twas times like this he appreciated his life. Now it was time to go home and let his own seven-year-old son know that he appreciated him too.

Johnny walked over to his son's bed and sat on the edge. He gently rubbed his large hands across little Johnny's head and over his face. Wanting to be the man and the father he should have been, he decided not to show any emotion but rather act as if he had been involved in his son's life all along.

"Hey there, son. Good to see you decided to wake up. I knew you was lazy, but goodness. You've been asleep for weeks."

"Very funny. Hey, Dad. Why am I in the hospital?"

"You were in an accident on your way home from school. Your school bus was hit by a tanker and...and, well, let's just say you had everyone scared for a while. But you pulled through, just like a champ."

"Where's Mom?"

"She'll be here. I just called her and left a message."

"Does she know you're here?"

"Ha, ha, ha. Yes, she knows. We're going to be a family again. This time, I promise, I'll be the kind of father that'll make you proud. How're you feeling?"

"I feel okay. I've missed a lot of school. I hope I still get to go to the carnival. Mrs. Steckenrighter has a rule that if you miss too many days you can't go."

"Believe me, she'll bend that rule for you, or there'll be no carnival. Hey, little guy. Can your poor old dad give his son a hug or will the other kids tease you?"

"I don't care if they do."

The Johnnys, father and son, wrapped their arms around each other and hung on for dear life. Big Johnny held on for all the years he had missed. He squeezed his son as hard as he could without rupturing anything in little Johnny's fragile body because the feel of his body against his son felt so good. He had forgotten that feeling of tenderness but now it came back tenfold. Little Johnny held on because he had missed his dad. Unwilling to hurt his mother under any circumstances, he had decided not to tell her that she had been wrong about throwing his father out. He held onto his father because, as a little boy, he needed his father's strength, to be there after his first fight, for his first touchdown and when he awoke kicking and screaming from his first nightmare. Most of all, he held on because his father was tangible, no longer a dream unfulfilled.

"Dad?"

"Yes, son?"

"I had a weird dream while I was sleeping."

"I bet. Could you hear us? I mean could you tell there were people in the room?"

"Not really. I mean I could hear voices but I didn't know where they were coming from. Inside or outside."

"What do you mean inside or outside? Outside of what?"

"Outside of my dreams. People were talking to me but I couldn't touch them. I couldn't play with them but they always wanted to talk to me."

"But could you see them?"

"Most of the time. Sometimes I heard voices from people that I couldn't see. I think those came from outside of my dream."

"What were the voices on the inside saying?"

"I don't remember everything, but they was always talking about a fire. They said a fire was coming to clean the dirt off the streets."

"Dreams can be different, son. Well, I can't wait for you to get out of here. The first thing we are going to do is take you..."

"Dad, I'm not finished telling you about my dreams."

"I m sorry. Go ahead. I won't interrupt."

"In one of my dreams, there was nobody around. Just voices. I was sitting on a rock and the fire was all around, but it wasn't burning me. I think it burned everyone else."

"Wow. That's a pretty wild dream. Were you okay?"

"I was okay but I didn't see Mom or Nigel. Or you. It was just me and this bird."

"Did the fire ever burn out?"

"I don't know. I woke up."

"Wow! Well, you're okay now. If you have any more bad dreams, I'll be there to help you through. Is that a deal, champ?"

"Deal. When can I go home?"

"The doctor says in a couple of days."

"Are you going to be there?"

"Not at first, but I'll be by every day. Your mother is going to be so overcome by my charm, she'll have to let me stay. We're going to be a family, again. You'll see."

"Baby? My little Johnny?" cried Arizona from the hospital room door.

"Hi, Mommy. Where ya been?" asked little Johnny.

"Yeah, where ya been? The kid's been looking for you," said big Johnny, wearing a huge grin on his proud face.

"Oh, my baby! Thank you God! Thank you for bringing my baby back!"

She let down her guard and unleashed the emotions she had held back. Racing to her son's bedside, she wrapped him in her arms and rocked him back and forth. Tears ran from everyone's eyes as the Kodak moment lasted for several more.

The emotional roller coaster ride had worn her down, but now, she was at the top of the nine story drop, with the brakes on. There would be no downhill for her. Her baby had come back to her and for that she would never feel sorrow again.

"Oh, Johnny. Oh, my precious Johnny," she sobbed.

"Don t cry, Mommy. I'm okay."

"He's back, baby, piped in Johnny. My little champ pulled through. Now we can be a family again, Arizona. Just the four of us. We can be a family again."

VERSE THIRTY

Four and a half billion burned
during Armageddon.
—The World

"Hey there, Ricky! Come on in. We want to show you something," shouted Jeff from the control room. He had noticed Ricky pacing outside the door and decided to invite him in. Over the past few weeks, they had become very fond of the lonely and somewhat confused security guard. They would often invite him into the control room and give him demonstrations on how the assorted lot of buttons and levers operated. Ricky was a good pupil and learned fast, which excited both Stan and Jeff. So seldom were they offered the chance to show off the importance of their jobs that, to them, Ricky was a breath of fresh air.

"What's going on, Jeff?" asked Ricky as he walked through the door. "Where's Stan?"

"He's running a little late this evening. I think he's having car problems. Or so he says. Why don't you sit in his chair and rest your feet awhile."

"Don't mind if I do. You don't think Stan the man will get mad if I sit in his chair, do you?"

"Of course not. Someone else sits there during the day and on his days off. What's one more person? Besides, Stan likes you. Told me so himself. Hey, Rick. You ever thought about getting a job here?"

"I already work here."

"I mean as a part of the Folsom Dam Project. Being one of us."

"Oh, no. I don't know nothing about operating a dam. Hell, first time I ever even seen one is when I was sent here to guard it."

"What are you talking about? Me and Stan taught you well. Besides, you learn quick and have more interest than most of the people who already work here."

"Are there any openings?"

"Not at the moment. But something will come up. It always does. I'll put in a good word for you. Maybe they'll add you to my shift. We'll have a blast."

"Yes, indeed. We would have a blast."

Ricky wished he had kept that last thought to himself but Jeff, a trusting and naive soul, did not pick up on what he meant. Totally convinced that neither Jeff nor Stan knew about the war, he was able to relax around them and at the same time learn everything he needed to know about the facilities. It was absolutely amazing to him how easy things were actually going to be. While the white devils were busy running down sisters in the streets, knocking off their foes one by one, Ricky had designed a plan to annihilate the whole lot of 'em.

"I guess now since it doesn't seem as if it's going to rain any more this year, you guys can rest a whole lot easier," said Ricky.

"Oh, contraire. We're on a closer flood watch now than ever before," responded Jeff, sitting straight up, beginning his teaching ritual. "The temperature has taken such a dramatic turn that the snow in the Sierra Nevada is melting at a record pace. Hell, the worst flooding the valley has ever seen could be on the hottest day of the year."

"What can you guys do here to prevent that?"

"When the dam reaches a certain level, we will open one or two, at the very most, of the flood gates and release the water into the rivers. If we do it manually, we monitor its flow and pace. Do you know the Yolo Causeway?"

"Sure. Who doesn't?"

"Do you know why the freeway is elevated in just that small section?"

"Never thought about it."

"Well, that area is used as a runoff. It's the place where the excess water goes to keep it from flooding our populated areas. When we raise the flood gates, we can direct the water to go into the causeway basin and other designated areas to prevent widespread damage."

"So if the snow melts in the mountains, and you don't have time to open the flood gates..."

"Then me and you and the rest of the city will be swimming to work. You see here, this entire section operates Gate Number One. This area is for Gate Number Two and so on. While under no circumstances would we ever open all four at once, we have that many in case we have problems with the others. A sort of checks and balances."

"You must have to have some sort of secret clearance to work here. I just can't see them letting any Joe off the street oversee the controls."

"Oh, sure. There's a background check. But I'm sure you'll do okay. You don't use drugs, do you?"

"And poison my body?" Ricky scoffed.

"Haven't been arrested for murder or anything like that, I take it."

"Never been arrested for anything like that."

"I'm sure you'd be fine. There is an extensive training program. Kind of interesting, kind of boring, but it'll do you a world of good. I'll keep my eyes and ears open. Let you know if I hear anything."

"I'd appreciate that, Jeff. Hey, I better get back on my rounds. Never know if someone is casing the joint."

"I'll be talkin to ya. Hey, come back in about an hour. I'm sure Stan will want to say what's up to you."

Ricky stood up after glancing down at the controls and briskly walked toward the door. He walked outside, lit up a cigarette as soon as he was safely out of the non-smoking building, and stared into the night. Eleven o'clock, and the cruel and unusual heat persisted. The thick, humid air clung to his clothes, causing them to stick to his already sweaty skin. What had happened to the rain? He and the rest of the city wished it would return.

Leaning against a light post that stood directly in front of the main entrance, Ricky blew rings of smoke through his mouth after taking in long drags of the cancer stick. The circles of smoke drifted into the air and dissipated as they floated away. Ricky watched each ring until they had all disappeared and there was nothing of his cigarette left to smoke.

He flicked the bud to his left and walked the perimeters of the building in a mocking attempt at guarding the palace. He laughed out loud at the acknowledgment of the fact that in this crazy world they called civilization, they needed a guard to guard the guard to guard the guard. Where did the treachery ever end?

He could hear the sounds of the water running, thrashing about in its protective hole. Closing his eyes, he imagined how utterly amazing it would look with all four gates open as one hundred sixty thousand cubic feet of water rushed through the passages per second. Every second. The Dave Roberts and Remmy Steels and the host of other blue-eyed devils would be helpless to defend themselves against the onslaught. The few who somehow managed to stay dry, would look up at the top of the hill and see Mr. Swift standing tall and they would bow down at his feet. It would be his world and be run his way.

Up the hill and over the small bridge, Stan drove into the parking lot. Ricky watched with dull interest as the other fool finally arrived. As Stan parked his car, Ricky pulled out another cigarette, lit it up, and waited for the jester to approach.

"What's up, Ricky, man? How's the criminal world treating you tonight? Anyone try to break in yet and steal the water?" teased Stan as he approached.

"Not yet. But don't you worry none, cause I'll be watching. No one will get past me."

"We're happy to hear it. Jeff here?"

"Oh, yeah. In the usual spot."

"Good. I better hurry inside. I'm already over an hour late. Stop on in when your feet get tired."

"I'll do that."

Up the stairs and through the door, Stan unknowingly entered the site of the modern day Pearl Harbor. Ricky blew another ring of smoke, then crushed the butt beneath the heel of his right boot. He raised his hands toward the sky and pulled them down fast, then pushed them back up, continuing the motion in rapid succession. Poking his lips in out, leaning forward on one leg, and fanning his arms in a circular motion, his unnerving resemblance to a giant grasshopper was maddening. He closed his eyes and envisioned the locus, traveling in a destructive swarm. Ready to feast on fresh kill. Greedily devouring every morsel in sight. Angrily taking its vengeance out on the world.

VERSE

THIRTY-ONE

Ozone layer depleting.
—Earth's Atmosphere

"Yeah, Larry. I got his address off the computer," Brooklyn returned, speaking into the telephone receiver. "The Tyler kid's attorney is ready to settle but I need to get the driver's statement. He actually lives right by me. About five miles south of my marina in the town of Hood. I figured I'd cold call him bright and early. Maybe he'll give me a statement, maybe he won't, but at least I'll know."

"Do you think Mr. Jackson took your offer of $750,000.00 back to his clients?" asked Laurence from the other end of the telephone.

"I'm sure he did. He seems ethical. A bit demanding, but then what else would one expect from a plaintiff's attorney?"

"Any word on the kid's condition?"

"Unchanged."

"If you can get this one settled for less than he's demanding, my hat will go off to you."

"Thanks, Larry. I'll see you around noon."

"I'm not sure if I'll be here. This one is getting a little hairy. I think I'll pay a visit to Dave Roberts. Force him to cooperate."

"What? You're going to get actively involved in a claim? I thought you swore that off."

"If this one goes sour, it'll be my head. I want to walk out when I retire. Not get thrown out."

"I hear you. I appreciate the help. Let me know if you find anything out."

"I will. Hey, I'm proud of you, Brooklyn. You're doing a fine job. Always have. I think it's safe for me to say that they'll probably ask you to fill my shoes."

"Thanks, Larry. I'll see you soon."

Brooklyn placed the phone on the receiver, then poured himself a cup of freshly brewed coffee. Walking onto the deck, he was met with heat so intense and unsuspecting that he stumbled back into his cabin, spilling his coffee as he did so.

"Damn, it's hot!" he yelled.

He quickly cleaned up the spilled coffee, decided against another cup, and scurried off to the bathroom for a quick, cold shower.

Once dressed, he gathered together the information he needed for his unscheduled appointment and walked out of the door. Sweat immediately appeared on his forehead, and his white shirt stuck to his body, creating an uncomfortable unison. As he walked past the marina store, he looked at the thermometer and gasped at the height of the mercury. "102. It's only eight o clock in the morning."

"Unbelievable, ain't it Brook?"

Brooklyn turned around and spotted Scott as he unloaded his crawdad traps.

"Hey, what's going on Scott? Hot as hell ain't it?"

"Not quite that hot, but it's gettin' there. With the temperature rising and the fires blazin', if I didn't know better I would swear this was the end."

"I wouldn't say all that, but I am going to start saying my prayers on a daily basis. I want no part of anything hotter than this. Hey, I'll see you later Scott. Try and keep cool."

"It's useless, but I'll try. Be good, Brook."

Brooklyn jumped in his car after waving a goodbye to the old sailor and drove off down the road. He had never known Scott to be a religious man, but he guessed that when one day rain is falling from the sky like a waterfall and the next, it's a hundred fucking degrees, a lot of people would get religion.

In no time, he was getting off the river road and turning into the town of Hood. Following the directions he had made for himself, he wound through the tiny town until he came to Cain street. Being able to turn only left, he did so and drove to the sole house at the end of the short block. He parked in front, rummaged through his notes and hopped out before recognizing the fact that he was disturbing someone at eight in the morning.

Knock...knock...knock.

No answer.

Knock...knock...knock.

Silence. A bit disappointed, Brooklyn turned away from the door and walked back toward his car. Halfway across the lawn he heard a loud creak and turned back around to see if someone had answered the door.

Like a bad dream or an old friend, neither of them knew which, the sight of one another caused goose bumps and the hair on their arms to stand up on end. Ricky peered out of his door then opened it wide, hardly believing that the warrior had arrived. Brooklyn dropped his notes on the ground, refusing to believe that the world was so very small. Time passed, and the two men stood frozen, not knowing who should make the next move.

"Are you Richard Swift?" asked Brooklyn, after clearing his throat.

"That's me. So, you decided to come," replied Ricky, now grinning from ear to ear. He looked around his environment and for the first time, was embarrassed at the filthy display. He felt ashamed, but hoped the warrior would look past his neglect and join him in the Cause.

"You sound like you've been expecting me."

"Ever since the day we met."

"So you remember me from the laundromat?"

"Of course I do. What did you expect? I'd forget? Hurry up. Come on in."

A bit astonished at how smoothly things were going, Brooklyn walked back across the lawn, up two steps, onto Mr. Swift's porch, and into his house. The stench met him first, then his eyes focused on the pig sty the man was living in. Trash and discarded chunks of half-eaten food littered the floor. The odor was so strong that Brooklyn easily equated it with death. Not wanting to stay any longer than absolutely necessary, he stopped at the door and prepared to question Ricky.

"How are you doing, Mr. Swift?" Brooklyn asked politely.

"Ricky. The name's Ricky. I'm fine. Look, we don't have time for idle chatter. Have a seat, I'll be right back."

Not wanting to appear rude, Brooklyn brushed some papers off the chair nearest the door and waited for his host to return. *What a small world,* he thought. "Damn this place is disgusting," he said in a barely audible voice. Ricky reappeared as quickly as he had disappeared carrying an easel and a large pad of paper. He set up the stand and positioned the pad on the shelf and turned toward his guest. A maddening gleam blazed in his eyes. Brooklyn instantly recognized it as the same one he had seen in the laundromat on that rainy spring night. He pulled out his dictaphone and prepared for the quickest recorded statement he would ever take in his life.

Ricky saw him break out the recorder and laughed out loud at the naivete of the warrior.

"You won't be needing that. You'll remember, my brother. But I appreciate your thoroughness. I have some bad news though."

"What would that be, Mr. Swift, I mean Ricky?"

"It's just the two of us. Everyone else backed out. They're scared. I don't blame them. It's dangerous right now, and only the strongest men should be on the battlefields. We're better off without them at this point. We can't afford to have any weak minds carrying the torch."

"I'm sorry, Ricky, but I don't know what you're talking about. I just came here to..."

"I got all the information we need to end the nightmare we've been living. By midnight tonight, any devil that remains will be bowing at our feet. Ha, ha, ha! I can hardly believe the day is here, but it is. And we have to take full advantage of it. Time is running out. They've already started to attack. I'm sure you know a sister was killed a few days ago by them. I'm certain that's just the beginning.

They're probably planting explosives in all of the black neighborhoods as we speak. But that don't matter, 'cause what we've got planned is going to knock this entire city, the entire world for that matter, for a loop."

Brooklyn thought back to that night in the laundromat and tried desperately to remember what Ricky had said. With his eyes open, he closed his mind, concentrating on the past and all the events that had led up to Ricky handing him his card before speeding off into the rainy night.

"Look, I can't talk now. I imagine that rent-a-cop is on the radio to the police department. The last thing I need is Johnny Law hassling me. I don't know if I would stand for it. But take my number and call me. I'm part of an organization that I know you will find worthwhile."

"What kind of organization is it?"

"It's one filled with brotherly love. That's all you need to know. Give me a call and I'll fill you in. I gotta go."

Brooklyn went over the conversation over and over again in his mind while Ricky pointed to the graph he had made with the depiction of the Folsom Dam on it. He then thought of the white men who were found dead in the Delta and tried to piece the puzzle together, but it would not fit. It just would not fit.

"...then when we've taken care of the two idiots we can pull open all the gates and flood this motherfucker. Hell, before they know what the fuck has happened this whole son-of-a-bitch will be forty feet under water. Get it? Forty feet. Forty days and forty nights. Brilliance right?"

Ricky marveled at his own witticism while Brooklyn conjured up an excuse to leave. What had he stumbled into? What was the crazy man talking about? He looked around the room, trying to find the quickest and most unobstructed passage to the door. He no longer cared if he appeared rude, only that he got the hell out before Ricky realized he was not one of them.

As he turned his head to the left, he stopped dead, focusing his gaze on a pile of thrash which lay in the adjacent room. His heart flew up into his throat and his nerves began to clank together. Rubbing both eyes with the tips of his fingers, he refocused and stared harder at the pile of garbage, not wanting to believe what he was seeing. Buried in a pile of rubble, sticking out just enough for him to see, was a purple folder. The same type of purple folder they used at Wexington to house their automobile claims. The same type of purple folder that was missing from the office because Remmy had taken it to work on the Roberts Oil claim.

Uncertain of even his own sanity, Brooklyn tried to maintain a resemblance of calm. He turned back to the psycho who continued to ramble on, either not caring or not noticing that his listener wasn't listening. Brooklyn stood, wasting no more time and backed toward the door. Ricky woke up from his trance and his crazy eyes followed Brooklyn.

Their gazes met, each trying to cause the other to blink, but it did not happen. Two men, Africans living in the same world, now fighting a different war. Brooklyn realized suddenly what Martin Luther King Jr. had tried to get across all along. It was not the color of one's skin but the content of their character. Remmy had been white by color but decent by nature. Ricky was black as night with a demonic character making up the very foundation of his soul.

Ricky found himself fighting a war that he and others like him had created. He initially believed that all the bad creatures would come in one form. They had been taught that the white man was their enemy but now he realized that the leaders were wrong. The man he thought was the chosen one, picked to save them and lead him to salvation, the one who they had prayed to and honored turned out to be nothing more than a bump in the night. Another disguise, covering his true identity. Satan himself had walked through his door, and now the real test was in store.

"You tried to trick me again, you devil bastard! Haven't you learned you can't fool me?" screamed Ricky in a fiendish tone. His eyes faded into tiny slots. Sweat crept through every pore of his body and his blood boiled like never before.

"Calm down, man. Just relax. I told you before that everything's cool. I told you. It's just thunder," replied Brooklyn. Eyes turning red, muscles tightening, he had hated the realization that he had come to, but he was prepared to see it through. One of them was going to die, and if it took every ounce of his strength, he was going to make sure it was not him. "Look, Brother. I'm with you, okay? Let me hear the plan. Let me help you work things out."

"Don't mock me! You better not fuckin' mock me! I'll kill you, you hear me! I'll kill you!"

Ricky grabbed a bat which lay against the wall and frantically ran toward Brooklyn. He took several swings, but Brooklyn managed to back away each time, avoiding the blows. Quickly, he scanned the room and spotted the fireplace. He ran to it, never taking his eyes off the madman, and grabbed the pointed ore. Like a cheetah, he reacted with lightning quick speed. The ore caught the bat as it came down with enough force to send both men tumbling backward.

Meeting in the middle, they held their weapons before them, imitating knights fighting over the princess' honor. Neither blinked, knowing a second lost would be one too many. Circling the room, they postured, hoping to catch a weak spot in the other's stance. This did not happen. The warriors had met.

Ricky was the first to swing, landing a solid blow against Brooklyn's ribs. Brooklyn wanted desperately to scream out in pain but could not afford the energy. Cringing, he swung his own weapon, packing a blow powerful enough to send his opponent careening to the floor. Ricky hit the turf, landing on his back. Brooklyn leapt on top of him, extending his weapon back, preparing to drive it downward and into his foe. Ricky spit into the air before kicking his right leg left. Brooklyn jerked to avoid the spittle, tumbling to the ground and dropping his weapon on the descent. The ore hit the floor and rolled toward the door. Before the clock could record another second, Ricky was on his feet with bat fully extended in his hand. Wanting to gloat in his victory, he forced himself to hold back the laughter and finish off his arch rival while he still had the chance.

"I told you I'd kill you, didn't I? Well, next time you'll listen!"

Ricky brought the bat sailing downward, connecting with profound intensity against Brooklyn's head. With the click of the switch, Brooklyn's lights went out and the sounds of the drums stopped. Ricky pulled back to get one more solid blow when the sound of the voice coming through the door stopped him in his tracks.

"Is everything alright in there? Hello? Is anyone there?"

Ricky paused. He looked at his victim and, after assuring he was not getting up, he casually walked to the door.

"Hello. Is anyone there?"

"Can I help you?" asked Ricky, opening up the door wide enough to allow the unwanted visitor the opportunity to only see the eyes of the man who greeted him.

"Federal Express," replied the man in the blue uniform. "We found your package. It was sent some time ago from Roberts Oil Company but somehow it ended up in Cucamonga. Another Richard Swift. Sorry about that."

"Just leave it on the porch. I'm not dressed."

"Is everything alright in there? Sounded like you were falling or something."

"My dog. I'm cool. Just leave the package on the porch."

"I have to have you sign for it."

Ricky reached his hand through the tiny opening and signed the computerized clipboard. In an attempt to hand the deliverer back his pen, it dropped to the ground. Federal Express bent down, picked up the pen, then offered the package to his customer.

"Thank you, sir. And again, I'm sorry that it was late. We at Federal Express try to provide the best quality..."

The door was slammed. Federal Express threw up his middle finger then turned and walked back to his truck. He pulled off his hat, rubbed his hair, then shook his hand to rinse off the excess sweat. Looking back at the house, he stopped for one second and wondered if the heat was causing his mind to play tricks on him. *Naw. There wasn't a man lying on the ground in there,* he thought. "It's the heat," he said just before boarding his truck.

Inside the house, Ricky examined his work. He walked around it, bent over it, and even kicked it just to see if it would move.

"You're not so tough, are you?" he said as a smile spread across his face. He pulled out a cigarette and took a seat on his trash-strewn sofa while continuing to stare at his prize. "So, what did you have in mind? Did you think you were going to come into my house and take over? Fooled you, didn't I? I'm the king of this motherfucker. You better believe that. You and every fuckin' other person who crosses my path. I'm the king up in here. You got that? I'm the king!"

Ricky looked at his watch and gawked when he noticed the time. There was so much to do and so little time to do it. His first instinct was to finish the job and kill Lucifer, but he knew that he would simply come back in another form. He instead chose to tie and gag him and dump Brooklyn's body in the garage. He would tend to his prisoner later.

After securing Brooklyn's hands behind his back, he rolled the man up in a blanket then wrapped several more yards of rope around his body to assure that he could not move. Opening the car door, he lifted the body into the back seat of Remmy's vehicle and slammed the door shut. Breathing profusely, he flicked the light off in the garage before closing the door. Grabbing his keys, Ricky raced through the front door, jumped into his own car and sped off. Tonight was the night. He had to gather all he needed to assure all went right.

VERSE
THIRTY-TWO

> Commandments altered
> to fit lifestyle.
> — Social Conscience

I t was early evening when Laurence pulled into the parking lot of Roberts Oil Company. He found it somewhat odd that there was only one car in the lot but did not dwell on this notion for more than a few seconds. He paused before turning his car off. The air conditioner was on full blast and still the auto was only slightly cooled. Preparing himself for the intense heat, he took in a large gasp of air, then killed the engine. The coolness evaporated and was immediately replaced by hot thick air. The air was so was dense that he could feel it wrap around his body and penetrate his pores. Perspiration formed quickly as his survival instincts attempted to keep him from vaporizing.

After wiping his brow, he loosened his tie and downed the remaining soda he had purchased on his way over. Sucking on hot air, he crumpled the cup in his hand before tossing it on the ground, somewhat irritated that he had settled on a large rather than a giant-sized Thirst Buster. It would not have mattered anyway. His belly would have busted from the amount of liquid he could have consumed, and yet his thirst still would have persisted.

Stepping out, he waved his right hand across his face and walked toward the front of the store. The closed sign caught him off guard but as there was only one vehicle left in the lot, he was hopeful that it belonged either to the owner or someone who could tell him where the owner was. He knocked on the door, but no one answered his call. Pressing his face against the glass, he was able to see the entire store, but no one was in sight.

"What the hell am I doing here anyway?" he thought. "Trying to help this idiot save his company," he said.

Turning to walk back to his car, he heard a noise coming from the fenced yard near the building. He walked in the direction of the sound but was kept from going inside by the locked gate. He peered as far as he could in both directions but could not see where the noise was coming from. Baking in the strong sun, his first thought was to call it a day and make way back for his air-conditioned car, but he figured he was here so he might as well follow every lead.

"Hello!" shouted Laurence. "Is anyone here?"

"Who the fuck is it?" returned a voice from the other side.

"Laurence O'Shante. I'm with Wexington Insurance Company. I'm looking for Dave Roberts."

"Hold on. I'll be right there."

Seconds later, Dave Roberts appeared from behind a sixteen-wheel mac truck. The chrome on the cab and chaise was so shiny that it sparkled like diamonds, demonstrating a dazzling glow. There were several others in the yard but none caught Laurence's eye like the one that was in plain view from the gate. The yard was litter free except for a few scattered parts from old trucks and other pieces of equipment.

Laurence waited patiently while Dave Roberts seemingly took his time in finding his way to the gate. When he finally was within earshot, he stopped suddenly on the other side and eyed his visitor cautiously. He was completely flushed, his pale skin now as red as the devil himself. His eyes resembled an old sick owl, clothes dripping with sweat, hands cracked, garments ripped. He still remained as proud and as arrogant as if he were wearing an original Armani suit.

"What can I do for you?" asked Dave Roberts.

"It's a hot one, isn't it? You better be careful working in the sun. Liable to get heat a stroke," returned Laurence, bearing a pleasant smile.

"Come on. I don't have all day. What can I do for you?"

"I'm looking for Dave Roberts."

"Are you deaf? Are you fucking deaf? I'm Dave Roberts. Now for the third and final time, what may I do for you?"

"As I stated, I'm Laurence O'Shante, and I'm from your insurance company. Wexington. We are handling a pretty big claim for you but we are having problems getting ahold of one of your employees. I was hoping you would have some information on where we could reach him. I generally wouldn't stop by unannounced, but I couldn't seem to get an answer at either of the numbers we have on record."

"I don't know where anyone is. I have shit to do."

"I'm sorry to bother you, Mr. Roberts. But as a provision of your policy, you are required to cooperate with us during our investigation. Not to mention, this claim is pretty serious. I'm sure you're aware that the Department of Environmental Services has sent a clean-up bill in excess of two million dollars. We're going to try and contest it as being unreasonable, but I don't know what kind of luck we'll have."

"Fuckin' commies! That's what they are! A bunch of fuckin' commies! I hope the oil contaminates all the fuckin' drinking water in this entire town!"

"I know how you feel, Mr. Roberts. That's why we need you to cooperate. You see, the possibility exists that if we could just speak to the man driving the truck at the time of the accident, we may be able to get comparative negligence from the city or the manufacturer of the truck. We have never been able to get his side of the story. All we've got is a contaminated river and a seven-year-old boy in a coma."

"Are you looking for that jig?"

"Excuse me?"

"Are you looking for that fuckin' jig-a-boo who crashed my truck?"

"I think his name is Richard Swift. Do you know where we can find him?"

"Ha, ha, ha! I gather that you have no clue what's going on, do you?"

"I don't follow."

"Let me give you some advice. You look like a decent white man. Stop worrying your head over a bunch of niggers. That little boy in the hospital, fuck him. That crazy jig who crashed my truck, fuck him too. You got it. Now, what you should be doing is heading on home and making sure things are okay at your house. You never know if they've already done to your wife what was done to that good white woman whom those savages tossed into the river a week ago. There's a war going on, brother. You think I give a shit about my policy or this whole damn company. I'm fighting over a country. Do you hear that? And you can be assured, I'm going to save it. Then when you wake up in the morning, and your white ass is still on top, you'll have me to thank. Now, like I said four times now, I've got things to do."

With that, Dave Roberts, turned his back on his ignorant brother and proudly walked away. Laurence stood in the same spot, completely dumbfounded by what he had just heard. In the year 1998, speaking to the president of a prestigious oil delivery company, Laurence was suddenly thrust back into time. He simmered in the blazing sun as he thought of the days when his countrymen had come together. He envisioned John F. Kennedy, cruising down the streets of Dallas, Martin Luther King Jr. waving from a hotel balcony in Memphis, and Abraham Lincoln enjoying a play from the balcony of the Ford Theater. He thought of all that but realized with all the velocity of a bomb landing on Hiroshima tragic deaths bonded the three great men together.

He watched as Dave Roberts walked away, absorbed in his angry world. He wanted to run behind him, wielding a sledge hammer, and knock some sense into Dave Roberts' bigoted, self-serving head but knew it would do no good. Creatures like him were filled with hate through and through. On their dying day, they would embrace their ideology, no matter how backward it had come to be.

Slowly turning, he found the will to walk back to his car. He tried to unscramble the confusing words the man had just said but was unable to make sense of the senseless. Laurence had grown up with decent parents in a humane town where all men were created equal.

Only two months to go until his retirement. More than ever before, he counted down the days.

Inside the gated yard, on the other side of the Mac-10 truck which blocked the view of his unwelcome guest, Dave Roberts was hard at work. He stuck the nozzle of a twenty-foot hose into the opening of the gas tank of the shiny truck. The other end of the hose was connected to an enormous loading rack which was attached to a ten thousand gallon, above-ground tank. While he filled the second compartment of the tank, he carefully loaded a hand torch and a small box of dynamite into the cab and chaise. Knowing that there was no more time, he had earlier in the day closed down his business, sending all of his workers home early and turning would-be customers away. Now on his third truck, he worked as hard as he did when he had loaded the first. The sun was wearing him down, his heart was starting to give out, but the power of the mind proved true. Will power could indeed conquer all.

He had driven the first truck to the north side of town, parking it in an empty lot on the corner of Grand and Marysville, right in the heart of Del Paso Heights—an enclave of hard-working African-Americans. The second truck was left at the underpass on Alhambra, near Broadway on the outskirts of Oak Park—a historically Black section of the city. The third and final truck would be driven to the intersection of Meadowview and 22nd, smack in the middle of the Meadowview area which was also populated with the despicable race. He had planned it so well that there was no way it would fail. Once he was a safe distance away and on his command, he would detonate the explosives located inside each of the trucks, which were filled to capacity with the most flammable and combustive fuel Roberts Oil Company had to offer.

A smile escaped from his lips as the thought of flying niggers crossed his mind. A second later, the nozzle clicked, indicating that the truck was full. He looked at his watch, removed the nozzle and jumped inside the gleaming Mac truck. Plastered to the dashboard was a large photograph that he had retrieved from an issue of *TIME Magazine*. Dave Roberts looked at the photo, then bowed his head in submission. When he looked back up, the demonic eyes of Timothy

McVeigh seemed to be looking directly at him. Dave Roberts shook his head to remove any doubt and once he refocused, realized that his hero had come to him.

"Good boy, Dave. Good boy. Now are you sure you got every-thing?" asked McVeigh.

"I'm sure. I checked the list a dozen times. This is no Oklahoma, but I'm going to send this town to kingdom come. You hear that, Timmy old boy? I'm going to blow this fucking city to smithereens!"

"Good boy, Dave. Now you have to listen to what I'm saying very carefully."

"I'm listening."

"They'll be watching. They may even catch on, but you'll have to follow through with the plan even if it means your life. Are you willing to give your life for the cause, Dave?"

"Yes. I'm willing to give my life to save this fuckin' country. Whatever it takes."

"Good boy. White Power!"

"White Power!" Dave Roberts replied.

Dave raised his right arm in the air and saluted the ideology that had killed an entire generation. He saluted more than just white power or any neo-Nazi political movement. He raised his arm, not in honor of the Klan or anti-government rebellion, but in honor of evil, plain and simple. He raised his hand to salute death by destruction and self-annihilation by the very beings who built the roads they were hell-bent on destroying. Dave Roberts saluted the revolution, the one which existed only in his mind.

With a turn of the key, the Mac truck roared to life. Not wasting any more valuable time, he threw the vehicle into gear and roared forward, taking the locked gate with him.

VERSE

THIRTY-THREE

World offered a chance
at redemption.
— Heaven

That's right, Frankie. He's okay. My baby's okay! Isn't that wonderful?"

"Yes. Wonderful, Arizona. A blessed miracle."

"Are you going to come down to the hospital?"

"I won't be able to come today, but I'll make it first thing in the morning. When is he going home?"

"The doctors want to keep him here for a few more days. Run some tests. Monitor his condition. Pretty routine stuff from what I hear."

"Will you be spending the night?"

"No. I'm going to go home and get his room together. I want to make sure everything is just perfect when he comes walking through that door. We're going to do everything in our power to keep any long-lasting traumatic effect to a minimum. We just want to be a family again."

"You and the kids?"

"And their father, Johnny."

"Going to give it another try I take it."

"We have to. If this isn't fate then I don't know what is."

"I know this isn't the time to talk business, but you know you still have a pretty substantial claim with the insurance company. Six weeks of your son's life is still worth a pretty penny."

"Frankie."

"Yes, Arizona?"

"We don't give a damn about that money. God gave us our son back. That's worth all the riches in the world. All we want is for his hospital bills to be paid. The doctor may want to conduct follow-ups for a few months to come. Of course, we'll want all that paid for, but we don't want to profit one dime. We've got our child back. What more can we ask for?"

"Now, let's not close the books to soon. You deserve that money. I know you're grateful for having your son back, as you should be. But the money has our, I mean your, name on it. Just a pot of gold sitting at the end of the rainbow, ready for the taking."

"A pot of gold mixed with little Johnny's blood. No thanks, Frankie. God don't like greed. Or haven't you read your Bible? His father and I have discussed it. This case is closed, Frankie. We just want to make sure his medical bills are taken care of. We'll do the best we can with the rest of his life. I'll talk to you soon."

Franklin Jackson heard the phone click several seconds before he placed his own end on the receiver. He sat motionless for a few seconds more, then stood up and walked to the window.

Darkness overtook the city and the night lights demanded center stage. Looking toward the sky, however, he saw nothing. The stars that were usually present were nonexistent and the half-moon was somehow dimmer than usual, as if embarrassed to come out. The man-made lights did their best to imitate the sky, but the scattering of street lamps and traffic signals seemed dismal and dull in comparison. Franklin pulled the long string that hung next to the window, causing the blinds to block out the disheartening scene.

Walking over to the bar, he glanced at the television but quickly turned away when the reporter cut to a scene which reminded him that the wild fires were still burning out of control. The air conditioner had been set at fifty, but the torturous heat managed to infiltrate the perimeters anyway, raising the temperature of the luxurious building to eighty-five degrees.

He reached the bar and immediately mixed himself a dry martini. Tossing it back in one gulp made him feel lightheaded and somewhat confused. He quickly mixed another drink and carried the full glass back to his desk.

The large file sat open, staring directly at him. Mocking him. Reminding him of the riches in store. Riches that he had deserved. He and his wife already had the money spent. They were going to take a trip to the west coast of Africa in an attempt to create their own roots. A trust was going to be set up for their son, so that he would not have to scrimp and scrape to pay his way through the college of his choice. They were going to move from their home on the river to one in the hills and show the world once and for all that Franklin Jackson had made it.

Now the dream was losing steam, running out of breath. His prized client was suddenly nothing more than a rear-ender, a whiplash. Not even worth the price of a new suit or the down payment on a car. He thought of this and scowled as the American dream slowly drifted out of reach.

Downing his martini, he threw the glass against the back wall of his office and watched as it shattered into a thousand pieces. Noticing the heat, he pulled off his necktie and stormed back to his private stock and filled a fresh glass, eyes dilating and blood pressure rising. He downed one drink after the other until he was barely able to stand. Reaching for the bottle of vodka, he was astonished to note that it was completely gone. He pressed the canteen against his lips, allowing the remaining drops to wet his tongue and slide down his throat, moving his blood alcohol level well past the legal limit.

Staggering back to the window, he separated the blinds so he could see outside. He looked in the direction of the hospital and cursed the people who took residence inside. *They can't do this to me,* he thought. "That's my money too," he said.

Giving it no further consideration, he grabbed the keys to his car, picked up the now-closed file and stormed out of his office.

*****

"I'm sorry, sir, but visiting hours are over," said Nurse Janice as she watched the man walk right past her and toward little Johnny's room.

"Out of my way. Those are my clients in there, and I need to speak with them," replied Franklin, completely ignoring her request. Without knocking, he barged directly into the room which housed the majority of the Tyler clan.

"Frankie! What a wonderful surprise," announced Arizona in a shocked tone. "You made it after all."

"How's it going, Mr. Jackson? We appreciate you coming by," said Johnny.

"I had to come by. After the conversation Arizona and I had, I felt it was best that I rush right over and try and talk some sense into you," Franklin stated, slightly slurring his words.

"I'm sorry, Mr. Jackson. I m not sure I know what you're talking about," replied Johnny, frowning in confusion.

"If I understand correctly, you have decided not to pursue a claim for the tragic accident your son was involved in. I think that's a big mistake. You are entitled for full compensation for the trials and tribulations that you have been unnecessarily put under. It's not a wise move for you to forsake what is yours by right."

"What is ours by right!" exclaimed Arizona, sitting straight up in her chair. "Nothing is ours by right. Not my home. Not my car and definitely not some money I've never had. How dare you walk in my son's hospital room and disrespect us like this!" Arizona tried to re-main calm as not to awaken little Johnny

"If anyone is disrespecting anyone it's you and your husband. What about your son's needs? What about his future? My God! The boy was in a coma for crying out loud. We're not talking about a sprained ankle. You don't know what internal damage, or for that matter, mental damage that could have been caused. If you don't want to think about your own future, then I appeal to you to think of his."

"What do you think we've been doing for the past forty days but thinking of our child's future? Frankie, we appreciate everything you have done for us, but we can't go there. No one, not the doctors, not our families, not even our minister thought Johnny would survive. By the grace of God, we have another chance for his future, and we're not about to ask for anything more. Thank you, Frankie, but we'll manage. We'll be okay," stated Arizona calmly

She sat in her usual seat, near the window. Johnny had pulled in another chair between his ex-wife and his son. Little Johnny lay still in his bed, peacefully sleeping and quietly dreaming of his perfect world. Realizing his argument had failed to convince his clients, Franklin moved closer, preparing to put on the case of his life. He glanced at the sleeping little boy and tried to force a smile from his own lips. The attempt failed, and instead, a frown appeared.

Being completely observant of the entire scene, Johnny saw the attorney's expression and could not quite comprehend what it meant. He looked at Arizona and saw pain return to his love's face. Turning, he looked at his son. Little Johnny, Nigel, and Arizona were his world, the beginning of his new life and new chance for a productive go at it. His son had awakened in his presence and was thrilled that his father had been there. Arizona had accepted the fact that she had to pull her family back together and had accepted his recent proposal to move back into the house. His life had come full circle, and he was not about to sit back and let anyone fuck with that.

Standing on his strong legs, he walked over to the unwanted guest and stopped once he was within arm's reach. Johnny was a new man and, in the first encounter since their reconciliation, he wanted Arizona to see.

"Mr. Jackson, I think you heard my wife. We appreciate you coming by and can understand your concern, but we've talked it over and have made our decision. You see that little boy over there? Well, he's my son. The only memorable thing old Johnny has done right with his life. For awhile, I thought I was going to lose him but, for whatever reason, he's stayin around with us. Now, I'm not really a religious man, although I do believe in divine creation. But something just doesn't seem right to us about making money on my boy's head. Man, I know you can't understand. But my boy is alive. That's enough. Do you hear me? That's enough. I'm not sure what kind of agreement you and Arizona had, but if we owe you something, we'll make sure you get your money. Right now, you should leave. I think you heard the nurse. Visiting hours are over."

"You'll make sure I get my money. Is that what you said? You must have no clue what kind of money we're talking about. On behalf of you and your family I have demanded three million dollars from the insurance company of Roberts Oil Company, and I'm pretty damn sure they're going to pay it. Last time I checked, I'm entitled to twenty-five percent of that. If my math is correct, that's $750,000.00. Now when can I expect the check?"

"Get out!" shouted Arizona through clenched teeth. Little Johnny was awakened by the sounds of his mother's shriek but he was still weak and groggily fell back to sleep. "Get out of here, you son-of-a-bitch, and don't you ever come back!"

"I think you'd better leave, Mr. Jackson. You're upsetting my family. And next time you decide to intrude on your clients, bypass the bar. Smelling like a distillery doesn't make a very good impression," interjected Johnny.

"You're making a big mistake. Biggest one you'll ever make. Does it really matter how you make your first million? If it were my son, I would have prayed that he stayed under long enough for me to get that money in my hands. Nothing's wrong about making the best out of a bad situation," argued Franklin.

"Make him leave, Johnny! Please make him leave," cried Arizona, no longer able to control her emotions.

"Mr. Jackson, I'm going to ask you one more time to leave. If you don't adhere to my request, I'll need you to refer me to a good criminal attorney, brother. One that can help me convince a jury that I was totally within my rights to throw you out of a ten-story window."

"When will our people ever learn how to play the game? What a waste."

Preferring to take the elevator to the ground floor, Franklin Jackson said his piece and made haste for the door. Johnny returned to his Arizona and took her into his arms. She slipped her arms around his neck, buried her face in his chest, and shed silent tears. Johnny held her tighter, reassuring her that he was there to protect her, until his dying day. They were a family again. He would never allow anyone to change that.

Franklin sped down the freeway, driving to nowhere in particular. The wild fire had reached the county's edge and even in the still of the night, the black smoke could easily be seen. He thought of the fire and how it was burning a swath through the land and compared it to the one that the Tyler family had just burned through his heart.

Opening the glove compartment, he reached to the rear and pulled out a box of Negal Cuban cigars. When the car lighter popped out, he lit the specialty smoke and felt his nerves finally begin to calm. He exited the freeway onto Pocket Road and turned left into the gated community of Garcia Bend. His house sat at the end of the court with its backyard right up against the levy of the Sacramento River. Deciding to finish his smoke before going into the house, he walked up the stairs of the riverbank and stared into the calming waters. He ripped off his jacket, trying to fight off the thick air and warm temperatures, but it was useless. The sky was pitch black but the sultry conditions made it feel like high noon in the Sahara Desert.

Finishing his cigar, he flicked the butt into the river and turned to walk down the stairs and inside his house. The alcohol had started to evaporate and his conscience had started to rear its head. What had he done? Images of his own son filled his mind, and suddenly he wanted nothing more than to rush inside his house and hold him in his arms. As he reached the stairs, though, the still-lit cigar butt rolled down the contaminated bank, landing on top of a pile of rocks which were still saturated with unleaded fuel. Combining elements, the fuel and cigar butt fused together, igniting a tiny spark which instantaneously grew into a full-fledged inferno.

VERSE

THIRTY-FOUR

...Revelations:
Behold the pale horse.
The man who sat on it was death.
And hell came with him.

Brooklyn returned to consciousness and was greeted by a headache so fierce he longed to go back under. His temples throbbed with so much pressure, he was almost unable to open his eyes. He lay still, trying to ride out the waves of pain, but the constant ringing of the bells in his head never let up. Realizing the pain had no immediate plans to subside, he decided to open his eyes and face the hurt in Technicolor.

Like a reoccurring nightmare, the previous surreal scene played over in his mind. Being grateful he knew his whereabouts, he said a silent prayer, thanking the Lord for his survival. As bad as he felt, he knew things could have been so much worse.

Opening eyes shone no more light on the scene than when they were closed shut. He was wrapped in a thick blanket, inside of a vehicle under the shelter of a dark garage. The heat inside the garage was unbearable. Brooklyn lay in a pool of his own perspiration, his head covered in his own blood. He tried to move his limbs but was barely able to wiggle his fingers as the ropes seemed to be welded to his body. Fortunately for Brooklyn, he was a calm man, otherwise the lack of oxygen would have added a dangerous dimension to his already bleak situation.

He laid still, not necessarily by choice, and thought about his options. After a brief thought process, he realized he had only two choices. He envisioned a sheep walking up the plank into the slaughterhouse, head bowed, unresisting, and accepting the fact that he was about to die. Not wanting to end up like the sheep, Brooklyn bucked and kicked and fought with all his might, trying to gain his freedom, attempting to save his own life. The rocks continued to bang around in his head, but he managed to ignore the resounding pain.

The struggle continued for what seemed to be an eternity, exhausted, he gave up and laid still once more. He could feel the air evaporating. He could feel his eyes beginning to close from the lack of oxygen, and the pain beginning to subside. He wanted so desperately to fight some more, but knew that the struggle had become useless. Never showing a weaker side, not even to himself, he refused to acknowledge his dire situation. Brooklyn Hunter knew that he was going to die, but would not allow the terror associated with death to enter his mind. While his demise would be untimely, he had had a chance to live. He had traveled the world, tasted the finest foods, made love to the most beautiful women. Having no regrets, he cherished the memories and bid them all farewell.

As strong of a man he was, he was still just that, a man. Deciding he had one last request, he squeezed his eyes tight and prayed to his Lord. "Dear God. Thank you for all you have done. But if I may, I have just one last thing to ask. Please let me die before he comes back." Unable to talk anymore, he closed his thoughts and laid quietly in the garage and prepared to meet his maker.

On the other side of the garage door, two sheriff patrol cars, carrying four deputies total, pulled in front of the house. They turned off the engines and stepped out with their hands never venturing too far from their guns. In the back seat of the lead car was the Federal Express delivery man. Refusing to believe his young mind was playing tricks on him, he had phoned the police and told them what he saw. Now he sat in the back of a sheriff's vehicle, pointing to the house that he had delivered a package to earlier that day, a house which appeared to contain a dead man lying face down on the living room floor.

The Federal Express courier remained in the vehicle while the trained officers converged on the house, covering all four sides of the dwelling. The first officer knocked on the front door, looking as relaxed as possible. After receiving no response, he knocked again, and this time backed away, putting his hand on his revolver as he did so. The second deputy, walked around to the back of the house, his back against the wall, eyes wide open, and his trigger finger flexed. The third deputy—who was also the highest ranking of the four and therefore in charge—stood in front of the garage. He looked to his partner who stood at the front door, then turned and signaled the fourth and final lawman to join the deputy on the porch steps. The fourth officer immediately rolled into place as the emergency response action was prepared to be put in motion. The sergeant looked back to the witness who sat in the car. The officer looked into the courier's eyes just to reassure himself this man was for real. He had been on enough assignments that he could tell what was a false alarm and what was the real thing. With so much craziness happening in his jurisdiction lately, he had no problem recognizing this house as being trouble. Trash piled up outside the house. Grass grew three feet tall, as if it had not been cut in weeks. And a stench coming from the general vicinity made his eyes water and his nose hurt. He looked at the young Federal Express agent and recognized the fear in his eyes. The courier had witnessed something out of the ordinary, something that just was not right.

With the fourth deputy in place, the sergeant gave the signal and, on command, Deputies one and two kicked in the door. Simultaneously, the sergeant shot out the lock on the garage while the second deputy kicked in the back door gaining entry into the house. Now indoors, all four deputies drew their guns, holding them steady, aiming forward. They cautiously scanned their respective areas, clicking on all of the light switches as they passed. After verifying that no one was in the house, they began to carefully inspect items which stood out among the disgusting rubble. The first deputy stopped at an easel which had been set up in the living room and tried to interpret the words and symbols scrawled on it.

"What the hell is this?" questioned Officer One. "Looks like some kind of plan."

"Look at this place," interjected Officer Four. "Filthiest damn house I've ever seen. Doesn't this guy believe in a broom and a dust pan?"

"Hey, Pete. Go to the car and radio in for backup. Something doesn't look right here," said Officer One, still studying the outline on the easel. Looking down, he stared into a pile of trash that was underfoot. He bent down into a squatter's position to get a better look at the object which caught his attention. "Gary. Come look at this. What does it look like to you?"

Gary—Officer Two—walked over to the area where his partner stood and stared down at the inamiate object. With his shotgun, he lifted the soiled piece of cloth and examined it under the light.

"Looks like blood to me, Mike," offered Deputy Gary Foxford.

"That's what I thought. Hey Pete, tell them to send the fucking investigation unit. Tell them to get out here, now!"

"Hey guys! Get in here!" shouted the sergeant from the garage. Pete ran out of the front door while Gary and Mike joined their commander in the rear of the house.

"What's going on, Jay? Is everything alright?" asked Mike, while entering the room.

"Hell no. There's someone in the car wrapped up in a blanket. I think they're dead," replied Jay who was standing next to the car and looking inside. He was a veteran on the force and knew it was best not to move the body until the appropriate people had arrived. But what if he was not dead? He knew something would have to be done. "Cover me. I'm going to open the door."

"Careful Jay," coached Mike.

Jay slowly opened the door and stood directly over Brooklyn's body. Barely conscious, Brooklyn jerked sporadically, thinking the crazy man was back to get him. Officer Jay pulled his gun and stumbled away from the car in surprise. Brooklyn kicked and bucked, determined to fight to the end. He pictured the crazy man, standing over him with a knife in hand, waiting to cut his throat.

"Oh, shit! He's alive. Hey, help me get him out!" shouted Jay.

Gary and Mike flew to his side and tried to calm Brooklyn while they released him from his prison.

"Calm down, buddy!" coaxed Mike in a soothing voice. "We're going to get you out of here."

"Come on man, relax. It's the police. We're here to help," said Jay.

Hearing the sounds and the words of the police, Brooklyn relaxed and lay still. The three deputies worked quickly, attempting to set the hostage free. Carefully, they pulled him from the car and cut away the wrap which restrained him. After the gag was removed from his mouth, he gasped for air which reignited the numbing pain in his head. Barely able to focus, Brooklyn laid on the garage floor, fighting the urge to vomit and trying to accumulate enough strength to speak to the men who had saved him.

"Hey, Pete!" yelled Jay through the open garage door. "There's a critically injured man in here! Call an ambulance! This guy needs help!"

"And ask them why that back-up ain't here yet!" shouted Mike.

"It's alright, sir. You're going to be alright. Can you understand what I'm saying?" asked Jay.

Brooklyn nodded his head in the affirmative. The three deputies in unison breathed a sigh of relief. The celebration, however, was brief for the sounds of screaming in the distance told them that all hell had broken loose. Jay stayed at Brooklyn's side while the other two officers ran out of the garage and looked west, toward the direction of the screams. In a spectacular show of energy, a monstrous fire blazed from the direction of the river. Flames shot twenty feet into the air, causing a cloud of black smoke to fill the sky. More screams, explosions, the sounds of cars crashing, then sirens. Deputy Mike Dudley changed directions, looking now toward the east. Although he could not see it, he knew that the fires in the foothills were there, still burning uncontrollably and descending upon the city. He turned back toward the river and watched as the flames seem to grow more intense, more angry. The already balmy temperature rose another notch, making the night nearly unbearable. The men looked at each other, then back toward the fire. They felt the heat on their skin and, for the first time since the day they slid from their mother's womb, truly wondered what in God's name was going on.

"Is that a fire burning over there?" asked Gary.

"Yes, sir. It's coming from the river," replied Pete, still hanging onto the dispatch radio.

"Damn! When did that erupt?" asked Jay. "This whole damn city will be on fire in a short time. Hey, did you dispatch an ambulance? There's a man in here who needs immediate attention."

"The dispatch says they'll send someone out as soon as they can. Said they must of received a thousand calls in the past few hours. The department is stretched thin. Seems the fire is burning up and down the river. A few homes have already burned to the ground."

"Damn! What the hell is going on in this city?"

Preparing to turn left onto Cain street, Ricky stopped suddenly when he noticed police cars in his driveway. Panicking, he backed up and slammed on the brakes, attempting to make a U-turn. The sound of the wheels skidding on the concrete caught the attention of the officers, who looked south, noticing the erratic driver.

"Holy, shit! You see that son-of-a-bitch!" hollered Mike. "I'll bet he lives here. We'd better go after him!"

"Go ahead Mike. Take Pete with you. We'll stay here until the ambulance arrives. Radio into dispatch. Tell them we got a fuckin' chase on our hands!" yelled Jay.

Sergeant Jay Roth remained by Brooklyn's side. His strength dwindling, Brooklyn was determined to hold on. Mike and Pete jumped into the second patrol car, turned on the sirens, and started their pursuit of the suspect. Gary ran to the lead car and grabbed the radio. With no set agenda in mind, he planned to inform dispatch of the direction of the high speed chase, the injured man clinging to life in the garage, and the fact—in case they had not noticed—that the whole damn city was burning down around them. The Federal Express agent remained in his seat, completely stunned by the events unraveling right before his eyes.

Racing up Highway 160, Ricky zigzagged through heavy traffic which had recently formed due to the townsfolk attempting to escape the blaze. With the fire burning in the river, boat owners had abandoned ship and hopped into their cars, causing a massive traffic jam on the two-lane road. Sitting in the passenger seat of Ricky's vehicle were as many rifles and guns as he could physically carry. He had earlier paid a visit to Malik's home and was able to break inside their hideout to obtain the weapons. He was grateful that no one was there; otherwise, he would have had to kill them, and he did not want to do that. A sudden gust of wind shot up from the delta and added a new level of destruction to the wall of flames. Pieces of the fire broke off in the wind, formed into large fireballs, and took flight, sailing over the crammed roads and into the Cavanaugh's Public Golf Course, igniting the dry, brittle grass in seconds.

When he reached the interstate, Ricky could hear sirens blaring behind him. He initially thought it was a siren from a fire truck, but discovered he was wrong as he checked the rear view mirror. The sheriff's patrol car, donning red and blue warning lights, raced behind him, gaining ground in their pursuit.

Pressing the accelerator, Ricky leapt onto the Interstate—north-bound—at record speed. The enemy had found his hiding place. There was no more time.

Mike was on the radio while Pete drove with precise expertise, beginning to catch up to the suspect. They followed suit as he led them on a high speed chase over the streets of Sacramento. The sky was black, but the lights from the fires circling the city made the night look like day. Ricky crossed his way onto the final leg of his journey, heading eastbound on the US 50 freeway, in the direction of Folsom Dam. City police cars joined in the high-speed chase as the sirens followed Ricky's blue Mustang as it headed toward the foothills.

Moving in a direction parallel to the US 50, and on foot rather than by car, Dave Roberts hobbled away from the third truck that had been set on Meadowview Road and 22th Street. He could hear the sirens, completely surrounding him. He could feel the heat of the fires burning deeper into his skin. And he could tell that his heart was slowing down as the pressure of the past few weeks finally caught up with it. Only a block away from the truck containing the explosives, cardiac arrest set in, sending old Dave Roberts collapsing on the ground. In order to save himself, he needed to be at least another block away. With the condition of his heart, he knew he would never make it. The police sirens were closing in on him, and there was nothing he could do.

Closing his eyes in pain, Dave Roberts slowly pulled the detonator from his hip pocket. Repeating his promise, he said the words aloud one more time: "Yes, I am prepared to die for my country." Opening his eyes briefly, he pressed down on the device just as his heart gave out.

The sound of the explosions echoed throughout the city as the truck bombs erupted, spreading death and destruction in their wake. Five city blocks at each location caved in, as the explosion caused the ground to open up, sending valley residents scrambling about. Hundreds of people were killed instantly as the blast ripped the foundations from their homes. Many survivors believed the jolt to be an earthquake. A few recognized the sound of the bombs, but only a handful actually realized the end was here.

Back on the interstate, Ricky and his army of pursuers continued eastbound, either ignoring or not believing the coming of the end. In the vicinity of Folsom Dam, Ricky exited the freeway, almost overturning his vehicle as he took the curve on two wheels. He continued speeding up the hill, choosing not to look back. He knew they were just behind him.

He had hoped he would have been able to revel in his victory but was prepared to offer his life for the Cause. He would get but one chance to strike and was determined he was going to make it count. The forest fires had dropped down in elevation and now could be seen from the hill that housed the dam. Swirling infernos. Crackling conflagration. A holocaust, the Armageddon. The world had set itself ablaze.

The police and sheriff's patrol cars began ascending the hill just as Ricky pulled into the parking lot. Grabbing his biggest gun, he ran toward the door, pulling the keys from his pocket in the process, and scurried inside. Kicking in the door to the control room, he aimed the Uzi at the men he had once befriended. Stan and Jeff were in their usual locations. They turned around to greet the intruder to discover the crazy security guard was aiming a gun at their heads.

"Get the fuck up, you bastards! Get up before I blow your fuckin' brains out!" he yelled.

"Hey, Ricky. What's the problem? What's going on here?" asked Jeff nervously.

"Shut upppp! Shut upp and get up before I kill you!" he howled.

Both Stan and Jeff leaped to their feet and stared at the man with the gun. They could hear the wail of sirens outside of the building. They felt the explosions that had sounded off minutes before. Their clothes were drenched in sweat as the relentless heat overpowered the high-tech air conditioner. And now they stood face to face with an insane man with a gun.

"Pull the lever, Jeff! Pull the fuckin lever!"

"What lever? What are you talking about?"

Activating the Uzi, Ricky sent a round of ammunition into Jeff's thin frame, not allowing him the chance to hear the answer to his question. Barely able to stand under his own strength, Stan's eyes nearly popped out of his head in shock as he watched his friend fall lifelessly to the ground.

"Pull the gates open! Pull them all open!"

"We can't do that. Do you know what would happen? Just calm down, Ricky man. Everything will be okay," stuttered Stan. He did not mean to disobey the commands but was helpless to do anything about it. His limbs were frozen. His body numb with grief, and his mind paralyzed by fear. The insane man would just have to shoot him, for there was nothing he could do.

Ricky could hear the sound of the stampede as the barrage of policemen entered the building. Time was up. He had to act. In a blink, he emptied bullets into Stan, killing the innocent bystander instantly. Running over to the control panel, he remembered what he had been told. Frantically, he pressed the appropriate buttons, then began pulling the levers which operated the flood gates. After pulling the first two, a warning light sounded, and bells began to ring throughout the building.

Before he could pull the next lever, the first policeman appeared in the doorway and drew his gun, taking aim at the criminal whom the officers no longer deemed a suspect. Ricky glared at the policeman, looked him right into the eyes. Having no fear in his soul nor any compassion in his heart, he pulled down the third lever before dropping to the floor behind a counter which served Ricky as a barricade.

Instantaneously, the Folsom Dam was transformed into a gushing waterfall, spilling its contents into the passageways below. One hundred, sixty thousand cubic feet of water per second roared through three open gates, overflowing the rivers and rapidly demolishing low-lying bridges. The powerful surge of water overcame a handful of unsuspecting boaters. Before they could even imagine what had hit them, the massive wall of liquid death capsized their vessels and sent them tumbling helplessly downstream.

"Throw your gun down, you son-of-a-bitch, or I'll blow your brains out!" shouted the cop.

"I bet you didn't know what we had in store, did you!" screamed Ricky from behind the shelter. "This is my world! Do you hear me! All mine!"

In seconds, the entire police crew had found its way inside the control room. Ricky rose slowly with his gun out before him. He tossed it forward, offering his weapon as a sign that he was planning to surrender. Waving the white flag. Giving up on the war. Before the cops could apprehend him, Ricky turned back around, grabbing hold of the fourth lever, determined to bring it down. Not knowing what he had planned, the officers opened fire, sending twenty rounds into Ricky's body. Falling backward, he somehow managed to wrap his right hand around the lever, and pulled it back with him.

Like the final act of a Greek tragedy, the bad guy hit the floor. Unlike the last scene of an American western, however, the good guys could not prevent him from living out his twisted dream.

With all the velocity of an atomic bomb, the coveted dam burst. And, with that, all hope was lost. Mankind had once again done itself in. Only this time, there was no going back.

****

Perched on his throne, high among the clouds,

the Good Lord leaned forward, and viewed the
world with much doubt.
All that He was, but not enough for thee.
For the world had forsaken their promise and
neglected what was He.
He promised eternal life and riches
beyond their dreams.
"Live by My word and ye shall all see,
that heaven is a great place,
where you'll soon find Me."
But the world had turned ugly and angry, you see.
And now He must show them,
that they'll never be free.
Rising from His throne, he prepared for the end.
The world had asked for His vengeance,
which now he had to send.

When the first horn sounded, Arizona was gazing out of the window. She had decided to spend the night in the hospital room, not wanting to leave her son's side. The enormous wail forced her to cover her ears, but there was no way to block out the sound. Johnny covered his ears as well and dropped to the ground as did the entire staff of the UC Davis Medical Center. Little Johnny, however, lay sound asleep in the hospital bed that had become his final home.

With the sound of the second horn, the windows to all the buildings shattered. Chunks of flying glass flew around the city, slicing into the citizens who were finally realizing the Lord was in their mist. The sturdy structures began to tremble. Brick by brick all of the buildings came crashing down.

By the time the third horn struck, priests and nuns had already taken shelter inside the sanctified walls of churches. They were on their knees, hands clasped together, eyes shut tight, trembling while begging their Lord to take them with Him. Instead, they were crushed by the falling beams that fell from the roof of the chapels. They, however, were the lucky.

The thunderous fourth horn forced screams so loud from the humbled beings that their cries nearly drowned out the sound that descended from the heavens. The previous horn also brought the locusts which swarmed the lands, attacking anyone that moved, as well as anyone who did not. Millions of grasshoppers viciously feasted on the vast array of delicacies that they had been offered. The humans still alive, wished they had been the chosen few to die by flying glass or collapsing buildings.

Some thought they could actually outrun the wrath. Traveling at unheard of speeds, down all the major freeways. Humans, completely mad with fright, drove aimlessly as the sound of the fifth horn brought the fire-breathing horses, which suddenly appeared on the roads. So large, they easily dwarfed the speeding cars and stomped each one out.

With the sound of the sixth horn, the sky opened, revealing the King of kings, Himself. He stood above the world: Omnipotent, the Alpha and Omega, the first power, the true warrior. With rod in hand, He signaled to the angel holding the trumpet. Raising the instrument to his mouth, the angel took in a deep mass of air, then blew into the horn with all the conviction of a million men, basking in holy water.

As the seventh horn sounded, fire streaked from The Creator's rod and shot down to the earth, sending the entire planet up in flames in one final dazzling display of power. Without so much as a second thought, He destroyed the world He had created, much the same way He had done so before. He had told them that He would be back. And God Almighty always lives up to His Word.

EPILOGUE

THE BEGINNING

ittle Johnny awoke from his peaceful slumber and stretched his arms toward the sun. He felt more rested than he had ever felt in his entire short life. It was not an undisturbed sleep, for it was full of dreams and disturbing images. Even with the continual visions running through his mind, his young body seemed lighter, somehow rejuvenated. He wiggled his toes, then his fingers, to make sure he was no longer a part of the dreams but rather in the land of the living. Things were a bit blurry as his eyes opened. Balling his hands into loose fists, he gently rubbed the sleep from his eyes.

His first sign that things were different was the fact that he no longer was stretched out in the clean hospital bed. He now lay limply over a large rock, like the one he had seen in his dreams. A little frightened, he sat up so that he could observe his surroundings closer. Panic had started to creep into his mind, but calmed down upon realizing he had not woken up after all. Continuing to sleep, he marveled at how vivid this dream was compared to the rest. While it was the same rock and the same desolate, smoldering surroundings, things just seemed more real. More tangible.

He waited patiently on the rock, for he knew he would awaken soon. This place, afterall, seemed familiar. He heard a sound in the distance and looked in the direction of the noise. A small white dove fluttered overhead, then graciously drifted down, landing right next to Little Johnny, just like in his previous dreams. He looked at the bird who appeared to be watching him forcing a tired smile from his face.

Leaning back on the rock, he noticed the bird staring off into the distance. Wanting to know what had caught its attention, he did the same, anticipating this new addition to his dream. From out of the blue came a lamb with a grayish-black wool coat. As humble as can be, it trotted toward the rock, then stopped when it was within Johnny s reach.

Becoming alarmed, Johnny shied away from the sheep, afraid of what it might do. He moved back on the rock but dared not get off. While there was nothing around to burn, a fire surrounded him, emitting a spectacular glow. Deep gold flames scorched the earth, appearing to rise from the very ground itself. Other than the flames, the land was completely barren. No trees, no grass and no houses were around that he could see. In this dream he was having, he was alone with the exception of the tiny white bird and the humble young sheep.

Deciding he had had enough of this dream, he tried to wake up. Pounding his fist against the rock, he called out for his mother. But it was of no use. He remained asleep. While he continued to pound his fist against the rock, he looked downward, noticing what he was doing. He stopped suddenly, then opened his closed fist. Palm flat, he rubbed his hand across the rock, feeling every crater of its rugged surface. Completely confused, he looked back at the sheep. Leaning forward, he touched its wool then retracted his hand as if he had been cut. This dream was different. He could feel the rock. He could touch the lamb as if they actually were real.

The sound of voices suddenly filled the air, but he could not see who was speaking or where they were coming from. He looked in all four directions, but the fire blocked his view. Ready to cry, he covered his ears and silently wished he would wake up. The voices continued, circling around him. Moving closer, almost touching him. Closing his eyes as tightly as they would go, he tried to block out this dream which was going much further than he had ever wanted it to go.

In time, the voices stopped. He opened his eyes to discover the fire was out. A raven, one similar in size yet opposite in color to the dove, had joined them on the rock. He looked at the sheep to discover a white lamb was standing next to it. Puzzled, he decided to stand to try and get a better view of the new and foreign land. As he stood, he looked at himself for the first time, and noticed he was naked. Thinking this a little odd, but not caring in the slightest bit, he scanned the area around him trying to locate the people belonging to the voices. Feeling something wet on his toes, he looked down and noticed the black sheep was licking his toe. In shock, he left his foot in place, marveling at the fact that, in this dream, he could touch and feel. Then, little Johnny Tyler, only seven years old, was forced to arrive at the conclusion that he was not sleep at all. He had entered a new land, a new world. One that had only existed in his dreams.

When the voices returned, he closed his eyes, so that he could understand exactly what they were saying. He knew that whomever the voices belong to would not hurt him. In fact, he knew with all his heart that they were actually trying to help.

When the voices stopped, he once again opened his eyes. This time, he saw things in a whole new light. While time did not seem to change, Little Johnny had aged and was now an adult. Stepping off of the rock, he landed in fresh, green grass. The fire had burned out and in its place was now an entirely different land. Walking east, the lamb and birds followed, never venturing too far from his side. Blue skies replaced the black one, and tall beautiful trees now stood where a ferocious fire had burned seemingly moments before.

Bending down, he picked up a long stick, shaped like a cane. The full robe that covered his tall body came as no surprise. Nor did the sandals which adorned his feet, nor the long hair that draped down his back. In the distance, he could see it, a lake so clear that the sun's rays actually went through it, giving off a brilliant sheen. The lake was so large that two animals of every species, even those long extinct, surrounded it. They were all taking mouthfuls of the precious water and were relishing it's cool, refreshing taste.

Johnny stopped just shy of the body of water and watched the sheep and birds join the others and bask in the glory of the holy water. Rich, healthy trees stood nearby and beautiful roses bloomed before his very eyes. The sound of the animals quenching their thirst and cleansing their souls filled him with elation as he literally watched the sins of a thousand years being completely washed away.

Then, as if on command, the multitude of animals ceased their consumption and backed away from the water. Now it was his turn. Johnny walked to the edge of the lake and stared at its beauty. The water was so clear, and the sky so very, very blue. Dropping to his knees, he leaned forward and cupped a handful of water to his mouth. He brought the water closer to his lips and was about to drink when the bounty of animals became excited, causing him to drop the water from his hands. The elephants raised their trunks, making enormous sounds. The monkeys jumped up and down, birds sang; wolves howled in unison. Johnny wondered what it all meant. He knew he was supposed to drink from the water in order to cleanse his soul but could not understand why the animals were trying to prevent him from doing so.

Placing his hand back into the water only rose the howls of the animals to a higher level. Johnny crawled back and leapt to his feet. Scratching his head, he continued to wonder what it could be. As he stared back into the water, his purpose became clear. He held his cane in the air, easing the minds of the animals who became calm and relaxed. Taking in a deep breath, he turned around and welcomed the arrival of his bride.

When she reached him, they joined hands, then walked back toward the edge of the lake. Dropping his cane, they bent down together, dipping their hands into the holy water. Wanting to be certain she had some of the holy water in her hands, he waited for her before drinking. Turning to her mate, Rebecca brought the water to her mouth and without further hesitation the twosome drunk of the water that would wash away their sins.

The Lord sat back down on His throne and the trumpeter walked away. He was giving them another chance, but refused to allow nearly as many mistakes. He knew that the world would not be as perfect as He, but expecting kindness, and love was not to much to ask of His children. "Go, my children," he intoned from above. "Multiply and prosper and shed lots of love. But remember my words, when you all start to hate. I am the provider of life and the decider of fate."

Amen

PEACE Books

Enter the worlds of
Kendall F. Person
and you will never want to leave.

The Remembrance
Universities are liberating and beautiful, overflowing
with intelligent young adults filled with dreams.
Yet for some, universities and dreams
become nightmares. Horrible places filled with
humiliation and pain. They become places where living
in our minds leads us to relive past sins.
Sins, whether committed by us or against us, must be dealt with.
Trade Paperback ($12.00)

Capturing Spring
is a story of love, courage and life as it really is.
It is filled with honesty, hope and tragedy.
This is one story which will linger long after the last page is turned.
Hardback ($13.00)

Send your orders or fan mail to:
PEACE Books
P.O. Box 15355
Sacramento, CA 95851
RockPeace@aol.com
Add $1.24 for shipping and handling.
Allow 4-6 weeks for delivery.